TOUCHDOWN

"Those two announcers in the booth seemed to think you were pretty terrific," Jess informed him.

"Do tell. And what did you overhear?"

She grinned. "I shouldn't tell you. You might get a swelled head." Darn! There was one of those double entendres again. She'd never had so much trouble keeping her mind out of the gutter. "They said you had great hands, and you didn't fumble very often," she related, managing to keep her tone flat. "But they also said you've got to avoid the sack and have better protection."

Ty drew in a deep breath, an unsuccessful attempt to tamp down his rising libido. "Did they now? Well, I have to agree to some extent. Good protection is a must. But eluding the rush isn't always possible, is it, Jess?" He took a deliberate step toward her, his sharp, searching gaze boring into hers. "Like now, for instance. I'm getting quite a rush."

Jess gulped and stepped backward. "You throw a smooth pass, on or off the gridiron, but I'm not much for playing 'bump and run,' Ty."

"Me, either. I like to retain possession as long as possible," he said, matching her quip for quip. He took another stride forward and she retreated again. "Don't back down now, sugar, just when the game is starting to get interesting."

One last step and he'd backed her to the edge of the bed. Jess lost her balance. As she fell, she reached out, grabbing for something to hold her upright. Her hands caught at Ty's shirt, and she wound up dragging him down on top of her.

"Nice tackle," he said, before his mouth shrouded hers in a long, blistering kiss. . . .

Critics sing the praises of Catherine Hart's novels:

"Action-packed, thrilling, HORIZONS is an ~~exhil~~ courage, ingenuity and survival.

"Humor, intrigue, and red-hot

"A good story. . . . Bold and a

"Takes lucky readers on a wo bines magic, history, and romanc

D0684788

<u>BOOK YOUR PLACE ON OUR WEBSITE</u> AND MAKE THE <u>READING CONNECTION!</u>

We've created a customized website just for our very special readers, where you can get the inside scoop on everything that's going on with Zebra, Pinnacle and Kensington books.

When you come online, you'll have the exciting opportunity to:

- View covers of upcoming books
- Read sample chapters
- Learn about our future publishing schedule (listed by publication month *and author*)
- Find out when your favorite authors will be visiting a city near you
- Search for and order backlist books from our online catalog
- Check out author bios and background information
- Send e-mail to your favorite authors
- Meet the Kensington staff online
- Join us in weekly chats with authors, readers and other guests
- Get writing guidelines
- AND MUCH MORE!

Visit our website at
http://www.zebrabooks.com

IMPULSIVE

CATHERINE HART

Zebra Books
Kensington Publishing Corp.
http://www.zebrabooks.com

ZEBRA BOOKS are published by

Kensington Publishing Corp.
850 Third Avenue
New York, NY 10022

First Printing: October, 1998
10 9 8 7 6 5 4 3 2 1

Printed in the United States of America

I dedicate this book to football fans everywhere, especially female fans, like me. Also, I would like to assure everyone that I intend no disrespect to the various NFL teams (or their players) that I mentioned in the course of writing this book to enhance the story line. They're all great, in my estimation.

CHAPTER 1

Whoa! Talk about tight ends and backfields in motion! Jessica Myers squeezed her eyes shut once more and leaned her hot, damp forehead against the inside of the locker door. One peek through the vent slats at the chaos in the locker room beyond was enough to give her a whole new perspective on these much-used football terms—not to mention the male anatomy—in a very up-close, in-your-face kind of way. Now, if she could just keep herself from hyperventilating in this claustrophobic tin box she'd chosen as her hiding place, she might survive the experience!

When she'd decided to snoop around the locker room, she hadn't counted on practice breaking up early, or having to stow away in an empty locker so she wouldn't get caught. So much for Plan A! Now, thanks to a badly timed chance glance, Jess would never be able to look these fellows in the eye without recalling the sight of their bare behinds and turning beet red in the face.

Her only remaining hope was to stay hidden until she could sneak out undetected. Given time, perhaps the memory of all those hairy, bulging thighs, sweaty Godzilla-like chests, droopy jock straps, and assorted tatoos would fade into oblivion. Then again, maybe not. But with luck, at least it would be her secret cross to bear, for this was one escapade Jess didn't care to reveal to anyone.

A bead of perspiration rolled down her face and dripped from her chin onto her chest to join others that had preceded it. Jess grimaced, forced to ignore the growing discomfort, and the itch in the center of her back and the end of her nose, neither of which could she scratch at the moment. Wedged into the locker like a canned sardine, she couldn't even raise her arm far enough for a glance at her watch. At five-foot ten inches tall, the only way she'd fit inside at all had been to scrunch herself in with her knees bent, her toes overlapping, her shoulders hunched together, and her arms crossed.

Her back was protesting the strain now, and—God help her—her knees were beginning to wobble. Jess could only pray they didn't begin to knock against the thin metal door, the latch of which she was holding onto with near-numb fingers, lest anyone try to yank it open. Of course, with all the racket these gridiron jocks were making, cracking towels and jokes at each other and clanking equipment and lockers to beat the band, she doubted they would hear any noise she'd make anyway.

Though it couldn't have been more than half an hour, or forty-five minutes at most, it felt as if she'd been stuck here for an eternity already. How long did it take these guys to shower and change clothes, for crying out loud? She could have done it in half the time, and curled her hair to boot!

The pungent odor of muscle liniment tickled her nostrils, and Jess squelched the urge to sneeze. Drat! Couldn't these macho Goliaths use the newer brands that didn't stink so badly? Didn't they worry that the smell would clash with their after-shave and make them reek to high heaven? Obviously not. After years of inhaling the stench of the locker room, which had undoubtedly dulled their olfactory capabilities beyond redemption, they probably thought they smelled like veritable roses.

Liniment, varied colognes, several brands of soap and shampoo and deodorant, talc, foot spray, mud, blood, sweat, grass, musty showers, grimy shoes, and clothes filthy enough to defy any detergent—these scents and more combined to create that unique fragrance familiar to locker rooms the world over. Whereas under normal circumstances it would not have bothered Jess in the least, the odor totally permeated what little moisture-laden air seeped through the door slats to her, and she was fast becoming queasy. Hot, nauseous, even slightly light-headed. If these gorgeous galoots didn't speed it up, so she could make good her escape, Jess was apt to do something she'd never done in all of her twenty-seven years. Faint. The question was, would she do so before or after she up-chucked her lunch?

Gradually, the locker room cleared out. The noise faded as one by one and in small groups the men exited through the double doors to the outer hall. Jess heard them calling farewell, trading a last joke or ribald comment. Finally, all was silent.

Jess ventured another look. Big Willie Watson was just rounding the far end of the row of lockers, hiking his jeans over his abundant "love handles" as he went and offering Jess a parting glimpse of the crevice between his buttocks in the process.

Jess made herself wait for several more minutes, listening for footsteps or other indications that anyone else was still around. She heard nothing but the hum and splash of the jacuzzi, which someone had left running. She was really going to have to mention that to Tom. Here he and the other owners were trying to make a go of a new NFL expansion team, and the players were already squandering tightly budgeted money by leaving lights and equipment on when they left for the night.

She had to flex her stiff fingers several times before she could get any mobility back. Then, when she tried to manipulate the lock, it wouldn't cooperate. She jiggled it. She smacked it with her fist. It gave a satisfying rattle, but the door remained shut. Jess pushed on the thin metal panel, and kicked at the bottom corner with her tennis shoe. Though she had little leverage to her benefit, she shoved with hands and knees, applying all her weight. But to no avail. The locker door was wedged tight. Jammed.

Again and again, Jess rammed her body against it, gaining

nothing but a bruised shoulder. The door shook and resounded like a Chinese gong; with each effort, it would bow outward only to snap back into place. Though not normally prone to panic, Jessie was precariously close to it now. The more she tugged and lunged and squirmed, the more excited she became, the quicker she depleted the muggy supply of oxygen in the locker. Not that she was in any danger of suffocation. Additional air continued to enter the door slats, but she was rapidly consuming it in short, jerky breaths now—half cursing, half sobbing. Tears blurred her vision, soon mingling with the salty streams of perspiration running down her face.

"No!" she wailed, pounding on the jammed door. "I refuse to be stuck in here!" Briefly, she wondered if one of the guys had slipped a lock or something through the outer hasp, anchoring it fast. Could she have missed that while she'd had her eyes closed? Was that why the door refused to budge?

"Oh, please, no," she groaned. If that were the case, despite the embarrassment it would cause, her only chance of release would be to yell loudly enough to attract someone's attention. But whose? The players were all gone. No one else was likely to drop by the locker room at this hour—not even the malingering janitor who obviously needed to get the lead out—and the Lysol! Good grief, it stank in here! And she could be trapped, like a rabbit in a snare, until tomorrow, when the team returned to resume practice. They did have practice the following day, didn't they? What if they didn't?

At that thought, hysteria blossomed once more, full-bloom. Amid rising shrieks and several choice curses, Jess pounded fists and feet against the stubborn door. "Let me out! Somebody get me out of here!"

Ty was relaxing in the whirlpool, letting the swirling water soothe his aching, abused muscles. His mind and body were adrift in a warm, fuzzy state of bliss when the most god-awful racket yanked him rudely back to reality. It seemed to be coming from the connecting locker room, and was fast growing in volume, rising well above the rumble and splash of the jacuzzi.

Someone, or something, was banging on the lockers to beat hell.

"Hey! Knock it off out there!" Ty hollered.

The metallic din continued. "If I have to come out there, I'm gonna kick some ass!" he warned. As an afterthought, he hoped he hadn't just threatened "Sir Loin" Simms, a massive defensive tackle who weighed well over three hundred pounds if he weighed an ounce, with hide as tough as buffalo jerky. While no wimp himself at six-foot-three and tipping the scales at two hundred ten, Ty was still just a slim-line quarterback by comparison, and thumping "Sir Loin" was a task he'd rather leave to a hapless member of an opposing team, thank you very much.

The noise built, the clanging now accompanied by an unearthly shrieking. A week ago there had been a similar ruckus when, as a joke, one of the guys put a baby pig in a comrade's locker. Ty sighed in exasperation. "Here we go again. It's probably another pig, or maybe a cat this time, and it had better not be trapped in my locker or there will be hell to pay."

Reluctantly, Ty heaved himself up and out of the whirlpool. The towel he hastily knotted around his waist did little to impede the streams of water puddling in his wake as he trod barefoot into the locker room. The source of the commotion, while as yet unidentified, was not difficult to locate. Ty simply followed the nonstop clamor down the aisles until he stood opposite locker number thirteen.

He frowned at it, his brows knitting. "I should have known," he muttered irritably. The prankster had chosen the one locker in the entire place that invariably stuck—the reason no one used it, except any unsuspecting rookie recruit who could be momentarily duped.

As Ty was eyeing the locker, watching the door bulge and twang and wondering what the devil was in there and how he could free it, the "thing" inside issued a string of obscenities that nearly made Ty's hair curl. His brows rose in surprise, and remained arched halfway to his hairline. *Holy Toledo! This was no captive animal! It was human! And female, at that! What had those lamebrain teammates of his done now?*

"Hey! Hey! Calm down in there!" Ty had to yell to be heard above the ruckus. When that didn't have the desired result, he banged his fist on the outside of the locker. "I said shut up in there! If you'll settle a minute, we'll figure a way to get you out!"

She must have heard some of this, because her shouts reduced to whimpers, and she quit kicking at the door.

"Okay," Ty said. "Now, I'm going to have to find something to use to jimmy the door open. You just stay put and wait quietly. I'll be back as soon as I can."

"No!" she screeched hysterically. "No! Don't leave me! Let me out! Now!"

"Lady, I would if I could, but the door is jammed big time. I need something to use as a pry bar, or you're going to be in there until love beads and bell-bottoms are back in style. So just behave yourself, and I'll be right back to rescue you."

For several seconds, all he heard from inside was her frightened, heavy breathing. She was panting like some wild creature. Finally, she replied tearfully, "All . . . all right. But hurry, please. It's very close and hot in here. Like . . . like being locked in a coffin."

"I'll hurry," he promised. "Sit tight."

"As if I had a choice," she quipped shakily.

He stalked off, slipping and sliding with every squishy stride, delaying his mission of mercy long enough to ditch the wet towel and yank on his cut-off jeans and his running shoes. Then he headed into the workout room, considering it the best place to search. He was right. There he found a small toolbox with an odd assortment of tools used to assemble the exercise machines and keep them in running order.

Ty returned to the locker, gave a quick tap on the door, and inquired, "How you holding up?"

"Just dandy," she groused. "I'm swimming in sweat, my shoulder's numb, I think I've scraped half the skin off my knuckles, and my knees have turned to Jell–O."

"It could be worse," he suggested.

"Did I mention the nausea and that I've got to pee?" she

countered miserably. "So if you could speed it up some, I'd really appreciate it."

"I'll do my best." Screwdriver in hand, Ty set to work on the warped metal. "What's your name, and how in the world did you get locked inside there, anyway?"

After a moment of silence, she said softly, "Jessica. My name is Jessica, but most people just call me Jessie or Jess."

"I'm Ty. Ty James."

"The Knights' quarterback and duly appointed king of the team," Jess commented dryly. "Otherwise known as T.D. James, for touchdown, of course."

"And a lot handier with a pigskin than a screwdriver, I'm afraid," he added. Then, "You never said how you came to be stuffed in a locker in the team locker room. Did one of those idiot guys sneak you in here for a little fun and games or something?"

"Get real!" Jess huffed. "Do you actually think I'd let some jerk stow me away in a tin box for later use, like some play toy, and then forget me?"

"Sorry! So, what's the story, sister?"

There was a long pause before Jess admitted ruefully, "I was having a look around the locker room when I heard the team coming in from practice. I knew I'd never make it into the hall without someone spotting me, so I crawled inside the first empty locker I found and waited until all the players left. But when I tried to get out, the door wouldn't open."

"Obviously. However, that doesn't tell me why you were snooping around the locker room to begin with. What are you, one of those wacky groupies? An avid fan scouting around for a special souvenir, like maybe a spare jersey or a jockstrap?"

Jess groaned. "Give me a break! I'm not some star-struck loony, and I wouldn't touch your jockstrap if it were lined with gold!"

"Your loss," he snickered. "For all you know, it might be."

"Fat chance," she shot back.

"About the same odds as you electing to hide in the one locker out of a hundred that always sticks," he retorted wryly. "And you might try buttering me up, 'cause it wouldn't pay

to piss off the one person available to rescue your dumb butt.''
Half to himself, he muttered, ''Geez! You've got to be a
blonde!''

''Isn't that a case of the pot calling the kettle black?'' she
jeered. ''You're blond, at least until you go bald. Most athletes
do, you know. Must be from wearing those helmets and caps all
the time. And for your information, buster, my hair is brown.''

''Does it stand up in sharp spikes like your tongue?'' he
taunted. ''Lord, woman! For someone in need of help, you sure
are a smart-ass! But back to the topic at hand—if you're not
a groupie looking for a freebie, what were you doing in an area
that's off-limits?''

After another lengthy hesitation, Jess announced, ''I'm a
reporter.''

''Aw, for cripe sake!'' he exclaimed. ''Tell me you're kidding!''

Jess bristled. ''Why? What's wrong with being a reporter?''

''A female reporter, no less,'' he added. ''Nothing personal,
klutzenheimer, but ear wax is a step up on the biological ladder.
As a group, you're nosy, biased, uninformed, intellectual snobs
who wouldn't know a punt from a peanut.''

''As opposed to all you super-jocks,'' Jess snapped back,
''who are overpaid, undereducated, conceited jackasses who
run around slapping each other on the rear and scratching and
spitting in public? Wow! Am I impressed or what!''

Ty sat back on his heels and malevolently contemplated the
door, and the woman hidden behind it. ''You know, for two
cents, I'd walk off and leave you to fend for yourself, Miss
Bad Mouth.''

''You . . . you wouldn't dare!'' she shrieked.

''Why wouldn't I?''

''Because . . . it would be bad for your image. You're one
of the Columbus Knights for crying out loud. And knights are
supposed to be gallant, and slay dragons, and rescue damsels
in distress and all that sort of tripe. They certainly don't abandon
helpless women.''

''And you actually buy into that line of bull?'' he queried
curiously.

"Not really, but . . ."

"Oh, don't get your panties in a bunch. I'm not going to desert you. I fully intend to spring you, so I can march you up to the office and toss you into the lion's den. I, for one, have had it with snotty, know-it-all, female reporters who feel it's their God-given right to invade anyone's privacy at any time, and in any place or set of circumstances. Sheesh! Next thing you know, a fellow won't even be safe from you in the john!"

Jess gave a haughty huff. "Like I'd want to watch a row of guys whiz on a wall and all over the floor! Yep, that's my idea of prime-time entertainment, all right."

"Hey! Whatever trips your trigger, babe! As long as it's not on my turf." He changed the subject. "Okay, let's give this a try now. You push, and I'll pull. On three. One, two . . ."

On the count of three, Ty levered the upper corner of the door into place and gave a hefty yank. At the same time, Jess threw her full weight against it from the inside. For a moment, the door still refused to give. Then it emitted an ear-splitting screech and popped open with the velocity of bread from a revved-up toaster.

Ty's momentum sent him crashing into the bench behind him. The bench toppled backward, and Ty with it, as Jess tumbled out of the locker atop him. They landed in a jumble of arms and legs, with Jess's elbow planted squarely in Ty's stomach.

"Ooof!" The air whooshed out of him in a pained gust, and for several seconds, all Ty could do was fight for the next breath and try to nudge Jess's arm aside. At last, swatting a clump of her damp brown hair from his face, he managed to wheeze, "Get off of me!"

Jess, slanted head-first over him, was helpless to do so. She tried, but after being bunched into the locker for so long, her numb limbs refused to obey her mind's commands. Finally, with him shoving at her, she simply slid to the floor at his side and lay there in a limp heap, gulping in breath after grateful breath. Laden though it was with fungal foot spray and other assorted foul scents, the air outside the locker seemed ever so much sweeter than it had from the inside.

"Free at last!" she puffed. "God, it's glorious! I wonder if this is how that poor whale in the movie felt?"

"I have no idea, but he was undoubtedly more graceful and didn't have needle-sharp elbows. I've been tackled by men twice your size and had it hurt less."

"You're not exactly Fred Astaire, yourself, you know. Still, I'm glad you came along and got me out of there. Thank you."

"Your appreciation may wane when I get you upstairs and you have to answer to the big boys," he warned.

"Maybe, but anything's better than being trapped in that sweat box."

He rolled his head to the side and got his first good look at her. She looked like a rain-drenched waif. Stringy brown hair stuck in moist clumps to a face as red and shiny as a ripe apple. Even her chest, above the droopy, sopping-wet T-shirt she wore, was slick with perspiration and tomato-bright. "Are you all right? You look as if you've just spent a week in a sauna."

"No joke, Einstein. That's what it felt like. I think I'm one heartbeat away from heatstroke."

Jess levered herself up on her elbows and closed her eyes as dizziness assailed her. "I really could use a breath of fresh air, some that doesn't reek of mildew and old sneakers. And a glass of water, if it wouldn't be too much trouble."

Ty untangled himself from the bench, rose to his feet, and extended one big hand toward her. "Come on. Let's see if you can stand up without falling on your keister."

He hauled her upright, his features registering surprise as she straightened to within a few inches of his own height. She swayed precariously. Reflexively, he grabbed her shoulders to steady her. "Whoa, gal. Guess I'll have to carry you."

Jess let loose a wobbly chuckle. "Don't make me laugh. You try to lift me, and you'll give yourself a hernia."

"Well, you are tall, but you're all skin and bone. How much can you weigh?"

With that, he bent, hooked one arm behind her knees and lifted her into his arms. His eyes widened as he staggered a couple of steps before regaining his balance.

Jess yelped and squeezed her eyes shut. "Put me down, you fool, before we both end up on the floor again!"

"Oh, clam up, will you?" he grumbled. "Geez, for such a skinny thing, you must pack a lot of muscle. Guess they're right. It does weigh more than fat." He juggled her a bit to better equalize his load, gained a better grip, and stumbled toward the double doors to the hall with Jess clutched tightly to his chest.

"I wonder," he huffed, "if it's recorded anywhere that a knight ever rescued an Amazon?"

Jess hissed a one-word reply. "Wagara."

"How's that?" Ty asked.

"Wagara," she repeated succinctly. "It's an acronym. Each of the letters stands for a word. Figure it out for yourself, hotshot."

CHAPTER 2

Shades of Gone With the Wind! Jess still couldn't believe this was happening. Not to her, and certainly not with someone as handsome and sought-after as Ty James. Never had one of her boyfriends dared pick her up and carry her like this. She was simply too tall, too lanky, for any of them to risk it. Of course, this particular situation was not precipitated by romance, but it was nonetheless a unique experience for Jess.

Unfortunately, she was too apprehensive to enjoy this once-in-a-lifetime event to its fullest, especially when Ty reached the end of the hall and despite her protests began trudging up the stairs with her. By the third step, Jess was dizzy. Then Ty teetered slightly on the fifth step, and she went ballistic. On a frantic shriek, her hands balled into fists, each clutching a big wad of his shaggy blond hair, while her arms tightened around his neck to the point of strangling him. "Oh, God!" she wailed. "Put me down! I'll walk! I'll crawl! Just let me down!"

Though he didn't release her, Ty did stop. Leaning against the handrail for support, he craned his head around in an effort to ease her choke-hold on his neck. "Geez, lady! Chill out, will you? My ears are going to be ringing for a week!"

"Down!" she hissed. "Now!"

His lip curled in a derisive smile. "You know, you're one bossy broad. And nothing toasts my Twinkies quite like a bossy broad." He hefted her, as if to toss her in the air, then laughed when she let loose a high-pitched squawk. "Now, where were we? Oh, yeah, I remember." Tightening his grip on her, he proceeded up the stairs.

Jess caught a quick glimpse of the long flight of cement steps before she squeezed her eyes shut and shoved her face into his neck. Between hasty prayers, she railed at him. "If you drop me, I swear I'll . . ."

"I'm not going to drop you. Even if I did, the worst to happen would be your bony butt putting a crack in the concrete."

"Funny. I didn't know gorillas had a sense of humor." A second later, "Don't fall. If we fall . . ."

"You'd land on top of me, and maybe break a fingernail. Big deal. Besides, if you're so blasted worried, why don't you pipe down and stop wiggling? And it would help if you'd get your thumb out of my left eye so I could see where we're going."

"Sorry." She moved her hand, but kept her grip on his hair. "So, how long have you had this Rhett Butler complex?"

"Didn't know I had one," he wheezed. "But this ought to cure it once and for all."

They stopped again. Jess kept her eyes closed. Waiting. Gulping deep breaths and inhaling the clean, crisp scent of him with each one. He smelled of chlorine, shampoo, and warm male flesh.

"Let loose of my hair and give a knock on the door," he told her.

"Put me down and do it yourself," she countered, relieved to see they were finally off the staircase and standing in the upper hall.

Contrarily, rather than do something so logical, he rapped at the door with his knee.

From inside, a male voice called, "Who is it?"

"Ty James. You got a minute?"

"Sure. C'mon in."

Ty couldn't quite grasp the doorknob past Jess's derriere.

"I don't suppose you could open the door?" he asked her dryly.

She smirked. "Would the hen unlatch the chicken coop gate for the fox?"

"Forget I asked."

By squashing her between himself and the door panel, with his nose wedged flat against her breast, Ty got hold of the knob. The door flew open, aided by their combined weight, and the two of them stumbled into the room. Somehow, Ty kept his feet beneath him as he lurched for the office couch and dumped Jess unceremoniously onto it. As he hovered over her, Jess griped loudly, "You can back off now, he-man."

"Only when you let go of my hair," he retorted. "I'm sort of attached to it, you know."

Jess had the grace to grimace sheepishly as she unwound her stiff fingers from his golden mane.

"Good grief, man! What in the world is going on?"

Ty swung around to face the other man, one of the team owners. "Tom. I'm sorry to barge in here like this, but I caught this woman, who claims to be a reporter, hiding in a locker in the team locker room. Now, I know we have to keep a good rapport with the press, but this—"

"She is a reporter," Tom broke in, peering around Ty's shoulder and recognizing Jess. "And a damned fine one at that."

"You know her?" Ty asked, his face a reflection of surprise as his gaze swept from one to the other.

From the couch, Jess waggled her fingers at the older man. "Hi, Tommy. Can I use your bathroom while you two chat?"

"Uh, yeah. Sure. Your purse is in the bottom, right-hand desk drawer, honey. Right where you left it."

"Thanks." Jess levered herself off the couch and quickly skirted past Ty. She retrieved her purse and headed for the private restroom adjacent to the office. "I won't be long."

"Take your time, Jessie," Tom advised, shaking his head in wonder. "Lord knows, this isn't the first time I've caught you looking a fright, but this really takes the cake. What in blazes have you been up to, anyway?"

With a full head of snow-white hair, twinkling blue eyes, a robust laugh, and a moderate-but-growing potbelly, Tom more resembled a clean-shaven version of jolly old St. Nick than the staid bank executive he actually was. Santa's look-alike didn't appear very jovial, however, as he leveled a warning frown at Ty. "If this randy stud has dared . . ."

Ty threw up both hands and backed up two full steps. "Whoa! Wait just a doggone minute here! In the first place, I'm the guy who pried her skinny bones out of that jammed locker, or she'd still be in there sweating and cursing to beat the band. In the second place, I wouldn't touch her with a ten foot pole, even if the pair of you weren't a hot item."

"A hot item?" Tom echoed, the furrow in his forehead deepening as his eyes narrowed. "Care to enlarge on that statement, James?"

"Oh, for the love of Mike!" Jess stopped dead in her tracks, swiveling to glare at Ty. "Talk about stupid jocks! You, Tyler James, have got to be the prize idiot! Tom and me? Having a fling? Pray tell, how did you, in a few scant seconds, arrive at such an asinine conclusion?"

"Yes," Tom added in a huff. "I'd like to know, too."

"Well, let's see." Ty mockingly pretended to contemplate the notion. "First, you two know each other well enough to call one another by your first names. And it's Tommy and Jessie no less. Then there was a 'honey' thrown in for good measure, and the little matter of her purse in your desk drawer, and the fact that she obviously knows her way around your private office well enough to find the restroom on her own. Last, but not least, was that comment about you having seen her looking a wreck before, which led me to assume you've seen her mussed after a rousing bout in bed perhaps—especially after you jumped to her defense like a jealous lover."

"Or an irate godfather, which is precisely what I am," Tom informed him tersely. "If I wasn't afraid I'd break your damned jaw and put you out of commission for the season, I'd ram my fist down your throat! Why, I'm a married man! And Jessie . . . well, that'd be the next thing to incest! Just the thought is a preposterous insult to both of us! For two cents, I'd trade you off to the worst team in the league.'' Tom paused in his tirade, then added grumpily, "Problem is, *we're* the worst team in the league. In both leagues.''

Ty, his face hot with embarrassment, stammered, "Lord . . . love a duck! I sure have stuck my big foot into it this time, haven't I? Look, Tom, Jess, I apologize. I was reading things all wrong, I guess, but it was an honest mistake. I don't know what else to say, but I'm sorry.''

"You certainly are!'' Jess agreed vehemently. "You're the sorriest son-of-a—''

"Jessie. The bathroom.'' Tom pointed toward the door. "Go. I'll take care of this myself.''

When Jess emerged from the bathroom ten minutes later, she looked marginally better than she had before. Her hair, while neatly combed, was just as limp and lackluster as ever. Her face, free of the sheen of perspiration, was also void of makeup at the moment. Also, without a change of clothing, her top was only slightly less damp than when Ty had first freed her from that hot locker—though she did smell of soap and water now, and less like sweaty old sneakers—a major improvement in itself.

Through the closed door, she had heard the men arguing, though she couldn't make out their words. Now, as she entered the room, Tom was wearing a cat-that-ate-the-cream expression, while Ty was slumped in his chair looking decidedly sulky.

"Welcome back, Jessie. You'll be glad to know that everything is settled.''

"Yeah,'' Ty muttered. "According to dear old Tom, we're going steady.''

"Pardon me?'' Jess inquired.

"Dating. Seeing each other. Spending time together. Tripping the light fantastic,'' Ty enumerated sarcastically. "As in, I'm your guy, and you're my girl, until Tom doth us part.''

"You're kidding, of course,'' she concluded with a sickly grin. "He is joking, isn't he, Tommy?''

Tom gave a satisfied smile. "On the contrary, my dear. He's one hundred percent on track."

Jess's face clouded. "Back up. I think I've missed something vital here."

"It's really quite simple, Jessie. After hearing about your problems today, it struck me that you need a little help getting your foot in the door with the team," Tom went on to explain. "And what better way to be a part of the 'inner circle' than to be dating one of the members? The players will open up to you much more readily if they think that's the case, more so than they would if they thought you were simply interviewing them for your in-depth report on the Knights. In fact, I don't know why I didn't think of it before. It's ingenious, if I do say so myself."

"You just did," Ty grumbled.

"And I don't think it's quite as clever as it is ludicrous," Jess added. "For heaven's sake, Tommy. Who in his right mind would ever believe I could be dating Ty James?"

Ty gave a vigorous nod. "See there? I'm not the only one who thinks your idea is full of holes, Tom. The guys just wouldn't buy it. She's not my type at all. So, that lets me off the hook, right?" Ty started to rise, eager to make a swift exit.

"Wrong," Tom declared. "Sit your butt back down, boy."

For her part, Jess glared daggers at the handsome quarterback. "Wow! Your ego is alive and well, isn't it?" she sniped. "Listen, hot stuff. When I said nobody would believe it, I meant that no one would believe I would lower myself so far as to date some muscle-bound jerk with a toothpaste smile and his brains in his jockstrap."

"For both your sakes, you'd better make them believe it," Tom inserted seriously. "Jessie, you have a job to do here, and I'm depending on your story to help give the team the shot in the arm it needs. We're the new kids on the block, the newest NFL expansion team. We need some good, up-beat media exposure. We need the new sponsors it could pull in, the revenue it could generate. I'm counting on you, girl. All us co-owners are. We've got a lot invested here, more than most of us would care to lose.

"As for you, Ty James, you have more at stake than that paltry fifty-thousand-dollar fine I'm willing to dismiss. Your pro-football career could be in jeopardy should we decide to cut you and give your position to Jack Hays. Who else would sign you up this late, except maybe as a third-string back-up quarterback? Team rosters are already filled for the year. So make up your mind, son. Do you want to play the game, or warm a bench on the sidelines? The decision is up to you— and Jess, of course."

Ty bounded from his chair. "That's blackmail, and you know it!"

"Powerful persuasion. Maybe even dirty pool. But blackmail?" Tom shook his head. "Besides, it's not as if I'm asking you to marry her. Just escort her around. Take her to team functions. Parties. Rallies. Whatnot. What'll it hurt? Furthermore, if you make it clear that she's your girl, it'll keep the other guys from trying to hit on her—and from sucking up to me through her—once word gets out that she's my goddaughter."

"Gee, thanks for the vote of confidence and all the praise, Tommy. I'm surprised you didn't try to get me a spot as the team mascot, complete with a suit of armor," Jess groused. "Why don't you just let me do my job the way I see fit, and let it go at that?"

"Because the future of this team is too damned important, that's why," he retorted heatedly. "All I'm asking is a little help from you two, just a few weeks of your time, and we'll all reap the benefits. Jess, you'll get your story, with all the inside information and exclusive interviews. Ty, your position as quarterback and your full salary will be guaranteed. And, hopefully, the team will get the backing and the boost it needs so badly. Then you can both go your separate ways, and never speak to each other again for all I care. What do you say, kids? Will you do it? For me? For yourselves? For the Columbus Knights?"

Ty rolled his eyes, slanting a look at Jess. "If he says, 'For the Gipper,' I'm gonna puke." Then, "Okay, okay, but I want that fine revoked in writing. Signed, dated as of today, witnessed, and duly notarized. I don't trust you, you crafty old codger. Not after this.''

Jess groaned. ''Why do I just know I'm going to regret this, big time?''

''You?'' Ty exclaimed in disbelief. ''My entire reputation is about to go down the tubes.''

''What reputation?'' Jess scoffed. ''Your status as Stud of the Month, maybe? Or Gridiron Playboy? Big whoop! It might do you wonders to be seen, for a change, in the company of a woman whose IQ is larger than her bust size.''

He slid a lingering leer over her torso, boldly assessing her chest. With a shrug, he jeered, ''Well, they say more than a mouthful is a waste, anyway. I guess we're about to find out, aren't we, sweetie pie?''

CHAPTER 3

Ty hit the turf so hard he heard his teeth rattle, despite the protection of his mouth guard. This made the third time he'd been sacked this afternoon, and the team had only been practicing for an hour and a half. He couldn't blame his blockers, though he would have liked to. No, the fault lay entirely with him—and with Jess Myers. She hadn't shown up yet, but he was sure she would. Which was why his concentration had been shot to hell and back since he'd first walked out on the field. Just waiting for her to appear, even while he was hoping against hope that she wouldn't, was fraying his nerves to shreds.

He hadn't seen her or spoken to her since they had parted company outside Tom Nelson's office the previous evening, and he was dreading the moment he'd see her again and have to begin acting as if he actually liked the smart-mouthed witch. His teammates were going to think he'd lost his mind, taking up with such a homely Amazon.

Hopefully, he'd seen her at her worst yesterday, all sweaty and red-nosed from crying, without a stitch of makeup. Still, heaven only knew what she might look like normally, in the full light of day. He prayed she wouldn't look too awful, that she would spruce herself up a bit for her role as his girlfriend.

But not too much. God forbid she would overdo it and show up looking as if she'd applied her cosmetics with a trowel! Or wearing some atrocious outfit and tons of cheap costume jewelry. Even mousy-drab was better, he supposed, than having people believe he'd taken up with a two-bit hooker who moonlighted as a circus clown! If she was plain as a mud fence, he could at least claim he was attracted to her personality or her intellect or some such foolishness. And later, he could claim temporary insanity, or the phase of the moon, or the peculiar alignment of the planets, or one concussion too many.

"How many fingers, T.D.? C'mon, Ty, blink or something, will you?"

Ty jerked back to reality to find himself still prone on the ground, his coach leaning over him with a concerned frown. "What?"

"Fingers, big guy. How many?" the man repeated, holding his hand in front of Ty's nose.

"Three. Why?"

"Why? Shit-fire, man! You been lyin' there staring at the clouds for five minutes. We thought you'd been knocked clean out, but for the fact that your eyes were wide open. Now, where does it hurt most?"

"Nowhere but my pride, and my tongue. I bit it."

"What about your neck? Are your ears ringing? Twiddle your fingers for me."

"Dammit, coach, I'm fine. Just got my bell rung a little, that's all. Nothing serious."

"You're positive? Your timing's been off all day."

"I know. It happens sometimes, okay?"

The coach nodded. "Sure, but that being the case, why don't you take a breather and let Jack get in some practice?"

"Suits me," Ty agreed, as he allowed the man to help him to his feet. "Let Hays enjoy a little abuse for a change. Maybe it'll wipe that smug expression off his face. Besides, he's looking entirely too spiffy and spotless over there. It's like playing with Mr. Clean, for God's sake!"

"Don't worry, T.D., we'll muss him up good for you," Dean

"Dino" Sherwood promised. "Sorry about hittin' you so hard, man. I didn't hurt you, did I?"

"No," Ty assured him. On a laugh, he added, "But if you find any marbles or teeth rolling around out here, don't throw them away. They're probably mine."

He had his helmet off, and his water bottle halfway to his mouth, when he spotted her. She was in the lower section of the stands, sitting next to her devious-minded godfather, who was obviously not above a little bribery to get his dowdy goddaughter a steady date. From this distance, she didn't look too bad. She was wearing cut-off shorts and a sleeveless blouse knotted beneath her breasts, what there were of them, to leave her midriff bare. Her mouse brown hair was parted in the center to fall in a sleek bob that curved along her jawline, with a fringe of bangs cut straight across her forehead. Not a great style for her—it reminded Ty of the little Dutch boy on the paint can—but at least it appeared neat and clean this afternoon.

As Ty had feared he would, Tom waved for him to join them. Grudgingly, all but dragging his feet with every step, Ty made his way to the stands and trudged up the few rows of seats.

As he drew nearer, he was glad to see his worst fears laid to rest. She hadn't lathered on the makeup. In fact, she didn't seem to be wearing any at all, other than a bit of mascara and a hint of lip gloss. Now that she wasn't ready to faint or keel over from heat exhaustion, her natural complexion was neither pale nor ruddy, but lightly suntanned and blemish-free, discounting the spattering of freckles across her nose and cheeks. If she'd been shorter, and several years younger, she would have been the perfect Norman Rockwell picture of the all-American tomboy. Or, in Ty's opinion, a female version of Tom Sawyer.

Ty was still a few feet away from them, morosely contemplating his misfortune, when Tom leaned toward Jess and said something that must have struck her as terrifically funny. In an instant, her entire expression was transformed as she tossed her head back and let loose a laugh. Even as he witnessed it, Ty couldn't believe it. Her hair fell away from her face, revealing high, strong cheekbones that would have been the envy of any fashion model. Her eyes lit up with delight, and suddenly they weren't just a nondescript hazel, but an intriguing shade of golden-brown, ringed by a wide band of green. Straight, pearly white teeth came into view as her lips curved upward and parted on the most enchanting smile Ty had ever beheld.

She still wasn't beautiful, not in the usual sense of the word. But "pretty" didn't quite measure up, either. "Striking" was the term that came immediately to Ty's mind. Followed by "stunning," which was precisely how Ty felt. Stunned. That a mere smile could change a common plain-Jane into a downright attractive female, all in the blink of an eye. It was akin to watching a magician perform one of those sleight-of-hand maneuvers that left you shaking your head in amazement.

Okay, so maybe the boobless wonder isn't a total zero after all, Ty thought to himself. *The tricky part is going to be to keep her amused the majority of the time. At least when we're out in public together. As long as she smiles like that, maybe no one will find it odd that I supposedly find her appealing. And if I can talk her into stuffing a pair of falsies in her bra, her figure wouldn't be bad, despite her height. Lord knows she has the longest legs I've ever had the privilege of ogling! Add a touch of eye shadow and some makeup to cover her freckles, and a new hairdo, and who knows, and she could turn out to be rather alluring, in her own way.*

Tom's greeting drew Ty out of his private musings. "Hey, boy! Are you okay? You had me worried for a minute or two there."

"Yeah. Coach Danvers just thought I could use a break, that's all."

Jess's lovely smile converted itself into a smirk. "I'd be pleased to oblige, now that you're all rested up from your little siesta out there on the field. What would you like broken first? An arm? A leg? How about a kneecap, for starters?"

Ty returned her look with a false smile of his own. "Now, is that any way to talk to your main squeeze? You might actually hurt my feelings with that sharp wit of yours."

"I doubt it," she rebutted. "You've got the hide of a rhino, and the disposition to match."

"Be still my heart! The woman's mad about me!" Ty quipped.

"You're supposed to like each other, remember?" Tom growled, rolling his eyes. "So shape up and behave like adults, if that's possible."

"Consenting adults, I hope," Ty amended in yet another attempt to get Jess's goat.

"I wouldn't hold my breath if I were you," she informed him. "Or maybe you should, just for the fun of it."

"I'll pass, thanks."

She faked a simper. "Pass? Oh, golly gosh! Do you really know how to do that? And here I thought all you could do was get knocked on your backside and count stars every couple of plays. My grandmother could dodge a sack better than that."

"Your grandmother's dead," Tom reminded her dryly.

Jess nodded. "Then I guess that says it all."

"Not quite." Tom directed his next mandate toward Ty. "After practice, you can introduce Jessie to the other players. The sooner they meet her, the sooner she can start interviewing them for her story."

"Sure," Ty agreed, with a grin. "I'll march her straight into the locker room as soon as practice is over. You'll be right at home there, won't you, Jess? Surely it won't bother a seasoned reporter like you if the fellas strip down to their skivvies in front of you. No doubt you saw more than that yesterday while you were hiding out in that locker."

Jess's face flushed guiltily, but she managed a fair retort. "Whether I did or not, I have to assume there's less blubber on a pod of whales than on several of those guards and tackles. It thoroughly amazes me that any of them can walk upright, let alone run."

"That's beside the point," Tom put in. He leveled a hard look at Ty, jabbing a finger at the quarterback's chest. "Listen up, James. You will introduce Jessie to the team outside of the locker room, just as you would any woman for whom you had the highest regard. Say, your mother, for instance. You will

continue to treat her with the utmost respect for the entire time
you two are dating. She's not some floozy you picked up on
a street corner. She's a lady. I trust you know the difference?''

"Loud and clear, boss. I'll treat her like my kid sister. Just
don't blame me when this farce you've cooked up doesn't fly.
I can't pretend to be bonkers over her and keep her at arm's
length, too. The guys simply wouldn't buy it.''

"I realize that. Just know where to draw the line.''

"Better yet, let me draw the line,'' Jess proposed. "You
two seem to be forgetting that I have a say in this as well.''

"Hardly,'' Ty scoffed. "Not with you running off at the
mouth every two seconds. Tell you what, *sugar plum*. We'll
just play this thing by ear, and if you're real lucky, I might let
you seduce me.''

Jess laughed outright. "Are you kidding? You can't even
score on the football field.''

He sent her a decidedly salacious wink. "Lady, you just
watch and wait. They don't call me T.D. for nothing.''

Jess had the horrible feeling she was heading for deep trouble
with this pretext of being Ty James's girlfriend. The primary
problem, other than trying to fool everyone else, was that she
found the smart-ass quarterback altogether too attractive for
her own good. Moreover, he was a "toucher." As he led her
around, introducing her to his fellow team members, his arm
was either slung across her shoulders or around her waist,
holding her close to his side in a none-too-subtle signal to the
guys that she was his exclusive property.

Jess's skin positively tingled in every place he'd touched;
and foolish as it was, each time he tossed a false endearment
her direction, accompanied by a smile that could have charmed
a cobra out of its hide, her heartbeat jolted into double time.
Worse, she had the awful suspicion that he knew exactly what
his actions were doing to her, and was enjoying it immensely.
The best clue, no doubt, was the big goofy grin she couldn't
seem to wipe off her face the whole while.

Then, just as she thought this first ordeal was over, one of the guys suggested they all go out for pizza. Naturally, the invitation was extended to Jess, since several of the others intended to call and have their wives and "significant others" come, too. Before she could politely decline the offer, Ty accepted for both of them.

In an evasive move, Jess told Ty she would meet him there, since they both had their own cars, and she didn't want to leave hers in the stadium lot. Besides, she had a couple of errands to run first.

Ty responded by giving her a look that said, without words, that he knew she was trying to give him the slip and wouldn't show up at the restaurant if she drove away by herself. "That's okay, honey," he said, loud enough for the others to hear. "We'll take your car, and leave mine here for now. But hand over your keys, because I'm driving. Not that I have anything against women drivers, you understand," he added with an ingratiating smile. "I just trust my own driving skills over anyone else's."

Drat! She'd been outflanked before she'd gotten off the line of scrimmage! Jess fished her keys out of her purse and slapped them into Ty's outstretched palm, aware that without them she couldn't leave while he was showering and changing into his street clothes, which she most certainly would have done otherwise.

To further push her off-stride, Ty leaned over and planted a swift kiss full on her lips. "Miss me while I'm gone," he told her with a devilish grin. He sauntered off to the locker room, whistling a merry tune—and leaving Jess breathless and fuming at his sneaky tactics.

Half an hour later, in the close confines of her little Honda Civic, Jess marveled at how much smaller the interior felt with Ty crammed into it. His shoulders took up two-thirds of the front seat space, for crying out loud! If that wasn't enough, he had the nerve to criticize her choice of transportation!

"How can you stand driving this sardine can?" he complained. "Where's your sense of national pride, woman? Couldn't you buy American-made, at least?"

"For your information, smartzenheimer, this car rolled off an assembly line here in Ohio. Therefore, I do not consider it a foreign model," she informed him stiffly. "Moreover, I'm thoroughly satisfied with it. It gets super gas mileage, and has a terrific warranty."

"I'll take my Trans Am over this, any old day."

Jess gave a haughty sniff. "Figures, the pro player has to have his sporty hot wheels. Well, I've got news for you. Your big old gas-guzzler cost you twice the money on the lot and the road."

"At least when I hit the gas pedal, I've got some horsepower under me," he pointed out in a superior tone. "It's a wonder you haven't gotten yourself killed just trying to pedal this Tinker Toy across the street before the signal light changes four times."

"Ha-ha. I did my research, buddy, and let me tell you something. This 'Tinker Toy' has more leg and headroom than your big bad Pontiac, a wider wheel base, and the resale value over a four-year span is significantly higher. Not to mention that it corners tighter and probably has a lower insurance rate."

Ty's eyebrows rose. "Hey! I'm impressed! You really did your homework. But you're still not going to convince me your car is better than mine. I've definitely got more elbow room, and as for headroom, I've also got you beat there."

"How do you figure that?"

Ty laughed. "Mine's a convertible."

She wrinkled her nose at him. "I should have known. I'll bet you bought a bright red one, too. The better to be seen by your adoring public."

"Nope. Teal, with an ivory interior and the gold package. Now, aren't you sorry we didn't take my car?"

"No, I simply regret we had to ride together at all. Or that we have to eat together and paste phony smiles on our faces while we do it. I can feel the indigestion building already."

"Speaking of phony smiles, keep yours in place if you please," he suggested bossily. "It vastly improves your appearance. And remember to stand up straight. I'm half a foot taller than you are, so you don't have to slouch.''

"Five inches, tops," she amended. "I'm five-ten, and you're six-three, if your stats are accurate. I pulled your file, by the way. I know all kinds of facts and figures on you."

"While I know next to nothing about you, except that Tom Nelson is your bulldog godfather. So tell me a few things about yourself. Stuff a guy should know about the woman he's dating."

"Like what, my measurements?" she sneered.

"Nah." He shot her a grin. "I like to find that sort of information out for myself. For starters, despite the lack of a wedding ring, I hope you're not married. For all my faults, I don't mess around with married women."

"No. I came close a couple of times, but I managed to avoid the matrimonial pit."

"I fell smack into it," he told her. "I've been divorced for three years now. My son, Josh, is five years old. How old are you, by the way?"

"Twenty-seven," she admitted readily.

"Birthdate?" he pressed. "God forbid I should miss your birthday while we're 'dating.' "

"You won't. It's May 8th. You'll be history long before then."

"Mine's November 12th, so you have three months if you want to knit me a sweater."

"I know, and I don't knit," she said smugly. "You'll be thirty-two. That's getting rather long in the tooth for a starting quarterback."

He zapped her with a dark look. "Gee, I guess somebody ought to let Young, and Elway, and Marino in on that tidbit of news, so they can order their rocking chairs and stock up on Geritol. In case you missed the punchline, sugar dumplin', they're all older than I am, and I haven't even hit my prime."

"Your conceit is showing again, not that it ever fades completely, I assume. Rather like that Southern drawl of yours."

Ty contemplated this with some surprise. "There are folks who would differ with you there, and claim that Kentuckians don't have a true Southern accent. Not like people in the deep South, anyway. So, where are you from?''

"Originally, from Dayton. But I went to OSU for my degree, and Columbus seemed to suit me, so I stayed.''

"Dayton's only a little over an hour away, isn't it? I suppose you get home to see your family fairly often.''

"Mom, yes. Dad died when I was in high school. He and my older brother were killed in a boating accident when I was sixteen.''

He grimaced. "Sorry. That must have been tough. Any other siblings?''

"Not unless you count my stepsister, Allison, but we're not close. Mom married her father four years ago. To this day, at twenty-two years old, Ali resents having to share her daddy's attention with anyone. She's such a pita!''

"Pita?'' Ty echoed. "Like in pita bread?''

Jess laughed. "Hardly! It's another of my favorite acronyms, like wagara. The letters stand for Pain in the Ass, which, come to think of it, describes you to perfection.''

CHAPTER 4

"Good grief! That doctor must have really stretched you out when he delivered you! How ungodly tall are you, anyway?"

Jess scowled down at the buxom shrimp seated next to her at the table. "Tall enough to tell that your hairdresser isn't the only one who knows you're not naturally blond," she retorted tartly. If the little cheerleader could be catty, Jess had no qualms about dishing it right back.

From her other side, Ty abruptly popped a wad of his pizza into Jess's mouth. "Here, honey, try some of mine. I ordered extra cheese."

It was shut up and chew, or choke. Jess chewed.

Across from Jess, a statuesque black woman, the undeniably gorgeous wife of one of the players, and a famous fashion model in her own right, leaned forward and said, "Don't mind Heidi, Jess. Besides being defensive because she's the shortest cheerleader on the squad, she thinks she's Hitler in disguise."

Jess still couldn't get over the incredible names of the team cheerleaders. There was Heidi, of course, and Starr, and Destiny, and Pepper, and Jazz, all of whom were present this evening. She had yet to meet the other half of the squad, which consisted of Candy, Shasta, Tawna, Desiree, and last but not

least, the inevitable Bambi. Not a Mary or Linda or Susan
among them, which led Jess to the conclusion that many of
their names must be made up, like those chosen by actors and
singers and popular deejays. Or perhaps a few were nicknames.

At least the majority of the other women dating or married
to the guys on the team had what Jess considered normal names.
There was Corey Rome, the model, Lisa Harvey, Shannon
Baxter, Amanda Orwig, Beth Chambers, Kim Hardesty,
Michelle Tanner, and Tara Jones. Most appeared nice enough
at first meeting. Just a couple of them struck Jess as a bit
standoffish, or perhaps they were merely shy. Of the five cheerleaders, only Heidi and Starr had put on airs thus far. Destiny
came across as slightly ditzy, but amicable. Jazz nearly bubbled
over with energy and talked practically nonstop. Pepper had a
low, raspy voice and a delightfully lusty laugh to match, one
of those contagious laughs that made you join right in despite
yourself.

As Tom would have expressed it, and as was to be expected,
all the cheerleaders had figures like brick outhouses, with all
the bricks in the right places. Busty, beautiful, and built. The
other women weren't slouches, either, by anyone's estimation.
In fact, Jess knew beyond a doubt that she was less attractive
than any one of them—even Tara Jones, who was eight months
pregnant, and timid little Beth Chambers, who acted as if she
wouldn't say boo to a goose.

But Jess was used to being the odd girl out. After all, she'd
been thrust into that role for most of her life. Since childhood,
she'd towered over her female classmates, and many of the
boys as well. Too tall, too skinny, with braces on her teeth and
blah-brown, baby-fine hair, she'd slouched through her teen
years—mostly in a vain effort to disguise not only her height,
but the fact that while other girls were sprouting breasts, hers
more resembled grapes. Even now they were more like poached
eggs than those succulent fruits to which romance writers
always compared their heroine's breasts. Unless you counted
a pair of puny tangerines, perhaps.

It wasn't until she'd gone to college, and found her niche
on the women's soccer team, that Jess had begun to blossom.

There, she'd learned to appreciate her latent athletic talent, her intelligence, and her innate sense of humor, and to focus on her assets instead of her shortcomings. She'd made new friends, both male and female, and by the time she graduated with a bachelor's degree in journalism and communications, she'd grown into a new sense of herself as a valid, valuable person.

Happily, she'd soon found her way into investigative reporting, and had done so well at it, from behind the scenes, that she was now free-lancing on a regular basis for several major network news/magazine programs. These days, it didn't matter so much that she was plain. She had her work, which was satisfying and exciting, she had good friends, a nice apartment . . . her own place in the world. She was content, for now. At least she had been before she'd had the misfortune to fall into Ty James's arms and start daydreaming again about things that could never be.

"How did you and Ty meet?" This from Corey Rome.

"Uh, we sort of bumped into each other at the stadium one day," Jess ad-libbed.

"I've seen you around there a couple of times," Jazz commented. "Aren't you some relation to Tom Nelson, or something?"

"Jess is a reporter," Ty put in hastily. "She's going to be doing a big story on the Knights."

"Is that right?" Dino Sherwood leaned past his tablemates to look down the long table at Jess. "Does this mean we're gonna get our pretty mugs in the paper?"

Jess shook her head, but before Dino's good mood had a chance to evaporate completely, she told him, "More likely on television. I often free-lance for the major networks, and they usually like whatever ideas I present to them. If I can get a good angle on the newest NFL expansion team, its players and their backgrounds, I could quite possibly sell it to the national sports network."

"Hey! That'd be great!" another player exclaimed. "Then my boys could brag about their old man to their new classmates and the neighbors. They're kind of the new kids on the block right now, and they could use some clout in their corner."

"I know the feeling," Jess commiserated. "Maybe we can include them in the piece, too, if it doesn't run too long."

From there, to both Ty and Jess's relief, the talk revolved around the Knights and this latest project of Jess's, instead of her personal life and her fictitious alliance with Ty.

Jess shut her apartment door behind her and immediately sagged against its sturdy panel for support. This had to qualify as one of the longest, most stressful evenings of her life, and she was so darned glad it was over that she could have cried. But that would only have made her tension headache throb even worse, not to mention clogging up her sinuses.

Her head wasn't the only thing aching, either. She'd be lucky if her ankle wasn't black and blue by morning. Every time Ty had thought she might say something out of line, or blurt out some bit of information she shouldn't that would make a lie of their pretense, he had nudged her with his foot to keep her quiet. After a dozen or so times, even the rubber sole of his sport shoe had felt like a sledge hammer. In retaliation, she'd taken to surreptitiously ramming her elbow into his rib cage. She sincerely hoped he was hurting at least as badly as she was, the rotten rat!

Slowly, so as not to jar her head, Jess made her way down the hall into her bedroom. After ridding herself of her clothes, she went into the adjoining bathroom, popped three aspirin and took a long, hot shower. Attired in her cotton Ohio State University nightshirt, she was brushing her teeth when she heard a familiar mechanical sound from the spare bedroom, which she used as her office. It was her fax machine, printing out a message.

Curious as to who would be faxing her at this hour, she ambled barefoot into the office. There were already four sheets of copied pages lining the tray, and another still printing. Plucking them up, she scanned them, and just as swiftly felt her temper rising to the boiling point. That blasted ape! That bossy, arrogant snot! How dare he presume to dictate to her! And how had Tyler James gotten her fax number, anyway? She hadn't even given him her regular phone number, or her address. If she had to hazard a guess, she'd say he'd called Tommy, and her buttinski godfather had provided him with the number, and heaven only knew what other private information about her as well. She was going to wring both their necks!

The first of the lot was the cover page with Ty's name and return fax number and a short, succinct explanation. He wanted her to fill out the questionnaire he'd devised, the better to exchange necessary data between them. In turn, he would send one back to her with the personal facts on himself.

Jess glanced at the four-page, single-spaced document, her eyebrows and her blood pressure rising at the number of questions and the nature of them. How in the heck had he typed this up so quickly? She'd only dropped him off at his car a little over an hour ago! And the things he'd had the gall to ask her! Why, this guy had more raw nerve than a decayed tooth! Beyond full name, address, age, height, weight, schooling, work experience, and the usual statistics you'd expect to find on, say, a job application, he was requesting some very private information, the nosy damned twit!

One line wanted her to list the names of close relatives, living or deceased, and include any relevant or interesting details about them. Another actually inquired about sexually transmitted diseases, and if she'd ever been tested for AIDS! Additionally, there was a query about any medical problems, such as diabetes, allergies, ulcers, recent or pending operations, or drug addictions! Was there a family history of heart problems, migraines, or—the topper—mental illness? Then he got really nit-picky and wanted to know if she wore dentures, eyeglasses or contact lenses, if she snored, and how severe she would rate her PMS.

The list went on and on, asking about everything from her favorite color and food preferences, to the type of undies, nighties or pajamas she wore—or did she sleep in the nude? What size was her bed? Did it have a regular mattress or was it a waterbed? Did she prefer one side of the bed to the other? Could she swim? Did she have any annoying habits, other than being a wise-ass? What were her hobbies? What games or sports did she like? Was she a health nut? Did she exercise regularly? By the time she was finished reading, Jess was surprised he hadn't inquired if she suffered from irregularity, though he had thought to ask what brand of toothpaste she used, and if she preferred a shower to a bath.

To say she was ticked was an understatement. Talk about brass balls! This guy had to be sporting a pair of stainless steel bowling balls! Her headache forgotten, or more likely overridden by fury, Jess sat down at her desk. Within minutes, she was firing a return fax message back to him:

> *If you think for one minute I am going to answer your asinine questions, you are certifiably insane. For all I know you'd broadcast my answers on the Internet. Furthermore, this is not a game of "you show me yours, and I'll show me mine." I'm only doing this for Tommy, who is on my black list right alongside you for giving you my fax number. So shove your questionnaire where the sun doesn't shine, super jock.*

As soon as the fax signaled "message sent and received," Jess shut off the machine, pulled the plug for good measure, and stomped angrily back to her bedroom. She'd scarcely put her head on the pillow when her bedside phone rang.

Yanking the receiver up, she barked out, "Buzz off, pond scum!"

"Oh, come on, Jess." It was him. "We really need to get to know some of these intimate details about each other if we're going to convince everyone we're hot for each other. And I'd certainly never put such information 'on line.' I'm not that much of a cad."

"How am I supposed to know that?" she countered stiffly.

"You would, if you'd give me a chance—if you'd cooperate with me instead of bucking me at every turn. So, how about it?"

"No way, José. You'll find out on a 'need-to-know basis.' "

"And risk blowing the whole scam? What will your dear Tommy think of that?"

"Frankly, Scarlett . . ." her voice trailed off, letting him fill in the rest.

"Neither would I, except that I'd like to keep my job, so why don't you stop being such a prude? These are the nineties, after all."

"I know the year. Unlike you, I'm also aware of the hour. Good night. Don't call me again."

She hung up, but before she could unplug the phone, it rang again. Even knowing better, she answered it. "Can't you take a hint?"

"If you won't fax your responses, give them to me over the phone. I promise confidentiality on the really personal stuff."

"Look, James, give it up. While I appreciate this modern technical age, I don't trust it with private matters. That goes for computers, modems, fax, phone, and mail. Now, if you don't mind, I'd like to get some sleep."

"Wait! Don't hang up yet!"

She sighed audibly. "What is it now?"

"Meet me in the morning. Here. There. Wherever you choose. We can have breakfast and go over the list of questions one by one. For every reply you give, I'll match it. You can even add to the list if you want."

"And delete those I don't like," she bargained.

"It's a deal. Where and when?"

"Neutral ground. Denny's, near me, at nine. You pay."

"You're late." Jess speared Ty with a put-out look.

He slid into the booth seat opposite her. "It took me a while to find the place," he told her, his voice rife with exasperation. "I'm not all that familiar with Columbus as yet, and your directions, 'Denny's near me,' weren't very explicit, you know."

She offered an indifferent shrug. "Sorry about that."

He snorted in disbelief. "And pigs fly, too." Placing a sheaf of papers on the table, he said, "Did you bring your copy?"

"Yes. I thought about using it for toilet tissue, but I figured as stubborn as you are you'd only run off another batch."

He grinned. "You bet your sweet tush, I would. Shall we get started?"

"Can we at least order breakfast first, Mr. Impatience?"

Ty ordered eggs, bacon, blueberry pancakes, juice, and a pot of coffee on the side. Jess requested French toast, juice, half a melon, and a glass of chocolate milk.

"Chocolate milk?" Ty teased. "No grown-up beverage?"

Jess scowled at him. "I intend to have coffee, too, but I want my calcium."

"Then why not order white milk? I recall hearing somewhere that you deplete all the vitamins and minerals in milk when you add chocolate to it."

"Hogwash. Pure, unadulterated tripe. All the chocolate does is add flavoring, which is the only way I'll drink it. I detest plain milk; have since I could toddle."

He pointed his fork for emphasis. "See there? That's the kind of thing I was talking about. Common everyday details. Wouldn't it seem odd if we went someplace and I ordered white milk for you? People would naturally assume, if we're seeing one another regularly, that I would know you didn't like it."

"I suppose so," she conceded. "That or you're just a big snoop."

"And you, as a reporter, aren't?" he huffed.

Jess held up her hand, signaling for a truce. "Okay, okay. Point taken."

Ty drew his pen from his shirt pocket. "Let's start with the easy stuff. What books have you read, and what movies have you seen lately?"

Forty-five minutes later, Jess sat back with a sigh. "Whoa. Stop. Enough. I'm drowning in trivia here. I need some time to assimilate what you've told me already."

"Me, too," Ty admitted. "Let's adjourn and pick it up later. Say tonight, for dinner? Just you and me?"

She thought about it for a moment, then agreed. "As long as it's not someplace swanky. I don't do swanky unless it's absolutely imperative."

"Why?"

"Because I hate to wear flats or those stupid-looking dinky heels. Even I know they don't complement an evening dress worth beans. I might as well wear army boots and have done with it."

"So wear regular high heels."

She wrinkled her nose at him. "Right. And look like a giraffe? Besides, I don't even own a pair."

"Buy some. You can wear them when we go out, if no other time. I'll still be taller than you." He paused a minute, then added, "You should stand tall and proud, Jess, with your back straight, and your chest thrown out. You can't do diddly damn about your height, anyway, so why not flaunt it instead of creeping around all hunched over, as if you think you're some freak?"

"Easy for you to say," she muttered. "You're a walking, talking ad for physical perfection, and you darn well know it. You're the type of guy all the girls go ga-ga over. Couldn't you at least get your nose broken, or chip a tooth, or something to make yourself a little less gorgeous? Just one tiny flaw or two, so the rest of us don't feel so inferior?"

As she spoke, she unconsciously rubbed at the small bump on the bridge of her own nose, evidence that she'd had it broken at one time.

Reaching across the table, Ty brushed her fingers aside. His fingers replaced hers, stroking the almost indiscernible lump. "How'd you break it?"

"Playing soccer." It irritated her that goose bumps had popped up on her nape and her words emerged on a breathless whisper. She was reacting to his mere touch like a moon-struck calf!

"Didn't they set it at the hospital? Not that it's all that obvious. I didn't even notice it until you started rubbing at it."

His hand had dropped away, and she could speak normally again. She explained. "For some reason, the X-rays didn't show the break, maybe because they were wet when the doctor reviewed them. Anyway, the doctor didn't catch it right away. By the time the mistake was discovered, my nose was well on the way to healing. There was no way I was going to let them rebreak it and go through all that pain again. Not to mention running around looking like a giant raccoon for several more weeks, with two huge neon shiners.''

"Can't blame you there," he concurred. "Besides, like I said, it's not that noticeable. Now, if they'd left you looking like Karl Malden, that would be another matter altogether.''

Jess had to laugh. "I guess I should be thankful. It could have been worse.''

"Lots of things could be worse," he agreed. "We should all remember more often to be thankful when they aren't. They say that to an optimist, a half-filled glass is always half full. To a pessimist, that same glass is half empty. Sometimes, it's all in your perspective.''

Jess's wry grin mocked his curbside philosophizing. "To my way of thinking, it's still a glass that needs washing.''

CHAPTER 5

Jess had some research to do on her computer, so she didn't see Ty again until he showed up at her door that evening. She'd dressed casually, in lightweight slacks and boat neck pullover, and had exchanged her comfy tennies for a pair of sandals. Ty was even more casually clothed, in shorts and summer knit shirt.

He glanced over her attire and approved it with a nod. "Nice, but if you want to change into shorts, I'll be glad to wait. It's hotter than Hades, and twice as humid. I wouldn't want you to be uncomfortable, and we're not going anywhere fancy. In fact, if it's all right with you, I figured we'd pick up a bucket of chicken and the fixings and head to the park, or maybe find a spot down by the river, on the off chance of catching a breeze."

"Sounds fine with me, and in that case I'll take you up on your offer and switch to shorts."

He followed her into the apartment, gratefully sucking in the dry, cool air. "Ah, air-conditioning. God bless the man who invented it!"

"Make yourself comfortable," Jess told him, heading down the hall. "I'll be back in a jiffy."

"Mind if I take a look around the place?" he asked.

"Go ahead. Help yourself to some iced tea if you want."

Like Jess, her apartment wasn't showy. Her living room furniture appeared more comfortable than trendy, though instead of the usual couch or loveseat she had chosen a futon. Ty had seen them in stores, but had never sat on one before. He lowered himself onto the puffy cushion and bounced lightly.

"Hey! Is this thing really comfortable to sleep on?" he called out to her.

"The futon?" she yelled back, hazarding a guess.

"Is that what it's called? This couch-thing that folds out?"

"Yes, it's not bad at all, but I wouldn't want to be relegated to it on a nightly basis."

Skirting an oak end table, Ty zeroed in on her entertainment center. Her TV was a color portable with a built-in VCR, nice but nothing to rave about. But her stereo system, now that was state-of-the-art! Ty perused her collection of tapes and CDs.

"I see you like some of the same music I do," he shouted over his shoulder.

"You don't have to yell; I'm right here." She'd come into the room so quietly he hadn't heard her.

"Sorry. I thought you were still changing." His gaze, when he turned, traveled lingeringly over the super-long, shapely expanse of her legs. His eyes widened and seemed to grow darker, becoming more midnight blue than indigo. He coughed to clear his throat, and said huskily, "I'll take you up on that iced tea if you don't mind. I haven't made my way past the living room yet."

"So I see." Jess headed for the kitchen, with Ty trailing behind. She walked to the refrigerator, retrieved the pitcher of tea, turned around and bumped smack into him. He was peering over her shoulder into the refrigerator.

"If you're that hungry, I can make you a sandwich," she said, pushing past him to the cupboard where she kept the glasses. "Or we can leave now if you prefer."

"No, I'm fine." His head was half-buried in the fridge as he inventoried its contents.

Jess didn't know whether to be perturbed or to laugh. "Uh, Ty. What are you doing?"

"Finding out what kinds of foods you like."

"Oh. Well, move, will you, so I can get to the ice cubes?"

Instead, he opened the freezer and handed her a tray, getting a look at the frozen goods inside.

"Real ice cream," he commented. "And not a diet entree in sight. It's going to be fun going out for a change with someone who isn't counting calories. I hate sitting down to a dinner of country fried steak, mashed potatoes with gravy, creamed peas, and rolls slathered with butter, while my date is munching on a plate of rabbit food. It makes me feel guilty, and takes a lot of the enjoyment out of the meal."

"You certainly won't have that problem with me," she assured him, passing him a glass of tea. "If it isn't chock-full of calories and fat, half the taste is gone. And if it's made of chocolate, get out of my way or I'll mow you down to get at it. I sincerely pray that I never become overweight, because my willpower in that department is totally nil."

By now, Ty was out of the freezer and had spotted her cappuccino machine. "Wow! Look at that!" He tugged open a cupboard door, then another. "You have real food in here, too, and pots and pans that actually look used, and a mixer, and a Crockpot, and a food processor. Tell me you cook, honest-to-God cook, and I'll marry you tomorrow."

Jess shook her head, amused at his overblown enthusiasm. "Down, boy! Down! Let's not get carried away, here. Besides, you'd be the last man I'd choose to marry."

Ty blinked in surprise and tendered a frown. "Why? You've already admitted that you think I'm handsome, I'm semifamous and make good money, and"—he winked—"I've never had any complaints in the bedroom. All in all, most women would consider me a prize catch."

"I'm not most women," she reminded him, "and if you'd think about it for a minute, you'd know why I'd be nuts to marry you. Do you really suppose I'd want to go through the rest of my life with the name of Jessie James?"

Ty roared with laughter, as once again she caught him off guard. "Oh, that's choice!" he hooted.

"To you, maybe, but not to me."

"But you do cook?" he urged, nodding toward a rack of cookbooks he'd just noticed.

"When I have time," she told him. "When I'm not on assignment somewhere and living out of a suitcase."

"Do you do that much?" he questioned. "Travel, I mean."

"I try to hold it to a minimum, but often there's a story I want to research, something that just won't gel via phone or computer, or some event or incident that needs that hands-on touch. Then I drive or fly to wherever it is and get the scoop firsthand. Sometimes being there—seeing, touching, smelling, experiencing it up close, getting face-to-face interviews— makes the difference between a so-so story and a really great one."

"That makes sense, I suppose," he granted. After a quick peek into the laundry area, Ty sauntered back through the living room and headed down the hall. With Jess trailing behind, he found the hall closet and the guest bath, giving them a swift once-over and continuing on. Next to be discovered was her office.

"I take it this used to be the second bedroom?" he ventured.

"Yes, but I converted it into an office for myself, since I do a lot of my work at home. When I have overnight guests, they camp out in the living room."

He wandered around the room, checking out her desktop computer, her printer, her bookcase, her fax. "You've got some quality equipment here," he remarked. Bending over, he noted the read-out on the fax and chuckled. "I see you remembered to turn it back on."

After admiring her laptop computer, he made a beeline for the only remaining room off the hall. Without bothering to ask permission first, he opened the door and walked in. "The master bedroom, or in this instance I suppose it's the mistress's bedroom," he stated, looking around with interest. "Cozy. I forget, what's that design on the comforter and curtains called?"

"Paisley."

"Oh, yeah. Those curved jobbies always remind me of sperm." Her stunned reaction to his blunt statement was lost on him as he strode into the connecting bath.

To Jess's annoyance he opened the cupboard beneath the sink, then the door to the medicine cabinet. "What do you think you're doing?" she snapped, slamming the cabinet door shut again.

"I can't believe you! Didn't your mother teach you any better?"

He had the nerve to grin at her as he slipped past her into the bedroom again. "Just checking your supply of Midol, my dear. No need to get your dander up. On second thought, if you're getting that strung out, maybe you should pop a couple of those babies before we leave. And I noticed you're low on tampons."

"Shove it, James."

At this juncture, she really shouldn't have been surprised when Ty marched over, yanked open the door to her closet, and began rifling through her clothes. "What are you looking for now, pray tell?" she inquired sharply.

"Nothing particular," he told her. "Just trying to get a sense of your style, and the colors you prefer." He dragged out an army green tailored blazer, held it up, and grimaced. "Oh, puke! Don't tell me you really like this thing?"

She grabbed it from him and rammed it back in the closet. "That's it, buster. The tour's over. You've worn out your welcome."

By the time she slammed the closet door, Ty, ignoring her obvious pique, was cataloging the contents of her dresser drawers. He'd found the one with her underwear and was rifling through it before she could stop him.

"Okay, where are they?" he muttered.

Jess shoved at his hands, all the while plying her weight against his in an effort to shut the drawer. "Where's what?" she snarled. "Damn it, Ty! If you're on a hunt for drugs, I don't have any. I don't sell, and I don't use, and I don't associate with anyone who does."

"I already figured that," he stated flatly. "You wouldn't

want to mess up your brain, since that's how you make your living. I'm trying to find your bras, but all I can locate so far are these shapeless sports things that look like sawed-off T-shirts.''

"My bras?" she repeated stupidly. "My bras?" This time she shrieked the words. "Look, you pervert. If you're into ladies' underwear, go buy your own and get your big paws off mine!"

He turned and gave her a disgusted look. "I'm as normal as the next guy. Maybe more. I just needed to see what size you wore, and I figured if I asked, you wouldn't tell me."

"Damn straight, Sherlock." She glared at him, her eyes blazing like lit coals.

He held out his arms, palms up in a conciliatory gesture. "I can explain."

"Uh huh. Sure you can," she said snidely.

"The reason I needed to know your size was . . . well, I got you something today, and I wanted to make sure they'd fit."

Jess shook her head, as if to clear her ears. "Care to run that past me again?"

"What the hell. You can't get any more pissed at me than you are already." He reached into his rear pants' pocket and pulled out a small paper sack, holding it out to her.

Jess reached for it hesitantly, as if it might contain a family of tarantulas.

"Go ahead," he prodded. "Open it."

She did. Inside were two badly mashed, squishy flesh-tone objects. She pulled them out, holding them by the tips of her fingers.

Her enunciation was exaggerated to the extreme, her tone deadly calm as she inquired, "Are these what I think they are?"

"What do you think they are?" he hedged, his expression as guilty as sin.

"Falsies." She all but spat the word at him.

"Actually, the correct term these days, according to the saleslady who waited on me, is 'breast enhancers.' ''

"I don't care if they're called booby balloons!" she shot

back, waving them in front of his nose. "It amounts to the same thing! And you can take them right back! Maybe you can get a refund. If not, wear them yourself for all I care. I certainly won't!"

"I knew you'd take this all wrong," he griped. "Look, Jess. I was just trying to help."

"Help?" she mocked. "If this is your idea of help, I can darned well do without it."

He sighed. "I didn't mean to hurt your feelings. I just figured you must be self-conscious about the size of your breasts, and maybe you were too shy or sensitive about the subject to buy something like this yourself."

"But you weren't at all shy about doing it for me, were you?" she exclaimed in disbelief. "My God! I can't believe you actually purchased these yourself! Or did you have someone else do it for you?" Her eyes narrowed with suspicion. "Fess up, you cad. Who else is in on this nasty little joke of yours?"

"It's no joke, Jess, and no one knows but you and me. I honestly did buy them myself, and believe me when I tell you it was anything but funny. I had to talk my ass off to get that woman to believe I was buying the blasted things for my poor, embarrassed, underdeveloped little sister."

"Well!" she huffed. "Thank you too much for your blunt analysis of my attributes, or lack thereof. However, your efforts and any embarrassment you suffered—and I hope you were humiliated to the hilt—were all in vain. I learned a long time ago not to attempt to make myself over into something I wasn't meant to be. I also learned this particular lesson the hard way," she added, wagging the falsies at him for emphasis. "Believe me, the lesson stuck."

"You, uh . . . you tried some already?"

"To my everlasting regret," she admitted. "I was fifteen, and all the other girls in my class had chests. All but me. I was still in the training bra stage, being teased to death by my older brother. Finally, Mom took pity on me and bought me a padded bra. Overnight, I went from a minus-A to a B cup, and

I took a lot more ribbing from brother Mike about that. He liked to claim I'd sprayed them with Miracle Grow.''

A chuckle spurted from Ty's lips. At Jess's scowl, he pursed them in an effort to quell any further outbursts.

She resumed her tale. ''Some of the other kids at school were really unkind about it, too, but I ignored them all in favor of my new, improved shape. Until the day the washer broke and Mom and I went to the laundromat to do the clothes. Everything went fine until we got home and I couldn't locate the foam inserts to my bra. To make a long story short, we drove back to the laundromat. Mom went in and came out just as fast. She got back into the car, clutched the wheel, and in a strangled voice told me that if I wanted those things back that badly, I would have to go in and get them myself, because someone had tacked them to the bulletin board.''

''Oh, my Lord!'' If his life had depended on it, Ty could not have kept from laughing.

Even Jess was wearing a wry grin, remembering that long-ago day. ''Oh, go ahead. Mom laughed, too. So hard she could scarcely see to drive, as I recall.''

''What did you do? You left the falsies there, I presume?''

''On the contrary. I went in there, in front of a packed audience of males and females of all ages, I might add. With a face as red as a ripe apple, I snatched my 'boobies' off that wall and ran out as fast as I could. Mom peeled rubber for half a block making our getaway.

''Not long afterward, I decided the embarrassment and the heckling weren't worth it. God forbid something even more mortifying should happen. The padded bra hit the trash, and from that day forth my motto has been, 'What you see is what you get, like it or not.' ''

Ty reached out and plucked the offending objects from her grasp. ''Jess, if I'd known, I swear to you I would never have bought these things. I didn't do it with malicious intent.''

''I believe you, but that doesn't help much right this minute. You see, Ty, I realize that you're used to being seen with beautiful women, with well-rounded figures, and I don't fit that bill by a long shot. Whether you admit it or not, you and I both know that your underlying motive was to make me over into someone more suited to your I-deserve-the-best standards. Well, I've got news for you, Studly Do-Wrong. I'm not going to play that game. Not for you, or any other self-centered male on the planet. Along with other hard-learned lessons, I've concluded that any man worthy of my respect and affection will accept me just as I am. If not, he can just trot on down the road, because he's not welcome here.''

Ty grimaced. ''So basically what you're saying is, 'You are woman, hear you roar'? Thanks for cluing me in to your feminist leanings, because I think I've finally figured out what that acronym you threw at me the other day means. Wagara must stand for Women's Association of Grandiose and Ridiculous Attitudes.''

Jess dredged up a fake smile. ''Sorry. Nice try, but no cigar.''

''Okay, so the falsies are out. How about a nice underwire bra? My sister claims they do wonders to push everything up and in or out or whatever.''

''I'm so glad for your sister,'' Jess professed blandly.

''The least you could do is buy some sexy silk undies. What's with all the cotton? You planning to join a convent?''

''I doubt they'd accept me. I'm a Methodist. Now, I hope you'll understand if I ask you to leave. And take those stupid falsies with you, if you please.''

''Oh, come on, Jess. I've apologized. Let bygones be bygones. I don't want to eat alone, and it's too late to make a date with someone else. Besides, I'm supposed to be seeing you exclusively, which, if you really want to know, is putting quite a crimp in my social life these days.''

She jerked her thumb toward the street outside, her expression unrelenting. ''Wagara, Romeo. Wagara.''

CHAPTER 6

The Knights had their third preseason contest that Sunday. It was a home game against the Minnesota Vikings, and the new climate-controlled Castle-Dome, built to accommodate a whopping hundred thousand fans, was barely half-filled. Perhaps because it was still preseason, or maybe because the Knights had lost their first two matchups, one at home and one away. The Seahawks had really dented their armor last week in Seattle, but to be fair they had made a fair showing against the 49ers in the preseason opener, losing by only six points, the total of two missed field goals by their rookie kicker.

Corey Rome must have been watching for Jess. The minute Jess saw her, the woman waved for Jess to join her down front, on the first section of seats behind the home bench.

"I saved you a seat," Corey told her, then laughed. "Not that there aren't plenty to choose from, but these are reserved for us." "Us" being the wives, children, and special friends of the players.

"Thanks," Jess said with a smile. "And thank you for your help the other day. I know you probably don't get such strange calls every day."

Corey chuckled. "I've had weirder calls, believe me."

For two days after Ty had left her apartment, Jess had stewed. She'd fumed. She'd cursed Ty for the arrogant ass he was. Then she'd phoned Corey Rome, the only woman she'd met lately with a figure anywhere comparable to her own, and presumed to ask the model's advice. Corey had been a doll about the entire subject, not at all bitchy or superior—which was why Jess was sitting next to her now, wearing a stretchy new satin-and-lace, barely padded "Magic" bra beneath her ribbed knit top.

Corey's eyes twinkled. "So? It looks good. How does it feel?"

"Odd," Jess confided in a near whisper. "More confining than my sports bras, but lighter, too. I didn't know they made them so pretty these days, without those stupid removable pads."

Corey winked. "Hey! We've come a long way, babe. A little polyester fiberfill in the right places, and whallah! Instant cleavage! And who's to know? In the heat of passion, a guy is going to be eyeing what's popping out over the lace, not what's supporting you underneath or on the sides."

"Are you sure it isn't too much? Too drastic a change?" Jess asked self-consciously.

"Absolutely not," Corey assured her. "Now, sit up straight before I'm tempted to strap a yardstick to your back. Show those puppies off, girl!"

Once the game got under way, Jess got caught up in the action and forgot all about her slinky new undies. Having attended OSU, she'd been a dyed-in-the-wool Buckeye fan, and had evolved into an enthusiastic football fan overall, enjoying both college and pro games. While so many women complained of being football widows on weekends and Monday nights, Jess was usually glued to her TV set, happily munching popcorn and playing "armchair quarterback." That, or freezing her buns off in Ohio State's horseshoe stadium, bravely courting pneumonia and the flu.

Of course, this was still August, as muggy and buggy as it could get outdoors. Contrarily, while it was a relief not to have to sweat and swat mosquitos, in some inexplicable way, being

ensconced in such a perfect-weather atmosphere took away
from the spectator ambience somehow. All this comfort at a
football match would take some getting used to, Jess supposed.

The first quarter was slow and relatively uneventful, ending
in a scoreless tie. "I realize no one wants to get injured in
preseason, but this is ridiculous!" Jess griped.

"I know," Corey agreed with a bored yawn. "You'd think
they were all afraid of getting those boss uniforms dirty, as if
they had to do their own laundry!"

The team uniforms were undeniably sharp. Crimson and
silver, they were designed to emulate as closely as possible the
battle outfits of knights-of-old. From a distance, the jerseys
actually looked as if they were made of chain-mail armor, the
front of each adorned with a pair of crossed swords and the
player's number on a scarlet shield. Likewise, the helmets were
fashioned to resemble a knight's helmet and sported a horse's
head on the sides, the symbol used in chess to designate the
knight's piece. For each touchdown, sack, or other important
personal achievement, a silver spur would be added, affixed to
the wide band of red that encircled the outer edge of the helmet.

Naturally, the cheerleaders had to have outfits to complement
the team, though in their case a lot of liberty had been taken
with the theme. Known unofficially as the Columbus Dames,
the formal title given to a female member of the order of
knighthood in olden days, they had chosen not to dress as
"ladies." Rather, they wore short skirts, which again appeared
to be made of metal, much like the skirts of tasses on a suit
of armor. Their sleeveless, bare-midriff tops were cunningly
cut in imitation of a breastplate. By contrast, those cute little
cowgirl getups the Dallas cheerleaders wore were almost
modest!

Thankfully, the pace picked up in the second quarter, as if
the players had finally gotten the feel of the field and the
measure of their opponents. Moreover, the players were still
vying for various slots on the teams, needing to prove to their
respective coaches that they were the best men for their positions, before final cuts were made in preparation for the regular
season. No one wanted to be relegated to second or third string

for the year, warming the bench until a player was injured or ousted.

The Vikings made the first touchdown, and the Columbus crowd booed their disappointment of the Knights' defense. It wasn't until the final minutes of the half that the Knights' offense caught fire. They marched steadily down the field, down by down. Then, from the Viking forty-yard line, Ty aired a bomb. Gabe ''Rocket'' Rome made a spectacular diving catch, landing in the end zone. With the others, Jess and Corey leapt to their feet, cheering madly. The point-after was good, and once again the quarter ended on a tie.

Toward the end of halftime, as everyone was getting settled again for the second half, Jess noticed a couple of cheerleaders staring pointedly in their direction. One in particular seemed displeased about something. Jess nudged Corey. ''Who is that redheaded Dame giving you looks that could kill?''

Corey looked, then laughed. ''Oh, that's Bambi. Isn't she a deer?'' she joked. ''And those daggers she's shooting are aimed at you, girlfriend, not at me.''

''Me?'' Jess exclaimed. ''But I haven't even met her. Why would she be mad at me?''

''Because you've got Ty, and she wants him. Rumor has it he took her out once, before you came along. I'd say a single date wasn't enough for her. After all, in these circles, dating the starting quarterback is quite a coup, especially if you manage to hang on to him for a while.''

''I see. So my dating him automatically makes me her enemy,'' Jess deduced. ''Seems rather sophomoric to me, but then what do I know?''

Corey shrugged. ''As they say, forewarned is forearmed. Don't be surprised if she or some of the others, out of pure jealousy, try to make trouble between you and Ty.''

That was a new concept for Jess. As far as she could recall, she couldn't name one person, particularly another female, who had ever expressed jealousy toward her. If anything, that shoe had always been on Jess's foot, envying other girls for their more attractive looks and greater popularity.

Trying not to be obvious about it, Jess studied her ''rival.''

Though Bambi was of average height, there was little else average about her. Her fiery hair fell in a thick tangle of curls halfway down her back. It framed an incredibly pretty face, complete with a cute little nose that made Jess feel like an aardvark by comparison. Then there was the girl's abundant chest, perhaps her most outstanding feature. Jess wondered how long it had been since Bambi had seen her own hooves . . . er, feet! Years, most likely.

Not having met her, Jess didn't know how Bambi, even with that ridiculous name, measured up in the brains department. But with her other attributes, Jess supposed it didn't really matter if the woman was a certified airhead. The guys would still be stumbling over each other to gain her attention.

As the team came back onto the field to begin the third quarter, Jess was grateful for the distraction. She'd learned years before that it did little good to dwell on her own deficiencies, though at times like this they were hard to ignore.

The Vikings were all revved up now, and out for blood. They scored three touchdowns, adding twenty-one points, in quick succession. Try as they might, the Knights still couldn't get their act together. Because of their weak offensive line, Ty was sacked twice. When he did connect with a receiver, his teammate either dropped the ball or was hit for a loss. Finally, they did score, and even made the two-point conversion afterward.

In the first minutes of the final quarter, the Knights' kick receiver—a lightning-fast little guy by the name of Carlos "Chili" Rodriguez—ran the ball back seventy-two yards for a spectacular touchdown. The spectators came to their feet, cheering wildly, then groaned in tandem as the kicker missed the follow-up point.

Somehow, for the duration of the game, the defense held the Vikings from further scoring. With fifteen seconds showing on the clock, the Vikings fumbled. The Knights gained possession of the ball on their own fifty-two-yard line. It was obvious to all that with no time for anything else, this was going to be a "Hail, Mary" attempt. The Vikings went for the rush, but the Knights' defense held long enough for Ty to set his feet and throw. It was the most perfect pass Jess had ever seen, as the ball spiraled toward the end zone, hitting Shane Griffin square on the numbers. The crowd went collectively nuts.

The score was twenty-eight, twenty-seven, in favor of the Vikings. One point would tie the game. Two would win it. It seemed every fan in the stands was shouting for the two-pointer, for though a tie would automatically send the two teams into overtime and perhaps give the Knights another chance to score, it would allot the Vikings that same opportunity.

For reasons Jess would never understand, the head coach opted for the kick, instead. She and the rest of the crowd held their breath and prayed. All for naught. The kick went wide to the right as the clock ticked down to zero. The game was over, lost by one lousy point. Rather, as Jess saw it, lost by two missed kicks by the most inept kicker she'd ever had the misfortune to witness.

What they had hoped would be a victory party turned out to be a pity party at the Romes' house. Several of the major players and their partners gathered there to commiserate with each other. The coaches and team owners were noticeably absent, as was the shame-faced kicker. Though Jess had tried to back out as well, Corey was having none of it. Moreover, Jess was still supposed to be Ty's current flame, and was therefore expected to show up to lend her fellow a sympathetic shoulder.

"We almost did it, dammit!" one disgruntled player grumbled, aping the various comments of his comrades. "I could throttle that Alan Crumrine! What the hell did that boy do, put his shoes on the wrong feet?"

"More likely, he screwed his head on backwards," a running back offered. "Sort of like our little Destiny here." He hugged the cheerleader to his side, ruffling her hair affectionately.

"I resent that remark," she piped up.

"No, you resemble that remark," Dino told her with a chuckle. "Come to think of it, so does our *deer* Bambi."

Bambi struck an offended pose, her lower lip projecting in

a sultry pout. "As if you're some sort of genius, Sherwood. I saw you fumble that ball tonight. Maybe you ought to try Super Glue next week."

Dino shook his head. "Nah. I might get high on it, like you do, carrot-top. Warp my fantastic brain cells."

"Get a life, you creep," she shot back.

Gabriel Rome chuckled. "Better watch it, Dino, or Bambi will whack off your ponytail. You don't want to lose your talent like Samson lost his strength when Delilah cut his hair short."

"God forbid!" someone else put in. "Lord knows we need all the talent we can muster right now, and then some."

"I vote we let the cheerleaders play the next game," Heidi suggested with a sneer. "We sure couldn't do any worse than you guys have been."

"Right!" came the derisive reply from a linebacker. "And what're you gonna use for muscle? Boobs, maybe?"

"Good idea," Shasta said, thrusting out her ample chest. "We might do better with these than you big apes do with your hammy thighs and beer bellies."

"Hey, woman! I've worked hard for this excellent physique," Sir Loin Simms objected. He patted his protruding stomach. "I've got a lot of pasta and beef invested here. You ought to learn the difference between fat and muscle."

"Well, buddy, this *is* muscle," Shasta contended, bringing her arms in to her sides to accentuate her cleavage.

The cheerleaders all nodded, each mimicking Shasta.

"I'd wager there are more rubber bumpers here than there were in the parking lot tonight!" Jack Hays proposed on a brusque laugh.

"More silicone, anyway," Corey muttered in disgust.

"Or maybe they just used Miracle Grow," Ty suggested, winking at Jess, as if they shared a private joke.

Jess was not amused at his comment, particularly since she wasn't sure his jest wasn't aimed at her. She was sure he'd noticed her improved figure, and wondered if he wasn't poking fun at her. Anger and embarrassment combined to render her pink-faced and momentarily speechless.

At the same time, Bambi, ignoring Jess entirely, approached Ty and wantonly pressed her chest against his. "Now, honey," she purred silkily, batting her long lashes at him, "you know these are the genuine article. Every single morsel. Heaven knows you inspected them thoroughly enough, and I've still got the love bites to prove it!"

Despite himself, Ty felt a blush creeping up his neck. The damned brazen hussy! So he did get into a hot and heavy petting session with her the one night they had gone out! Did she have to announce it to the whole world? Right here in front of Jess, to boot?

He stared down at Bambi, his gaze stony and unblinking, as he took her arm and put her away from him. A humorless smirk slanted his lips as he said softly, but audibly, "Trouble is, Bambi, a man might suffocate in all that surplus flesh. I wouldn't care to risk it again. I'm just thankful we stopped at the preliminary stages, or you might have smothered me. Besides, I've been saving myself for Jess."

Sporadic chuckles broke out, tentative at first, then heartier as Ty's friends overcame their initial discomfort and rallied around him.

"Saving yourself for Jess? That's a good one, T.D."

"Can I get that on tape?" someone else hooted.

As Bambi stalked off in a huff, Gabe walked up, slapped his pal on the back, and teased, "Yeah, Ty. I always did suspect you were as pure as a lily. That must be why you're so uptight most of the time. Jess, you ought to help him loosen up a little. Maybe it'll improve his timing."

Corey took pity on her new friend, who now looked as if she'd been dipped in poppy red paint. "Cool it, guys. Especially you, Gabe. You're embarrassing Jess. She's not used to your ribald humor the way I am."

She looped an arm across Jess's shoulders. "Come on, gal. Let's go rustle up some chips and dip and other goodies while these yahoos fire up the barbecue grill."

Corey then turned and surveyed her guests, her lilac-gray eyes glittering. Her perfectly sculpted face, with its flawless café-au-lait complexion, took on a regal expression, one that had graced the covers of magazines the world over. "Ladies, feel free to join us. You'll note I used the word *ladies*. Those of you who must behave like ho-bags, feel free to leave or shape up, whichever suits you, but in my home I reserve the right to set high standards of decorum. Abide by them, or don't bother to darken my door until you can."

Jess and several other women followed their hostess into the kitchen. "You didn't have to say that on my account," Jess told her.

"I didn't do it for your sake alone," Corey assured her. "I simply won't abide bad behavior in my own house. That goes for the guys as well as the women, and everyone might just as well learn the guidelines from the start."

"Then maybe you'd better post a list of no-no's," Shannon Baxter suggested wryly. "I'm sure there are people here who wouldn't know proper manners if they stumbled over them."

Corey merely laughed and fluttered her brightly manicured fingers in a nonchalant manner. "They'll learn fairly quickly what I will tolerate and what I won't. Believe me, Gabe and I have been through this before, with other teams in other cities. I'm an old hand at reforming the irreformable, and at politely booting the rest out."

The party went smoothly from that point on. Bambi and a couple of her cohorts had opted to depart the premises, but most of the guests had remained and were on their best behavior.

Jess actually enjoyed herself, despite the fact that she was totally miffed at Ty. Not only had he put her on the defensive with that remark about Miracle Grow and that oh-so-obvious wink at her, but all evening she'd caught him stealing glances at her when he thought she didn't notice—looks she could swear were aimed at her chest more often than her face. But what really rubbed a raw spot was knowing that the rotten lecher had not only dated Bimbo Bambi, but hadn't denied fondling the cheerleader's bountiful assets. Sure, he'd claimed it hadn't gone far, and had also professed to prefer Jess, but she knew that was all for show, part of the act to convince everyone that they were a couple. In reality, he was one of countless men Jess had met who would choose boobs over brains any day of the week.

The gathering broke up around midnight. After thanking Gabe and Corey for their hospitality, Jess headed for her car. She was halfway down the walk when Ty caught up with her. "Hey! Wait up. Don't I even get a goodbye kiss?"

Jess rounded on him, her face furious. "I'll tell you what you can kiss, mister," she snarled. "A maggot-infested garbage can!"

Ty held up his palms and backed off a step. "Whoa! You're really ticked! Care to tell me why?"

"As if you didn't know, you swine!" she hissed. "How dare you humiliate me like that in front of all those people! Staring at my chest! Making snide remarks about Miracle Grow! But I guess I shouldn't expect any better from a man who has the temerity to publicly admit dating someone named Bambi."

He had the gall to grin. "So that's what has your britches in a bind! You're jealous!"

"Oh, grow some brains, James! Preferably somewhere other than in your pants!"

"As soon as you cultivate a sense of humor," he countered bluntly. "You're entirely too sensitive, Miss Know-It-All. That Miracle Grow comment was made as a joke between you and me, a silly dig at Bambi and company. It was not in any way meant as an insult to you or to divulge your intimate secrets."

"You're doing it again," she stated testily.

"Doing what?"

"You're staring at my breasts, you oversexed beast!"

"Well, hell!" he exclaimed with exasperation. "I'm a man. All normal, red-blooded, sighted men do it. Furthermore, you can't tell me women don't check out a guy's physique."

She offered a nasty smirk. "Of course we do, but we do try to make eye contact once in a while during the course of a conversation, if only for propriety's sake."

In a move that took her completely by surprise, Ty stepped closer, raising his hands and clasping them around her midriff. His palms skimmed her ribs, coming to rest along the curve of her breasts. Despite the barrier of her knit top, his fingers found the outline of her bra beneath it, brushing over the lace-adorned cups. As his thumbs whispered across her nipples, even through two layers of cloth, Jess shivered. She stood spellbound as his mouth lowered toward hers.

"Lace," he murmured. "Over silk?"

"S . . . satin," she stammered, her mouth suddenly desert-dry.

His mouth brushed hers, so lightly she might have imagined it. "What color?"

"Peach."

"I love peaches," he claimed huskily.

"I could be wrong. It might be apricot," she said breathlessly.

"Sounds delicious."

His thumbs grazed the aroused peaks again. Jess quivered anew, her sigh melting against his lips as they claimed hers. His kiss was hot, inviting and demanding in like measure. His tongue traced her lips, exploring their shape, their texture, then slipped between them to leisurely twine with hers. His lips sipped at hers, learning her taste.

The ground tilted beneath Jess's feet, but Ty's arm was there to keep her from falling. He pulled her close, allowing only enough space between them for his hand to cradle her breast, for his fingers to ply their skillful magic on the dimpled crest. His lips and tongue teased, advancing and retreating, until Jess caught his head between her hands and anchored his mouth to hers. A groan rumbled in his chest as her tongue slid seductively past his teeth, initiating her own bold foray into his mouth.

They were both breathing heavily, lost in the heat of their embrace. Ty's hand was tugging at her shirt, trying to dislodge it from the waistband of her slacks, when loud laughter brought them abruptly back to earth. Jess gasped, lurching backward, and would have tripped had Ty not held on to her arm—though he didn't appear to be all that steady himself at the moment. He looked as dazed as she felt.

Three couples leaving the party trooped past them, issuing friendly taunts as they went.

"Administering a little mouth-to-mouth there, James?"

"What did Corey put in that jalapeño dip, anyway?"

"I don't know, but I hope you had some, honey."

"Carry on, folks. Don't mind us."

Jess wanted nothing more than to find a large hole, crawl into it, and pull it in after her! She'd never been so mortified! At least not since the "falsie" incident. Ty, blast his hide, just shrugged and chuckled along with them, as if it were no big deal to get caught necking in his friends' front yard.

From the porch, Corey flipped the light switch off and on again. Gabe called out, "Can't you wait until you get home?"

"Indeed!" Corey added, her tone as amused as her husband's. "This is a respectable neighborhood. Now go make out someplace else, before someone calls the cops. And Ty, get your big feet off my pansies, before I take a broom handle to your head!"

CHAPTER 7

Ty was at Jess's apartment at nine o'clock the next morning, apparently intent on beating her door down, from the sounds of it. Still in her jersey-nightie, Jess peered at him through the peephole. Even distorted by the minilens, he looked gorgeous! It just wasn't fair!

"Open up, Jess!" he hollered. "I know you're in there. Your car's still here."

"Go away!" she called back through the door.

"Oh, c'mon!" he wheedled. "I was counting on a couple cups of cappuccino."

"There's an espresso place two blocks south of here," she informed him. "Now, stop banging and yelling at me or I'm going to sic my dog on you."

He laughed. "You don't have a dog."

"I bought one this morning," she lied blatantly. "A big Doberman with a penchant for biting annoying quarterbacks."

"I don't hear him barking."

Jess waved her foot in front of the motion-activated rubber frog sitting on the floor just inside her front door. It gave its customary "ribbet . . . ribbet."

Ty let loose with another laugh. "Since when do Dobermans croak?"

"He has a cold," she ad-libbed.

"It's August, and so hot you can fry eggs on the sidewalk," he reminded her.

"It's a summer cold. Or maybe an allergy. It's pollen season."

"You're nuts, you know that?" he claimed. "Speaking of which, I brought donuts. Those gooey pecan twists you said were your favorites. Now, will you please open the door?"

Jess relented. He'd hit her weak point with the donuts.

Ty stepped inside, triggering the frog again as he entered. He stared down at it, his mouth quirked in a wry grin. "A poor excuse for a security system, if you ask me. But better than my first assumption, which was that you were in here kissing toads, trying to turn one of them into a prince, and risking warts in the process."

"Been there. Done that," she quipped. "It doesn't work. You're still a toad this morning."

He ogled the long expanse of leg beneath her sleep shirt. "Want me to check you over for warts?"

"Do you want to wear those donuts?" she countered.

"Your moods are as changeable as the wind," he complained, docilely following her into the kitchen. "You didn't seem to mind my hands on you last night. In fact, I'd swear you were enjoying yourself immensely."

"The kiss was nice," she admitted, "until we got caught looking like two sex-starved teenie-boppers."

Ty chuckled. "Yeah, that doused the flames real fast, didn't it?"

"I'm glad you found it funny. Personally, I was embarrassed to the hilt."

"Your parents never caught you smooching on the front porch with your date?" he asked.

Her sheepish expression gave her away. "Once, and that was enough. I was dating a basketball player, one of the few guys who was taller than me. The trouble was, we both wore braces. Our first, last, and only kiss was a disaster. His braces got tangled up with mine. Luckily, or unluckily, depending on your viewpoint, my dad was a dentist. He managed to extricate us, though not without quite a bit of work, during which he gave us a long sermon on the perils of 'swapping spit and germs' with another person, particularly someone of the opposite sex.''

Ty tossed back his head and roared with mirth. By the time he could speak coherently, he was holding his ribs and wiping tears from his eyes. ''You've got to be making all this up. The braces, the falsies, the whole bit.''

''I wish!'' she exclaimed, setting his cappuccino down in front of him and selecting a donut for herself. ''I must have had the most embarrassing childhood on record.''

''At the risk of offending you, I wish you had those times on tape. You'd win that hundred-thousand-dollar prize on 'America's Funniest Home Videos' hands down!''

He picked up his cappuccino and took an appreciative sip. ''What are you planning to do today?'' he inquired, changing the subject suddenly.

She slanted him a sideways glance. ''Oh, I thought I'd knit an afghan or two, write a best-selling novel, and maybe dash off to Washington to have lunch with the president's wife in between. Nothing too taxing. Why?''

Ty rolled his eyes. ''Hundreds of comedians out there starving, and you're trying to be funny. I just wondered if you were coming to watch us practice this afternoon.''

Jess frowned. ''I thought you got the day off after the game.''

''So did we, but there was a message on my answering machine when I got home last night. Until further notice, we will be having practice sessions every day.''

''I shouldn't wonder!'' Jess snorted. ''In that case, they ought to make Crumrine practice twice a day. Where did they recruit that guy from, anyway? He can't kick worth a tinker's darn.''

''Damn.''

''What?''

''If you're going to swear, do it right. It's a tinker's damn.''

Jess shrugged. ''That's beside the point. Crumrine is still the worst kicker I've ever seen.''

Ty's face clouded. ''You know, it really burns my butt when

you armchair pros spout off the way you do, especially when
you don't know what you're talking about half the time. It's
easy to criticize from the sidelines, but you should walk in a
man's shoes before you come down too hard on him. Sure,
Alan's having a bad streak, but it's not as if you could do any
better."

"Want to bet?"

"Ha!"

"I'm not kidding, Ty," she assured him.

He gave her a hard look. "Okay, babe. Time to put your
money where your mouth is. In other words, put up or shut
up."

Jess brushed the crumbs from her hands and stood. "Fine
with me. What'll it be? The wager, I mean."

He gave her the once-over, from head to toe.

"Not that, stud muffin. Think of something else."

"Kind of hard to do, with you wearing that shortie shirt and
flashing those long legs at me," he told her. Then, "If you can
kick better than Alan, I'll trade you cars for a week. If I
win the bet, you make me seven of my favorite home-cooked
meals."

She grinned. "You're on. How, when, and where do I prove
my point?"

Ty glanced at his watch. "We've got a couple of hours
before practice, which means we should have the field to ourselves. What do you say we go now?"

Jess nodded. "Wait here while I get changed."

"I could come help you," he offered devilishly, reverting
to form. "I'd still like to get a gander at that new peach-apricot
bra."

"No way."

"I don't suppose you bought panties to match?" he suggested.

She sent him a sassy wink. "As a matter of fact, I did. French
cut. Chew on that while I'm gone."

"I'd love to. Just toss them out here. Better yet, I'll gnaw
them off of you."

"In your dreams, big boy," she shot back, trying to keep

her voice from cracking. Just the thought of him doing that was getting her hot and bothered.

He sighed, casting a prayerful gaze toward the heavens. "Just go get dressed, will you, before I turn into a raving, drooling maniac?"

This early, the only other people at the stadium were the clean-up crew, busy clearing the debris from the stands. The field had already been swept free of spectator trash left from last night's game. Ty got a couple of footballs from the equipment room while Jess donned her cleated soccer shoes. She was squatted down, doing what amounted to half a leg split, when he returned.

"What are you doing now?"

"What's it look like? I'm stretching out. Warming up. It's been a few years since I've played soccer."

He tossed a football from hand to hand. "This is a football, not a soccer ball, in case you haven't noticed. There is a difference."

"Uh-huh." She went on with the exercises intended to limber her muscles. On her feet now, she kicked her foot high over her head, then repeated the move with the other leg.

"Stop that!" Ty snapped. "I can see right up those loose legs of your shorts."

"Shut up and enjoy the view. I'm busy."

"Busy displaying everything you've got to the whole world, not to mention the cleaning crew," he informed her tersely.

"I'm wearing underwear, the thick athletic brand I've always worn to play soccer, so I know nothing improper is showing."

Done with that exercise, she began jogging in place, and progressed to an intricate series of stagger-style sidesteps and kicks. Three steps and kick with the left leg, three steps and kick with the right.

Ty covered his face with his hand, in a gesture of dismay, and peered through the gaps in his fingers at her. "Pray tell, what are you doing now? You look like an overgrown fairy who's lost her pogo stick. Or a drunken ballerina, at best."

Jess stopped, planting her hands on her hips, and stared him down. "Cut the crap. You and I both know that numerous coaches are sending their football players to dance classes now. It improves their agility. So does this, and I prefer it to ballet."

He grinned. "Ah, flunked out of dance class, did you?"

"No, I quit. Right after my instructor informed my mother that she was wasting her money."

"Let me know when you're done wasting *my time*," he told her.

She dangled her arms at her sides, shaking them. "It's only fair that I get to limber up first, Ty. You wouldn't want to win by default, would you?"

Finally, she was ready. "I'll hold the ball for you," he said, "but try not to bash your foot into my hand. It's hard to play with broken fingers, and Coach wouldn't be real thrilled, either."

"Oh, stop being such a whiner, James. I'm not going to injure your precious digits."

"Where do you want to start?" he questioned, still wearing a skeptical expression. "Is the twenty-yard line okay?"

"Just dandy," she assured him.

He planted the ball. She rushed it in three well-measured steps. It left the toe of her shoe and sailed over the crossbar with room to spare.

"Child's play," she taunted, shooting him a wide smile.

"A fluke, more likely," he grumbled.

He set it up again, and once more she nailed it.

He eyed her cynically. "Let's try one from off center."

She simply shrugged, as if she couldn't care less. In quick succession, she effortlessly popped three from the left, and four from the right, each on a more severe angle than the next. "This wouldn't be quite so easy if not for the dome," she admitted charitably. "Then, I'd have to account for windage, too."

"Right," he grumbled. The woman hadn't been kidding. She was good. From close up, at least. "Let's try a few from farther out. Field goals aren't always made from the twenty."

They added ten yards, which would have constituted a forty-seven-yard field goal. She threaded it through the goal posts without breaking a sweat. At thirty-five, the ball still spiraled dead center between the posts, with a good twelve inches of clearance, and Jess indulged in a little victory dance. With her arms over her head, her fists punching the sky, she whirled in a circle. "Yeah! When you're good, you're good!"

Ty's expression had run the gamut from smug to sullen and now astounded. "Holy Moley! I can't believe the foot you've got! And the power behind it! You're absolutely incredible! Where did you learn to kick like that?"

"I told you. I played soccer, right here at Ohio State."

"Yes, but . . . what else can I say, but wow!"

"Shall we try one from the forty-yard mark?" she suggested. "If I make it, you owe me a full tank of gas on top of our original bargain."

Ty nearly swallowed his tongue when the ball cleared the bar by inches and only a little right of midpoint. She'd just made a fifty-seven-yard field goal!

The cleaning crew had long since stopped to watch, and were rooting for her. "From the fifty, lady!" one called out. "From midfield!"

Ty shook his head at her. "Can't be done," he informed her. "The longest official field goal on record is sixty-three yards, originating from the forty-six. That's held since 1970, when Tom Dempsey did it for New Orleans, in a game against the Detroit Lions. No one has equalled it since, let alone broken it."

"Aw, let me try," she pleaded. "If I miss, I miss, but it'll give my cheering section a thrill either way. Besides, records are made to be broken, even if this wouldn't be official."

She gave it her best shot, amid encouragement from her impromptu gallery. The ball had the distance, but fell just short in height. It hit the crossbar near the left-hand post, and ricocheted backward. Had it taken a forward bounce instead, it would have been a legitimate score—and Ty would have fainted dead away. As it was, he was ready to kiss the ground she trod upon.

He gathered her into his arms and twirled her around, her

toes barely skimming the ground. "Woman, you are truly something! I've never seen the likes of you!"

Jess giggled. "Then you admit I'm better than Alan?"

"Ten, twenty, a hundred times over!" he conceded readily. "The coach would kill to have a kicker like you. You know that?"

He put her down, but didn't release her. "If the coach would approve it, would you consent to practicing with Alan? Teach him how to kick like that?"

"Like a personal trainer?" she queried.

Ty nodded. "Yes."

Jess's brow furrowed. "I'm not sure that would work, Ty. In the first place, the coach probably won't agree. In the second, Alan would most likely resent anything I, as a female, would attempt to teach him. Third, I'm not certain I can teach someone else how to kick the way I do. At the risk of sounding egotistical, a lot of it is simply natural talent, and some of it is just dumb-luck instinct."

"Whatever it is, babe, it's pure gold."

She didn't have a chance to refute his claim as his lips covered hers in a kiss that was instantly hot and urgent.

When the two of them finally came up for air, both breathing erratically, Jess was all but limp with desire. "Whew!" she declared fervently. "If I'd known making field goals was such a turn-on, I'd have started kicking them sooner."

Like Ty, the head coach had been scornful at first, but after witnessing Jess's amazing skill, he was properly impressed. However, the special teams coach was quite defensive about having his position usurped, if only in this one area, by a novice, and a woman at that! Had it been up to him alone, he would have nixed the idea. Danvers outranked him, though, and once he'd convinced the manager and the three co-owners, the deal was done. They had even agreed to pay Jess for her efforts, with a bonus if Alan improved significantly.

The biggest fly in the ointment, and the thing that bothered Jess most, was that of the three co-owners, Tom had been the only one to vote against her. That really hurt. When she cornered him in his office at the bank the next morning, she asked him why. He told her he simply didn't want her neglecting her primary job as a reporter.

"A bird in the hand is worth two in the bush, Jessie. Don't jeopardize the career you've worked so hard at."

She promptly assured him that her new assignment as Alan's trainer would not interfere with her article. "Besides, Tommy, this 'coaching' bit is only temporary, and it might even get me in better with the other players, especially if it pans out. At this point, they're all thoroughly ticked at Alan."

"That, or they'll come to resent you for interfering in what they consider their male domain," Tom warned. "Crumrine, at least, is not going to like it one bit. Come to think of it, neither is your mother. Have you told her about it yet?"

Jess wrinkled her nose at the thought of the phone conversation she'd had with her mother the previous evening. "Yes. I figured I'd better do it before you did, or before the news leaked out by some other means. She had a hissy fit at first. Her baby daughter, working around all those sweaty, spit-and-curse men! As if I were still sixteen and she had to protect my virtue, for heaven's sake!"

"She worries about you, Jessie. So do I."

Jess grinned at him. "That's why I told her good old Tommy was right there to watch out for me and see that I didn't come to any harm. Then I reminded her that being surrounded by all these men might be a blessing in disguise, if she's still holding out hopes of me getting married and providing her with grand-children one day. It does better my odds, considering I'm such an odd duck, after all, and can't afford to be too picky."

Tom shook his head in mock dismay. "Jessie, Jessie. What are we going to do with you, girl? Oh, well, I hope you sent your mother greetings from me. Are you going to be seeing her soon? If she's coming to Columbus in the near future, I'd love to take you both out to lunch."

"I wouldn't count on it. She's awfully busy right now, getting Halloween and holiday molds set up for the fall circuit of craft shows."

"Still tinkering with those ceramics, is she?" Tom commented. "What about that husband of hers? Can't he support her properly, so she doesn't have to mess with it?"

"Now, Tommy. You know she loves John dearly, and he earns darned good money. Mom just likes puttering around with her ceramics. She's even bought a pottery wheel, and is turning out bowls and vases of her own design now. It's very creative and satisfying for her."

"I suppose she needs a hobby, an outlet of her own," Tom conceded, not too graciously. "Living with a shrink could drive a person nuts, otherwise. What is it with Claudia, anyway? Married first to a dentist and now to a psychiatrist?"

"Guess she has a 'thing' for doctors who work on some part of the head," Jess commented lamely.

Jess was well aware of the crush Tom had had on her mother for years. Honoring Claudia's bereavement and the memory of his best friend, he'd waited a year after Mike Myers' death, and then proposed to her. But Claudia had declined the bank executive's offer of marriage, telling him that she did, indeed, love him, but only as a dear friend, not in any passionate way.

Tom had pursued Claudia for the next seven years, trying to change her mind, but to no avail. Six months after Claudia had married John Derry, Tom wed another widow. Anita was bright, funny, outgoing, a thoroughly wonderful lady. Jess adored her, and so did Tom. It seemed a match made in heaven, and for a while, he and Anita had been very happy. Then, a year and a half ago, Anita had been diagnosed with Alzheimer's. Much to everyone's heartbreak, she'd been rapidly declining ever since.

"How's Anita doing?" Jess asked now. "I've been meaning to stop by and visit with her, but I don't want to intrude at an inopportune time."

Tom gave a sad sigh. "She has her good spells and her bad, but the bad seem to be winning out more often. That's why we've hired a full-time companion for her, though there will come a day when we'll have to place her in a nursing home, I suppose. It's so damned pathetic, and confusing as hell. Some days she doesn't seem to know her own name. Then, she'll turn around and relate verbatim a conversation that took place years ago. You know how she loves her music, playing her piano?''

Jess nodded.

Tom went on. ''She could play anything, from pop to Bach. Now there are times she can't play chopsticks, let alone Chopin.''

Jess walked over and gave him a huge hug. ''I'm sorry, Tommy. I'm so sorry.''

''So am I, honey-girl. So am I.''

CHAPTER 8

Alan Crumrine did not welcome his new kicking tutor with open arms. Overall, he was sullen, sulky, and uncooperative, projecting a typically superior male attitude, despite the fact that his "teacher" was more skilled than he. After two days of this, Jess was done with being nice. She walked up to him, faced him squarely, nose-to-nose, and laid it on the line.

"Look, Crumrine, I've had it with you. Either you want to better your kicking ability, or you don't. If you do, then I'm the person to help you. If not, you're more stupid than you look, because your teammates are sick and tired of having you lose games for them. They're busting their butts out there, and you're dragging them down. For my money, the next butt stomped into the mud is likely to be yours, and frankly I wouldn't blame them one bit. Now, are you willing to take on half a dozen hefty guards and linebackers and come out looking like a crash victim? Or are you ready to buckle down and learn something that just might save your hide from a royal beating? Think about it. It's your health, buddy."

Prudently, Alan decided to at least give Jess the benefit of the doubt. They set to work, both skeptical of the results.

Every day, Jess arrived dressed in ragged denim cut-offs or

running shorts, an old-but-clean T-shirt, socks, soccer shoes, and wearing her short ponytail tucked through the slot at the back of her favorite red baseball cap. Not exactly stylish. In fact, with his semilong brown hair sticking out of his cap in a like fashion and their similar height, from a distance she and Alan probably looked like twins. But her old clothes served the purpose, and her hat was definitely one of a kind. On the front of it, in big white block letters, was the word "WAGARA."

Like Ty, Alan was curious to know what it meant. Jess told him that the day he made ten field goals in a row, she'd let him in on the secret, on the condition he didn't tell Ty. In the meantime, he was free to try and guess.

Upon spying Jess's cap, Ty renewed his own efforts to uncover its meaning. It became a ritual between them that each day began with Ty making a new, and usually outrageous, suggestion as to what the letters represented.

"I've got it. Women And Girls, American Revolutionary Activists."

Jess shook her head and laughed. "Pitiful attempt, James. Really pitiful. Keep trying." Her attention then returned to her recalcitrant pupil. "You, too, Crumrine. I know you can do better than that."

She drilled the kicker hard, giving him plenty of praise when he did well, but no slack when she felt he wasn't applying himself. She pushed herself equally as hard. This kid was going to learn if it killed them both!

Jess taught him her warm-up exercises, which meant the pair of them took a lot of flack from the other guys on the team. At least at first—until Danvers decided they could all benefit from more dexterity. Soon the entire team, Ty included, was on the field at the beginning of each practice, prancing around like a bunch of burly, bilious munchkins. It was a sight to behold!

When it came to the mechanics of Alan's kicking, Jess found that he had a tendency to kick to the right. To compensate, the ball was angled to the left, which seemed to do the trick for the time being. Eventually, Jess hoped that Alan would be able to straighten it out, because his holder wouldn't always have time to tilt the ball.

Other problems were dealt with differently, and Jess wasn't always congenial when Alan failed to heed her advice. "How many times do I have to tell you? If you hit the ball too high, it's going to roll. You've got to get your toes under it. Now do it again, correctly this time!"

And—"Alan, you're not following through with your kick like I showed you. You've got to follow through or the ball is not going to have the proper momentum."

Or—"You're wasting valuable seconds, not to mention energy, by pulling your foot back so far before swinging it forward for the kick. Your opponents are going to have you flat on your back before you know what hit you." She demonstrated, for the thousandth time, the proper method. "Snap, place, step, kick. One, two, three, kick. Got that? Now you do it. Get some rhythm going."

"I'm a kicker, not a dancer," Alan complained.

"More's the pity," she retorted. "Now, either get your act together, or I'm going to suggest dance lessons for you at Arthur Murray's!"

She'd only worked with Alan for five days, two since he'd begun to cooperate, when the team headed to Indianapolis for their final preseason game against the Colts. Alan had improved minimally, and Jess wasn't holding out much hope as yet. However, as his new coach, she more or less had to go along, if only to bolster his morale and lend last-minute advice. Additionally, she would gather more material for her article, and would have a free front-row seat on the team bench. All in all, she figured it was a pretty good deal.

Rather than fly such a short distance, the team manager had rented buses for the drive to Indianapolis. Some of the guys opted to go in their own cars, as did Ty. His ex-wife and son lived there, and he intended to spend some extra time with the child. Everyone naturally assumed Jess would be traveling with Ty. Not that she minded. She hadn't been looking forward to a cramped three-hour bus ride, listening to off-color jokes and off-key singing. Nor had she wanted to drive the distance herself, or get stuck riding with the cheerleading squad.

To accommodate Ty's desire to spend as much of the weekend with his son as possible, he and Jess were driving over on Saturday, hours ahead of most of the team. When Ty stopped by early that morning, Jess was set to go, her bag packed and stowed in the trunk of his car, which she was still driving as per their wager.

She answered the door to find Ty decked out in well-worn jeans and a cobalt blue shirt, a color that made his intriguing indigo eyes seem all the more mesmerizing. Perhaps that was why the lyrics of an old song popped immediately into her mind, and why a fiery tongue of desire skipped up her spine at the mere sight of him. Yes, the handsome devil knocking at her door did, indeed, have blue eyes and blue jeans! Not to mention shaggy sun-blond hair that simply begged a woman to run her fingers through it. Now, if he started whispering sweet nothings, she was going to flip out!

"Ready?" he asked. "I'm really looking forward to this. Something tells me we're going to have a devil of a good time this weekend."

At his words, Jess's eyes went wide and her mouth dry. His phrasing was close enough to the lyrics in that song, that it was downright eerie! As if he'd read her mind, or somehow had the very same tune running through his brain. She shook her head. No, that was impossible—wasn't it? If not, she was a goner for sure, because this man was tempting enough, without their subconscious minds trying to get in on the act and weaken her already flagging resistance to him. He was Seduction with a capital *S*, or to coin another expression, "to-die-for," and Jess knew she was teetering on the edge of disaster, one step away from falling for him like the proverbial rock.

"Hey! Are you okay?" he questioned with concern. "You look a little pale, like you've seen a ghost or something."

"Or something," she murmured, trying to get her senses back under control before she made an absolute fool of herself. "It's nothing, really," she assured him. "Let's get going."

Ty held out his hand for his keys. "I'll drive, if you don't mind, especially since we're taking my car."

She turned the keys over to him. "Okay, but you owe me an extra two days to make up the difference."

He chuckled. "Oh, so you like my gas-hog after all, huh?"

"As long as you're footing the fuel bill, I do."

"Do you want to go for broke and put the top down?" he suggested. "Or are you afraid of getting your hair all messed up?"

"As if anyone would be able to tell the difference," she retorted. "Besides, I've been driving like that all week."

They arrived in Indianapolis too early to check into their hotel. The rooms reserved for the team would not be free and cleaned until mid-afternoon. Instead, Ty drove directly to his ex-wife's house, to pick up his son.

"Josh is going to love meeting you," he predicted. "His school doesn't have a football team for his age group, but they do have a soccer team." Here, he shrugged. "Guess they think the kids are less likely to get hurt. Anyway, he'll be starting kindergarten in a few days and is considering joining the soccer team if his chicken-livered mom will let him. If you could give him a few pointers, sort of give him a leg up on the other players, you'll be his friend for life."

"I'd be glad to, but I wouldn't want to encourage him at something his mother is dead set against, either."

Ty gave her a conspiratorial wink. "Oh, she'll come around in the end. Josh can talk anybody into just about anything. Barb's just not very sports oriented, that's all."

Jess's brow rose. "You're kidding! I thought, being the former Mrs. T.D., she'd really be into the game."

Ty shook his head. "Nope. That was all for show, until she had me hooked. Oh, she liked all the extra attention, and the big bucks and all they'd buy her, but football itself? No way. She's more into tennis lessons, so she can wear those cute little outfits. And a smidgeon of golf, because she and Dave—that's her new hubby, the one she ditched me for—belong to the country club. But I'll bet she hasn't played more than a few dozen holes in the past three years. She's probably too busy with other games, like musical beds.''

"Oh, so that's why the two of you divorced," Jess guessed. "She was playing around on you? With Dave?"

"And any number of others. Her main criterion was a fat wallet, and mine was getting too flat to suit her.''

"What does her present husband do for a living?"

"He's a corporate attorney, but he was so smitten with Barb that he offered to handle her divorce from me, free of charge. For her, of course. Me, they took to the cleaners.''

Jess's lips pursed. "Ouch! Tough break. But, if Barb wasn't into sports, how did you meet her?"

"At a bar," he admitted ruefully. "In Detroit. I played for the Lions back then, and was pretty tough stuff, or so I thought. Evidently, so did she, at the time. Or maybe we were both so damned drunk that first night that anyone would have looked good to us. To make a long story short, we dated hot and heavy for several weeks, and the next thing I knew, she was pitching a fit, demanding that we get married. She'd goofed up on her pills, and we were going to have a baby. Josh was born eight months later.''

"I take it she went with you when you signed on with the Colts, and that's how she and Dave became acquainted?"

Ty nodded. "That was also the year I broke my leg, and sat out the entire season. The following year, I injured it again, and my future with the Colts, or any other pro team for that matter, was looking pretty dim. Needless to say, being married to a broken-down, washed-up jock was not Barb's cup of tea. She didn't hang around to see if things would improve.''

"Are you sorry?" Jess asked hesitantly.

"For a long while, I was. Not because of Barb so much— the glow wore off the romance long before the divorce, almost before the wedding. But being away from Josh was difficult for me, and for him. I really love that little guy, and it hurt not to be able to be a full-time dad. It still does, but Josh is bigger now, and starting to understand. He knows I love him and miss him. I just wish we could spend more time together.''

Ty wheeled the Trans Am onto a long, curving driveway that led to an impressive brick house. "This is it," he told her. "The twelve-acre estate of Barb and Dave Savoy, Esquire. Complete with sixteen rooms, swimming pool, tennis court, maid's quarters, and one Joshua James."

"Don't they have any other children?"

"Not yet. It seems old Dave, esquire or not, is shooting a lot of blanks. Scads of cash, but short on . . . what's the word I'm looking for? Oh, yeah." He snapped his fingers. "Paisleys! Anyway, unless they get awfully lucky, there won't be any Davie Jr. to carry on the family name or tradition in law. Also, as it stands now, Josh isn't the least bit interested in following in his stepfather's footsteps."

"I suppose he wants to be a quarterback like his dad?"

"No, he wants to drive in the Indy 500." Ty laughed. "I knew I should never have taken the little snot to this year's race."

Josh was waiting and raring to go. Ty had scarcely shut the engine off when the front door flew open and three and a half feet of gangly kindergartner came dashing down the sidewalk, dragging an overstuffed duffel bag with him.

"Hi, Dad!" he yelled excitedly. "Guess what? I lost my front toof yesterday!" The wide gap in his smile was evidence of that.

Ty leapt from the car and swept his son into his arms just as the boy started to trip on his untied shoelace.

"Hey, sport! If you want to keep your remaining teeth for a while, you'd better tie those shoes," Ty informed him, enveloping Josh in a huge bear hug.

"If I've told him that once, I've said it twenty times in the last half hour. He's absolutely impossible on the days he knows you're coming!"

Still in her seat, Jess turned to see Barb Savoy sauntering down the walk toward Ty. Her initial thought was that the name suited the woman. Ty's ex resembled nothing less than a walking, talking Barbie doll, complete with wavy blond hair and a face so flawless it looked as if it had just been peeled from a toy mold. Moreover, dressed in an immaculate white tennis outfit, she was slim, trim, and tanned. Jess would have bet her last dollar that "Barbie" was a perfect 36-24-36. The sum of which made Jess feel all the more like a dowdy freak.

"We'll take care of it, won't we, son?" Ty said in response to Barb's opening comment.

"Uh huh," Josh agreed, bobbing his blond head. Then he spied Jess. "Who's that?"

"That's Jess. She's going with us today."

Without waiting for Ty to introduce them, Barb walked up to the car and put out one expertly manicured hand. "I'm Barb, Josh's mother."

Jess shook her hand, only now wishing she'd thought to file and shape her own nails. They were clean, as usual, but heaven knew when they had last seen a coat of nail enamel. "Jess Myers. Pleased to meet you."

"Are you . . . uh . . . are you . . ." Barb appeared to be at a loss for words, something Jess would bet didn't happen often.

"Yes, Barb," Ty put in, guessing what his ex was trying to say. "Jess and I are dating. Do you have a problem with that? Not that it matters, you understand."

Barb's smile was trite. "Why, not at all, Tyler. I was simply wondering. However, since you brought it up, I would hate to hear from Josh that there is any monkey business going on between the two of you while he is present."

"Holy—" Ty bit off the last half of his angry expletive, for his son's sake. "I can safely assure you that there will be no 'monkey business,' as you put it, in front of Josh. Jess and I aren't into such antics. Unlike you and Dave, apparently, we have better things to do than swing from trees, suck bananas, and pick lice off of each other."

"You . . ." Barb sputtered. "You are an uncouth barbarian. God alone knows what I ever saw in you."

Ty lowered Josh into the backseat of the car and began fastening the child's seat belt. "The same thing that attracted you to Dave. My income bracket."

Barb stalked off without saying goodbye to any of them.

Her parting words were, "Have Josh back here tomorrow night by nine o'clock sharp, and not a minute later, or there will be hell to pay."

"Mommy said a bad word," Josh declared with wide indigo eyes, a perfect match for Ty's.

"Yeah," Ty replied with a forced smile. "Mommy must have been watching *The Wizard of Oz* again, huh? That wicked witch is her all-time favorite character."

They had gone several blocks, with Josh and Ty exchanging information about their respective lives since they had last gotten together, when Ty suddenly turned to Jess. "You're awfully quiet over there. What's up?"

Jess said the first thing on her mind, actually the thought that had been consuming her for the last ten minutes. "Your . . . Barb is very beautiful. I can see why you were attracted to her."

"Oh, yeah. She's a real piece of art," Ty mused drolly. "But, in all honesty, I've got to say she's improved over the past three years. Primarily thanks to Dave's bank account. Otherwise, she could never have afforded the nose job, the breast reduction, the tummy tuck, and those special beauty treatments at an exclusive spa. And she's stopped letting her roots grow out before getting them touched up at the salon."

Jess was dumbfounded.

From the rear seat, Josh, who had been hanging on his dad's every word, piped up with another revelation. "Mom gots some new stuff from the doctor now, Dad."

"What kind of new stuff?" Ty prompted.

"Eye colors, and lipstick that don't come off like before. But she sure did look funny for a while, after she had it put on. Her lips was real big, and she had two big black eyes. Then they turned purkle, an' green, an' yellow, like rainbows."

By now, Jess was holding her hand over her mouth to hide an ear-to-ear grin. Ty didn't bother trying to hold back. "Ah, the miracles of modern science! Isn't it grand? Reminds me of that old song Granddad James used to sing."

"What song, Dad?"

"Well, it went like this." Ty began to sing. "After the ball was over, she took out her glass eye. Put her false teeth in salt water, and hung up her wig to dry.''

Josh clapped enthusiastically. ''Do it again, Dad!''

''Only if you two sing along with me.''

With the convertible top down, they cruised down the high-way—the three of them happily serenading anyone within ear-shot.

CHAPTER 9

Given his choice, Josh opted for lunch at McDonald's and an afternoon at the zoo.

"But we went to the zoo last time," Ty reminded him. "Wouldn't you rather go to the Children's Museum? It's air-conditioned."

"But, Dad, I wanna ride the elepunt an' the camel again."

"Me, too," Jess whined, sticking her lower lip out like a pouty child.

"Oh, no! Not only am I outvoted, but now I have two snivelers to put up with!" Ty complained mockingly. "Okay. You win. The zoo it is. Maybe I'll get lucky and they'll draft both of you for the chimp exhibit."

It was a delightful afternoon, despite the heat. Bright, breezy, and not unbearably humid. Jess had the time of her life, trailing along with Ty and Josh. It helped that Josh was so pleasant, and surprisingly accepting of Jess. As for her, she couldn't help but compare the five-year-old to his father. With their dark, denim blue eyes, blond hair, twin stubborn chins, and winning smiles, they looked like carbon copies of each other at different ages. Josh even had similar mannerisms: his slightly strutting walk, certain inflections in his speech, and a habit of tugging at his left earlobe, as Ty was prone to do. In no time flat, Josh had Jess's heart wrapped around his little finger.

Berating herself for not thinking to pack her camera, Jess splurged on one of the disposable kind, exorbitantly priced at the zoo's gift shop. "I just have to get some pictures of you two together," she told them.

"We'll probably break your camera," Ty warned her. "Especially since it's so cheap, regardless of the ridiculous sum you paid for it."

Despite his disclaimer, the camera held up fine, and Ty and Josh were thrilled to pose for her. Actually, they were a pair of hams, intent on seeing who could make the funniest faces, noises, and imitations of the animals. They passed the camera around, Ty taking a few shots of her and Josh, Josh snapping a couple of Jess and Ty. They even got a bystander to take one of the three of them together.

They stuffed themselves with popcorn, peanuts, and soda pop, though most of their munchies went to feed the animals. They rode the sight-seeing train, the antique carousel, the camels and the elephants. By the time they trooped wearily through the exit gate, the adults were as tired as Josh, or more so. But Jess didn't care. She would have turned right around and done it all again, because despite her aching feet, she couldn't remember when she'd had so much fun.

"What do you say we take a breather, go check in at the hotel and give Josh a chance to catch a quick nap, get cleaned up, and go out to supper afterward?" Ty suggested.

"Sounds great to me," Jess agreed.

"No nap, Daddy," Josh protested testily. "I'm not a baby."

Discounting his claim, Josh was sound asleep in the backseat of the car before they got out of the zoo parking lot. He didn't even wake when Ty plucked him from the car and carried him into the hotel. "Just get your own bag if you need it now," Ty told Jess. "I'll have one of the bell boys collect mine and Josh's after we check in."

The team manager had reserved rooms for the players and coaches. As usual, Ty was paired with Gabe.

"Does Gabe mind Josh sharing the room?" Jess questioned.

"Nah, he and Josh are good buddies. Sometimes Josh even sleeps with him, instead of me. Then there are times when Corey comes to the games and she and Gabe get a room of their own."

"She's on a photo shoot this weekend, isn't she?"

Ty nodded. "For another week yet. In the meantime, Gabe is back to baching it."

"When we get back to Columbus, why don't you and Gabe come by my house one night for dinner?" Jess offered. "I know you didn't win our bet, but I suppose I could break down and make you a home-cooked meal, anyway."

"Great! I was hoping to weasel at least one out of you."

When the desk clerk checked the roster, Jess was disgruntled to find that the team manager had put her in a room with three of the cheerleaders. "Do you have anything else?" she asked the man. "A single room, on any floor, would do. Naturally, I'll pay for it myself."

"Sorry, miss. With the game and two conventions going on, we're booked solid."

Ty glanced at the register himself. "It'll work out, Jess. They've got you rooming with Destiny, Jazz, and Pepper. They're all nice. Now, it would be another story altogether if they'd put you in with Bambi. One of you would probably come away bald, and from where I stand, I'd put my money on you keeping your hair."

Jess sighed, and accepted the room key the clerk handed her. "I suppose you're right. They did seem fairly personable when I met them before. It's just that I'm not used to sharing quarters with other women. I haven't had to do that since college."

"Think of it as a pajama party. Isn't that what they called them, back when my sisters used to have a horde of giggling girls sleep over?"

"Yes, but I never thought I'd see the day when I would attend one of those goofy gatherings."

Ty, still carrying his slumbering son, ushered Jess ahead of him into the waiting elevator. "What? Didn't you go to scads of those things in your teen years? I thought all girls did that."

"Not me," Jess informed him with a shake of her head. "I

wasn't all that popular in high school, and I didn't date much. Therefore, I didn't really fit in with most of the other girls, when all they could talk about were boys, clothes, who was going steady with whom, et cetera.''

''Oh, well, you probably didn't miss much,'' Ty said. ''It all seemed pretty silly to me, even from a distance. When Karlie, Cheryl, or Lynn threw one of those shebangs, I was exiled to a pup tent in the backyard or shuttled over to my best friend's house for the night.''

''Good grief, that's right. You did put down on that questionnaire that you had three sisters. Two older, and one younger than you, if I recall correctly. And no brothers, to help even the odds?''

''Nary a one. Just me and Dad against four females. The worst of it was trying to get some time in the one and only bathroom. Dad finally tacked a schedule on the bathroom door. Not that they abided by it too faithfully, but at least it gave us guys some small chance at the shower and toothpaste.''

''About the same chance I'm going to have rooming in with three other women,'' Jess surmised. ''Which means I'd better hustle if I want to wash this cotton candy out of my hair.''

The elevator stopped on her floor first. She was out and in the hall before she thought to ask, ''When and where should I meet you?''

Ty stuck his foot out to hold the door open long enough to call back, ''Six-thirty. In the lobby. Don't wear anything too fancy. Unless I miss my guess, we'll be dining on pizza at the Mouse House.''

Jess lucked out. Pepper was the only one who had checked into their room before her. She was sitting on one of the two queen-size beds, painting her toenails. ''Oh, hi, Jess. I was beginning to wonder if my deodorant was failing and everyone was avoiding me.''

''Hi, Pepper. Where are our other two roomies?''

''Out shopping. They barely took time to drop their bags off at the desk before hailing a cab.''

"Didn't you want to go with them?"

"If you'd ever been shopping with Destiny, you wouldn't ask such a dumb question," Pepper replied with an exaggerated shudder. "That girl has an incredible knack for finding the most bizarre boutiques. You know, those little holes-in-the-wall stocked full of old sixties styles that look like they're straight out of a 'Brady Bunch' rerun. Bell-bottoms, beads, headbands, you name it. Weirdest stuff I've ever seen. Personally, I wouldn't be caught dead wearing any of it."

Jess laughed. "Sounds really 'far out.' "

Pepper returned her grin. "Almost as spacey as Destiny."

Jess plopped her suitcase on the empty bed. "Are you going to need the bathroom, or can I monopolize it for about half an hour? I've been to the zoo with Ty and his son, and I'm in sad need of a quick shower."

"Go ahead. But don't lock the door, okay? I'll try to run interference for you, but like as not Jazz will dash in here about to wet her pants. I swear that gal's got the weakest bladder in the world."

Jess had gathered her clean clothes and her shampoo and was halfway to the bathroom when she thought to ask, "By the way, Pepper, what do you know about a restaurant called the Mouse House? Ty said that's where we were going tonight."

Pepper's eyes went wide and began to sparkle. Then her lusty laugh broke forth. "Maybe you ought to put off that shower until you get back. You'll probably need another one, anyway. The Mouse House is one of those kids' places, where they have video games, and all sorts of other hyper-activities for children. Mostly designed with breaking the sound barrier in mind, I think. They also serve a variety of ultrafattening junk food."

She went on to add, "If you're extremely nimble, you'll make it past all those screaming, jumping kids, and the obstacle course of horn-honking clowns and midgets dressed up as cartoon characters, without wearing your meal all over the front of you. Don't quote me on this, but I think they award the kids with free tokens for every adult they bowl over. And if you haven't got ear plugs, for God's sake find someplace to buy a pair beforehand, or I can promise you'll be deaf for hours afterward.''

Jess grimaced. ''Oh, yippee, skippy! And me without my raincoat. That would have provided some protection, at least.''

''I've got a dry-cleaning bag you can wear, instead,'' Pepper offered gleefully.

''Don't laugh,'' Jess responded wryly. ''I just may take you up on that.''

The Mouse House was a far cry from Jess's idea of the dream date, but it wasn't as awful as Pepper had portrayed it, either. Her major mistake had been wearing her cream-colored jeans instead of her blue ones. They were now finger-painted with pizza sauce, bearing the imprint of Josh's small hands after he'd excitedly grabbed her without first wiping his hands clean.

Immediately after it had happened, Ty apologized profusely. ''I'm sorry, Jess. He just gets so carried away sometimes that he forgets to be careful.''

''No harm done,'' Jess told him, not wanting Josh to get into trouble over one little accident. ''It'll wash out, and if it doesn't, it's no great tragedy. I'll just say it's the latest in designer jeans.''

She didn't realize her mistake until Ty instructed her to stand up. He did likewise, coming around to her side of the table. ''Turn to face me, and hold still.'' With no more warning than that, he stepped close, put his arms around her, and planted his hands firmly on the seat of her pants. Then he swung her around to view the result of his ''handiwork.''

''Perfect!'' he gloated. ''The only thing better would be two more handprints to match, on the front of your blouse, but that will have to wait until later. Not here, in front of the kids,'' he added in a staged whisper.

Jess couldn't turn her head far enough to see her own behind, but she didn't doubt she now wore matching imprints of Ty's hands on the rear of her jeans. ''Ty!'' she exclaimed. ''You idiot! Do you know what that is going to look like to everyone?''

He chuckled. "Like I've been copping a feel?"

She whirled to face him, torn between laughter and exasperation. "Precisely. You might just as well have autographed the darned thing!"

His eyes lit up. "Great idea. Let's do it." He reached for his pen, but she swatted his hand away.

"Don't you dare!" she hissed, though her intended scowl emerged as a smile. "There are impressionable children here, including your own very attentive son, who is going to go home and give his mommy a blow-by-blow description of everything that went on this weekend."

Ty resumed his seat, his face still alive with mischief. "Spoil-sport!"

Privately, Jess wished they had been somewhere else, alone, and he could have signed his name to her jeans. As it was, she was tempted never to wash them again, unless she could be sure of setting the stain in for all time.

Later, Ty apologized again, not for the pizza prints on her jeans, but that they couldn't have gone somewhere nicer to eat, like a supper club, maybe one of the local comedy clubs, or out dancing.

"I really didn't mind," she told him sincerely. "After all, this is your time to spend with Josh. I'm the one who's intruding, but I'm glad you invited me along because I had a lot of fun."

"So did I," he said. In deference to his son's presence, he gave her a peck on the cheek. "Good night, Jess."

Josh raised his head from Ty's shoulder, giving her a sleepy smile. " 'Night, Jess," he echoed. "Sleep tight. Don't let the bed bugs bite."

Jess laughed and reached out to ruffle his blond locks. "You, too, tiger. See you in the funny papers."

After breakfast the next day, the Knights had a light practice at the RCA Dome, what amounted to an early warm-up for the game. Remembering her promise to Ty, Jess let Josh watch as she gave Alan a few last-minute pointers. Then, to the boy's delight, she let Josh kick a few balls, and gave him a short lesson on some simple soccer maneuvers. Josh was elated, so excited that he could barely eat his lunch, which he did with the entire Knights' team.

The game, which was to be televised, was scheduled for a one o'clock kickoff. Jess was disappointed that she and Josh couldn't sit together; but she had to be on the sidelines with the other coaches, and Josh wasn't allowed to stay there. Aware of this, Ty had already arranged for Josh to sit in the reserved section with Lisa Harvey and her children.

The Colts had the home-ground, home-crowd advantage from the start, though many Knights fans had driven the relatively short distance to Indianapolis in support of their new team.

"I'd really like to win this one," Ty told Jess. "Not only for the Knights, but for Josh. But it's going to be a hard row to hoe, since many of the Colts are guys I used to play with. They know my style, my favorite moves, which will make it twice as difficult to surprise them."

His prediction proved true. Though Ty and his teammates did their best, the Colts were reading many of the plays and held the Knights to two scores. Fortunately, Alan made both points-after, but at the half the Colts were leading by two touchdowns. The down-hearted Knights followed their coaches, Jess included, into the locker room for the traditional halftime pep talk.

"Things aren't looking real good out there, fellas," Danvers said. "I know you're doing your best, but you've got to dig deeper if we're going to pull ourselves out of this hole." He listed a couple of changes he thought would help, matching his players against different opponents. "Ty, since the Colts are evidently so familiar with your technique, I'm thinking of putting Jack in at the start of the second half. Sort of mix it up more. We've got to get them off our scent, so to speak."

Though Ty hated to admit it, Danvers was right. "I understand, Coach, but I'd still like to keep my hand in. If we alternate sporadically between Jack and me, it might confuse their defense even more."

Danvers nodded. "I like that, James. It just might work."

They returned to the game, their deflated spirits somewhat renewed. Jack Hays took over as quarterback for the first possession, with a revised offensive line. The baffled Colts' defense, not expecting such a drastic change in the lineup, faltered. Several downs and mixed running plays later, the Knights were finally on their opponents' forty-five-yard line. From there, Hays, not noted for successful long passes, made a short shovel-pass to Tornado Jones. Like the whirlwind he was nicknamed for, Tara's hubby made straight for the end zone, outrunning three Colts to get there. Then, Alan, unable to handle the pressure, missed the crucial kick.

Jess nearly bawled. Damn! A conversion kick, straight in and short, and Alan had to miss the blasted thing! Josh could have made it from there! Well, not really, but after making the first two Jess was hoping for a third. Obviously, she was going to have to work harder with him.

Fortunately, the realigned defense held the Colts from another score. Hays loped back onto the field, confident and cocky. Impossibly, the Colts were already onto him and the Knights' new offense, almost as if they were plucking the plays straight out of Jack's head. It was a fast one, two, three, and punt.

Again, the defense managed to hold the Colts, and Ty ran onto the field to lead his offense once more.

It was right about then that Jess's headset, which all the Knights' coaches were required to wear, went on the fritz. Suddenly, she was listening to the television broadcast of the game, though that should have been impossible. She heard the announcers talking, about Ty, evidently.

"When he's on his toes, James can really drill it. I've seen him shoot some real zingers, straight from the pocket, for the score."

A second speaker agreed. "He's got great hands, and he can fake-pump with the best of them, but he's got to have better protection."

The first man again, "I agree. He's got some good moves, but he's got to avoid the sack. At least he doesn't fumble the play very often."

Jess nearly choked on her Gatorade. Lordy! Maybe it was just her frame of mind tonight, but she'd never realized before how downright *sensual* football talk and the terms could be! Why, there were more double meanings, just in this conversation between the announcers, than she could shake a stick at! Great hands, good moves, balls and pumps. And let's not forget "protection" in the "sack," or from it, to be more precise. Still, it was all very provocative when you thought about it in the right light, which she seemed to be doing now. Since meeting Ty. The guy who could shoot a real "zinger," from his pocket, no less!

Her headphones fuzzed up, and she lost the connection, which she should never have had to start with. Jess's attention, or half of it at least, returned to the field. She'd missed the first handoff, which had gone to Rambo. Apparently, he'd only made three yards or so. Ty called a second audible from the line. Cutter Callahan was stopped for a yard loss on the play. Though the offense was doing its best, the holes simply weren't opening up—oh, heaven's, there was another one of those suggestive phrases!

Through the static, Jess heard the next play-call through her headset. "Right, thirty-seven, on three."

She watched as the play evolved. It didn't go as planned. Instead of going right, per the play-call, Ty pulled a fake pump and threw left, hitting Rome wide open at the fifty-yard line. Rome eluded two tacklers and ran the ball in for the touchdown. This time, praise heaven, Alan made his point, and the Knights only trailed by one.

The remainder of the game was nip and tuck, with neither side scoring. It seemed the Knights were destined to lose another game, again by a single point. Then, miraculously, Dino made a pass interception, running the ball back to the Colts' thirty-four-yard line before being tackled from behind. Three tries, and the Knights could advance the ball only to the twenty-five, three yards short of a first down.

Like a bad dream repeating itself, it was all up to Alan again. A do-or-die situation. Jess leapt to her feet and rushed to meet him as Alan snapped his helmet strap. "You can do this Alan," she told him. "I know it's a forty-two-yard attempt, but it's a straight shot. Just get your toes under that ball, and give it all you've got." With a pat on the back, she sent him onto the field—and started to pray.

The coaches, the fans, the players on the sidelines, all seemed to be frozen in place as they watched the team assemble for the kick. Ty, who was sitting out this play, came to stand beside Jess. "Can he do it?"

"He'd better, if he knows what's good for him," she murmured. "He has the foot for it if he just doesn't hook it."

Alan's stride was off a bit, but he got the kick off without mishap. The ball sailed through the air, missing the right post by a fraction as it skimmed over the crossbar, the underside brushing the top of it as it passed.

Jess clamped her hands to her mouth. "Oh, God! He did it!" she screamed over the roar of the crowd. The next she knew, Ty had caught her by the waist, lifting her a good foot and a half off the ground. His dark eyes were shining up at hers, his lips drawn up in a jubilant smile. "Lady, you're beautiful!" he declared, twirling her around in dizzying circles.

The spinning, the incredible kiss afterward, did not make Jess as giddy as what he'd just told her. With those three precious words, she fell headlong, irretrievably in love with Tyler James.

CHAPTER 10

"Dad, you kissed Jess." Josh spoke around the bite he'd just gnawed off his fried chicken leg.

"Don't talk with your mouth full, rug rat," Ty replied, hoping to steer his son away from the topic.

It didn't work. Josh swallowed hastily. "But I saw you. You kissed her."

"Yes, I did."

"Does that mean you an' Jess like each other?"

Ty nodded, casting a quick glance at Jess, who looked as if she were sitting on a pile of tacks. "Of course we like each other, don't we, Jess?"

"Sure."

"Will you and Jess get me a baby brother?"

It was hard to choke on mashed potatoes and gravy, but Ty almost did. "Good grief, Josh! What a question!"

"Well, will you?"

"I doubt it," Jess told him, coming to Ty's rescue. "You have to put your order in way ahead of time, and baby brothers are in short supply right now. Like when Santa has trouble finding a toy you want for Christmas, and you have to wait until later."

"Oh." Josh thought a minute, and said, "Order one soon, okay?"

"Maybe you ought to ask your mom and Dave to do that, instead," Ty suggested.

Josh scowled. "I did already, a long time ago, but they can't get one. I think their letter got lost in the mail or something.'

Ty grinned. "Could be, son. Maybe they didn't use the proper postage. Tell them to try again."

Because they had won their game, the coaches had given the players the next day off, with no practice. As soon as Ty had learned this, he'd asked Jess if she'd mind staying over in Indianapolis another night, so he could see Josh off on his first day of school. Jess could see that it was important to both of them, and since she didn't have anything pressing the next day, she'd agreed.

As they delivered Josh home that evening, at precisely nine o'clock, the little boy asked for the umpteenth time, "You won't forget to come and see me get on the school bus, will you, Dad?"

"I'll be here," Ty pledged. "Cross my heart."

"Jess, too?"

"Me, too," she promised. "And we'll be here at eleven-thirty, when you get home again."

After walking Josh to the door and safely inside, Ty said, "Well, the night's young yet. What would you like to do, Jess? How about taking in an act at one of the comedy clubs?"

"You don't have to entertain me, Ty. After two days with that live-wire son of yours, not to mention a terrifically tough game today, you must be tired. We could go back to the hotel, have a drink in the lounge, and call it a night."

"Or maybe rent a movie to watch in our room," he suggested. After a slight hesitation, during which Jess said nothing, evidently not having caught his full meaning, he ventured, "I . . . uh . . . when I called to have the hotel save our rooms for another night, they'd already rented yours out again. And there wasn't another available. I did check, Jess. Honest, I did."

Jess stared at him, her jaw slack and her eyes wide. "And you didn't think to tell me this before now?" she questioned skeptically.

Ty gave what he hoped was an innocent shrug. "It's no big deal, Jess. My room has two beds, and we're both adults. I won't turn into a ravening beast the minute the lights go out."

"We could just head back to Columbus right now," she told him stiffly, offering an alternative. "We could be home by midnight."

"You're forgetting our promise to Josh," he reminded her. "I, for one, intend to keep mine."

Jess sighed. "Okay, okay. But you should have told me right up front."

"So you could take the bus home with the team? And how would that have looked, when we're supposed to be lovers?"

"Lovers?" she echoed in a squeaky voice. "Since when did we evolve from 'dating steadily' to being lovers?"

Again that irritating shrug. "Since tonight, I guess, though everyone probably thinks we've already slept together. After all, we have been seeing each other for a couple of weeks already."

Jess gave an irate snort. "And you're not usually the type to let any grass grow under your feet, I take it. So what does that make me? Just another notch on your bedpost? One more silver spur on your helmet?"

"No," he snapped, becoming irritated himself now. "It makes you my woman, at least in the eyes of anyone who cares to notice."

For several blocks, Jess didn't say a word. Then, suddenly, she commanded, "Pull in there." She indicated a convenience store.

When he'd parked in front of the store, she got out.

"What are you doing?" Ty asked. He had some idea she might intend to call a cab to take her to the airport or the bus station.

She grabbed for her purse. "I like popcorn with my movies," she informed him tartly. "I'm also going to buy a couple of cold cans of cola and a package of candy bars. There is no way I'm going to buy any of that stuff they sell in that minifridge.''

Ty heaved a silent sigh of relief. She wasn't taking this as well as he'd like, but it sounded as if she was willing to cooperate. At least to a point. ''Wait a sec. I'll come with you. If we're going to binge on junk food, I want to choose some of it.''

''Suit yourself.''

Inside, he headed straight for the cold beverages. ''Pepsi or Coke?'' he asked her.

''What? No beer?'' she jeered.

''I thought you wanted cola.''

''I do, but I thought all you jocks preferred beer.''

''I drink it occasionally, when I'm out with the guys, but I try to limit my alcoholic intake. And I rarely touch hard liquor anymore. Guess I exceeded my quota when I was going through that bad stretch.''

''The divorce?''

''That, and nursing a bum leg two years in a row, and losing my son except for weekends, alternate holidays, and a few weeks each summer. I was feeling pretty sorry for myself back then. In fact, I came damned close to becoming an alcoholic.''

''I'm glad you didn't,'' she said more mildly. ''It would have been a shame to throw your life away on booze, not to mention your career or how it might have affected Josh.''

''Josh is the primary reason I pulled myself together,'' he admitted. ''I didn't want to set that kind of example for him to follow.''

By the time they reached their hotel, they had formed a truce, albeit a tentative one. Jess couldn't help feeling apprehensive about spending the night in the same room with Ty. She didn't want to make a fool of herself over him—not that she intended to throw herself at him and beg him to make love to her. Nor did she want to come off as a complete prude. And she had no idea what she would do if Ty made an honest-to-goodness pass at her. Faint dead away from the shock, more than likely. But this buddy-pal roommate business was going to take some fancy footwork, lest she slip up and reveal just how much she was coming to care for him—which would be totally mortifying to both of them, no doubt.

Upon entering the room, Ty dropped his bags by the door, went directly to the television and flipped it on. Following his example, Jess tossed her purse and overnight bag on the far bed, picked up the movie guide, and began to scan it.

"See anything interesting?" Ty inquired.

Yes, you, her subconscious replied silently. Aloud, she said, "Not really." She handed him the guide. "Have a look. Maybe something will appeal to you."

You appeal to me, he thought to himself. Briefly, he skimmed the listings. "Nope. Nothing here I want to see. Suppose we just channel surf until we hit something interesting?"

"What about the sports channel? Maybe they're reviewing today's games, and we'll get to see a few highlights of the Knights beating the Colts."

Ty vetoed that idea. "I don't usually watch those until later in the week. Coach will run a tape of the game Tuesday, before practice, and point out all our flaws then, which is soon enough. Why ruin a perfectly good victory by watching reruns of all the mistakes you made along the way, not to mention the commentator's comments, which aren't all that complimentary at times."

"Well, those two announcers in the TV booth seemed to think you were pretty terrific," Jess informed him.

Mistaking her meaning, Ty glanced quizzically at the television, currently set on the weather channel, then back at Jess. "What are you talking about? What announcers?"

"The ones covering today's game. At the stadium, Ty."

He gave a shake of his head. "I'm still confused. When did you talk to them?"

"I didn't. I heard them discussing you over my headset."

He stared at her, confounded. "You couldn't have. Those things are locked onto a preset frequency, so transmissions can't be picked up by anyone but your own coaches and team."

"Maybe they're supposed to be, but mine must have gotten a short in it or something, because I could hear those two discussing you as plainly as I hear you now."

"Do tell. And what did you overhear?"

She grinned. "I shouldn't tell you. You might get a swelled head." *Darn! There was one of those double entendre phrases again!* She simply had to stop this! She'd never before had such trouble keeping her mind out of the gutter.

Ty's initial thought was, *I'll probably get a swelled head anyway before the night is over, and not the one above my shoulders.*

"They said you had great hands, good moves, and that you don't fumble very often," she related, managing to keep her tone as flat as if she were reading from a textbook. "But they also said you've got to avoid the sack and have better protection."

Ty drew in a deep breath, an unsuccessful attempt to tamp down his rising libido. "Did they, now? Well, I have to agree to some extent. Good protection is a must. But eluding the rush isn't always possible, is it, Jess?" He took a deliberate step toward her, his sharp, searching gaze boring into hers. "Like now, for instance. I'm getting quite a rush—from you and all the subtle signals you seem to be sending my way."

Jess gulped and stepped backward. "I get the feeling you throw a smooth pass, on or off the gridiron, but I'm not much for playing 'bump and run,' Ty."

"Me, either. I like to retain possession as long as possible," he told her, matching her quip for quip. He took another stride forward, and she backed up again. "The truth, Jess. Since we met, haven't you wondered what it would be like to get a quarterback—this quarterback—in the sack?"

"Talk about an enormous ego!"

Ty gave an indifferent shrug while his words and dark eyes continued issuing the challenge. "Don't back down now, sugar, just when the game is starting to get interesting. What say we huddle, cuddle, and see what kind of action develops?"

One last step, and he'd backed her to the edge of the mattress. Jess lost her balance. As she fell, she reached out, grabbing for something to hold her upright. Her hands caught at Ty's shirt, and she wound up dragging him down on top of her.

"Nice tackle," he said with a chuckle. "A bit unorthodox, but it felled me nonetheless."

Before she could catch her breath, his mouth, so warm and enticing, shrouded hers in a long, blistering kiss. His lips feasted on hers. Her tongue darted out to meet his. The heat between them built, fueling itself on their mutual desire.

"I want you," Ty murmured, peeling his lips from hers to pepper kisses across her face. When he reached her ear, his teeth nipped at her lobe, eliciting a quiver that shook Jess to her core. "Tell me you want me, Jess. Please say you do."

"I . . . I want you," she murmured, barely able to speak past the lump of longing lodged in her throat. "I want you so badly, Ty."

He sighed, as if he'd feared she would reject him, though Jess couldn't see how any woman could withstand this man's advances. Not for long. Not when he could swamp her senses with just one kiss, one caress, one look from those compelling eyes.

"Oh, babe," he whispered. "I'm going to love you like nobody has ever loved you before."

Jess had no doubt that he would, physically, at least. She had the distinct feeling that until now she'd been dealing with amateurs, on more than one level. Now she was playing with a pro, and way out of her league. But she was going to give it her best shot, because it could be the only one she ever got.

He was caressing her now, his hand skimming the length of her body, creating shock waves in its wake. Her lips trembled beneath his. Jess's hands rose of their own volition, her fingers fumbling blindly with the buttons of his shirt. When at last her fingers tunneled into the mat of golden brown hair to knead at his chest, Ty's groan was akin to the rumbling purr of some great jungle cat. He aided her quest, shrugging quickly out of his shirt and tossing it onto the floor, his lips never breaking contact with hers.

Given free rein, her hands roamed at will, exploring the width and breadth of him, delighting in the texture, the warmth of his skin, the muscles rippling just beneath the surface.

His lips deserted hers as he swiftly tugged her top over her

head. Before she could cover herself, his lips were tracing the
lace trim of her bra, his tongue lapping at the exposed flesh
along the inner edges. His hands caught hers, bringing her arms
in close to her sides, and her hands back to his chest. "Yes,"
he murmured. "Touch me. Let me touch you."

With passion-glazed eyes, Jess watched his lips sip at her
skin. His tongue explored the valley between her breasts, then
swept up the slight slopes to seek out the peaks, first one and
then the other. As if by his command, they leapt to alert attention. She clutched at his shoulders as an intense ache raced
through her.

With deft fingers, he unhooked the latch of her bra and swept
it aside. He palmed a breast in each hand, his long fingers
surrounding each in a tender embrace. His thumbs reached out
to caress the rosy centers, his eyes darkening as he watched
the nipples pucker even tighter.

"They're like the most delicate of rosebuds," he breathed,
as if in awe of the treasure he'd uncovered. "So pink and pretty
and dainty."

His head lowered, his hair tickling her breast as his lips
sought out the rigid crest. His tongue swirled around it, over
it, dampening it. His breath cooled it even more. Then, as if
to heat it again, he drew it into his mouth, suckling gently at
first, then stronger.

With every tug on her breast, the sweet ache built within
her. Growing. Expanding. A yearning that curled low in her
stomach and spiraled outward, until it engulfed her whole body.
When he released his hold, she grabbed his head, trying to
force it back to her once more.

She heard him chuckle. "Like that, do you?"

All she could do was plead. "Please."

"Oh, I intend to, darling. I'm going to please you like you've
never been pleased."

His lips clamped down on her other nipple, sucking with
such force that a good portion of her breast was pulled into his
hot, damp mouth. Jess gasped, her back arching nearly off the
bed as a lightning bolt of desire shot through her. Fire sped
through her veins, searing her from head to toe.

He had her shoes off, and her slacks undone and sliding down her legs before she was aware that he'd moved. His mouth left her breast, blazing a trail of flame across her bare stomach. His hand slipped between her legs, nudging them apart. His fingers found her through the sleek satin of her panties. Rubbing. Teasing. Then his mouth was there, scalding her through the thin cloth.

It was heaven and hell wrapped into one delicious torment. Jess's fingers tangled in his hair, half tugging him away, half prodding him on, as if she couldn't decide which to do. Ty solved the dilemma for her. He whisked her panties off, hooked her long legs over his shoulders, and with something that sounded like a growl, buried his face between her wide-spread thighs. Suckling, licking, spearing her with his tongue, he led her to the edge of ecstasy. She writhed, she whimpered—she fell into the whirling pit, spinning helplessly out of control.

By the time she could think and breathe again, Ty had rid himself of the rest of his clothes and was lying beside her, stroking her damp hair from her forehead and smiling down at her with those devil blue eyes. "Lady, I love the way you lose it."

"You should be charged with illegal use of hands," she claimed weakly. "And mouth."

He chuckled. "With what penalty? Loss of down?"

"No." Jess levered herself up on one elbow, her face level with his. Her hand skimmed along his bare thigh, raising goose-flesh in its wake. "New rules. The opposition gets equal time and access. Think you're up to it?"

His hand caught hers, leading it to his groin. "Judge for yourself."

Her fingers curled around his turgid manhood. "I'd say so, but let's make sure, shall we?" she suggested with a smile as old as Eve.

"I'm all yours," he vowed with a wicked grin. "Do your worst. Just don't drop the ball, babe."

Her hand moved, curving downward to cup his scrotum. "I think you'll find I can handle a ball or two without fumbling them too badly." She squeezed lightly, playfully. "Of course,

I'm more accustomed to kicking them than I am fondling them,'' she taunted.

"Not this time, if you please," he said. "We don't want the poor things 'whistled dead' before the game really gets going, do we?"

"No way," she agreed. "We've got to keep everything pumped up nice and firm. Which is why I'm going to check out your equipment, big boy."

She began with his chest, nuzzling her nose into the golden fleece, kissing, nipping, lapping her way leisurely down his torso. "You taste delicious," she told him.

"So do you," he countered on a blissful sigh, one that reversed into a gasp as her teeth nibbled a new path up his inner thigh. "Careful there, darlin'."

Her laugh was delightfully provocative, her hands soft and sure as she caressed him. Her tongue swept out to lap a dewy drop from the tip of his engorged penis, sending a shock wave bounding through him. Reflexively, he lurched upward as she took him into her hot, slick mouth. His fingers caught in her hair, binding her to him as she worked her wanton wiles, suckling him until he thought he would die of the pleasure.

When he could stand no more, was sure he would explode if she didn't cease her sweet torture, he tugged her away from him, pulling her up and beneath him. As he sprinkled kisses across her breasts, he reached for his trousers. Seconds later, he was ripping open a foil packet. Her hands reached to help him slip into the protective sheath, and to guide him to her own.

He entered her slowly, surprised at how tightly she gloved him. She grabbed his buttocks, urging him onward.

"I don't want to hurt you, sweetheart."

"I want you. All of you." She arched upward, engulfing him further.

It was more than he could withstand, and in one swift lunge, he buried himself to the hilt. Her sigh echoed his. They lay motionless for a moment, savoring the exquisite sensations, until she shifted her hips restlessly beneath his. He answered her siren's call, retreating only to plunge deeply again—and again, and again, in a driving rhythm that lured them ever higher. Blind, breathless, driven by the ruthless demands of their bodies, they surged toward the pinnacle. Together, they hurtled past it, into a fiery abyss, welcoming the flames that consumed them.

CHAPTER 11

"God! They were right!" Jess panted.

"Who was? About what?" he rasped.

"Those announcers, about you. They claimed when you're on your toes, you can really drill it."

Ty dredged up enough energy to chuckle. "I wonder what they'd say about you? You've drained me dry."

"Will you do a small favor for me?" she asked, lying limply at his side.

"If it doesn't require any energy, yes."

"Just raise your head, look down, and see if either of us smokes after sex, will you?"

He laughed outright. "You screwball."

"No, I think that's your department."

It felt good to banter back and forth with Jess this way. At any rate, it was certainly a novel experience for Ty. Much better than a trite exchange of "Was it good for you?" afterward, or a tearful, "Do I mean anything to you at all?" or an equally awkward silence. Come to think of it, he couldn't recall the last time he'd laughed with a woman in bed.

She nuzzled next to him, and he realized anew just how well the two of them fit together, like adjoining pieces of a jigsaw puzzle. Hip to hip, chest to breast—she was just the right height for him. It was a relief not to have to bend himself in half and get a crick in his back every time he went to kiss her.

She sighed contentedly.

"Go to sleep," he suggested softly. "I'll turn off the TV and check the lock."

"I should shower first, so we won't be so rushed in the morning." Reluctantly, Jess got up, wobbling weak-kneed to the other bed. After fishing through her overnight bag, she toddled toward the bathroom. "Dang! My legs feel like over-cooked spaghetti! I sure hope the fire alarm doesn't go off anytime soon!"

"Me, too, because I sure as heck don't have the strength to carry you down eight flights of stairs. In which case, we'd just have to slide down the banisters."

Ty, nibbling at the nape of her neck, woke Jess the next morning. "C'mon, sleepyhead. Rise and shine. Josh's bus will be there to pick him up in an hour."

Jess bunched her pillow under her face and mumbled something that sounded vaguely like "coffee."

"Right. I'll have room service send some up. We can drink it while we're getting ready."

He flipped back the sheet and reached for the phone, smacking Jess on her bare bottom at the same time. "Up, woman."

Still half asleep, Jess fumbled her way to the bathroom, grouching all the while. How could that dratted man be so ever-blasted cheerful this early in the day? The answer was obvious. He was full of himself this morning, after two glorious sessions of lovemaking the night before. Meanwhile, she hadn't gotten her quota of sleep, and was walking like a bow-legged octogenarian.

One look in the mirror, and Jess was glad she'd been cuddled next to Ty with her back to him. Undoubtedly the rear view had to be better than the front. She looked as if she'd spent several hours under a street sweeping machine.

The coffee still hadn't arrived by the time she relinquished the bathroom to Ty. ''What are they doing, picking fresh beans by hand and transporting them by donkey?'' she groused.

The phone rang just as Ty emerged from the bathroom, looking bright-eyed, bushy-tailed, and perfectly groomed—while she was still bleary-eyed and barely presentable. It simply wasn't fair!

Jess answered the call. It was room service, wanting to know if they still wanted their coffee delivered to the room. They apologized for having to double check, but upon seeing the sign on their door, the boy who had taken it up a short while ago had returned for further instructions.

''What sign?'' Jess asked. Then, to Ty. ''Did you hang the 'Do Not Disturb' sign out?''

Ty shook his head. ''Tell them not to bother now, we'll grab a cup on the way.''

Jess relayed the message, and they finished packing their belongings. On the way out, Jess was holding the door for Ty when she caught sight of a large sheet of stationery taped to the outer door panel. ''Oh, my lands!'' she declared in astonishment.

Ty took one look and started to laugh. ''No wonder we never got that coffee.'' Someone, most likely the person or persons in the next room, had printed in large letters, ''Do Not Disturb. Rabbits Busy Humping!''

''It was that darned headboard!'' Jess hissed, as though it would do any good to be quiet now, long after the fact. ''It kept knocking against the wall.''

''Or you giggling, and shrieking like an Indian on the war-path,'' Ty reminded her.

''Well, if you hadn't kept tickling me . . .''

Ty grabbed the paper, folded it, and tucked it into his shirt pocket.

''What did you do that for?'' Jess wanted to know. An expression of horror crossed her face. ''You're not going to complain to the management, are you?''

''Lord, no!'' Ty told her, chuckling. ''I'm going to keep it, as a memento of our first night together. Now, let's get moving.'' His eyes took on a merry twinkle as he added, in a fair imitation of Elmer Fudd, "And be vewy, vewy quiet. Weahr humping wabbits!"

"And you're Looney Tunes!"

It was on the long ride home, during a discussion of the game, that Jess told him, "I liked that surprise move of yours in the fourth quarter."

"Which one was that?"

"When you switched direction, and threw left instead of right, and made that spectacular pitch to Gabe for the touchdown run. That was very sneaky, and very effective. Up 'til then, the Colts seemed to be reading every play almost before you or Jack could make it."

"That's why Coach and I decided to change it."

"It must have been an awfully last minute decision," she concluded. "I heard the original call over my earphones, just before you broke the huddle."

"Wait a second. I'm getting confused. Are we talking about the same series?"

"Well, you only threw one T.D. to Gabe," Jess recalled. "He was on the fifty-yard line when he caught it."

"And it was third down, right?"

Jess nodded.

"Babe, that call was decided on the sidelines, while our defense was still on the field. I knew it three plays ahead of time. It was never delivered via audio transmission."

"Oh, well, maybe Coach Danvers was simply relaying the information to the other coaches upstairs."

"Not if you heard the old play call," Ty pointed out.

Jess frowned. "So why did I hear the false play call go out? It doesn't make sense."

"No, it doesn't," Ty concurred. "Was it Danvers' voice you heard?"

"I'm not sure. There was a lot of static. It could have been anyone. I just assumed it was him. Why?"

A thoughtful expression furrowed Ty's brow. "It could be that somebody else, someone who was unaware of the change in plans, was transmitting our plays to the opposition. Which would explain why they were always one step ahead of us, until then. And you've already said that your headphones were messing up. Maybe . . . just maybe . . . you caught a signal no one on the Knights team was meant to hear.''

"But . . . that's illegal!'' Jess exclaimed, her eyes wide.

"You bet your booty it is. Logically, the next question is, who was giving our plays away?''

"And why?'' she added pensively.

"For money, most likely,'' Ty said in response to her last query. "Damn!'' He hit the steering wheel with his fist, his anger building. "It's hard enough starting out with a new team, without having a rat in the pack.''

"But who? One of the players? A coach?''

"That, my lovely Jess, is the big question. And I intend to get some answers before all is said and done.''

They were on the loop that circled Columbus when Ty took an off ramp much too early. "Are you lost?'' Jess asked. "This isn't my exit.''

"No, it's mine,'' Ty informed her calmly. "I thought maybe you'd like to see where I live.''

Jess shrugged. "I suppose I should, just in case someone asks me about it, or mentions something I should know.''

"Is that all?'' Ty inquired, his mouth quirking with humor. "Aren't you even the tiniest bit curious, just for yourself?''

"I've wondered a time or two,'' Jess admitted nonchalantly. "Does this mean I get to go through your drawers, too?''

Ty chuckled, and gave her a sexy wink. "Honey, you can search my drawers any time you want.''

Jess rolled her eyes. "Boy, you're easy.''

Ty had rented a two-story town house in an elite suburban community enclosed behind a vine-covered brick wall—a complex which came complete with security gate and guards, landscaped gardens, lighted tennis and sand-volleyball courts, heated swimming pool, and exercise/spa facilities. At the gate, he slipped a plastic card into a slot, punched in a series of numbers on the key pad, and the gates swung open.

"Wow. I'm impressed. Do they have guard dogs, too?" Jess commented.

"No, but the security personnel have weapons, and the top of the wall is imbedded with ground glass to keep out any intruders. I guess they thought dogs were superfluous, and would probably be more of a nuisance and a menace than anything, especially to families with children."

"They actually allow children to live here?" she mocked.

"Don't be facetious. The kids even have their own playground, with all the latest, safest equipment, and there's a twenty-four-hour child-care center on the premises."

"Now I truly am impressed."

Jess noted with interest that unlike other apartment complexes, hers included, the units here were not identical to each other. Here, the planners had gone the extra mile, and each town house was uniquely fashioned and constructed to resemble a single-family residence. Ty's was the end house on a cul-de-sac. Instead of abutting a neighbor's property, his backyard bordered a golf course, providing a pleasant expanded vista. The large brick duplex was of Spanish design, with half-round roof tiles, arched windows, wrought iron gates, shutters, and window planters. At either end was a curved driveway, leading to a garage which faced the side yard rather than the front, to further the impression of a stately home rather than a condo.

"Nice. Very nice," Jess said. "I can't wait to see the inside."

She wasn't disappointed. Through the recessed front entry, she stepped into a marble-tiled foyer. To the right, along the brick wall dividing the apartments, a spiral staircase curved upward to the second story. To the left, a wide arch and two semicircular steps led down to a spacious living area with ten-foot-high walls, vaulted ceiling, ultraplush carpeting, recessed lighting, and a stone fireplace with built-in bookcases on either side. The shelves were sparsely filled with a few books, randomly positioned knickknacks, and several framed photos of Josh. The furniture was dark oak, rustic but elegant, the thick cushions covered in a diametric southwestern pattern.

"Compared to this, my place looks like a garage sale in progress," Jess declared, surveying her surroundings appreciatively. "Did it come furnished?"

"No. Corey helped me select some of the new stuff. The rest I already had, or chose myself. And your apartment may be more cramped, and therefore more cluttered, but it has that lived-in look and feel to it. Unlike this place, which is nice enough to look at, but lacks the warmth and welcome of yours."

Jess grinned at him. "Just throw a couple of pairs of dirty socks around, scatter some newspapers and magazines here and there, an empty pop can and candy wrapper or so, and you, too, can have that homey aura of disarray and disorder. It's not difficult to achieve, Ty. Believe me. All you have to do is spend a little time here and not pick up after yourself so well."

"I don't," he told her. "A cleaning lady comes in twice a week. Even if I did make a mess, she'd clear it out again. So you see, there's just no hope for it, unless I fire her. But then I'd be up to my neck in dirty laundry and pizza boxes in no time flat."

"Not to mention having to clean the tub and toilet yourself, which I'll bet you've never done in your life," she teased. She glanced around again, with a more critical eye. "I suppose if you got some plants it would help. If you like fish, you could put up a fish tank. Or get a big, hairy cat and buy it a ton of toys."

"The cat would starve to death, or eat the fish," he predicted. "Then there's that litter box issue. Helen might consent to feeding the creature, and vacuuming up after it, but I doubt she'll agree to changing a litter box."

"Then both of you are wimps," Jess decided. "Show me the rest of the place."

The far end of the living room doubled as the dining area. In keeping with the overall theme, double glass doors with ornate grillwork led out to a roofed patio, surrounded by a low brick wall and arched pillars. The patio extended in an L-shape around the far corner and across the back half of the house. The kitchen featured Mexican tile floor and countertops, light oak cabinets, and a butcher block island—above which hung an array of empty hooks for pots, pans, and utensils, and a wine and goblet rack, equally void.

"This room is criminally barren, to the point of sending back an echo," Jess observed balefully. "You need some shiny, copper-bottomed cookware, and some stemware." She eyed the bare counters. "Copper canisters would be nice, too, maybe a teakettle to match, and some decorative covers for the range burners. A colorful throw rug or two and a couple of pretty dish towels would help absorb the sound, since you have those louvered wood shutters over the windows instead of curtains."

Behind her, Ty chuckled. "Typical female. Show her your home, and she immediately wants to remodel it."

Jess shrugged. "Sorry, but . . ."

"Oh, you're going to be more than sorry, Miss Big Mouth," he told her. "Now that you've spouted off, you can help me shop for the items you suggested. Let's see what else we should add to the list, shall we?"

They resumed their tour. Off the kitchen was a small laundry room. The rear patio was partially enclosed and sported a recessed hot tub; latticed panels were strategically placed to ensure privacy from the neighbors on either side while still allowing a view of the golf course. There was a half bath downstairs, and two full baths up, one for guests and the other off the master bedroom. There were three bedrooms. The first was a guest room, as yet unfurnished except for a multitude of unpacked boxes, poking out of which Jess saw several trophies and award plaques.

"You should have those on the shelves downstairs."

Ty shook his head. "No. While I appreciate having them, I don't want them on display for one and all. Regardless of anything you may have heard or read about me, I'm not that egotistical."

The middle bedroom, and the smallest, was obviously Josh's. Against one wall was a set of loft beds. Pooh Bear, looking a little ragged and much loved, held the seat of honor on the top bunk. A Mickey Mouse lamp sat on the dresser. A small bookcase was crammed with children's books and small toys. A nearby toy box overflowed with larger ones. Tossed into one corner was a beanbag chair, while a race track was half-erected in another.

Jess smiled. "Ah, a kid after my own heart. Josh goes for the jumbled look, too, I see."

The master bedroom was the rearmost, farthest removed from any annoying street noise and offering the best scenery. A king-size bed dominated the room, matching mahogany bedstands flanking it. Along the wall opposite the bed was a mirrored chest of drawers. In one corner, a portable TV rested atop a highboy. The furniture, while beautiful, was also massive.

Jess stared at it in wonder. "How in the world did you get this bedroom suit up that skinny spiral staircase?"

"We didn't," Ty said with a wide grin. He gestured toward the over-sized bay window taking up most of the far wall. "The architect allowed for that problem, thank goodness. That center section of windows opens like French doors. Of course, we had to remove the screen and stand on the patio roof to haul them up here, but it worked."

Jess ambled over to the bed and made a production of inspecting the bedpost.

"Just what are you doing?" Ty questioned, though he already suspected what she was up to.

"Just checking for notches," she admitted readily. "Curiosity, you know."

"Wondering how many women slept in that bed before you?" When she nodded, he added, "None."

She glanced at him through her lashes, saying nothing, but her expression was dubious.

"No, I'm not a monk. Never have been, never will be. The bedroom suit is new, Jess. Bed, mattress, the whole shebang." Now it was his turn to gaze at her askance. "Care to initiate it with me?"

"I don't know, Ty," she hedged, even as a smile began to blossom. "I was rather hoping we could do that in the hot tub."

"Why stint?" He walked toward her, slowly but determinedly, as if stalking her. His eyes gleamed wolfishly above a devil-may-care grin. "We'll do both. And afterward, we can make love on the kitchen island, in front of the fireplace, on the staircase, in all the closets, and on top of the washer and dryer. Who knows? We might get really daring and try the laundry chute!"

CHAPTER 12

Though both worked hard at their separate and joint commitments, Ty and Jess were basically inseparable in the following days. If she didn't stay overnight at his place, he turned up at hers, carting a clean set of clothes and an extra toothbrush with him. Gradually, her laundry hamper came to contain as many of his clothes as it did hers, and vice versa. His toiletries found space in her bathroom, as hers did in his. A portion of their closet and dresser space was now allotted to the other person. Preferred foods were stocked in each kitchen. They were now actually and officially a couple, no longer having to pretend to be.

They worked, played, ate, and slept together. They even went shopping together—for food, items for Ty's town house, clothing. When Jess put off buying high heels, Ty dragged her into a mall shoe store and helped her select a few pair in the newer and wider-heel styles, which would go with almost any outfit she might choose to wear.

"If I break my neck trying to walk in these things, my death will be on your head," she warned him.

"Bull crap!" he retorted. "Those saleswomen claimed these are more stable than those spike jobbies, and you hardly wobbled at all in them. A little practice, and people will think you were born with them on your feet.''

Jess rolled her eyes. ''Right. And stink doesn't draw flies.'' Actually, Ty and the ladies were right. The wider heels were better for balance, and they looked really great. In them, her legs and ankles took on a more alluring shape, with curves never before accented.

Ty maintained they made her legs appear a mile long. ''If I didn't know better, I'd swear those gorgeous gams of yours go all the way to your armpits.''

Thus prompted, Jess found herself shopping for skirts and dresses, the better to display her newfound assets. To her amazement, it was actually enjoyable, especially with Ty tagging along, alternately poking fun and stating his preferences. Surprisingly, he had very good taste in fashions and wasn't shy about voicing his opinions, as many men might be.

''Be bold, Jess. Go for the red number,'' he'd say. Or, ''Get that sexy black dress, the one with the low top and the scarf hem that flares out when you whirl around. I want to take you dancing in it.''

Jess threw him a wink. ''I'll see if they have it in your size, dear,'' she teased.

But she bought it, primarily to please him, which was another abnormal reaction for her—just one among many these days, it seemed. Since Ty had come on the scene, Jess was suddenly feeling exceedingly feminine, appealing, and downright sexy for the first time in her life. Though she'd dated, been engaged once, even lived with a man for a while, she'd never felt this attractive, this wanted, or quite this alive and excited. It was like skydiving, she supposed—totally exhilarating, but somewhat frightening and potentially dangerous. Impulsive to the point of idiocy. She was flying high, and loving it, knowing full well she had no parachute to break her eventual fall.

Jess continued interviewing and video taping various team members for her article. She also talked with their wives, their children, the coaches, and the team manager. She had yet to corner Tom and the other two owners to get the story from their perspective, which would round out her report.

Obtaining Alan's input was especially easy, since they practiced together nearly every day. Spending so much time together, the two of them soon became friends, as well as coworkers. He was quickly learning to heed her advice and was improving by leaps and bounds.

In a home game the following Sunday, Alan added nine points to the scoreboard, assisting the Knights in their sound defeat of the visiting Bengals—though he still missed one field goal and a point-after attempt, which was blocked. Ty, however, was spectacular, throwing pass after perfect pass, and nary an interception. Unfortunately, his target didn't always catch the ball, or hold on to it. One receiver in particular seemed to fumble the ball or run the wrong pattern almost every time the ball came his way. Contrarily, Gabe had several good runs and made two touchdowns.

"That's my man!" Corey gloated, leaning over the barrier separating the team from the spectators to punch Jess on the arm. "He's got great hands, doesn't he?"

Jess grinned and yelled back. "You should know, Corey! But I have no idea what Butterfingers Baker's problem is. He's so good in practice that it's almost inconceivable that he'd be so lousy tonight."

Corey shrugged. "Who can tell? Maybe he laced his shoes too tight and cut off circulation to the rest of his body."

Since it was Labor Day weekend, and Josh had come to stay with his dad, Jess did not spend Friday, Saturday, or Sunday night at Ty's. Both she and Ty agreed that, for now, it was best not to do so while Josh was visiting. Jess spent part of Saturday with them, and most of Monday. Familiar now with Ty's kitchen, Jess prepared the side dishes for their Labor Day cookout while Ty broiled hotdogs and hamburgers over the outdoor grill. They all trooped down to the playground for a while. Then Jess, who hadn't brought her swimming suit and wouldn't have been seen in public in it anyway, opted for KP duty while Ty took Josh to the pool for a swim.

All too soon, it was time to drive Josh back to Indianapolis. Despite her protests, Jess was persuaded to ride with them.

"But, I have a ton of laundry to do, and umpteen million other chores I've let slide," she argued.

"They'll wait," Ty countered. "Besides, you can help keep me awake on the drive back. Six hours behind the wheel, after a busy day with Josh, and I'm all but comatose."

That convinced her. She certainly didn't want to be accountable—in any way, shape, or form—for Ty having an auto accident. She didn't stop to ask herself why she should feel responsible for his welfare, when a few weeks ago the notion wouldn't have entered her mind. Now, it was either go with him, or worry herself silly until he returned.

They arrived back at Ty's house shortly after midnight, both of them thoroughly exhausted. Both fell into bed, thankful to have the long day behind them. Ty drew her next to him and dropped a kiss on her drooping lids. "I hate to admit this, but now that we finally have the place to ourselves, I'm too pooped to pop."

Jess cuddled close, stifling a yawn. "Me, too. Let's just snuggle tonight, and forgo the bedroom calisthenics. Maybe we can conserve energy and get together in our dreams, instead."

"Only if you don't mind making love in the middle of the highway, darlin'," he told her with a weary chuckle. "I stared at that road so long that every time I close my eyes, I see white center lines whizzing across black pavement."

"Stop at the next roadside rest," Jess suggested sleepily. "And don't park next to any nosy truckers."

Jess first noticed the strangers that week at practice—two men at first, sometimes a third, lurking on the sidelines. Why she decided they were "lurking" and not just observing she couldn't say. It was just something about them—the way they stood, the way they dressed—nothing specific she could put a finger on, but there nonetheless.

"Who are those guys?" she asked Alan on Friday.

The kicker shook his head. "I don't know. I think one of them might be dating Bambi. Why?"

"Because they have no business being here, that I can see. How interesting can it be to watch a team practice day in and day out? And why would they bother? Besides, they give me the creeps."

Alan frowned at her. "Why do you say that? They're not doing anything wrong, that I can tell."

"I know. It's just a feeling I've got."

"Women's intuition?" he teased.

"More like 'reporter's nose,' " she said. "They just seem sort of disreputable, bordering on nefarious, don't you think?"

"Nefarious?" Alan echoed on a chuckle. "Like someone whose picture you'd find on the post office wall?"

"Or on 'America's Most Wanted' or 'Unsolved Mysteries,' " she added with a nod. "They even dress oddly. It's entirely too warm to be wearing sport coats. Why aren't they wearing jeans or Dockers or something more casual?"

"Maybe they're businessmen."

"In what kind of business?" Jess wondered aloud. "They look like goons, for crying out loud. Or drug dealers."

"Goons?" Alan hooted. "Geez, Jess! You've got to stop watching those old gangster movies, or whatever you're doing."

Jess cast him an annoyed look. "Go ahead, laugh. But those men are not Bible salesmen, dammit. More likely, they're as crooked as a dog's hind leg. Really shady characters."

Alan did laugh. "So define shady, Jess. And describe a criminal for me while you're at it. For all you know, those guys might be so clean they squeak. On the other side of that coin, I've heard Ted Bundy looked as normal as you or me."

Jess threw up her hands. "Okay. You've made your point. But I still don't like them hanging around all the time, watching us like vultures."

Alan gave her a congenial clap on the back. "Not to worry, Jess. With no more meat than you have on your bones, you'd be slim pickings."

Jess stuck her tongue out at him. "Wagara."

His brow wrinkled. "Warranty And Guarantee Are Revoked Again?"

Jess just laughed.

That night, Ty stayed overnight at Jess's. Because Sunday's game was in Phoenix, Ty would not be taking Josh for the weekend. Nor would he be able to attend Josh's first soccer practice, much to his son's disappointment. The team was flying out to Arizona late Saturday afternoon.

Saturday morning brought a surprise. It was nine-thirty, and Ty had just finished his turn in the bathroom. Jess was in the shower, singing off-key. When the doorbell rang, Ty yanked his jeans on his still-damp body and hollered, "I'll get it." He doubted Jess even heard him over the racket she was making.

Loping down the hall in nothing but his Levi's, he was still tugging the zipper up when the doorbell chimed again—and kept ringing as the caller leaned on it nonstop. Ty pulled the door open to find a middle-aged woman glaring with impatience. Upon seeing him, her expression swiftly changed to befuddlement.

"I . . . uh . . . is Jessica . . ." she fumbled.

There was some resemblance, and given the age difference Ty hazarded an educated guess. "You must be Jess's mother. Come on in."

He stood aside, letting her enter. "Jess is in the shower." He waved her toward the living room. "Why don't you make yourself comfortable, Mrs. Derry? I'll go tell her you're here."

Claudia started forward, then changed her mind. "Excuse me, but I don't believe we've ever met," she said, her brows knitting as she assumed her parental/investigator role.

"I'm Tyler James." Ty elaborated no further, not sure how much, if anything, Jess had told her mother about him or their relationship.

"Oh. The quarterback," Claudia commented. "Jess has mentioned you, but . . . well, I hadn't realized the two of you were so . . . involved." Blushing madly, her gaze traversed him from head to toe, noting his bare chest and feet, and his towel-dried hair.

"Yes, well, you seem to have caught us at an awkward moment, Mrs. Derry."

"So I see." Claudia took a deep breath and plunged in. "May I ask what your intentions are toward my daughter?"

Her question, rather passé for this day and age, brought a crooked smile to Ty's lips. "At this exact moment, my intentions are to go find my shirt and inform Jess that we have company. Then I'm going to see if I can rustle up a pot of coffee." He started down the hall. Two steps later, he turned again and said, "You wouldn't know how to operate that cappuccino machine, would you? I just can't seem to get the hang of it yet."

"Yes, but . . ."

"Bless you, Mrs. Derry. I assume you know your way around Jess's kitchen well enough to find everything you need."

Claudia eyed him oddly, not quite sure what to make of him. "I'll manage," she assured him dryly.

Ty scooted to the bedroom. Jess was just emerging from the bathroom. "Get something on, sweetheart, and try to be quick about it. Your mother's here."

Jess's eyes grew huge. "My mother?" she squeaked. "Oh, my God! Where? When?"

"While you were taking your good sweet time in the shower," he told her brusquely, thrusting his arms into his shirt and fumbling blindly for the buttons. "I let her in. She should be in the kitchen making cappuccino, unless she decided to wait for you to do it."

"Oh, Lord!" Jess wailed. "What did she say? You . . . you . . ." She gestured toward him, indicating his lack of attire.

"Right. That's similar to your mother's reaction, give or take a syllable. But she recovered enough to ask me what my intentions are toward you."

Jess groaned, hiding her face in her hands. "Tell me she didn't!"

"Oh, but she did. Now, will you stop standing there like your feet are glued to the floor and get a move on? I'll try to keep her occupied until you can join us." Ty planted a swift kiss on her forehead and dashed from the room.

He slid to a halt inches shy of the kitchen doorway and sauntered into the room as if he hadn't a care in the world. "Jess will be right out. Did you find everything all right?"

The espresso machine whirred. "I did," Claudia responded shortly.

Ty walked to the refrigerator, opened the door and peered inside. "Have you had breakfast, ma'am? I'm pretty good at scrambling eggs and making French toast, if you'd care for some."

"No thank you, but help yourself. I suppose *you* know where everything is, too?"

"Most of it," he replied with studied nonchalance. He removed the carton of eggs and milk and proceeded to make breakfast. At one point, he stopped, went to the memo board hanging near the phone, and jotted down a note. "We're almost out of butter," he explained, to no one in particular.

"Your coffee is ready," Claudia offered.

"Just set it on the table, thanks." He grabbed the toast as it popped up, buttered it, and carried it and the platter of scrambled eggs to the table. "Are you sure you won't join me?" he asked again, as he rifled through cabinet and drawer for plates and flatware. "There's plenty for all."

"No, coffee is fine for me." She waited until he was seated opposite her, and asked, "So, how long have you and Jessica . . . uh . . . known each other."

"About a month."

Fortunately, Jess sprinted into the kitchen at that point, with just enough breath left to say, "Now, Mom, don't interrogate Ty. It's embarrassing."

"Not nearly as much as that falsie incident, though," Ty inserted with a sly grin.

Claudia's eyes widened. "She told you about that?" she queried with interest.

Ty chuckled. "Yes. Did you really lay rubber for half a mile afterward?"

Claudia gave a nervous laugh. "I believe I did." She

switched subjects, back to the primary point. "You two seem to be exchanging confidences fairly soon."

Jess glowered. "Mother, I'm a grown woman. I'm entitled to some private life of my own."

"And I'm your mother," Claudia countered, "and therefore entitled to worm any information out of you that I can. I worry about you. Now sit, and eat your breakfast. You're still entirely too thin."

"Why didn't you call and tell me you were coming?"

"I thought I'd surprise you, dear," Claudia replied with irony. "But it seems I'm the one who was in for the greatest shock."

"Not by far," Jess muttered. "Still, I wish you'd phoned ahead. I could have saved you the trip. We've got to catch a flight to Phoenix in about five hours."

"Both of you?"

"The whole team," Ty put in. "We've got a game there tomorrow against the Cardinals."

Claudia faced her daughter. "From that, I assume you are still tutoring that kicker?"

"Yes, Mom, I am. It's working out nicely, and padding my bank account as well. I'm also finishing up my interviews for my television article. Moreover, I've made some very good friends."

"Besides Mr. James?" Claudia inquired archly.

Jess ignored the jibe. Ty grinned openly. "Please, call me Ty, or Tyler. No point in standing on formality at this stage, is there?"

Jess shot him a glare. "One of the other players is married to Corey Rome, the model," she said to her mother. "She's very sweet, and not in the least stuck-up, despite her fame."

"I'll bet she's also tall and thin, like you," Claudia supposed. "Maybe she could give you some pointers on the latest styles." Claudia's gaze swept over Jess's worn jeans and faded T-shirt, a look of weary resignation on her face.

"I'm already on top of that," Ty assured her. To Jess, he added, "Why don't you show your mother your new duds. I'll bet it's been years since she's seen you in a pair of high heels."

"High heels?" Claudia echoed incredulously. "My stars! This I've got to see to believe!"

By the end of her visit, short as it was, Claudia was duly impressed. After kissing Jess goodbye, she offered her hand to Ty. "I must say, you have excellent taste, Tyler. I wouldn't have guessed it."

He took her hand, but rather than merely shaking it, he brought it to his lips and kissed her fingers. Then, as if the courtly gesture was too much, he winked. "Modesty aside, I have to agree. I have superb taste. I chose your daughter, didn't I?"

CHAPTER 13

They were supposed to use their flight time to review the playbook and strategies, and to psych themselves up for the upcoming game, but it was nearly impossible to concentrate with one flight attendant or another interrupting every second or two. It got so ridiculous that Jess was becoming greatly perturbed.

"Good grief! You'd think you guys were rock stars or something, the way these women are hovering over all of you!"

"Jealous, love?" Ty teased.

Jess scowled. "Yes, blast it. They could at least have one good-looking steward to attend to us girls."

Ty frowned. "That's not what I meant, Jess. I was asking if it bothered you to have other women showing an interest in me."

"I know what you were fishing for," she grumbled, "and the answer, again, is yes. As absurd as it may seem, I guess I'm already used to having you to myself."

"Me, too," he admitted, taking her hand in his and stroking her fingers. "I just needed to know if you felt the same."

Phoenix was hot, but dry. Given even a smidgeon of humidity, the hundred-degree temperature would have been unbearable. The air-conditioned hotel felt wonderful. This time around, Corey had come along, so Gabe would be staying with her. Jess was slated to room with the cheerleaders again, but it didn't take much talking for Ty to persuade her to share his quarters instead.

"Should I at least make some pretense, for propriety's sake?" Jess asked in a low voice. "I could have my bags sent to my room and only bring what I need to yours."

Ty chuckled and shook his head. "What good would that do? Even if you waited until the others were all asleep and sneaked down to my room, they'd still know. You wouldn't be fooling anyone, Jess, so we might as well be up front about it."

"I suppose you're right," she conceded, "but I don't want to get you into trouble with Coach Danvers. After all, aren't you jocks supposed to conserve your energy the night before a game?"

"As in no sex?" he questioned with a wide grin. "Get real, sweetheart. That old myth went out with the Model T."

She grinned back at him. "I was hoping you'd say that."

Ty laughed and hugged her close to his side. "That's my horny little bunny," he whispered into her ear, his warm breath making her shiver. "We humping wabbits have got to stick together."

"Sure do, you wiley wascal," she retorted on a giggle.

The phone was ringing before they got their door open. "Oh, come on," Ty said wryly. "Our neighbors can't be onto us yet. We haven't even made it out of the hall, let alone into bed!"

Ty answered the call. It was Corey, wanting to know if he and Jess would join her and Gabe for dinner and dancing that evening. While Corey waited on the line, Ty relayed the request to Jess.

"I don't dance very well," Jess told him ruefully. "Not too many guys care to look as if they're dancing with a giraffe, so my experience has been severely limited."

Ty shrugged. "We can go along and enjoy the music if nothing else. Maybe try a slow number or two. You did bring that black dress and your heels, didn't you?"

Jess nodded.

"Corey, we'd love to join you. What time?" A pause, then, "That's fine. I'd like to get in a little pool time and enjoy some of this Arizona weather first. What? Sure. We'll look for you at the pool in about fifteen minutes, then."

He hung up, only to find Jess with a dismal look on her face. "Let me guess. You didn't bring your swimsuit."

"No, and I wouldn't wear it if I had," she told him. "Ty, when are you going to get it through your head that I'm extremely self-conscious about exposing my body for everybody's viewing. I don't need to advertise the fact that I'm skinny and have small breasts."

"Babe, you're being silly. There are women who would kill to have your shape, breasts and all. Just ask any of a zillion females who have been counting calories all their lives. You are slim, trim, and have the most incredible legs in the world. You'd be a knockout in a bikini."

"In your dreams, hotshot."

"There, and elsewhere," he vowed. He dug his swim trunks out of his suitcase, grabbed her arm, and steered her toward the door. "Come on. We're going down to that shop off the lobby, and I am going to buy you a new swimsuit."

"I won't wear it," she replied stubbornly.

"Yes, you will, if I have to go into the ladies' room and stuff you into it myself," he threatened in return.

Ty was as good as his word. When Jess refused to cooperate, he chose a couple of suits himself and literally pushed her into the changing stall. "If you're not out of there in two minutes, modeling one of those suits, I'm going in after you."

"Damn bossy jock!" she muttered, yanking off her top. "Give him an inch, and he wants a mile." Her bra went the way of her blouse.

"I heard that," he called from just outside the door. "That's what all the fellas say about you ladies. Give you an inch and—"

"Oh, shut up!" she snapped, dropping her slacks to the floor. "Just stick a sock in it, will you?"

She emerged wearing a red one-piece, similar to the style worn by Olympic swimmers. Ty studied her in it. "Nice, but it doesn't trip my trigger." He waved her inside again.

Next, she came out wearing a blue two-piece, with a little fringe skirt. Ty shook his head. "Too frilly. It hides your hips."

Jess almost laid a brick when she tried on the third suit and saw herself in the mirror. While it was probably modest compared to the thong things other women wore these days, it was still a bikini and covered less than the other two-piece. Not only that, but it was simply too bright, sort of a neon yellow, and extremely . . . noticeable. It was designed to attract altogether too much attention to the wearer, especially if that person were her.

"Ty, I can't wear this yellow suit," she called out to him.

"Why? Isn't it the right size?"

"Yeah, if you count wearing a couple banana-colored hand-kerchiefs as being decently covered."

"Let me see."

"No."

"Jess, get your butt out here."

She poked her head out first, glancing around to make sure no one else was looking in her direction. "Look fast, buster," she instructed, inching out of the booth. "God forbid anyone else should see me in this."

Ty stood gaping, his eyes all but bulging from their sockets. When he finally found his tongue, he let loose a low whistle. "Holy Moses! That's the one, Jess! That says it all!"

"You've got to be kidding!" she hissed. "I feel like an idiot!"

"Well, you look fantastic," he assured her. His grin grew. "I had a feeling this was the one I'd like. There's just something about those two big eyes on your breasts, and that smiley mouth on the bottom half. A touch of whimsy, if you will. And it makes your belly button look like a nose."

"I'm so glad you're amused." Her look said otherwise. "Who has ever heard of a smiley-face bikini?"

"We're buying it," he announced.

"You can buy it, but I am not wearing it in public," she informed him.

"That's what you think." In the blink of an eye, Ty darted into the changing stall, grabbed her clothes, and rolled them into a bundle. "C'mon. Gabe and Corey are waiting for us."

He started for the sales counter, her clothes tucked under his arm.

"Tyler! You get back here!"

"No way. Now, stop being such a child, and loosen up. If you don't trust my judgement, you can at least let Corey see you in it and give you her opinion."

Jess was left with little choice but to sprint after Ty, who was nearly running to keep ahead of her. She couldn't believe hotel security didn't nab her for indecent exposure as she loped down the hall toward the access door to the pool area. Moreover, she'd never in her born days felt so utterly conspicuous—so totally exposed! Or so righteously irate! When she caught up with him, she was going to kill Tyler James and stuff his drowned corpse down the pool drain!

Gabe was the first to see them coming. His greeting froze in his throat as his jaw dropped comically. A single word emerged. "Wow!"

Corey turned to see, and her expression mirrored her husband's. "Whoa, gal!" she exclaimed, her face bursting into a smile. "Now you're showing your true colors, and these guys don't stand a snowball's chance in hell against your arsenal, honey. They might as well surrender from the start and save their energy."

"Any other man gets within ten feet of her, and I'll lay him flat," Ty declared loudly.

By now Jess was breathless and next to tears. "Will you people please stop making fun of me?" she beseeched. "This wasn't my idea. It was Ty's. And I'm so mad right now I could spit!"

"Jess, sugar, we're not teasing you," Corey proclaimed sincerely. "Honestly. I meant every word. You are simply stunning in that suit, and any male with eyeballs will verify that."

"You can say that again," Gabe agreed.

"Seriously?" Jess asked querulously. "I look okay?"

"More than okay," Ty told her. "You're a knockout."

"So why aren't you dressed for swimming?" Gabe inquired of Ty.

"I was too busy trying to get Jess out here, but if you two will keep her corralled so she doesn't go back inside and change, I'll go get into my own suit. And don't let any of those drooling pool gigolos near her while I'm gone."

"Home, James." Jess giggled, and punched Ty on the arm. "I've always wanted to say that!"

Ty grinned and pulled her closer to him in the backseat of the taxi, making room for Corey to get in. "You're sloshed, love," he told her.

Jess fluttered her hand, as if swatting a mosquito. "Nah, I'm just feelin' good." That set her off, and she began to sing. "I feel good. So good. Yeah!"

On the other side of her, Corey laughed. "I'll bet you won't be feeling so perky in the morning."

From the front passenger's seat, Gabe added, "Just let us know if you need to have the driver pull over to the side of the road. Feel free to pass out any time you want, but please don't puke in the car."

"Oh, you guys are being so silly!" Jess hooted. "I just had a couple of margaritas."

"A couple?" Ty echoed. "You had two at dinner, and at least three at the nightclub, despite all the time we spent on the dance floor."

"I like that place," Jess announced. "The people are so friendly."

"Right," Ty agreed mockingly. "Even when you bump into them and step on their toes. God knows, I'll be hobbling all through the game tomorrow."

"Me, too," Gabe concurred. "But I guess it was worth it to see Jess loosen up the way she did. Who would have guessed it?"

Corey chuckled. "You were really shaking your booty out there, Jess, high heels and all."

"I never went to the prom," Jess mused in a faraway tone. "No one asked me, and it would have been foolish to buy a dress just to sit on the sidelines like some dumb wallflower." She ran her hand over the skirt of her new dress. "I felt so . . . pretty tonight, all dressed up like this."

"Sweetheart, you are pretty, even when you're not all dolled up," Ty assured her, giving her a hug.

"Of course you are," Corey added. "And don't you let anybody try to tell you differently."

"You do have sort of an extra glow about you tonight," Gabe put in kindly. "I thought it was your sunburn, but maybe it's just the real you showing through."

Jess pushed a lock of hair from her face. "It was probably all that dancing. Whew! I really worked up a thirst."

Ty's mouth twisted in a wry smile. "We noticed. Which is why I'll bet you're going to have one dandy hangover tomorrow and not remember half of what you did tonight."

In the hotel elevator, Jess leaned against Ty's side and hummed happily to herself. As the doors opened on their floor, Ty scooped her into his arms and carried her down the hall toward their room. "I'd better pour her into bed before she collapses face first," he remarked to the other two.

"I'd offer to help, but I'm sure you can handle undressing her on your own," Corey said with a grin. " 'Night, now. Have fun."

Over Ty's shoulder, Jess waggled her fingers at Gabe and Corey, who had stopped in front of their own door. " 'Night, all. Don't do anything we wouldn't do."

Ty rolled his eyes. "Oh, boy! Remind me not to ply you with liquor anytime in the near future."

He got her inside and set her on the bed. Kneeling beside her, he slipped her heels off and began massaging her arches.

Jess purred. "Oh, that feels marvelous. I'll give you a month to stop." She reached out to thread her fingers through his hair, savoring the silky feel of it. "It's like spun gold," she murmured. "So soft and shiny. Have I told you that you're the first blond I've dated?"

"I don't believe you mentioned it." He delved beneath her skirt to tug at her panty hose.

Jess giggled. "Is it true that blonds have more fun?"

"Yeah, it's a regular riot." He finally managed to peel them down her legs.

Reaching behind her for the zipper of her dress, he was already off balance when Jess leaned back, pulling him with her onto the bed. She pursed her lips close to his. "Kiss me quick, before I turn into a pumpkin."

They shared a long, slow, torrid kiss that left them both wanting when their lips finally parted. Jess, now lying half over him, sighed and rested her head on his chest. Her fingers found his shirt buttons and began working them loose, while Ty took the opportunity to unzip the back of her dress and unsnap her bra.

Jess burrowed her nose in Ty's chest hair, her hands now wandering to his belt buckle. "You smell so delicious. Good enough to eat." She lapped at his exposed nipple, giving a low laugh as it tightened into a rigid bud.

Ty shoved the sagging top of her dress to her waist, along with her bra. "Don't start anything you can't finish, darlin'."

Her dress pooled around her hips as she pushed herself up to her knees. "Don't worry about it, big guy." Her hand slid into the open gap of his trousers to cup him through his shorts. Her fingers kneaded gently, eliciting a groan of pleasure from him.

For someone he'd judged to be fairly intoxicated, Jess was remarkably dexterous and definitely in an amorous mood. Ty didn't know whether to let her continue, or to put a stop to it before she pushed him any farther. Like as not, she was two blinks from passing out and leaving him all hot and bothered.

Before he could decide which course to take, Jess had him free of his pants and engulfed in her hot, sweet mouth. Her hair fell in a sleek curtain around her face, adding to the torment by tickling his stomach. Ty reached down and anchored it back. He wanted to watch her, to revel in the look of desire blossoming on her face as she suckled him. It had to be the most sensual thing he'd ever witnessed—her eyes glowing through half-closed lids; her face all flushed; her lips, moist and rosy, gliding up and down over his engorged shaft.

Before she took him to the point of exploding, Ty reversed their positions, barely remembering to sweep her dress aside as he knelt between her thighs. His mouth claimed one pert nipple as he plunged into her, burying himself in her silken depths.

The dual assault sent Jess into a frenzy. She thrashed beneath him, her head thrown back and her hips arching upward to meet his. Her hands clawed at him, urging him on—faster, deeper, harder—until their entwined bodies burst into a million sizzling shards, flaring high above them, only to enshroud them moments later in a glorious glimmer.

CHAPTER 14

Jess's hangover wasn't nearly as bad as Ty had predicted, for which she was supremely grateful. Moreover, she remembered everything they had done the night before, including their passionate coupling, in vivid detail.

"I don't believe it," Ty groused. "You get soused to the gills and don't even have to pay with a hangover. However, now that I know you can handle your liquor that well, and how aggressive you become when you've tipped a few, I just may be tempted to ply you with it more often." He waggled his brows at her playfully. "You really were hot to trot last night, honey bunny. In fact, if I hadn't given in so readily, you'd probably have ravished me, whether I was willing or not."

"Ha! I told you before, you're entirely too easy."

"Hey, Jess! Where were you last night?" Pepper asked, sidling up to Jess as they stood on the sidelines awaiting the start of the game. "Your bed wasn't even slept in."

"Now, Pep, you know she was with Ty," Destiny put in before Jess could reply for herself. "Why would she want to room with us, when she can bed down with a hunk like him?"

"Why, indeed?" Jazz commented with a naughty wink.

"Okay, you three. Enough already," Jess told them, her face turning pink. She still wasn't used to being teased this way by other women. Not tormented, but teased in a friendly manner that held no rancor. Moreover, she was surprised to find that the more she got to know them, the more she liked these gals.

Pepper was a hoot, her sense of humor as earthy as her voice. That sexy, raspy timbre, Jess had learned, was a result of a childhood accident that had damaged Pepper's vocal chords. Thus the nickname. Jazz's name was a shortened version of her real one, which was Jasmine. Actually, Jazz fit her better, for she was energetic to the point of being hyperactive. Destiny's ditzy outlook on life, and her name, were a direct result of being raised by hippie parents. Though somewhat spacey, she didn't have a mean bone in her body.

"Hey! I really dig that new swimsuit of yours," Destiny said now. "A smiley face! Talk about super cool!"

"You saw it? Me?" Jess stammered.

"Sure did, along with about a hundred other people at the pool," Jazz told her. "And I've got to tell you, that suit is a winner. I just wish I could wear something like that, but I've got too much chest to pull it off."

Pepper laughed. "Me, too. Half my butt would be hanging out the bottom, and my breasts would droop too far for anyone to see those cute little eyeballs on the cups."

Jazz poked her friend. "Shoot, Pep, those flimsy straps would snap and your big flabby boobs would unroll like window blinds and break your kneecaps!"

Pepper swatted at Jazz, who was laughing uproariously at her own joke. "You should talk, girl! You could grow mushrooms between your toes and never see them. It's a wonder you don't get those things stuck going through a revolving door!"

"I did that once," Destiny admitted sheepishly. "Only, it was a sliding door. Hurt like the dickens, too! I had a flat nipple for a month—after the swelling went down, of course. Guess I was lucky I didn't get it caught in something more dangerous, like a garbage disposal."

By now Jess was laughing so hard she could barely stand

upright. "And to think I've always envied women who are
built like you," she blurted. "I always saw the advantages, but
never realized the hazards."

"Shucks, honey," Pepper said. "There isn't a woman alive
who is one hundred percent satisfied with the way she looks.
If it's not her figure she hates, it's her hair. Or some part of
her face, or her laugh, or the way she walks. It took me years
to adjust to the fact that I'll always sound like a frog."

"But you don't," Jess told her honestly. "You have a voice
so sexy men must dream about it at night."

"Tell that to my high school choir director," Pepper retorted
with a wry grin.

"Oh, she was probably just jealous," Destiny commented.

Pepper shook her head. " 'She' was a 'he,' but come to
think of it, he did have this high voice that made him sound
rather like Mickey Mouse."

"I've never liked my toes," Jazz contributed. "They look
like ugly little bent twigs. That's why I never wear sandals."

"I'll take your toes over my tattoo any day," Destiny
claimed.

"What tattoo?" Jess asked curiously.

Destiny wrinkled up her nose. "The one on my behind."

Pepper let loose a bark of laughter. "You've got to see this
sometime, Jess. No kidding. It's a picture of a cute little skunk,
on Destiny's right cheek."

Destiny gave a long-suffering sigh. "Well, tell the world,
why don't you, Pepper? It's bad enough Mom thought it was
such a nifty idea, without you hollering about it."

"Well, you've got to admit it probably made changing your
diapers a lot more fun," Jazz proposed past a chortle. "And
it certainly fits the spot. What else would she put there? A
rose?"

"I'll bet it is embarrassing," Jess commiserated. "If you
truly dislike it that badly, can't you have it removed?"

Destiny shook her head, adamantly opposed to the suggestion. "No way am I going to go through all that pain, and
possibly end up with a scar worse than the skunk. It's bad

enough that every guy I go to bed with notices it—not that I've had scads of lovers, mind you—but I can just see getting stuck with some smart-ass doctor who would call in everybody but the resident plumber to see my tattoo before he removed it. No, I'll keep it, thanks, and put up with all the razzing.''

The game against the Cardinals was a nail biter. For every score the Knights made, the Cards matched it. While trying to stay on top of the game, Jess fiddled with her earphones. Either they had been repaired or this was a different set, for no matter how she tried she couldn't get any signals other than those she was supposed to receive.

They were playing outdoors today, on a grass field in Sun Devil Stadium. Though hot, the dry breeze made it fairly temperate and kept the bugs at bay. Which was why Jess noticed the one reserve player on the bench who seemed to be terrifically uncomfortable. The poor fellow kept shifting and scratching and tugging at his clothes. Jess was soon itching herself, just watching him. Finally, out of self-defense, she approached him.

''I don't mean to be too personal, Ervin, but do you have a bad case of poison ivy, or hives, or something?''

The man looked up at her, startled. ''No ma'am. Why?''

''I've seen flea-bitten dogs who didn't scratch and fuss the way you have been,'' she told him bluntly. ''Frankly, you're making me itch. Maybe you should check this out with the doctor. Could be you're allergic to something.''

''I'll do that, Coach Myers.'' She was blocking his view of the field, and he angled his head to see around her. ''Uh, could you scoot over a bit, please?''

''Sorry.'' Jess moved to one side and stood there to watch the upcoming play. From the corner of her eye, she saw Ervin tug at his left ear. Not once, but three times. Then he gave his knee a couple of quick slaps. Probably no more than nervous gestures, but that reporter's instinct Jess had mentioned to Alan kicked in.

On a hunch, Jess stepped in front of him again prior to the next play. Though he didn't say anything, she saw him frown and shift to another spot on the bench. It struck her, however, that his new position was even less advantageous to viewing the game. He rubbed his nose, then bent to retie his shoelace—though it wasn't untied to begin with.

She turned in time to watch the rival defense make a quick realignment on the field. The ball was snapped, and Ty had to scrap his plan to throw to Gabe. He scarcely handed the ball off to another receiver before getting rammed to the ground. He got up slowly, and for a minute Jess was afraid he'd been injured. Fortunately, he didn't appear to be hurt as he plucked a chunk of grass from his shoulder pad—just supremely angry.

The Knights were now in a third down and ten situation, too far downfield for a field goal attempt. Once more, her own temper rising, Jess tested her burgeoning theory. As if unaware that she was again stepping into his line of sight, Jess stationed herself in front of Ervin. When he scooted to the right, so did she. He stood up and walked past the end of the bench, and even though she wanted to, Jess couldn't follow. It would have been too obvious. But she did watch, her lips tightening, as Ervin scratched his chest, first up and down and then across, and stamped his left foot twice.

Within seconds, the defense shifted into a more advantageous lineup. Again, the Knights' play was fouled, and they had to punt the ball away.

The moment she could, Jess cornered Ty. "There's something fishy going on with Ervin," she told him bluntly. "He keeps fidgeting and making all sorts of odd motions, and every time he does, the opposing defense changes position immediately afterward, and your play goes down the tubes."

Ty glanced at Ervin and back at Jess, a scowl growing. "Are you sure?"

Jess shrugged. "I was standing right there, and whenever I moved in front of him, he'd move to another spot. Then he'd scratch, or tie a shoe that didn't need tying, or some such thing. It may just be my imagination working overtime, but I could almost swear he's sending signals to somebody. I just don't know to whom, because he didn't seem to be in full view of anyone on the other team, at least not that I could tell."

"He's not squirming around now," Ty observed.

"No, he only seems to do it when our offense is on the field," she said. "Am I nuts, or does that strike you as a bit odd?"

Ty gave a sharp jerk of his head, his eyes narrowing into slits as he stared at Ervin. "More than a bit, darlin'. But we're still shy on proof here. Why don't we try a little scam of our own and see what happens?"

Ty hustled Jess to where Coach Danvers was pacing the sidelines. After advising the man of her suspicions, Jess listened as Ty and Danvers swiftly formulated a plan of action. When the Knights' offense next took the field, Ty was armed with a totally new series of unscheduled plays.

As Coach Danvers and Jess watched, Ervin began to fidget. For no apparent reason, he put his helmet on and abruptly removed it. He pulled at the armpit of his shirt. When the new play Ty called succeeded in garnering the Knights a first down, Ervin looked befuddled. He picked up his playbook and seemed to be studying it. As the second play was set up, he tipped his water jug to his mouth in four jerks and wiped his hand down his right thigh. This play also gained yardage, and Ervin frowned and checked his playbook again.

By now, Danvers was cursing beneath his breath. For a third time, Ervin made a series of odd motions, and when Ty made a surprise shovel pass to Chili that resulted in a touchdown, Ervin definitely appeared more frustrated than elated at his team's score. As the others cheered, his gaze was trained on the section of stands beyond the goal post, as if he were searching for someone there. Jess saw him shake his head and make a hand gesture, as if to say it wasn't his fault.

"That lousy son of a bitch!" Danvers cursed. "I'm gonna tack his traitor's hide to a wall and use him for target practice. And it won't be footballs I'm aiming at him, either!"

"I'm sorry, Coach," Jess told him. "I was hoping I was wrong."

"Don't be sorry, Jess. I'm glad you noticed, especially since no one else seemed to be aware enough to catch on. You may have just saved this team a whole season of defeats, and for that I can't thank you enough."

Two hours later, Jess was in the center of a police investigation, and up to her ears in her own feelings of guilt. "If I hadn't said anything . . . ," she lamented. "Oh, Ty, I feel so responsible."

Ty hugged her to his side. "Jess, it's not your fault. If you hadn't noticed what Ervin was doing, eventually someone else would have."

"I know, but . . . good God, Ty! The man hanged himself in the locker room! He's dead because I ratted on him! I might just as well have knotted the rope and handed it to him!"

Danvers stepped up to her other side. "Ervin wouldn't have resorted to this if he wasn't guilty, Jess. It's his fault, not yours, for getting himself tangled up in this situation."

"Did the police find a suicide note or anything?" she asked.

Danvers shook his head. "No. Just Ervin and his playbook. They took it as evidence, of course, to see if it contains any phone numbers or anything else that might be useful in discovering who was paying him in exchange for our plays. Right now, we're still in the dark about that, but it was probably Ervin, or someone he was signaling to, who was transmitting the plays you heard the other week over your headphones."

"Damn! What a mess!" Ty declared tiredly. He rubbed at the bridge of his nose, trying to alleviate the pounding pain in his head. "With Ervin dead, I don't suppose anyone else is about to admit to any wrongdoing, either. We may never know who is behind all this."

"It's a crying shame any way you look at it," Danvers agreed. "The kid was only a rookie, but he had potential—if only he'd had a little patience. I keep wondering if he did this out of spite, because he only made third string and would be warming the bench most of the season. Or if he'd gotten himself into a financial pinch of some kind."

Ty sighed. "Could be someone made him an offer he couldn't

refuse, for whatever reason. But it won't do much good to second-guess the matter at this point."

At long last, the police had finished questioning everyone, and they were free to go. The Knights, all of them stunned at Ervin's traitorous behavior and suicide, were still in their uniforms. None seemed inclined to change clothes, let alone use the showers where Ervin had hung himself. Dirty, sweaty, and down-hearted, they headed en masse to the airport. They had won the game, but the loss of their teammate made it a hollow victory.

"When I said I wanted you to generate some team publicity, Jessie, I sure as shit didn't mean this way!" Tom shouted. He waved the newspaper at her, the front page headlines blaring Ervin's death. A grainy photo of Jess, Ty, and Danvers also graced the page, along with a separate picture of Ervin. "Hell's bells, girl! You were supposed to report on the team, not investigate it!"

"Then you shouldn't have hired me to begin with," Jess shot back with a glower. "You know my forte is investigative reporting, not publicity pieces. I was only doing this as a favor to you. Now I'm sorry I ever agreed to it."

"So am I, dammit!" he concurred angrily.

"Then you'll be glad to know that my story is done, video clips and all, and ready to submit to the sports network. Of course, with this latest development, they may want me to add to it, but for the most part it's finished."

"Thank God for small blessings. Now you won't have to hang around here all the time poking your nose into team business. You can get involved with more interesting projects that are more up your alley."

His tone was brusque and cutting, wounding Jess to the core. She'd never seen him like this, or had him speak to her in this manner. Always before, since she could remember, he'd been kind, jovial Tommy. It was like meeting a stranger in her godfather's body. She could scarcely withhold her tears as she responded in turn.

"Oh, you're not getting rid of me that easily, Tommy. I'm still coaching Alan, don't forget."

He glared at her and snapped, "You're fired. How's that, Miss Reporter?"

"Not good enough. If you'll review my contract, you'll see that you alone cannot discharge me. Coach Danvers and the other two owners have to agree, and right now they're a lot more grateful to me for rooting out the rat in the woodpile than you are. Not that I'm proud of the resulting consequences, but you could still have a turncoat in your midst if not for me."

Tommy looked as if he were about to blow a gasket. "I'll still put it to a vote," he vowed. "And another thing," he said, pointing a finger at her accusingly, "just what is going on between you and that hot-shot quarterback?"

"That's none of your business, Nelson." Both Tom and Jess jerked around as Ty barged into the office.

"I don't recall inviting you to this meeting," Tom declared tersely.

"You didn't have to," Ty told him flatly. "Your little chat can be heard all over the building, so I assume it's not exactly confidential."

"Is that all you came to say?" Tom inquired. "If so, you can leave now."

"Not without Jess. You've dragged her over the coals long enough, Nelson, and you're placing blame where it doesn't belong. Ervin was the culprit here, not Jess. So back off."

Tom sneered. "Oh, how sweet. The irate boyfriend coming to the rescue. You drumming up brownie points, James?"

Ty's smile was as false as Tom's. "Don't need them, Tom, old boy."

Tom's features tightened even more. "So that's the way the wind blows." To Jess, he added spitefully, "I thought I warned you about letting any of these jocks cozy up to you, thinking they'd get in good with me that way."

Jess's eyes narrowed. "That tears it, Tommy. I've taken all the flak I'm going to take from you today. I'll be waiting for an apology, when you've had time to cool off and think things through properly. Until then, don't call me. I'll call you."

Ty took her arm, escorting her out the door. As they left, he sent a parting shot. "If you can't reach Jess at her place, Nelson, she'll be at mine. Just phone any time. Day or night. But like the lady says, don't bother until you're ready to apologize."

CHAPTER 15

Jess could not recall when she'd last been this depressed. First, this dreadful business with Ervin, then the fight with Tommy. For his part, Ty was angry on her behalf and equally mystified as to how to console her. But there had to be some way to cheer her up. He fell back on some of the things that always worked for his mother and sisters.

"Would you like to go shopping?" he suggested.

"Not really."

"How about getting gussied up and going out to dinner? My treat. The place of your choice."

Jess shook her head. "Thanks, but I'm not in the mood."

Ty figured it would be a bad move to buy her flowers at the moment. They would probably only remind her of a funeral arrangement.

"Do you want to rent a video, or go to a movie? Isn't there a new comedy playing?"

She gave him a weary look. "Wagara, James. Give it a rest, okay?"

"You keep hitting me with that word at the oddest times," he mused. "I'm going to guess it yet." He thought a minute, and said, "Women's Automatic Guy Alteration/Reformation Act?"

"Not even close."

But he had gotten half a grin out of her, so he tried again. "Wanted: Assorted Gods And Reverent Angels?"

She smothered a chuckle. "Not bad, but way off base."

"Okay, how about Who's A Grinning And Retarded Ape?"

Jess burst out laughing. "You are! Now stop this nonsense."

"Why? So you can go back to wallowing in your own guilt and feeling miserable? No way, lady. Say, why don't we trot down to the store and buy about a ton of ice cream and chocolate goop?"

"That doesn't sound half bad. Why don't you go while I wash my stringy, greasy hair?" She plucked at a limp strand, eyeing it balefully from the corner of her eye. "Yuck! I think I could wear a dirty mop and no one would tell the difference."

"A permanent might help. Curly hair doesn't get oily as fast as straight hair," Ty informed her.

Jess cocked an eyebrow at him. "Well, you're just full of surprising little tidbits. But a perm wouldn't do the trick, I'm afraid. Not for me. My hair is too fine. A body perm lasts me about a week and a half, and a full perm leaves me looking like Little Orphan Annie. Or Ronald McDonald's sister. Take your pick. Either way, it's not a pretty sight."

"Then why not get your hair frosted, or streaked, or highlighted? That usually adds a bit of body, besides giving you a change of color that's not too drastic. And if you do it lightly enough, you don't even have dark roots to touch up."

Jess eyed him oddly. "Just where are you picking up all this information, Tyler James? Are you secretly hooked on *Woman's Day* or *Cosmo?* Or are they putting this stuff in *Playboy* these days, just to give you guys something to discuss on a date?"

Ty scowled at her. "My mom's a beautician. I spent half my life hanging around her shop, watching her work her magic on little old ladies who wanted to look like Farrah Fawcett." He gave a sheepish shrug. "Guess my brain absorbed more than the perm fumes, huh?"

"Your mom is a hair dresser?" Jess was intrigued. "What does your dad do?"

Ty hesitated. "I'll only tell you if you promise not to freak out on me."

She gave him a curious look, but agreed. "Scout's honor."

"Dad is a mortician."

"A what?" Jess's mouth flapped open.

"So much for promises," Ty groused.

"Your father is an undertaker? Like in, working with corpses?"

"What's wrong with that?" Ty inquired defensively. "Somebody has to do it, or the bodies would be stacking up like cord wood."

"I suppose you're right, but of all the occupations you might have mentioned, that's the last one I would have guessed." She paused a moment, then asked almost tentatively, "So, are you planning on following in your father's footsteps after you quit playing football?"

"Well, I hate to disappoint you, Jess," he said with a grin, "but, no. Actually, I got my degree in accounting."

He'd done it to her again. Thrown her two curves in a row. "Accounting?" she repeated dumbly. "No announcing games? No coaching? No selling sporting goods? No sports bar?"

"Nope. Accounting and business administration. See there, Jess? I'm not just your run-of-the-mill super jock or ditso blond, after all, am I? You're talking to an actual Certified Public Accountant and investment management graduate. If I have to, I can even use words with more than two syllables."

"Don't get snide, Ty. I never said you weren't intelligent. I just thought you'd probably go into something related to football, since you like it so well."

He speared her with a knowing look. "C'mon, Jess. Admit it. You're harboring a few biased opinions of your own about me, the way I did about reporters."

"Perhaps," she conceded. "Primarily before I got to know you. You've already destroyed a lot of my preconceived notions, however, and I have a sneaking hunch you've still got a couple of surprises up your sleeve."

"If you really want to make me feel better, and yourself in the bargain, you could let me do your hair," he told her.

"Is that where all this was leading?" she asked suspiciously.

He gave her a look that might have passed for innocent if not for the twinkle lurking in his blue eyes. "Well?" he prodded.

"What did you have in that warped mind of yours?"

"I thought we might highlight it a little."

"How little?" she inquired dubiously.

"Not much. When it's done, it'll look sun-streaked. Basically, you'll still have your own color, only brighter, with strands of blond mixed in."

Her brows knitted, wrinkling her forehead beneath her stick-straight bangs. "Do you know how to do that, or would I just be some stupid guinea pig at the mercy of a novice dabbler?"

"Trust me, Jess. You'll love it."

Trust him. That was what it all boiled down to. Jess sighed. "Okay, but if you make me look ridiculous, I'm going to retaliate in equal proportion, buster. I'll dye your face green while you're sleeping. I'll paint your fingernails with a red permanent marker. I'll . . ."

"I get your drift, you vengeful witch. Now, go wash your hair, and I'll run down to the store and get the stuff I need and be back in a jiffy."

"Don't forget the ice cream and chocolate syrup while you're at it," she reminded him. "I've got a feeling I'm going to need the consolation. And a can of black spray paint for the mirrors might not be amiss, either."

He grinned at her. "Oh, ye of little faith!"

"Wait!" Jess threw up her hand to catch his—the one in which he was holding the scissors—and stared in horror at the lock of hair that had just fallen into her lap. "You didn't say anything about cutting it, too."

"I'm just going to reshape it, and get rid of the split ends," he assured her. "Nothing that drastic."

Jess let loose of him and groaned. "How did I ever let you talk me into this?"

He snipped another section. "Too late now, darlin'. So hold

still so I can get it even. And shut your mouth, unless you want a glob of hair in it."

"Give me a mirror first."

"Not on your life."

Jess closed her eyes and commenced to pray. Twenty minutes later, he ceased whacking at her hair. Jess chanced a peek. The floor was littered, as was she, and her head felt noticeably lighter. "Are you done with the scissors? Am I completely bald?"

Behind her, Ty chuckled. "Yes, and no, in that order. Now comes the fun part." For her perusal, he held out a shower cap dotted with tiny holes. "You get to wear this while I pull strands of your hair through the holes with this." He showed her something resembling a crochet needle.

"Oh, yippee!" she quipped, eyeing the items with growing dread. "What then? You make a sweater for Josh?"

"Not quite. Then we mix up the solution, glop it on, and wait the prescribed amount of time. About half an hour or so."

As he plied the pick, it felt as if he were yanking the remainder of her hair from its roots. "Ouch!" she complained for the umpteenth time. "Take it easy, will you?"

Then, when he applied the bleach mixture, her eyes began to water. "Are you sure you don't have it too strong?"

"Stop whining. I swear, Josh wouldn't complain as much as you are."

"Then work on Josh next time you get a whim to play beautician."

"You'll be singing a different tune when you see the final result," he predicted immodestly.

The last forty minutes seemed like a century. Finally, Ty deemed her hair the correct shade. "Now, we rinse, condition, and style."

"Can I look yet?"

"Absolutely not."

He brushed, he fluffed, he dried it with her hair blower. He spritzed, sprayed, turning her this way and that. At long last, he handed her a mirror, claiming as he did so, "Not bad, if I do say so myself."

Jess was almost afraid to look. On a deep breath, she held
up the mirror. That same breath rushed out again as she stared
at her image in total disbelief. "Oh, my gosh! Ty! What did
you do? That can't be me!"

Only now did Ty display the slightest apprehension. "Do
you like it?"

"Like it? I love it!" she squealed, angling for a better view.
"You're an absolute miracle worker!"

She swished her head back and forth, watching her hair
bounce and shimmer. It had body, and shine, and . . . pouf! Ty
had feathered it away from her face, leaving it long enough to
fluff out and over her ears. He'd cut the crown shorter, giving
it lift where it had hung limply before. He'd also layered the
back to give it more volume. And the color—streaks of pale
gold, artfully intertwined with her original brown, which no
longer seemed so drab now.

Her image wavered as tears gathered in her eyes. "Oh, Ty!
It's so pretty! And it makes my face look fuller. Not so long
and thin. I actually look . . ."

"Go ahead, sweetheart," he urged softly. "Say it. You're
beautiful. Downright, indisputably gorgeous. Which is precisely what I've been telling you all along. Until now, you
simply haven't been accentuating your best features, that's all."

"I really am pretty, aren't I?" she said incredulously.

"No. Pretty doesn't begin to cover it, Jess. What's it going
to take to convince you? You truly are beautiful, inside and
out. Now say it. Out loud. Say, 'I, Jess Myers, am a beautiful
woman.' "

"Ty, that's silly, not to mention outrageously conceited."

"It's the bare-faced truth. Now say it, dammit, or you don't
get any ice cream. I'll eat it all myself, right in front of you."

She felt foolish, and shaky, and unsure of herself as she
stared at the unfamiliar image in the mirror. But something
inside her, a skinny little girl with freckles and braces, was
pleading for her to do as Ty asked. "I . . . am beautiful," she
whispered.

"Louder. Stronger. With conviction this time, like you really
believe it," he prodded.

A smile tugged at her lips and traveled to her eyes. "I am beautiful," she stated more firmly. Swiftly, she turned, caught him around the neck, and pulled his face toward hers. "And it's all because of you, Ty. No one else but you."

Ty's smile was tender, his eyes glowing with something akin to love as he brought his lips to hers. "In that case, I wouldn't refuse a reward—a very special, intimate reward—if a certain lovely lady were to offer it."

Because of Wednesday's funeral service for Ervin, which most of the team attended, the Knights were cut short one practice session that week. Nevertheless, by the time Sunday rolled around, they were more than ready for their bout against the Portland Rangers. Like the Knights, the Rangers were a newly formed expansion team, still fledglings in the league. The Knights, with their fans rooting for them on their own turf, beat the Oregonians handily.

The following week, everything went downhill. Each practice session seemed to bring with it a new disaster. On Tuesday, Dino Sherwood broke his collarbone during the scrimmage. He'd be out of action for most of the remaining season. Wednesday morning, the coach announced that Brice Tackett, their best tight end, had been arrested for DWI and would be on temporary suspension until the matter was resolved.

This initiated an unexpected on-the-spot drug testing, or as the players had labeled it, a "whiz quiz." Doc Johnson, the team physician, handed each of them a name-labeled bottle at the rest room door and collected it again as each man left. Even the coaches had to submit a urine sample, though Jess was allowed to donate hers in the privacy of the ladies' rest room while Johnson waited in the outer hallway. While all this was done as efficiently as possible, it was still a lengthy procedure, causing practice that day to run over by an hour.

Havoc reigned Thursday when Doc Johnson proclaimed that two of the players had failed the drug test. The first was Rick Tanner, a veteran offensive guard. This came as a terrific shock to everyone, including Rick—particularly since it was well-known that he and his wife Michelle were devout Christians.

"Now hold the phone, Doc," he protested. "There's no way I could have flunked that drug test. I haven't even taken an aspirin in the past two weeks!"

"No, but it looks like you've been smoking some pot," Doc rebutted. "You're on the bench until I decide you're clean."

The second man on the list was Sir Loin Simms, who also protested his innocence, with the same results—though his test had shown traces of crack cocaine.

"This is preposterous!" Ty, as the team leader, was not buying it, and voiced his complaint loudly. "Doc, Coach, I know these men. Neither of them would jeopardize their careers this way."

Danvers held out his hands in a defeated gesture. "I'm sorry. My hands are tied. I have to abide by Doc Johnson's ruling. The only thing I can do is request that they be retested as soon as possible."

"But they're vital to us." Rambo pointed out the obvious. "Without them on the field, the Oilers are gonna walk all over us. On our first Monday night game on TV, too!"

"Well, I'm not taking this lying down," Rick declared. "I'm going to call my lawyer and have him meet me at the hospital, where I'm going to have them run another test. I want witnesses to the fact that I'm no druggie."

"What are you implying, Tanner?" Doc Johnson puffed up like a rooster, his face flaming in anger. "That I'm incompetent?"

"Not necessarily," Rick said, "but something went wrong with your test. Maybe the lab screwed up, or the container was contaminated. I don't know. All I'm sure of is that I have never smoked a joint in my life, and no one is going to say otherwise and get away with it."

"Hey, man! Can I come with you?" Sir Loin asked. "I ain't got a lawyer in Columbus yet, but I'd be glad to pay yours if he'd help me out, too."

"Now, let's all calm down here, fellows," Doc suggested. "I can take another set of samples to a different lab, and it won't cost either of you a dime. Maybe Tanner is right, and the first tests got messed up somehow. No sense blowing this thing all out of proportion.''

Rick didn't look too sure. Sir Loin was wavering. Finally, under Danvers' persuasion, they agreed, but only after Doc guaranteed the results would be back by the next afternoon.

By the end of practice on Friday, everyone was on pins and needles, waiting to hear the new lab findings. They got half their wish. Rick Tanner's test was clear. Sir Loin's wasn't. Still maintaining his innocence, Sir Loin marched off the field in a huff, defiantly stating that he was off to engage an attorney.

CHAPTER 16

With half of Friday and all weekend off, and no practice until Monday morning in Memphis, it was a perfect time for Ty to take Josh for a quick trip to Kentucky. Ty's parents lived in the small city of Bowling Green, about a hundred and twenty miles south of Louisville. To her surprise, Ty invited Jess to go along.

"How fast can you pack?" he asked her. "I'd like to take you down and introduce you to my folks."

"Really? Won't bringing me along make your family start asking a lot of questions?"

"Like your mom wanting to know what my intentions were?"

Jess nodded. "Precisely."

Ty shrugged. "I can handle it if you can," he told her. "Don't worry. There's plenty of room, and Mom always cooks for an army. One person, more or less, won't put her in a dither."

"Well," Jess hedged, though her curiosity was almost more than she could stand, "if you're sure your parents won't mind."

"Just pack casual clothes for there," he said. "We won't

be doing anything fancy. Mostly just hanging around the house so Mom and Dad can get a good visit in with Josh.''

''What about afterward? Are we going to drive all the way back to Indianapolis with Josh, then back here to catch the flight to Memphis Sunday night? That's going to cut your visit awfully short, not to mention all the driving you'll have to do.''

''It's all arranged. Mom and Dad are going to take Josh home on Sunday evening,'' he explained. ''You and I can drive back up to Louisville and catch a flight to Memphis from there, which will leave us a three and a half hour drive home on Tuesday.''

''But last-minute flights are so expensive, Ty.''

A sheepish look crossed his face. ''I bought our tickets two weeks ago, Jess, when they were running that fare-war special. I got them dirt cheap.''

Jess stared at him in wonder. ''You bought mine then, too?''

''Yes, and it's nonrefundable, so I was hoping you'd agree.''

Despite Jess's trepidation, the weekend was great, and so was Ty's family. Their home was large and welcoming, filled with a hodgepodge of furniture chosen for comfort rather than fashion. Overstuffed sofas and chairs, a trestle table and benches in the kitchen, cozy comforters and quilts on the beds, and country curtains at the windows. It was a home where children could feel free to play, without constantly being on guard against dirtying something or breaking some expensive knick-knack. Outdoors, there was a big fenced-in yard, complete with sandbox and swing set. The only drawback, in Jess's estimation, was that the house was located next door to the funeral home, albeit several yards away.

''You get used to it,'' Ty assured her, ''and I can categorically confirm that neither I nor any of my family have ever seen a ghost flitting around.''

''How would you like a tour of the mortuary while you're here?'' Wesley James offered with a grin reminiscent of Ty's.

"I think we can drum up at least one body that needs embalming, if you'd care to watch."

Jess fought not to turn green at the very thought. "No thank you, Mr. James. I'll take a rain check on that, if you don't mind. Say the second Tuesday of the fifth week in February?"

Wes winked at his son. "She's a quick one, isn't she, Ty?"

"You haven't seen the half of it, Dad," Ty told him.

"Josh really has taken a shine to you, Miss Myers," Ty's mother, Maggie, commented.

"Just call me Jess, please," Jess requested with a smile. "And I've taken quite a liking to Josh, too. Does he resemble Ty when he was young?"

"Like two peas in a pod," Maggie confirmed. "I'll show you some of Ty's earlier pictures later, if you like."

Jess shot Ty a wide grin. "I'd love to see them. Do you have any that might be useful as blackmail material? Say, Ty naked on a bearskin rug, for instance?"

Maggie chuckled. "No bearskin, but I think there's one of him on his training potty, with his drawers around his ankles."

"That'll do just fine," Jess said over Ty's loud groan.

"Geez, Mom! Give a poor guy a break, will you?"

"Sure, Ty. Just to be fair, I'll show Jess some of your sisters' pictures, too."

On Saturday, Ty's three sisters and their families came to visit. Unlike their brother, all three girls had settled within a few miles of their parents. Karlie, the oldest, lived a block down the street. She was married to an ex-coffin salesman, and the two of them now helped Wes run the funeral parlor. Karlie and Ken had two children, a boy Josh's age, and a little girl who had just turned three. Cheryl, a nurse/midwife, had married a local pharmacist. They had three youngsters, a boy and two girls, ranging in age from six years to six months. Lynn, the youngest of Ty's sisters, taught elementary school, and was engaged to a fellow teacher.

Josh was ecstatic that his cousins had come to visit. Within minutes, the house fairly reverberated with the sound of children laughing and shrieking. Used to such commotion, Maggie calmly ushered the older ones outdoors to play.

"What happens when it's raining?" Jess asked.

"We shove them into the cellar and lock the door," Karlie informed her, her blue eyes twinkling.

"Lord love a duck!" Lynn exclaimed. "Karlie, you'll have the poor girl thinking we're the most horrible people on earth!" To Jess, she quickly explained, "Mom and Dad have turned part of the basement into a play area for the kids. It's all paneled and carpeted, and they've even installed a bathroom down there, so it's not like we're tossing them into a dungeon or anything."

"Aw, darn!" Jess rebutted with a grin. "I was hoping to see some actual, old-fashioned torture equipment."

"Will Mom's old paddle do?" Cheryl offered. "It a real jim-dandy, with holes drilled through for less air resistance."

"Now, Cheryl, you know I retired that thing long ago," Maggie objected. "I don't believe it's been put to good use since your dad caught Ty smoking in his bedroom." She made a rueful face and added, "Of course, my azaleas haven't bloomed nearly as well without all the ashes he used to flick out his window, either."

Maggie was a marvelous cook and had taught her daughters the art as well. She was genuinely surprised when Jess offered to help prepare the meal. "My lands! Don't tell me Tyler has finally hooked up with a girl who knows her way around a kitchen. Why, I don't believe Barb could do more than open a can of soup and heat it in the microwave, and to hear her tell it, you'd swear she'd slaved over a hot stove all day just doing that much."

"Oh, Jess can cook like a dream," Ty volunteered. "Almost as good as you, Mom."

Once in the kitchen, surrounded by James women, Jess was bombarded with questions and freely tendered information.

"Did Ty tell me you're coaching one of the football players?"

"How serious is it between you and Ty? This is the first time since Barb that he's brought anyone home to meet the family, you know. After the number she did on him, I think he's been a little gun-shy about long-term relationships with women, especially if he suspects they're only interested in him for his fame or fortune.''

"Barb was a real bitch, if you'll pardon my French.''

"French? Cheryl, you can barely speak English.''

"Are you from around Columbus, Jess?''

"Has Ty met your folks yet?''

"Wait 'til you meet Grandma Arlyss. She'll be around tomorrow, no doubt, so be prepared to be grilled by the best. She's half deaf, and refuses to wear her hearing aid most of the time, so you'll have to yell some, mind you.''

"Have you met Ty's ex-wife? She's awfully attractive, in a different way from you—or she would be if she wasn't such a money-grubbing shrew.''

"Oh, I don't hold a candle to Barb when it comes to looks,'' Jess claimed.

"Don't kid yourself,'' Lynn told her. "Ty doesn't date homely women. Course, being a quarterback and semifamous and all, he doesn't have to, I suppose. Not with all the pretty ones after him.''

Jess shook her head, a wry smile curling her lips. "You wouldn't say that if you'd met me a few weeks before, or even a few days ago. I have to admit I was a mess.''

"Now, I don't believe a word of it,'' Karlie said. "Just look at you. Why, if Ty hadn't told us you're a reporter, which by itself was a major surprise since members of the press aren't exactly his favorite people, I'd swear you were a model or something.''

Jess waved that notion aside. "Me? No way. I'm more comfortable behind a camera than I'd ever be in front of one. I'd feel like a female Frankenstein.'' Out of habit, she rubbed at the small lump on the bridge of her nose.

"You're certainly tall enough, and thin enough to be a model,'' Cheryl noted. "And you have those high cheekbones they've all got. And I love the way you've done your hair.''

Jess laughed. "You ought to. Your brother did it for me.''

"Say what?''

"Ty?''

Maggie got the last word. "Ty styled your hair for you?''

"Cut it, highlighted it, the whole works," Jess confirmed with a nod. "Just this past week, in fact."

"Well, I'll be a monkey's uncle!" Maggie declared. "Turn around. Let me get a closer look." She inspected Jess's hairdo with a critical eye, then announced, "He did a right decent job of it, if I do say so myself."

"Thanks to you, and spending so much time in your shop, so he claims," Jess told her.

Maggie beamed. "I always hoped one of my offspring would inherit my talent, but God knows I never thought it would be Ty," she quipped with a chuckle. "Wes is going to have a bloomin' fit! His son, the quarterback accountant hairdresser!"

By the time their visit came to an end, everyone was on a first-name basis, and Jess felt as if she'd been adopted into the family. She felt so comfortable and welcome with them, she actually hated to leave.

"You bring Jess back real soon, Ty," Maggie told her son as they packed their bags in the car. "And don't stay away so long yourself."

"I will, Mom," he promised. "Maybe for Thanksgiving."

"Don't forget our date, Jess," Wes reminded jokingly. "Come February, I'll give you that tour of the mortuary."

As they drove away, Jess looked back. They were all standing in the drive, waving farewell—Josh with both hands flapping wildly. She wondered if she really would be coming back again with Ty. She hoped so. Lord, but she hoped so.

Memphis was a disaster from beginning to end. After spending the weekend in separate bedrooms at Ty's parents, Jess now found herself sharing quarters with the cheerleaders again, while Ty roomed with Gabe. Which might not have been so bad if Bambi hadn't been one of Jess's roommates this time around.

"We alternate now and then," Pepper explained. "This week, we've got Bambi and Shasta, while Destiny and Jazz are bunking in with Starr and Heidi. Eventually, you'll get

Tawna, Desiree, and Candy as roomies, or some combination thereof.''

Shasta's given name was Daisy, which she deplored, so she'd taken a variety of the flower and adopted it, instead. ''Daisy was my great-grandmother's name, and I've always hated it,'' Shasta said. ''It's so old-fashioned sounding. Maybe when I'm eighty, I won't mind, but for right now I'd rather be Shasta, even if some people do think I got it from a soft drink.''

Shasta was one of the younger members of the cheerleading squad, having never cheered for a pro team before, as some of the other girls had. Fresh out of high school, she hadn't set her sights on any other occupation as yet. This was Shasta's way to save money for her college tuition while she decided what she wanted to study when she got there. Destiny, on the other hand, was saving to open a boutique of her own someday, and Jazz wanted to start her own dance studio when her days as a cheerleader were done. Pepper, the squad leader, was already certified as a dental hygienist, and was merely biding her time until her dental student fiancé got his doctorate degree and the two of them set up shop together.

Jess found it quite enlightening that many of the girls did not intend for this to be their ultimate career. Mistakenly, she'd been under the impression that they were all fairly well stuck on themselves and out to bag a wealthy hubby, be it a football star or otherwise. Not that she was completely off-base in her prejudicial thinking. Case in point—Bambi, who made no bones about admitting that she was angling for a man who could keep her in the high style she felt she deserved, and to which she would like to become lazily accustomed. Just now, with no one better or richer on the horizon, she had her sights set on Ty. It mattered little to her that he was currently unavailable.

''You won't hold his interest for long,'' she informed Jess in a snide, superior tone. ''He's only dating you to get some good press, and to make me jealous. But any day now he's going to see that you're nothing but bad news—the way you were for poor old Ervin. Then you'll be history and he'll be mine. So go ahead, change your hair, get a nose job, spruce yourself up all you want. You'll only be wasting your money.''

"Now, Bambi, be nice," Pepper told her, "or I'll be forced to tell Jess your real name, so she can use it in her article and reveal it to the whole world."

Bambi wheeled on Pepper. "You don't even know it," she sneered.

Pepper's grin was wicked. "Want to bet? Remember Seattle, at the beginning of the season? Who answered the phone when your mother called the hotel room looking for you? She sure didn't ask for Bambi, I guarantee you."

"Ha! You're bluffing. Just a big bag of hot air!"

"Keep pushing me, and you're bound to regret it," Pepper warned.

"Oh, you think you're such hot stuff!" Bambi declared. "Just because you're the squad leader, when everyone knows you only got the position by sucking up to the coaches. Tell me, Pep. Did you have to screw them all, or just a few of them?"

If looks could kill, Pepper's would have. "Actually, I didn't have to do anything with any of them . . . Bernice."

"Bernice?" Jess and Shasta echoed the word as one.

"That's as bad as Daisy," Shasta added, wrinkling her nose.

"Pepper! You're going to pay for this!" Bambi exclaimed angrily. "I don't know how or when, but you'll pay!"

"Yeah, I'm shaking in my shoes."

In turn, Bambi shook a threatening finger at Jess. "If you dare disclose that name to anyone, I'll sue you for every penny you have."

"You can't sue a person for divulging the truth," Jess advised her blandly. "Besides, there are a lot of Bernice's out there who would probably love to know that a cheerleader of a pro football team shares the same name. Frankly, we're all getting a little tired of the Bambi bit."

A while later, Jess retold the tale to Ty. "That woman really despises me, Ty. I have a feeling I'll be sleeping with one eye open tonight, if I sleep at all."

"Waiting for her to creep up on you and try to smother you

with a pillow?'' he joked. ''You could always room in with
Gabe and me, I suppose. Of course, we'd have to blindfold
him, stuff cotton in his ears, and tie him to his bed.''

''Oh, sure!'' she scoffed. ''Corey would love that, not to
mention setting the old rumor mill grinding at high speed. In
no time flat, gossip would be that I was having kinky sex with
the entire Knights' roster. Thanks, but no thanks. I'm not that
desperate.''

As it turned out, even that rumor would have been preferable
to the one Bambi began circulating the next morning. For some
reason, Shasta had chosen to switch bedrooms and bunk in
with three of the other girls, leaving Bambi, Jess, and Pepper
to themselves. Now, Jess wondered if Bambi had talked Shasta
into it, and if it had all been a part of Bambi's scheme to get
back at her and Pepper, without another witness to refute her
claim.

Jazz was the first to approach them with the news early the
next day. ''Good God!'' she exclaimed to Jess and Pepper, as
she burst into their room. ''What did you do to set Bambi off?
She's running around telling everyone with ears that you're a
couple of lesbians!''

''What!'' Jess was aghast.

''Why, that lying-ass bitch! I suppose this is what she meant
about paying me back for blabbing her real name,'' Pepper
railed. ''And everyone already knows she hates Jess's guts.''

''Whatever,'' Jazz said. ''She's really making an Oscar-
winning act of it, too. She claims she woke up in the night,
looked over, and saw you two making love in the next bed.
According to her, she was so disgusted she ran for the bathroom,
locked herself in, and vomited.''

Jess groaned. ''I can't believe this! It's too outrageous! But
I'll bet there are plenty of other people who will. Damn that
witch, anyway!'' Then, as the thought occurred to her, ''Oh,
Lord! I've got to talk to Ty before anyone else does!''

Jess all but flew through the halls to reach Ty's room. He
and Gabe were just stepping into the hall as she rounded the

corner. In the process of pulling the door shut, Ty turned toward her.

Jess skidded breathlessly to a stop a few feet shy of him, her heart thudding triple time as she saw the anger reflected on his face. The question loomed in her mind—was his wrath directed at her or at Bambi? She stood silently—watching, hoping, praying. Then Ty held his arms out to her, open wide, and Jess rushed into his welcoming embrace.

"Oh, Ty! It's not true! Please, believe me!"

He hugged her tightly. "Sweetheart, if anyone knows that, I do. Hey, don't cry. It's not the end of the world. It's going to be all right, Jess."

"But . . . but . . ." she blubbered. "There are bound to be people who will believe it. How's this going to look for you? What if your family gets wind of it? Or Barb? What about Josh? And the team, the coaches, and . . ."

"Your friends will stand by you," Gabe assured her gruffly. "I, for one, would love to rip Bambi's tongue out and feed it to her."

Ty gently kissed a teardrop from Jess's eyelashes. "We'll handle it, babe," he promised. "Together."

CHAPTER 17

After all that had gone before, Jess could almost have predicted that the Knights would lose the game against the Oilers that evening. Not that they didn't make a good stab at winning, but it was as if they were playing under some infernal cloud of doom—predestined for defeat, no matter how hard they tried. It didn't help that they had several key players missing; that they were playing a night game (in Oiler territory, no less) when they were used to day games, which may have thrown their timing off a bit; or that, due to a vicious thunder storm, the officials stopped the game early, with ten minutes left on the clock and the Knights behind by only two touchdowns. All in all, it would have been a miracle if they had won.

"Well, you win some and you lose some," Ty philosophized. "I suppose we should be grateful that none of us got struck by lightning."

Jess nodded miserably. "That wouldn't have surprised me, either, at this point."

"I don't know about you all, but I could use a beer right about now," Gabe put in. "Care to join me? We can drown our sorrows together."

"Why not?" Ty agreed. "Maybe we can even find a country-western band playing an appropriate tune or two to match our mood.''

"Great!" Jess mused sarcastically. "Just what I need, to hear about somebody whose life is worse than mine. The lover ran off, the dog died, the truck won't start, and the spittoon runneth over. Meanwhile, back at the ranch, I've got to figure out where the devil I'm sleeping tonight, because it sure as heck won't be with Bambi, and I don't think it would be wise to share a room alone with Pepper at this point, either.''

"You're sleeping with Gabe and me," Ty told her, "and to hell with the gossip mongers. Let them have a heyday trying to figure that one out.''

As it happened, the rumor Bambi had initiated was soon put to rest. Several of the cheerleaders rallied to Pepper and Jess's defense, loudly refuting Bambi's claim. Destiny, bless her ditsy soul, had been the one to recall that Bambi couldn't see three inches in front of her without her contact lenses, which she removed each and every night. Therefore, if she had awakened in the night, she wouldn't have been able to see a herd of elephants trooping past her bed, let alone discern what was happening on the other side of the room.

Furthermore, all of the girls knew that Bambi complained she always had trouble falling asleep in any hotel room, especially if she had to share it with two or three other women. The light, the noise, everything bothered her—unless she took a sleeping pill, which she invariably did. Then, she slept like the dead until morning.

Once informed of this by Destiny and her friends, nearly everyone concluded that Bambi had fabricated the entire tale out of pure spite. Moreover, it was public knowledge that Pepper was happily engaged—and no one could imagine why Jess would want or need anyone else when she had Ty. Within days, the whole mess had blown over, leaving only residual resentment and mistrust toward Bambi.

* * *

Though they had lost the game, Alan had done well, earning the Knights several points by his efforts. His kicking had improved tremendously in the past few weeks. Jess was proud of him, as was the entire team.

"You keep this up, and I'm going to be out of a job," Jess told him by way of a compliment.

At practice on Wednesday, Alan exceeded her expectations. He made ten successive field goals from thirty yards or beyond. Following the last one, he leapt into the air, his fist punching the sky. "Yes!" he yelled. "Finally!" He swaggered up to Jess with a wide, self-satisfied grin. "Okay, Coach. Pay-up time."

Jess stared at him, at a loss.

"You said that on the day I made ten goals in a row you'd tell me what WAGARA means," he elaborated.

"Oh, I'd forgotten about that."

"Well?"

"You promise not to tell Ty, or anyone else who might tell him? It's driving him nuts, and I want to keep him guessing."

"Scout's honor."

When she told him, Alan whooped. "It figures," he said, "and it fits. I'd have hit on the right answer sooner or later."

"Maybe," Jess conceded. "You did come close a couple of times."

Finished with their own practice, she and Alan stayed to watch the rest of the team. After pacing the sidelines for several minutes, Alan loped back to the bench, where Jess was seated.

"Can I borrow your car? They shorted us on our delivery of Gatorade this week, and we're running low. Coach Danvers wants me to run down to the warehouse distributor's and pick some up. Trouble is, I rode my motorcycle today."

Jess dug into her pocket for her keys, handing them out to him. "Don't speed," she warned.

Alan laughed. "In that tinker toy? You've got to be kidding. I can peddle that fast!"

"Wisenheimer," she grumbled. Then she tossed him her red WAGARA hat. "It's yours. Wear it in good health."

His smile was a mile wide as he trotted toward the exit to the parking lot.

Forty-five minutes later, the rest of the team headed for the lockers, and Danvers approached Jess. "Where's Crumrine?"

Jess shrugged. "Your guess is as good as mine, Coach. How far is that warehouse, anyway?"

"About six blocks away. He should have been back by now. I hope he didn't get into an accident."

"Me, too," Jess added. "He borrowed my car."

"Well, there's your answer, then," Danvers replied. "The danged heap probably conked out on him halfway there."

Jess scowled. "I wish you guys would all stop ragging on my car."

By the time another quarter-hour had gone by, with no Alan, Jess was really beginning to worry. "Did you give him explicit directions?" she asked Danvers. "Maybe he got lost. Do you think we ought to send someone to look for him?"

"He's been there before, Jess. He knows where it is. He's probably just out joyriding."

"In *my* car?" Jess exclaimed incredulously.

Danvers just grinned. "Chances are, he's just stuck in traffic. If he's not back soon, we'll send out a search party."

As it was, the search party came to them, in the form of two uniformed patrolmen. Jess took one look at their grim faces and knew the news was not good. She just hoped Alan hadn't gotten himself into anything too serious.

"Anyone here know an Alan Crumrine?" the first officer inquired.

Danvers stepped forward. "Yes, sir. He's our kicker. I'm Coach Danvers. Has Alan been arrested or something?"

"No, sir. There's been an incident, and we need to notify his family. Also, he was driving a car registered to a Jessica Myers. We need to locate her, too."

"I'm right here," Jess said, approaching closer. "If that's

what's wrong, Alan didn't steal my car. I loaned it to him a little while ago.''

''Ma'am.'' The policeman nodded toward her, tipping his cap. ''I'm afraid your car is being impounded, pending an investigation. It'll be a few days, at least, before we can release it to you.''

''But, why? What's this all about?'' Jess questioned with a frown. ''Was there an accident? Was Alan cited?''

''Does he need bail? Or a lawyer?'' Danvers asked.

By now, some of the players had emerged from the locker room and were milling around curiously.

''Don't tell me he's not going to be able to play this weekend,'' one groaned. ''We're short-handed already.''

''Yeah,'' another fellow added, ''and Miller can punt, but he can't kick worth a darn, and he's our only back-up kicker. No offense, Miller, but it's the truth.''

''I'd suggest your punter bone up real fast, then,'' the officer told them gravely, ''because Mr. Crumrine won't be playing for the Knights again.''

The color drained from Jess's face. Ty grabbed her from behind. ''Oh, God! How badly is he hurt?''

''He's dead, ma'am,'' the man replied. ''I'm sorry to be so blunt about it, but there's no easy way to say it.''

''How?'' Ty queried. ''A traffic accident, I suppose?''

''As far as we can tell, he was the victim of a drive-by shooting.''

Jess inhaled on a gasp, her color fading even more.

''We can't tell you any more at this point, but we'll be investigating further. Meanwhile, we need to notify his next of kin. He had his team membership on him, along with his driver's license, which led us here after no one answered at his home address. But his I.D. didn't list any other names or addresses for close family.''

''Those would be listed on his personnel record,'' Danvers said weakly, as shocked as the rest of the team. ''I'll show you up to the office.''

The two officers followed Danvers, as others stood dumbly,

like a small herd of mute cattle. Finally, the murmurs began, and built, as the players voiced their stunned disbelief.

Ty led Jess to a bench and lowered her onto it. "Put your head between your knees, hon," he urged. "It'll get the blood flowing to your head again."

She fought the hand he pressed to the back of her head. Tears choked her as she exclaimed softly, "Somebody please tell me this is all a bad dream—that I'll wake up and none of this will be real. Oh, God, Ty! Not Alan. Not sweet, gullible Alan, with all his wisecracks and practical jokes."

"I know, sweetheart, I know. I'm having trouble believing it, too. Lord, it's like this whole damned team is living under a jinx. Some sort of weird witch's spell or something. It's just been one disaster on top of another. And it scares the hell out of me to think you might have been driving that car. That you could have been the one shot and killed."

"I should never have loaned it to him," she said. "If I hadn't, he'd probably still be alive."

"If that's the case, then Danvers should never have sent him on that errand to begin with," Ty injected. "No, Jess, there's just no way to foresee these things, especially something as unpredictable as a drive-by shooting. It's just that we feel so helpless at times like this, that we can't help but wonder if it could have been avoided."

She gave a shuddering sob. "I suppose so."

His arm tightened around her shoulders. "C'mon, love. Let's go home. I don't know about you, but I hate crying in public, and if I have to watch you very much longer, I'm going to sit down and bawl beside you."

That night, after Ty had plied her with wine and a long soak in the hot tub, and tucked her into bed, Jess's nerves finally began to unwind. Unfortunately, her mind wouldn't follow suit. Her thoughts kept leaping back to Alan. "Did I tell you he actually kicked ten goals in succession today, for the first time? I was so proud of him, and he was on top of the world. Full of himself, and rightly so, and demanding his reward—to know what WAGARA meant.''

''Did you tell him?''

Jess smiled sadly. ''Yes. Then I gave him my hat. That's how I'll remember him, just as I last saw him, I suppose. Strutting off, wearing that stupid cap like it was some kind of jeweled crown he'd won.'' She started to cry again. ''Damn! It's not fair, Ty! He was so young! He had his whole life ahead of him!''

He gathered her tenderly into his arms and held her until she finally cried herself out and drifted off to sleep.

In the wake of Alan's death, Tom Nelson immediately apologized to Jess for their earlier tiff. He showed up at Ty's house the next morning. ''Honey, when I think that could have been you in that car instead of Alan, why it just sends chills up my spine,'' he told her, giving her a big hug. ''What's the matter with the world today? Is everyone going crazy? Why, it's not even safe to walk out and get your mail anymore!''

Jess, her eyes still red and swollen from crying, hugged him back. ''I know, Tommy. It's awful. I feel just terrible about Alan. He was such a good kid, with loads of potential.''

''Uh . . . what about your car? I hear it's been impounded.''

''So they tell me, but I'm not sure I'd ever be able to drive it again when they do release it. Not after . . .''

''I understand, Jessie. So, what are you going to do for transportation?''

''That's where I come in, at least for the time being,'' Ty spoke up. ''In a few days, when Jess is up to it, we can see if her insurance company will cover some of the cost of a replacement. Then Jess can shop around for a new car.''

''Have you heard anything else from the police?'' Tom asked. ''Have they caught the guys who did this?''

Ty shook his head. ''Not a word, have you?''

''No, but Alan's parents have arrived from Pennsylvania. We're trying to set up a team memorial service before they take his body home to Erie. Most likely, it will be some time tomorrow, probably early afternoon. I'll let you know.''

Tom turned to Jess. "I guess this just proves all over again how suddenly those we love can be taken from us, and it made our little spat the other day seem so ridiculous by comparison. I hope you'll forgive me, Jess. I didn't mean half of what I said then. I've just been under a lot of stress lately, with Anita and all.''

Jess nodded. "It's all right, Tommy.''

"When I told you I didn't want you coaching Alan anymore, I certainly never meant for anything this horrible to happen," he went on. "Sometimes you really do have to be careful what you ask for, I guess. What a shame it all ended this way, but at least you won't be hanging around the team and the stadium so much. With all the disasters that have taken place lately, involving the Knights, I'll feel better knowing you're nowhere near, should any other tragedy arise.''

"I'll still be coming to the games, though, to root the others on," Jess told him. "Hopefully, in the future, to more victories than calamities.''

Almost happy to be consigned to the rank of spectator again, Jess was supremely surprised when Coach Danvers and one of the team owners approached her and Ty at the end of Alan's memorial service. "Jess, I believe you've met Keith Forsyth.''

Jess shook the man's hand. "Mr. Forsyth. It's good of you to come today. Alan would have been honored, I'm sure.''

"It's the least I could do," Forsyth commented gravely.

Danvers spoke up again. "Jess, I realize this isn't the time or place, but what we have to propose won't wait. We'd like to offer you the kicking position with the Knights.''

Ty's jaw sagged in surprise. Jess felt as if she'd just had the air punched out of her. As they stood, too stunned to speak, Danvers added hastily, "It's what Alan would have wanted, I think.''

"But . . . is that allowed?" Jess stammered. "For a woman to play on a pro team?''

"It would undoubtedly be a first," Ty said, his mind reeling. "Knowing Jess's skill, I certainly wouldn't object. It's for certain we need a good kicker, and she's the best. But some of the other guys might not cotton to the idea too well."

"We've considered all that, and we've gone over the rules with a fine-tooth comb. There is nothing that states that a woman cannot join a professional football team," Forsyth alleged. "In fact, the equal rights people will probably dance in the streets over this. Also, we've already asked some of the team members how they'd feel about it. The majority agree with you, Ty. Acquainted with Jess and her kicking ability, most are in favor of the idea."

"That's all well and good, but it's still so . . . unconventional," Jess claimed, for lack of another word. "I'm just not sure the world is ready for a female football player."

"As I said, I think Alan would approve heartily," Danvers repeated. "He idolized you, Jess."

Jess was all the more confused. "In some way, I do feel I owe him. He was driving my car when he was killed, after all."

"Now, Jess, let's not go through all that again," Ty told her. "You're not responsible for what happened to him."

"Suppose I did take the job," Jess suggested thoughtfully. "Would I sign a contract, like anyone else?"

"Of course," Forsyth said. "If it meets with your approval, we're prepared to offer you the same salary and bonuses Alan had."

"Could we stipulate that half of the money be donated to set up a college fund in Alan's name?" Jess proposed.

Forsyth's eyes widened in wonder. "Jess, that's more than generous, but you don't have to do that. No one would expect you to give up half your earnings."

"That's the only way I'll agree," she insisted. "Otherwise, it's no deal."

"We accept," Danvers said hastily, "and thank you." He grabbed her hand, pumping it up and down with grateful vigor. "I don't know where we'd have found another kicker of your caliber on such short notice. If you'll drop by my office this afternoon, I'll have that contract ready for you to sign, and we'll find a uniform to fit you. You will be ready to play this Sunday, I hope.''

''Jitters and all,'' she promised, even now second-guessing her rash decision. ''Tommy is going to have a conniption fit.''

''Tom Nelson?'' Forsyth inquired. When Jess nodded, he added, ''He's already had it, while voicing his objections very loudly and succinctly. The owners and the coaches got together this morning to discuss hiring you, and it was a wonder we didn't have to scrape your godfather off the ceiling tile. However, he was outvoted, and he'll just have to learn to live with it.''

Ty chuckled. ''Well, there goes your truce, Jess. Welcome back to the team. I just have one question. Does this make you a Knight, a Dame, or a Lady?''

CHAPTER 18

By Sunday, Jess was a nervous wreck, damning herself for having signed that contract. Playing soccer for OSU in a partially filled stadium had never sent her into a tailspin, but now, for the first time, she was getting a good taste of stage fright. Try as she might, she could not block from her mind that she would be kicking in a pro game broadcast on national TV—and if she screwed up, thousands of people would see it. Moreover, anyone who realized she was a woman would expect her to make a fool of herself on the field. They were probably making book on it at this very moment.

Not that the Knights were advertising the fact that they had just hired the first female kicker in the history of the NFL. On the contrary, they had simply listed her on the roster as number 11, J.D. Myers, kicker, and offered no further information as to her identity or background. This, in itself, would no doubt confound the sports announcers to no end. As a rule, they had access to all the players' statistics, everything from previous playing experience to personal data. But not in this instance, for which Jess was extremely grateful. For the time being, she would just as soon remain as anonymous as possible, in case she made a royal ass of herself.

178 *Catherine Hart*

As she took her place on the sidelines, Jess was thankful to be outfitted in a team uniform, the better to blend in with her fellow Knights. Her jersey was even loose enough, and long enough, to disguise the small bumps on her chest and her feminine derriere. As for her hair, it wasn't any longer than many of the players wore theirs, and she'd already mashed it down with her helmet, giving it a flat, mussed, unisex appearance. With any luck, she'd pass for one of the guys, no questions asked.

Another thing adding to her stress level was that her mother and stepfather would be among the spectators this afternoon. Claudia had done everything but have a seizure when Jess had informed her of this latest development. After ranting and raving on the phone for a full half hour, Claudia had firmly announced that she and John would be present on Sunday to watch Jess play.

"I want to be on hand when they haul your broken body off to the emergency ward," Claudia had claimed direly. "They'll probably need me to sign a consent for your medical treatment."

"Mom, the kicker rarely gets hurt during a game," Jess had rebutted. "It's one of the safest positions on the team, which is why a kicker can be smaller than the other members and still get the job done."

"Are those big galoots on the other team going to take it easy on you?" Claudia had persisted. "Will they know you're just a girl?"

"Just a girl?" Jess had echoed peevishly. "Mom! Get with the program. These are the nineties. Women can do anything and be anything they want, as long as they're equally qualified. And no, none of the Ravens will be aware that I'm a *woman*. Not if I can help it. The last thing I need is to have them all hooting and snickering at me."

"Maybe it would be better if they did know," Claudia had insisted mockingly. "If they're doubled over laughing, they can't attack you, can they?"

Jess knew that unless the Baltimore Ravens held the Knights scoreless, she would be called upon to kick for her team, either in a point-after attempt or to try for a field goal. Naturally, she didn't want the Knights to lose, but even more, she didn't want to be responsible for it happening. Especially since this game was being dedicated to Alan. Consequently, she was stuck between the proverbial rock and the hard place, with no one to blame but herself.

The Ravens won the coin toss and deferred, kicking off to the Knights at the beginning of the game. Baltimore's defense had been weak all season, so it came as no surprise that the Knights scored a touchdown on their first offensive drive, though it took several plays to accomplish it.

Jess's moment had come, much sooner than she would have wished. She stood immobile, until Danvers slapped her on the shoulder, jerking her out of her stupor. "Go get 'em, kid!" he told her, giving her a push onto the field.

She trotted toward Ty on wobbly legs, praying she wouldn't trip over her own feet. Upon reaching him, she blurted, "I'm going to throw up."

Ty laughed. "No you won't. You're going to pretend this is practice. Just you and me, like the first time. I'll hold for you, and you're going to ram that ball straight through the uprights, dead center." He winked. "I'd give you a kiss for luck, but that'd really set tongues to wagging, not to mention we'd probably get called for delay of game. Now, get set."

She measured off her paces, mentally marked her spot, and took a deep, steadying breath. "Okay, I can do this," she muttered. "If Alan could do it, so can I."

For the space of a split instant, she closed her eyes and imagined the ball sailing cleanly over the bar. The ball was snapped. Ty had it positioned perfectly. One, two, three strides. Jess's toe connected with the ball, wedging beneath it and sending it soaring between the goalposts. In her zeal, she'd put so much power behind the kick that the ball flew past the end zone into the section of seats beyond it.

Jess barely had time to heave a huge sigh of relief before her team mates converged on her with a barrage of traditional congratulatory whacks on the back and head. Jess, her helmet now pushed down over her eyes, was helpless to do anything but go with the flow as they herded her off the field—half carrying, half shoving her along with them.

When she was safely on the sidelines once more, she jerked her helmet off and glared at the bunch of them as she flexed her shoulders beneath the bulky pads. "Geez, you guys! Find another way to express your enthusiasm, will you? Not that I don't appreciate your accolades, but my chiropractor is going to be the richest man in town if you don't tone it down some."

"Yeah," Ty agreed with a mile-wide grin. "After all, Jess is just a little fella! Besides, I'm going to be super p.o.'d if she ends up in traction and my love life goes on the skids."

Her opening debut over, Jess was much more calm as she watched the game continue. When next she ran onto the field for a point-after, she did so with conviction. Just before half-time, she got her first chance at a field goal, a forty-yard attempt. Again, Ty was to spot the ball for her.

"Drill it, babe," he commanded confidently. "Show 'em how it's supposed to be done."

"This one's for you, Alan," she whispered. "Up and over."

The ball arched high into the air, well above the reach of the Ravens' special team's men who would have tried to bat it down, to rocket through the uprights. This time, when Jess's teammates picked her up and carted her off the field on their shoulders, she had no complaints.

The Knights dominated throughout the game. Altogether, they scored seven touchdowns and points-after, and three field goals, racking up fifty-eight points to the Ravens' seventeen. It was a decisive win, one they could all be proud of.

Only later, when they convened at Ty's house for an impromptu celebration, did Jess learn what the sports announcers had said about her. Corey was next to bursting, as she declared, "Oh, Jess! I wish you could have heard them! They were going crazy trying to figure out who you were and where you'd come from so suddenly. It was as if you'd materialized out of thin air."

"What were you doing? Listening to a radio in the stands?"

Corey nodded excitedly. "Yeah, one of those that pulls in the TV audio stations. Girl, when you kicked that first point-after and the football went clear past the end zone, those guys went totally berzerk. All three of them agreed they'd never seen anyone with such a powerful kick. Then, when you made that forty-yarder with room to spare, they really came undone. It's for sure they're going to be beating the bushes trying to find out everything they can about you.''

Jess grimaced. "I hope not, but I suppose it's inevitable."

"I think so, too," Claudia put in, draping her arm around Jess's waist. "So be prepared for it, honey. By the way, I hope you're serving crow with this pizza, because I deserve a big portion. You were fantastic out there tonight, despite all my predictions of doom and gloom."

"She's right, Jess," John Derry added, placing a peck on her cheek. "We're extremely proud of you. Your dad and brother would have been, too."

"And Alan," Ty said. "You did him proud, Jess."

"So did you." Jess returned the compliment, her smile edged with sorrow. "As did the whole team. It would have been a shame to lose this one, but we won it in grand style. I just wish Alan could have been part of it."

"I don't doubt that he was," Ty told her, his tone unusually reverent. "In spirit, if not in body."

The phone began ringing before nine o'clock the following morning. Ty made the mistake of picking up the bedroom extension on the first call. It was a reporter from a Columbus newspaper, wanting an interview with Jessica Myers, the new female kicker.

"Why call me?" Ty stalled.

"Because all I'm getting is her answering machine, and I was told you two are a couple. I figured maybe I could reach her at your place."

"How did you get my number?" Ty asked irritably. "It's unlisted."

"A friend of a friend," the guy hedged.

"Well, you've struck out, pal. No one's here but me," Ty lied. "And don't call here again. You know the drill. If you want any information about any of the team, call the Knights' office.''

''What was that all about?'' Jess asked when he hung up.

''Word's out that you're a woman.''

Jess made a show of lifting the sheet and looking down at her nude body. ''Well, what do you know!'' she mocked. ''I think they're right!''

''Cut the comedy. That was a local newspaper reporter. A 'friend of a friend' gave him my phone number, and yours, too, apparently—after informing him that our team kicker is one Jessica Myers, and my current flame. He wanted an interview with you.''

Jess sighed. ''Oh, brother! I knew it was bound to happen sooner or later, but I was hoping for later. And I'll bet I know who ratted.''

As one, they declared, ''Bambi.''

The phone rang again. Automatically, Jess reached for the receiver. Ty forestalled the movement. ''Let the machine get it. Chances are, it's someone else we don't want to talk to just yet.''

''You skirted the other call awfully well,'' Jess commented. ''Now that I think about it, you didn't admit anything. Not that J.D. Myers and Jessica/Jess Myers are one and the same, or that you're dating me or even know me at all. As I recall, the word 'she' never passed your lips. You're pretty slick there, James.''

''I've had a lot of practice handling reporters,'' he replied off-handedly.

''Yeah, I'll say you have!'' she chuckled. She knocked him back on his pillow and flopped atop his chest. ''How about 'handling' this one again, lover boy?''

That was just the start of things. By eleven o'clock, the message tape on Ty's answering machine was full, and a sheaf of faxes littered his desk. There were communications from several Ohio newspapers, all three major TV networks, plus the sports channel, the news channel, and a number of radio

stations. All left their numbers, requesting an interview with
Jess at the first opportunity. She'd also retrieved duplicate messages from her own phone and E-mail, via the laptop computer
she often left at Ty's place for convenience sake.

"Holy cow!" Jess exclaimed in awe. "I can't believe this!
You'd think I was just nominated for an Oscar or something!"

"Well, honey-bun, my advice is for you to get to work on
a press release that will satisfy them all in one fell swoop. As
for personal interviews, CNN would probably be your best bet.
That way the other networks could pick it up from them and
you could get by with doing just one. At least for now."

Jess's jaw dropped. "No way, José. There is no way on
God's green earth that I'll consent to a live interview and
have the entire U.S. and most of the civilized world criticizing
everything from my looks to my kicking ability, to my unmiti-
gated gall at joining a professional football team. Not to mention
digging into my background and personal life."

"The shoe pinches when it's on *your* foot, doesn't it?" he
commented wryly. "When it's your butt on the line, with
everyone shooting questions at you left and right. You should
have thought of all this before you signed that contract."

Jess groaned. "I did, but not thoroughly enough, I guess.
Mainly, I just wanted to do this for Alan, and to help out the
team."

"Which you are," he conceded. "You've also put the
Knights in the spotlight along with your own sweet self. Nothing
like a little notoriety to stir up team spirit."

"For which Tommy will no doubt be eternally ungrateful,"
Jess grumbled. "Lord, what a glorious mess I've gotten myself
into this time. You'd think, at some point or age, I'd learn not
to be so blasted impulsive. But no, not me. I just leap in with
both feet, regardless of the consequences."

"Hey! Impulsive is good," Ty argued. "You've just got to
learn to be selective along with it. Now, about that interview."

After much debate, Jess finally agreed—with certain rigid
stipulations. There would be no questions about her love life,

past or present. She would not answer any queries she considered too personal. She would discuss her career as an investigative journalist, and her accomplishments while on the OSU women's soccer team. Additionally, she okayed CNN's request for brief related interviews with her mother, some of the other Knights, and with a few select friends and former professors. Jess also insisted that the interview take place at the stadium, rather than her own home, and that she remain seated throughout, to distract attention from her height.

It took her three hours to select an outfit both she and Ty deemed attractive and feminine enough without looking frilly. She took extra pains with her makeup, had Ty do her hair and help with her manicure—something she almost never bothered to do—hooked her favorite earrings through her ears, and left the rest to Providence.

The piece, limited in length at Jess's request, ran on CNN Wednesday and was replayed on Thursday. Her succinctly worded press release also hit the newspapers in mid-week. In accordance with her present luck, it hit the UP wires and was printed nationwide. The phone and fax kept ringing, until both she and Ty were forced to have their numbers changed.

"I'm so sorry about all this hassle," she apologized for the tenth time in as many minutes.

Ty looked up from his personal phone directory, from which he was pulling names of those people to whom he had yet to relay his new number. "Don't sweat it, babe. Like I said, my number was out to too many people who shouldn't have it, anyway. I just don't want to forget to notify anybody who actually needs to know it. Like Barb. Unfortunately, I can't just skip her and give the number to Josh, as much as I'd like to."

The messages had continued to come in from across the country, and not just from the news media. How the average citizen had obtained her number, and her home address, Jess would have liked to know. Her best assumption was that they had tapped into some computer file somewhere. A mailing list, maybe. Heaven knew, once you subscribed to that first lousy magazine, everyone in the world was sending you junk mail, having bought your address from the original company.

At any rate, on top of all the E-mail, et cetera, she was also receiving cards and letters in abundance. Her mailman was about to have a hernia—or go into a maniacal rage and buy a gun! Not all of the missives were complimentary or encouraging, either. A woman from Iowa, obviously big on religion, wrote that Jess should be ashamed of herself. She should stop trying to be a man, get married, raise a family, and fulfill her God-ordained role as a woman. That was only one of a number of disparaging comments from both genders sprinkled among the good.

The messages that surprised Jess most, however, were from men—male admirers who sent more than casual greetings—encompassing everything from lewd offers to marriage proposals. Most were gushing, others graphic in the extreme. Some even went so far as to have flowers and candy delivered to her at the stadium. One fellow actually mailed her a pair of red satin thong panties, included his phone number, and asked her to wear the gift when she called him.

"When polar bears vacation in Tahiti!" was Jess's flabbergasted reaction. "Good grief, Ty! This is asinine! These guys don't actually think I'm going to respond to them, do they?"

He replied with an agitated frown, "I imagine they're hoping you will. Damn! This is getting out of hand. I never suspected you'd be collecting your own weirdos and groupies, like—"

"Like you and the rest of the hot-shot jocks?" she interrupted with a wry grin.

"Yeah," he grumbled. "Next, someone will want to start a Jess Myers fan club!"

She searched quickly through a stack of letters. Pulling one out, she waved it at him. "Got it right here, T.D. But you'll be glad to know this one is from a girl. She wants to join her high school football team, but so far they've succeeded in blackballing her. As of Wednesday, I am officially her most revered idol."

* * *

All in all, Jess was glad to accompany Ty to Indianapolis on Friday and escape the deluge of attention. They were finally going to get to watch Josh play in a soccer match.

"I hope his coach doesn't stick him on the bench the whole while," Jess fretted.

Ty chuckled. "You're worse than I am, Jess. Anyone would swear you were the kid's mom, the way you fuss over him."

"Does that bother you?" she asked hesitantly.

"Heck no. Especially since I know that with you it's sincere, not just some act you're putting on to impress me. You'd be surprised at the number of women who've resorted to such underhanded maneuvers in the past. Nothing ticks me off faster."

"I suppose, being a football star, you have had more than your share of women who would employ any kind of trickery to get into your bed," she mused sourly.

"You don't know the half of it, but you might by the time all is said and done. Wait until you find one of these guys who are mooning over you lurking outside your apartment, or sitting in your car after a game, or knocking on your hotel door and claiming to be someone from room service. You can't imagine how devious and persistent they can be, or how utterly annoying."

"Maybe this will all blow over soon. Anyway, it's nice to get away from it for a while, at least. Josh is going to be thrilled that you've been able to make it to a match at last."

"Just don't be shocked if he's happier to see you than he is to see me," he told her with a droll look. "You're the soccer champ, and now you're even kicking for the Knights, which ranks you right up there with the Mighty Power Rangers in his book."

"Don't worry. You'll always be his hero, Ty. After all, you're his superstar daddy."

"Speaking of which, you started your period this morning, didn't you?"

"Yes. No more PMS on top of all the other stress, thank

God. Sorry. I know I've been something of a bitch the last few days.''

"You've been great, considering. I was just a little afraid you—that you might be pregnant.''

"What!'' Jess stared at him in utter disbelief. "Ty, we've been going through condoms at a ridiculous rate. In fact, I've been considering buying stock in the darned company!''

"We skipped a couple of times, though, and I thought maybe we'd flubbed up.''

"When?'' she prodded. "When did we not use one?''

"That night in Phoenix, when you got plastered and all but attacked me,'' he related. "You had me so fired up, I completely forgot, and that's not the kind of mistake I'd like to make often.''

"Oh, so it's all my fault?''

"I didn't say that.''

"You implied it,'' she insisted. "It takes two to tango, Tyler James, and I wasn't the only one dancing.''

Ty gave a harried sigh. "I know. Listen, I didn't intend for this to escalate into a fight, Jess. I just said I'm glad you're not pregnant. I was railroaded into one marriage that way, and I wouldn't want a repeat performance, that's all.''

"Well,'' she sniffed, "thank you so much for your high opinion of me. May I echo that sentiment and inform you that you are one of the most distrusting, exasperating jackasses I've ever had the pleasure to bed down with? And here's another news flash, buster. If I ever do find myself pregnant with your child, you can rest assured I will not coerce you into marriage. I am perfectly capable of raising a child by myself, with or without your help.''

"Fine,'' he snapped back, his eyes flashing angrily. "Now let me tell you something, sweet pea. If you do end up bearing my child, you *will* marry me, Jess. I *will* be a part of his or her life, and yours—till death do us part. Any future kid of mine is going to see me day in and day out, not long-distance the way it is between Josh and me.''

Jess sneered at him. "You can lead a horse to water, but you can't make him drink. I won't be hustled into marriage before I'm ready, either. So stick that in your shorts and sit on it!''

"So, when do you think you'll be ready?" he asked, taking her completely off guard.

She shook her head, totally confused by his swift change of tactic. "I haven't got the foggiest notion. Why?"

"Because I think I've fallen in love with you, you aggravating shrew!" he declared loudly, clearly peeved. "At the moment, I'm not too thrilled about it, but there it is. I just don't want to rush into anything. I'd rather we take our time, get to know each other better, be absolutely certain it would work for us. Then, I suppose we could make that fatal leap into wedded bliss."

Jess's insides were hopping around like Mexican jumping beans. Ty loved her! Oh, sweet heaven, he really did! It was a dream come true—Cinderella and all her favorite fairy tales and fantasies wrapped into one! It was all she could do not to let out a wild whoop of pure joy. Instead, given his surly demeanor, which was less than princely by anyone's estimation, she replied huffily, "I love you, too, you arrogant toad! But wedded bliss? You and me? Don't kid yourself, James. More like scratch and squabble."

"Probably," he agreed with a nod. "But that could be fun, too, as long as we make up after every spat and the only scratching you do is in the heat of passion."

"You're horny again!" she accused. "Already. Still."

He grinned. "That's what being a toad is all about, sweetheart."

"Well, just cool your jets, Romeo. You've got a week's wait ahead of you," she reminded him smugly, then added smartly, "Gee, I hope you don't go into withdrawal and start twitching or foaming at the mouth. How would you explain that to Josh?"

CHAPTER 19

At the start of the game against the Steelers on Sunday, Ty thought to ask Jess, "Is being on your period going to affect your kicking any?"

Jess glared at him with feminine disdain. "Try to keep up, Tyler. We're almost into the twenty-first century. Today's women do not glisten; we actually perspire. We do not swoon at the sight of a tiny mouse; we go out and buy a mousetrap. Nor do we take to our beds at the first sign of a cramp; we pop a couple of Midol and go about business as usual."

She stalked off, leaving him to digest her impromptu lecture. Gabe, having overheard most of Jess's tirade from a few feet away, approached his friend. "Whooeee! What did you do to tick her off, T.D.?"

"The best I can figure, she's in a snit because I told her I think I love her. You'd think she'd be happier about it." Ty shrugged. "Go figure."

"Don't have to," Gabe said, almost before the words were out of Ty's mouth. "But I am trying to figure out how a guy with a college degree and thirty-two years under his belt can still be so stupid about women. Any idiot knows you never tell a woman you *think* you love her. You keep your big mouth shut until you're sure. It's a wonder Jess didn't rip your head off and present it to you on a platter.''

Ty glanced toward Jess. She was standing stiffly, her back to him. "She won't stay mad long. She never does."

Gabe was more skeptical. "I don't know, man. She might decide your ass is grass and play lawn mower, and then head for greener pastures—and some fellow who's more sensitive about her feelings. If I were you, I'd get a ring on her finger before someone else steals her away—at least an engagement ring. Unless you really don't care if she stays or leaves."

"So what do you suggest, oh wise one? Do I run out and buy her an engagement ring and present it to her in a big slice of her favorite chocolate cake?" Ty wisecracked.

Gabe's lips quirked. "Not unless you want to go fishing for it a couple days after she swallows it—and that's only if you're real lucky and she doesn't require major surgery to remove it. If you want my advice, you either take a more traditional route—down on one knee and the whole bit—or you come up with something more original. But whatever you do, Ty, remember that this is a sacred moment in a woman's life. Make it romantic."

Ty sighed and gave his friend a cynical look. "You sound like Ann Landers. What do you do in your spare time, Gabe? Scour advice columns and marriage manuals?"

Gabe grinned. "Nah. I just listen to Corey. With both ears and my whole heart."

"Will you please stop trying to sell me on some fast, fancy car, Ty?" Jess and Ty were out, for the third day in a row, shopping for a replacement car for her.

"Sure," he agreed. "When you stop considering models that look like Fred Flintstone's jalopy, or something your grandmother would drive. Get wild. Get crazy. Get something with a little pizzazz, Jess. After your second spectacular game, without a single missed kick, you've earned it. You deserve it."

"I can't afford your brand of pizzazz," she informed him

flatly. "I want something economical, with good gas mileage and a decent insurance rate."

"Okay, okay. But you have to admit, a station wagon is a stupid pick, and you need a van like you need three armpits."

Jess shrugged. "I want something substantial. What I'd really like is one of those sport utility vehicles. They're heavy enough to suit me, have lots of space plus seating, and four-wheel drive would really come in handy in the snow when winter sets in."

"Actually, those aren't too bad," he said after contemplating the idea for a moment. "They're sporty, in a rugged kind of way, and not truly ugly, either." He grabbed her arm, towing her toward that section of the car lot. "C'mon, let's take a closer look."

"Ty! Have you seen the sticker price on those things?"

"What is it with you and a dime, lady?" he griped. "You earn good money as a reporter, and now you're making a bundle as our kicker—even if you are giving half of that away. Take advantage of the windfall, loosen your purse strings for once, and buy yourself a decent car, will you?"

Her hesitation lasted only as long as it took her to spot a gold Ford Explorer. To Ty's amusement, she examined it thoroughly from bumper to bumper, inside and out—going back to the price listing at least half a dozen times, as if hoping it would diminish if she did so often enough.

He had to laugh. "Jess, you're like a kid in a candy store. You can dicker on the price, you know."

"Yes, but I've been through this before, and these salesmen always try to take advantage of a woman. It's downright maddening the way they throw technical terms around in an effort to confuse you, and then act as if you can't add past ten without removing your shoes first."

"Babe? All you have to do is ask, and I'll be glad to help out," he tendered. "That is if you can put your feminine pride aside long enough to let me."

Jess frowned. "Am I really that bad?"

"Only when you want to be."

"Okay, let's go make this guy's day," she decided. "Just don't exclude me from the conversation altogether. It is going to be my car, after all, and it really gets my goat when people talk over and around me as if I'm invisible.''

Actually, the salesman was quite nice, and wound up giving her a great deal on the car, after the company rebate was factored into the final tally. Jess's insurance check was a more than adequate down payment, and the additional financing went off without a hitch. By late that afternoon, she drove the Explorer off the lot, well-pleased with both her selection and a monthly payment that wouldn't send her straight into bankruptcy.

That evening, she took Ty for a short spin.

"Don't you just love that new car smell?" she sighed. "I think they should make a perfume like it. And men's aftershave.''

Ty chuckled. "I'll see if I can buy you some for Christmas. What I like are the heated side mirrors and seats.''

"And that gizmo that tells you the outside temperature," she added.

"The compass will come in a lot handier," he predicted.

"So, you like my new hot wheels?" she inquired, lifting an eyebrow in his direction.

"Yes. I think it suits you to a T. Modern, stylish, and sporty, all in one neat package.''

"Why, Tyler James," she gushed, batting her lashes in exaggerated flirtation. "You and that silver tongue of yours are enough to turn a girl's head.''

"Not while you're driving, sugar. Just keep those lovely eyes on the road.''

A severe bout of the flu kept Gabe out of their next game against the Patriots. He didn't even fly with the team to Massachusetts, but stayed at home with Corey—who nursed him as best she could, primarily with lots of liquids and large doses of sympathy.

Fortunately, Sir Loin Simms was back in action, albeit amid a flurry of controversy. The lawyer he'd hired was in the process of trying to ascertain why Sir Loin's supervised drug test at the university hospital had shown no traces of cocaine—clearly in opposition to the results obtained twice over by Doc Johnson's testing. Meanwhile, as a conglomerate of medical and law personnel worked on the mystery, Sir Loin was restored to his usual slot on the team.

Brice Tackett was also back in the line up. After tests determined that it was a double dose of antihistamine in his system, and not alcohol or illegal drugs, he'd been let off with a warning to limit either his medicinal intake or his driving during allergy season.

As was his habit when an out-of-state game was slated, the Knights' manager booked a Saturday flight from Columbus to Boston. The man was conscientious to the point of paranoia when it came to making certain that flight delays, weather, and so forth would not prevent the team from reaching their destination in time for a scheduled game. This also usually allowed the Knights at least one practice on the unfamiliar field.

To the layman, this might have seemed silly, since one football field is basically the same as any other. But some coaches insisted that—given the different surfaces, weather conditions, directional layout for sun, shadow, and wind—it often made a significant difference. Additionally, travel was wearing, no matter what the means of transportation, and you wanted your team as fresh as possible in preparation for the match on enemy turf.

They touched down at Boston's Logan Airport just before noon. After checking into their hotel, the team piled into rented buses for the twenty-odd-mile drive to Foxborough, where the stadium was located. After practice, it was back to Boston, with the rest of the afternoon and evening to enjoy themselves.

"What would you like to do?" Ty asked Jess. "If we hurry, I think we've got time enough to catch the last afternoon whale watch cruise."

"I don't do water sports anymore, other than swimming in the occasional pool and chancing a few of the water rides at King's Island," Jess told him. "But go ahead if you want. I wouldn't want you to miss it just because I'm too chicken to go. I can while away the time shopping, or take in some of the tourist sights.''

Ty declined. "It wouldn't be much fun without you. Are you sure I can't talk you into it? The weather is perfect, and the water is really calm. You shouldn't get too seasick.''

"I don't get seasick," Jess informed him. "At least not the way you mean." She sighed deeply. "Ty, I haven't gone close to a body of unchlorinated water larger than a mud puddle since Dad and Mike died. I hate driving across bridges, for pity sake. I'd probably keel over from fright if I got within ten feet of a boat again.''

Ty was immediately contrite. "Oh, God, Jess, I'm sorry. I'm a thoughtless ass for even mentioning it.''

"No, you're not. You just didn't know, that's all. Besides, you can't be expected to tiptoe around the subject whenever we're together simply because I've got this phobia about boats and deep water.''

Perhaps it was just that he wanted to make her feel better, or maybe his subconscious mind was replaying the advice Gabe had given him last week. Whatever it was, Ty found himself saying, "Why don't we go shopping before the stores close? Maybe hit F.A.O. Schwartz? Oh, and don't let me forget to get a new watch battery before this one conks off altogether. I've had to reset everything from the time to the date three times this past week. Then we can stop by this little place on the North End that is famous for its cappuccino. A trip to Boston wouldn't be complete without visiting there at least once.''

Jess chuckled. "You and your cappuccino. I swear I'm going to buy you your own machine for Christmas.''

Ty gave her his cute-little-boy grin. "Aw, gee! Do I have to wait that long? My birthday's coming up November 12th,'' he reminded her pointedly.

"I'll think about it,'' she told him, shaking her head over his antics. "You're worse than Josh at wheedling and whining.''

Unlike most people, who would dash into Walgreens or Kmart and buy a new watch battery, Ty had to choose the most expensive jewelry store in town in which to purchase his. As

he ushered her into the elite shop, Jess couldn't help but chide
him.

"Wal-Mart would probably have it for a tenth the cost. Why
come here, when you know it's going to cost you the earth for
the very same battery?"

"Because I bought the watch here," he informed her, "and
I know they'll stock it."

Jess had been in some fancy establishments, but this place
was really swank: Thick carpeting that absorbed every little
whisper of sound, making people inclined to walk and speak
softly. On the walls, interspersed by panels of mirrors, was
what appeared to be gold-embossed wallpaper. Scores of little
vanity stools were lined up along the shiny mile-long counters.
Inside the glass display cases, set against a colorful background
of silk and velvet, was every item of jewelry imaginable, all
polished to a high sheen, the radiance of which almost made
Jess reach for her sunglasses.

"Why don't you window shop while I see about the battery?"
Ty suggested, waving her toward a display case.

"It's for sure I can't afford to do anything more than look,"
she replied in a low voice. "Most of this stuff isn't even tagged,
which I take to mean 'if you have to ask the price, you can't
afford it.' "

Jess wandered around, peering into case after case, trying
not to drool at the exquisite merchandise within. Normally, she
didn't wear much jewelry, except for earrings, for which she
had a passion. But this array was enough to tempt even her.

"May I help you with anything?"

Jess glanced up at the saleslady. "No thank you. I'm just
browsing."

Ty stepped up beside her. "See anything you like?"

"Only everything," she admitted ruefully. "Now I know
what they mean about having a champagne appetite and a beer
pocketbook."

Ever so casually, Ty steered her over to a case containing
rings—solitaires, engagement rings, wedding sets—any and
every kind imaginable. There he stopped and leaned an elbow
on the counter, as if totally unaware of its contents. "It'll take

a couple of minutes to install the battery,'' he remarked lazily. ''You don't mind waiting, do you? It would be silly to have to come back later, when we're right here.''

''As long as they don't charge anything for breathing the rarified air in here,'' she quipped. ''You can almost smell the money, can't you?''

Ty laughed. ''That's gold and diamond dust, darlin'.'' He glanced down, into the case on which he was leaning. ''And little wonder. Get a gander at some of these, Jess. That one's bright enough to glow in the dark. And over there, look at the size of that rock.''

Jess stepped closer. ''They're all beautiful.''

''Which do you like best?''

''I can't afford to like any of them.''

''But this is only window shopping, Jess, where you're allowed to pretend you can buy anything your heart desires. At least that's how my sisters taught me to play the game. So how about it? If you didn't have to worry about the price, which one would you choose over all the others?''

She perused the display, nibbling on her lower lip as she examined each ring in turn. Finally she made her choice. ''That one,'' she said, pointing it out to him. She'd selected a round, brilliant-cut diamond of moderate size, flanked on either side by a smaller stone. All three gems were mounted over a brushed gold band.

Ty blinked in surprise, then wrinkled his nose. ''That dinky thing?'' he jeered.

''Dinky?'' she echoed. ''For crying out loud, Ty. The center stone alone has got to be a half carat. And look at the way it's cut, all the facets. I'm no expert, but even I can tell that it reflects the light much better than some of the others.''

''She's absolutely correct,'' the saleswoman agreed in her soft-spoken manner. ''Your lady has impeccable taste, sir. Size alone does not determine the quality of a gem.'' Unlocking the cabinet, she reached in and withdrew the ring Jess had selected. ''This is an excellent example of the four C's. Color, cut, clarity and carat weight. Still, no matter what it looks like in the case, it can look altogether different on a person's hand. You really can't tell if it's going to be flattering until you wear it."

She held the ring out to Jess. "Go ahead. Try it on, dear."

"Oh, I shouldn't," Jess protested, even as she reached for the ring. "After all, it's not as if I'm going to buy it."

The woman smiled. "Do you buy every pair of shoes you try on?" she rebutted.

Jess slipped the ring over her knuckle and gazed down at the gems winking on her finger. Holding it at arm's length, she twisted her wrist this way and that, watching the diamonds sparkle. "It's gorgeous," she said with a sigh.

"It looks fine to me. I guess you're a fair judge of what suits you after all. Anything bigger wouldn't have looked right on your slim fingers," Ty admitted.

"Absolutely," the woman concurred. "Except the band is about a half size too large. You want it snug enough that the setting won't slip off to the side."

Reluctantly, Jess removed the ring and handed it back. "It's lovely, but as I said, I'm just browsing."

"It's nice to daydream once in a while, though," the lady said, locking the ring away again. She spotted another customer. "If you see anything else you'd like to examine more closely, let me know. I'll be right over here."

As she walked away, the gentleman who had waited on Ty motioned him to the other counter. Jess gave the ring a final covetous glance on her way out of the store, then put it firmly out of her mind. She was not about to torment herself with wanting something she couldn't have.

It was a pity she couldn't apply that same attitude toward her relationship with Ty; but from the start her heart had overruled her head, and any common sense she might have possessed had flown straight out of her head. Fool or not, God help her, she was utterly, irrevocably in love with the man.

CHAPTER 20

After breakfast the next morning, Ty rented a car and they went for a drive in the country. The fall foliage, currently at its peak, was magnificent. Autumn had donned her most brilliant colors for their viewing pleasure. Reds, oranges, yellows, of every shade, intermingled in kaleidoscope fashion.

Merely by chance, they happened upon the observatory. When Ty suggested they go inside and get a bird's-eye look from the summit, Jess agreed enthusiastically. Atop one of the highest vantage points in New England, they were presented with a panorama of breathtaking beauty. Boston lay spread out below them, with the multihued mountains of New Hampshire as a backdrop and fields and forests blending into a wondrous burst of color. Even the harbor was gowned in splendor this morning, glittering like sun-drenched crystal.

"Oh, it's absolutely spectacular!" Jess gushed. "Can you imagine what it must be like up here at night, with all the stars out, and a full moon shining down?"

"A harvest moon," Ty added. "That would be something to behold. Unfortunately, while our timing is great for the daytime viewing, it stinks when it comes to a moonlight vista. We're about two weeks shy, or past, a full moon, whichever way you care to cut it. Furthermore, it's supposed to cloud up this evening.''

''Ah well,'' Jess sighed. ''The best made plans of mice and men, et cetera.''

Plans, practice, preparation—all went for naught when applied to the game that afternoon. The Patriots were on a hot streak and not about to be denied another win, most especially from a fledgling band of misfits called the Knights. With two of his main receivers missing, Ty was fighting an uphill battle all the way. Moreover, his blockers were definitely out-classed and out-muscled. As a result, Ty was sacked a total of five times, not to mention the numerous other hard hits he took. Every time he turned around, it seemed he was being tackled and tossed to the ground.

For her part, Jess made every point but one, a kick-after which was blocked by a Patriot who would have dwarfed the Jolly Green Giant. The final score, at the end of four long, grueling quarters, was twenty to fifty-four, in favor of the Patriots. Not a total shutout, thankfully, but still discouraging.

At the conclusion of the game, as the players and coaches gathered on the field to shake hands, Jess found herself adrift in a sea of Patriot uniforms. To her surprise and delight, she quickly spotted at least four familiar faces, all former OSU football players. Within seconds, she and they had converged and were soon chatting like old friends, though Jess had never before met any of them personally. The simple fact that they were all Ohio State alumni proved an instant bond.

It was several minutes before Jess became aware of Ty, standing apart from her group and glaring daggers at her—and several more minutes before she could politely extricate herself from the conversation. Timidity not being her style, she approached him boldly. ''Okay, sunshine, what crawled down your craw and stuck?''

His scowl deepened. ''What was that all about? Are you holding court now?''

Jess's eyebrows shot up, her temper immediately on the rise. ''Pardon me?''

"You're getting awfully chummy with our rivals, aren't you?"

"Oh, for heaven sake! They might play for the opposing team, but they're hardly enemies. Those guys are all former OSU players. If you would have come over, I could have introduced you."

"I've met a couple of them previously," he informed her dryly.

"Well, they're terrific," Jess went on. "It was great talking with them, if only for a couple of minutes. Like old home week on campus."

"With you as the queen bee," he stated accusingly. "I saw you smiling and batting your eyes at them, like some star-struck teenie-bopper."

"What?" Jess shrieked. "You're crazy, James. I was doing no such thing."

"The hell you weren't. You didn't budge an inch when that big ape slung his arm across your shoulders. You just looked up at him with those wide, innocent eyes and laughed."

Jess rolled her eyes in exasperation. "It wasn't as if he was trying to put the make on me, you dumb jerk. It was just a friendly gesture."

"Was your eyeing the punter's groin just a friendly little gesture, too?" he inquired snidely.

Jess stood firm, her own eyes blazing now and her lips tight. "I was not eyeing his groin, you jackass. He was demonstrating how to hold a ball for a punt. In fact, he gave me several good pointers."

Ty snorted. "Yeah, I'll bet he did, sugar. Did he offer to show you some of his better moves at a more opportune time and place?"

Jess squelched an irate scream. "Yeah," she retorted scathingly. "We've got a date to have a fling under the OSU bleachers the next time he's in town."

Ty grabbed her arms, hauling her up on her toes before him. "Over my dead body," he growled.

"Hey! I was kidding," Jess exclaimed. "For the love of

Pete, Tyler. Why are you behaving like such an idiot? What has gotten into you?''

"He didn't ask you out? You didn't accept?" he pressed.

"No, of course not. What kind of tramp do you take me for, anyway?" Jess reached one hand far enough to give him a solid whack on the side of his head. "Just because Barb had a roving eye, don't paint me with the same brush, buster. I don't poach, and I don't wander. As long as you and I are together, I won't go out with anyone else—and I expect you to abide by the same rules.''

He set her down and eased his grip, but didn't release her completely. "Okay, but no more flirting with other guys, either. It drives me nuts.''

Jess wrinkled her nose at him. "A short drive, evidently. And no matter what you say, I was not flirting. I was simply being friendly.''

"Then quit being so frigging friendly," he grumbled irritably. "Go back to being your usual cantankerous self. Damn! I've created a monster!''

Despite losing the game, despite Ty's seemingly irrational temper tantrum, Jess was absurdly happy. She'd figured it out. Ty was jealous, which meant he really did care for her. He wasn't merely mouthing the words and stringing her along.

Still, wanting another female to verify her opinion, Jess went to visit Corey. But Corey had her own problem, one much more pressing than Jess's love life. It was Gabe. He wasn't recovering from the flu—or what they had thought was the flu. In fact, he was steadily getting worse.

"What does the team doctor say?" Jess inquired.

Corey shook her head. "He still claims it's some sort of stomach virus, or maybe a touch of food poisoning, but I'm not so sure. In fact, I'm starting to wonder if Johnson got his degree out of a box of Cracker Jacks. He doesn't seem awfully knowledgeable to me.''

"Have you consulted another doctor?"

"Gabe finally agreed, and we set up an appointment for

Friday. It's the soonest we could get in, and we're lucky to get that. Not many doctors are taking new patients these days. Meanwhile, Gabe is determined that he's going to play in the game next Sunday, so sick or not, he's out there practicing as usual. I tell you, Jess, I'm worried. He's as weak as a kitten and has absolutely no appetite, which I can understand with all the stomach problems he's having. But, if this doesn't clear up soon, they're going to end up carting him off that darned field on a stretcher."

"Maybe this new doctor will find out what's wrong," Jess told her. "God knows, anyone would be better than Johnson."

By Friday even Jess could tell that Gabe's skin had taken on a gray cast. His eyes were puffy and ringed with dark circles, and he was dragging around with his energy level at rock bottom. In short, he looked like warmed-over death.

That afternoon, Ty and Jess drove to Indianapolis to pick up Josh, as it was his weekend to stay with his father. They arrived back at Ty's around six o'clock and were trying to decide what to do about supper when Corey phoned.

"They've admitted Gabe to the hospital," she declared tensely. "The doctor wants to run a whole series of tests."

"Do you want me to come keep you company?" Jess offered. With Josh in town, she wouldn't be staying the night with Ty anyway.

"No, most of my time will probably be tied up with Gabe and the doctors. I've already called and cancelled my photo shoot for the first of the week, which thoroughly pissed my company, but at this point I really couldn't give a rat's butt. Gabe comes first, and to hell with everything else. I've also notified Coach Danvers."

"Is there anyone else you'd like me to call for you? Or anything at all Ty or I can do?"

"Not that I can think of," Corey said. "Not right now, at any rate."

"Okay, but if you need anything, let us know. And keep us posted on those tests. What is the doctor looking for, anyway?"

"At this point, he's not sure, but he mentioned toxins more than once. Listen, I've got to go. Gabe is the world's worst patient, and I have to run interference for the nurses. I'll call later, when we know more.''

They decided to pay Gabe a short visit that evening, in spite of the fact that there was no further news as yet. Jess took Josh to the hospital snack shop and treated him to an ice cream sundae while Ty ran a bouquet of flowers up to Gabe. Then Ty sat with Josh while Jess dashed up with a get-well card, a book of crossword puzzles, and two newly released paperback novels.

On the way home, Ty said, "I've never seen Gabe like this before. It's as if someone has sucked all the energy out of him."

"I know," Jess agreed. "He's usually running circles around everyone else."

"He's putting up a good front, but it doesn't wash, does it?"

Jess shook her head. "No, and Corey is worried half out of her mind, no matter what she says in front of Gabe."

"Is Uncle Gabe gonna be okay?" Josh piped up from the back seat.

"We hope so, tiger," Ty told him. "The doctors are trying to find out what's wrong and fix it, so he'll get better again. But when you say your bedtime prayers, you might ask God to give Uncle Gabe some extra special attention while he's sick."

On Sunday, the Knights hosted the Eagles and by sheer dint of determination pulled off a three-point win, thanks in large part to Jess's unerring aim. More than ever, she was being touted as a phenomenon, not merely for being the first female pro football kicker, but for possessing a kicking ability that only came along once in a blue moon. The two together made her quite a sensation, and the latest media darling. On the other hand, everyone was watching and wondering how long her prevailing streak would last.

"That's the way it goes. When you're on top, it's not good enough that you've earned the right to be there. Along with

the congratulations, everyone's waiting for you to take a fall,''
Ty explained. "In fact, they're anticipating it, even while
they're singing your praises."

"I just wish they'd all shut up and pick on somebody else
for a while," Jess complained. "I don't want or need all the
attention."

"But, Jess, you kick so good," Josh told her with childish
admiration. "You might even get in the Hall of Frame."

Ty chuckled. "Yeah, not to mention the Hall of Fame."

"I'll leave that honor to you two," she said. "After all, I
only signed up to finish out this season, and then I'm back to
my old job again. Compared to this, being an investigative
reporter is a breeze."

When the phone rang early Monday morning, they let the
answering machine catch it, thinking it was probably another
reporter. Corey, her voice shrill and anxious, came over the
line. "Ty? Jess? Please pick up! I need you!"

Ty grabbed for the receiver. "Corey? What is it?" A second's
pause, and he exclaimed, "What in the hell are they doing
there?" Then, "Okay. Hang tight. We're on the way."

He hung up, amid Jess clamoring to know what was going
on.

"As we speak, the police are searching Gabe's house for
God knows what, and Corey's coming unglued."

Jess scrambled out of bed, making a beeline for the bathroom.
"Did they have a search warrant?"

"I assume so."

"And she has no idea what they're looking for?"

"She asked, but they wouldn't tell her. From the sound of
it, they're combing the entire house, and being none too timid
about it."

Jess dragged a brush through her hair, gave her teeth and
face the once-over, and yanked on the first pair of jeans and
T-shirt she touched. Her shoes were still untied as she and Ty
raced out the door. Fifteen minutes later they screeched to a

halt in Corey's driveway, parking behind half a dozen police cruisers.

A distraught Corey greeted them at the door, flanked by a dour-looking detective. "Ty, do something!" she wailed. "They're ransacking my house!"

Indeed, the place looked as if a tornado had swept through it. Cupboards, cabinets, bookshelves—literally every drawer and closet in the house had been searched, without regard to neatness or replacing items which were disturbed in the process.

Ty frowned, waving a hand at the resultant mess. "Is this necessary?" he inquired of the man whose name tag read Detective Haggardy.

Rather than answering, the detective posed a question of his own. "Who are you?" Obviously, he was not a football or Knights aficionado.

"Ty James, a friend of the family. Corey called me, but it looks like she should have called her insurance adjuster instead."

"And you?" Haggardy glowered at Jess.

"Jess Myers, also a friend. By the way, do you have a search warrant, or did you simply barge in here illegally?"

The detective sneered and patted his pocket. "Right here. I already showed it to Mrs. Rome."

At this point, another officer approached. "Nothing yet, sir," he informed his superior. "We've looked in every nook and cranny in the place. Garage, shed, basement, under the sink, in the pantry. We've got a whole stack of stuff tagged and ready for transport to the lab, but nothing looks promising."

"Go through it all again for anything you might have missed the first time around," Haggardy directed grimly. "Did you search both automobiles? What about the attic?"

"If you'd just tell me what it is you're looking for, I might be able to help," Corey suggested tearfully. "At least tell me who sent you."

"The judge did when he signed the search warrant," Haggardy said. He relented slightly. "I think this whole thing was started by some doctor. That's all I can say."

Jess mulled the information over a moment, then asked, "Is

Mrs. Rome being charged with something? Should she contact her attorney?''

"That might not be a bad idea," Haggardy admitted.

"Does this have something to do with Gabe?" Ty inquired. "Is it something he's supposed to have done? Or, since you mentioned a doctor, is it connected with his illness in some way?"

Haggardy stood firm. "I'm not at liberty to divulge that information.''

"Who is?" Jess pressed.

"Mrs. Rome's attorney will be better able to determine that," was all Haggardy would say.

Thirty minutes later, having all but demolished the interior of the house, the police departed, taking with them several large boxes filled with assorted confiscated items. Corey gazed around her in stunned dismay. "My God, they even searched the chimney flue! There's soot all over, and they tracked it onto the carpet!''

Jess shook her head. "Lord, what a mess! And I'll give you ten to one they won't send in a cleaning crew, either.''

"True, but on the bright side, they didn't haul Corey off in handcuffs," Ty pointed out.

"I expect that next," Corey added dismally. She sank to the floor amid a pile of books tossed from the bookcase and started to cry. "Why won't anyone tell me what's going on? What in heaven or hell is this all about?''

"Your attorney will get to the bottom of it, Corey," Jess assured her, kneeling down beside her. "It may just take a while to weave through all the red tape. Look, why don't you go visit Gabe, and get away from all this for a while? Ty can go with you, and I'll stay and start cleaning up if you'd like.''

"I . . . I can't," Corey sobbed. "Gabe's got enough to worry about without me adding this to his plate. He'll only get upset, and that can't be good for him.''

"On the other hand, maybe Gabe knows more at this point than we do," Ty proposed thoughtfully. "Why don't we go find out? Jess, are you sure you don't want to come along?''

"No. I've got my own agenda. First, I'm going to run back

to my place and grab the video camera and some film. Then I'm going to photograph every room in this house, so Corey's lawyer can see what a shambles the police made of it. That way, she might at least get reimbursed for any expense incurred to set things to rights again, like shampooing the carpets for instance. Then I'm going to attempt to forge a path, so she can get to the bedroom and bathroom without breaking her neck. You could be a sweetheart and bring back some sandwiches for lunch. I think I'm going to work up quite a hunger.''

Three hours later, and no sandwiches in sight, Jess was foraging through Corey's refrigerator when Ty called. "I've got good news and bad news," he began. "The good news is that we finally figured out, via Gabe and the lawyer, why the police searched the house. The bad news is they—the doctors and police, not Gabe—suspect Corey of poisoning Gabe.''

"Corey? Oh, that's asinine!" Jess exploded. "She worships the ground he walks on!''

"That's what Gabe told them, but they insist he's being poisoned. They just don't know how, or if it's deliberate or by chance, so they're covering all their bases, so to speak.''

Jess eyed the lettuce she'd pulled from the fridge, and promptly replaced it. "Did they say what kind of poison?''

"They're pretty sure it's arsenic.''

"Arsenic?" she repeated stupidly. "I didn't think that stuff was around anymore. At least not in the common household, like it was in the old days.''

"As I understand it, it's not as prevalent, or as easy to come by. But it is still around, predominantly in pesticides and the like, though not in any large quantities.''

"And they think he's been consuming it?''

"That, or absorbing it through his skin somehow. They fairly much ruled out breathing it in, or Corey would likely be sick as well. As a matter of fact, they're running some tests on her, too. She and her attorney are down in the hospital lab right now.''

"Is that wise?" Jess asked. "I mean, it's one thing to cooperate with the authorities when you're the victim, but when you stand to be accused of a crime, even if you're one hundred percent innocent, isn't that sticking your neck out? Our court system is not infallible, after all, and innocent people are sometimes convicted, while real criminals walk free.''

"You don't have to convince me," Ty told her. "But after consulting with Corey and Gabe, her lawyer advised her to go ahead with it. It's just one small step toward eliminating Corey as the perpetrator.''

"So that's why they took all those cleaners and odd bottles and cans from the house and garage," Jess mused. "They're looking for anything containing traces of arsenic. Anything from bug spray to baking soda.''

"Yeah, talk about shades of *Arsenic and Old Lace,* huh?" he said, alluding to the movie starring Cary Grant and Boris Karloff.

"So what's the prognosis for Gabe's recovery?" Jess inquired. "Is there an antidote or something? Is he going to fully recuperate?''

"They think so. He'll be hospitalized for a week or so, while they flush out his system, but after that their main concern is that he not ingest any more of it once he's home again. You don't necessarily have to get it in one large dose. It can build up in your body bit by bit and kill you.''

Jess grimaced. "A lovely thought. Okay, so for now Gabe is out of danger?''

"Yes.''

"And they're allowing Corey in to see him?''

"Only at Gabe's insistence.''

"Good for him. And her. Tell them I'm rooting for them, and I'll be up to visit with him soon, if that's permitted.''

"Will do. We'll see you soon. I'd guess about another hour should do it. Do you still want that sandwich?''

"Forget it. I've lost my appetite.''

CHAPTER 21

By the time Ty and Corey got back, Jess had made decent headway through the house. Everything was off the floor and approximately where it had been before the police had rifled through it. Corey could readjust things to their proper places later, but for now she wouldn't have to trip over anything.

Corey was appreciative, but still very distracted and distraught, which was to be expected. "At least Gabe is on my side," she sighed. "He knows I'd never do anything to harm him. Doesn't anyone understand that I'd give my life for that man?"

"We do," Jess told her sincerely. "And anyone who really knows you surely feels the same."

"Which brings us back to square one," Ty concluded. "Where in blue blazes has Gabe come into contact with arsenic? Since Corey tested negative, it probably isn't in anything around here, unless it's something Gabe has sprayed for weeds or bugs."

"And then the police will automatically assume I've been slipping it into his taco sauce," Corey added on a bitter note.

"More than ever, I feel like a jinx," Jess confessed. "Ever since I've come on the scene, awful things have been happening to people I know. First Ervin, then Allen, and now poor Gabe. Even Dino broke his collarbone. I'm beginning to think someone is deliberately targeting anyone I come into contact with, and if that's the case, I ought to stop hanging around Ty and Josh so much, before some disaster strikes either of them.''

''Now you're being silly, Jess,'' Ty told her with a frown. ''And your theory has a few holes in it, too. If—and I stress the word 'if'—someone was trying to hurt you in some way by causing calamities to befall people you know, what's the deal with Ervin? You hadn't said three words to the guy before you suspected him of giving away our signals. You barely know Brice, and he got tagged for DWI. You and the Tanners are cordial enough, but not bosom buddies, and it's not as if Sir Loin is your best pal. Furthermore, nothing has happened to me or anyone connected with you outside the team.''

Here he paused, as another possibility occurred to him. It hit Jess at the same time. ''The team!'' they cried in tandem.

''Of course,'' Corey concurred, her eyes wide. ''Why didn't we think of it sooner?''

''Because we weren't looking at the whole picture,'' Ty figured. ''Most likely, we're still not seeing it all. For instance, why would anyone target members of the team? For what purpose?''

Jess shrugged. ''To make us lose games?''

Ty shook his head. ''It's got to be more than that. We're just starting out, for pity sake. It's not all that likely that in our first season we'd end up knocking anyone out of the running for the Super Bowl. So where's the big threat?''

''Bookies?'' Jess hazarded. ''Point spreads?''

''Maybe, but I've got a feeling it's more than that,'' Ty concluded.

''Well, whatever the reason, and whoever is at fault, one thing is clear. All these 'accidents' and 'incidents' haven't been accidents after all. Someone is out for blood.''

Ty nodded. ''And completely without conscience, it seems. He doesn't just wound, he kills, too.''

''Let's back up a bit,'' Jess suggested, ''and put things into better perspective. Suppose someone is out to destroy the team and/or its members. We don't know who or what his motive might be.'' She began listing the incidents on her fingers. "One, Dino's mishap could be your run-of-the-mill football injury, but Alan's sure as heck wasn't, and neither is Gabe's. In that light, perhaps Ervin didn't hang himself out of remorse or fear of incarceration. Maybe someone did the deed for him.''

She'd ticked off four digits and went on to count three more. "Now we have Sir Loin and Rick Tanner, and those dubious test results. Plus, I have to wonder if Brice's DWI doesn't fall in there somewhere. Perhaps something to do with his allergy medication?''

"Doc Johnson,'' Corey deduced immediately, her eyes narrowing in righteous wrath. "He could have rigged those drug tests, and he probably prescribed Brice's medication. Moreover, he was the one who diagnosed Gabe's problem as the flu and kept tuning us out when we tried to tell him otherwise.''

"Did he prescribe anything for Gabe?'' Jess asked excitedly.

"No, he just advised us to do the usual—pump fluids, rest, take aspirin for the aches and pains.'' Corey's shoulders slumped, and suddenly straightened again. "Wait! He did give Gabe some special stuff a while back to treat athlete's foot. He claimed it was ten times better than anything Gabe could buy over the counter, but Gabe isn't convinced it was working all that well. Actually, his feet have gotten worse since he's been using it.''

"For how long?'' Jess inquired. "How long since Gabe began using it?''

Corey fluttered her hands, anxiously trying to recall the time frame. "I don't know, precisely. About six weeks or so.''

Ty leapt to his feet. "Where is this stuff? Did the police confiscate it, or could it still be here?''

"It wasn't here at all, I don't think,'' Corey informed him. "There's only one bottle, and Gabe kept it in his gym bag, so he'd have it both at home and at practice. On weekends, he'd bring the bag home, but through the week he left it in his locker. Since he expected to be back at practice on Saturday morning, I imagine it's still there.''

"Can you look, just to be sure?'' Ty asked eagerly.

"Yes, but this medication is applied topically, not taken internally," she stressed, "so I can't see how . . ."

"The doctor said it could be something that Gabe is absorbing through his skin," Ty reminded her. "It doesn't have to be in something he's drinking or eating."

Corey trotted off to the bedroom, with Jess and Ty close behind. "It's not here," Corey said moments later. "He always puts his bag on the closet shelf. Of course, with the police throwing everything hither and yon, it could still be here someplace, I suppose. That, or they might have taken it with the other things."

"I didn't see any sign of a duffel bag when I straightened the house," Jess put in.

"Then either the police have it or it's still in Gabe's locker." Ty headed toward the hall. "I'm going to the stadium, and if the bag's there, I'll bring it back."

Jess ran after him. "Wait! Shouldn't we call the police and have them look? Or phone Corey's attorney? You don't want to get arrested for tampering with evidence, or—God forbid—have them think you planted the stuff there."

Ty considered this. "I suppose you could call and have them meet me there. But I'm leaving now, before that bottle mysteriously turns up missing, if it hasn't already. Besides, we're working solely on our own theory here, and the police might not put much stock in it. Chances are, they'll think we're sending them on a wild goose chase, just to throw them off Corey's trail."

"It's a clear bottle, filled with some god-awful smelly green liquid," Corey clarified. "It looks just about like that name-brand liniment Gabe used to buy for sore muscles, only it's not labeled."

Jess hesitated, then dashed out the door on Ty's heels. "I'm going with you. Corey, call the cops and your lawyer. That way, maybe I won't be Ty's only witness, and a biased one at that."

* * *

Jess flat-out refused to stay in the car while Ty went into the locker room. "I'm too antsy to sit out here and wait. Besides, it's spooky out here in the dark."

It was no less spooky inside. First, the night watchman was nowhere to be found, and the entry gate, which was supposed to be locked, wasn't. "Fred must be making his rounds on the outer perimeter," Ty presumed. "He'll lock up again on his way back through. This sure made it easy to get in, though."

"Yeah, but just as easy for anyone else to do the same, with no one the wiser," Jess pointed out.

Then, Ty couldn't find the switch for the hall lights. "I have no idea where the main panel is. They probably put it in some oblique location, so John Q. Public doesn't have ready access to it," he submitted, "which is smart in one aspect, but not terribly convenient at the moment. Good thing I always carry a flashlight in the glove compartment."

"So you can play cat burglar?" she mocked.

"No, in case of emergency. You never know when it'll come in handy."

Their footsteps echoed eerily in the long, empty concrete corridors. Jess shivered. "This is downright creepy at night. Especially with only a dim beam to guide the way. You really ought to check your batteries more often, James."

"Sort of like touring the haunted house at Halloween, isn't it?" he said, shining the light in his face as he aped a wicked expression. "Or a mausoleum at the stroke of midnight."

She smacked his arm. "Knock it off, Ty. You're not funny. Oh, shoot!"

"What?"

"I have to pee. When I get nervous, my bladder kicks in."

Ty laughed, a sinister sound as it reverberated back, magnified in volume. "You mean when you're scared spitless."

"Then, too," she admitted. "Ty, I really do have to visit the ladies' room."

"Surely you can hang on until we reach the locker room?"

She wrinkled her nose at him. "I'm not exactly equipped to use a urinal, Ty."

"No joke," he rebutted. "We have regular toilets, too, you know, in addition to those."

"Okay, but I hope the janitor has cleaned in there recently."

He took her by the hand and quickened the pace. Jess was glad to reach the locker room, where the light switch was handy. She scurried off to the rest room area, flipping that light on as well. "Don't start without me. I'm supposed to be your witness, remember?"

"So hurry already, will you? I don't need wet car seats."

Jess was out of the stall, still tucking her shirttail into her jeans, when the lights outside the rest room went off. "All right, Ty," she called out irritably. "Enough with the trick or treat routine."

The only response was a muffled thump, followed by a dull thud and a metallic clang. Jess hastened to the doorway and peered cautiously around the corner. "Ty? Ty, if this is some sort of prank . . ."

Her voice trailed off uncertainly, leaving a silence so deep that she could hear her own heartbeat—no, not her heart . . .but footsteps, as someone ran from the locker area into the outer hall and beyond.

"Ty?" she called again, almost ill with dread as instinct told her that something was drastically wrong. "Please answer me. Are you all right?"

When he failed to reply, Jess glanced quickly around in search of anything she could use to defend herself if need be. The only thing immediately at hand was a dusty old toilet plunger that looked as if it might have come over on Noah's Ark, but it was better than nothing. Hoisting it before her like a spear, she advanced into the dark room, inching her way toward the hall entry and the light switch—all the while, wondering if Ty had gone running out, perhaps chasing someone, or if those footsteps she'd heard had belonged to another party entirely.

She was still several feet from the door, her path only slightly illuminated by the faint light from the rest room behind her, when she caught the sound of more footsteps, these rapidly approaching from the corridor. There was no way to know if they belonged to friend or foe. Galvanized into action by pure fear and adrenaline, Jess, in one huge bound, leapt behind a row of lockers. She hunkered down in the shadows, hardly daring to breathe as she clung shakily to her puny weapon.

Seconds later, the lights came on, the contrast nearly blinding her. "Anyone here?" a male voice boomed. When no one answered, the man said, "You sure you heard something, Mr. Nelson?"

"I could have sworn I did, Fred," her godfather replied.

Jess heaved a relieved sigh, which promptly turned into a panicked shriek as she turned her head and saw Ty lying face-down on the floor a mere yard from where she was crouched. His long, limp form was sprawled awkwardly in the space between the bench and the stand of metal lockers, his eyes closed. But what alarmed Jess most was the stream of blood trickling across the cement from beneath him.

Her scream was still reverberating through the room as Tom and the guard, his gun drawn, rounded the corner into the aisle. "Jessie?" Tom queried anxiously. Then he spotted Ty's unconscious body. "Oh, my God! What has happened?"

"I don't know! I don't know!" Jess wailed. On hands and knees, she crawled toward Ty. "Oh, please don't be dead! Please! Tommy, help him!"

"Fred, call 911. Have them send an ambulance," Tom barked, taking charge. "No, Jess. Don't move him. We have no way of knowing the extent of his injuries. You could do more harm than good." He scooted the bench out of the way and knelt down to feel behind Ty's ear for a pulse. "Calm down, Jess. He's alive. Help will be here soon."

Ignoring Tom's advice, Jess carefully wedged her knee beneath Ty's head, cushioning it as she stroked his hair away from his pale face with trembling fingers. "Th-the police should be on their way anyway," she stammered. "Corey called them before we left her house and told them to meet us here."

Tom blinked in surprise. "Why? What's going on?"

"It has to do with Gabe. We needed to get something from his locker."

"And it couldn't wait until tomorrow?"

Before she could say more, Ty let out a groan. "I think he's coming to," Jess said unnecessarily. She bent over him, crooning softly in an effort to comfort him. "It's okay, Ty. I'm here. Help is near, darling."

His lashes fluttered, but his lids remained closed.

To Tom, Jess whispered frantically, "Shouldn't we at least try to find out where he's bleeding from and stem the flow? He's losing an awful lot of blood."

"I think it's his head, Jessie. Maybe toward the back. Do you . . . do you think he could have been shot?"

"No, thank God. I was in the rest room when the lights in here went out. I heard some noise, but nothing like gunfire."

"Good, good. Then maybe he's not hurt too badly after all. I have heard that head wounds, even slight ones, bleed more profusely."

The metallic jingle of keys and handcuffs preceded the arrival of two police officers. "We got a message to meet a Tyler James here, and then a call about an injured party?"

"That's Tyler," Tom said, inclining his head.

"What happened to him?"

"We're not sure, but I'm so glad you're here," Jess answered. "Is the ambulance on the way?"

"Yes, ma'am. And you are?"

"Jess Myers."

Ty moaned again, and started to stir fitfully. Jess tried to calm him. "Stay still, Ty. You've been hurt."

One of the officers nudged Tom aside and took his place beside Ty. "Move your hand, Miss Myers. Let me see if I can ascertain how badly he's injured."

"We think it's his head. Can you stop the bleeding?"

From a packet concealed in his hat, the policeman removed a pair of sanitary rubber gloves. After donning them, he leaned forward and gently ran his fingers across Ty's skull. "Kenny, give me a little more light here, will you?"

His partner aimed his flashlight beam at the back of Ty's head as the first man continued to probe through Ty's blood-soaked hair. "Whoa! He's got a goose egg and a half back here! I'd guess a nice concussion to go with it, too."

"No bullet wound?" Ken asked.

"Nah. I'd say he either hit the concrete floor, or someone bashed him a good one."

Kenny's gaze roved from Fred to Jess to Tom, then lit on the toilet plunger lying on the floor next to Jess. "Any of you know anything about this?"

A trio of "no"'s resounded. Only Jess added an explanation to the denial. "As I told Tom, I was in the rest room when the lights out here went off and I heard noises. A couple of thumps or thuds, then footsteps running away. When Ty didn't answer me, I didn't know if he'd left, or if something had happened to him. Just to be safe, I grabbed the toilet plunger and came out to investigate. That's when Tom and Fred arrived, flipped on the lights, and we found Ty lying on the floor."

"We haven't touched anything, or moved Tyler, except for scooting the bench aside and supporting his head," Tom put in quickly.

"How'd you get in?" the officer inquired of Jess. "Isn't this area usually locked?"

"It wasn't tonight," Jess informed him. "Neither was the front gate. Ty figured Fred was checking the outer perimeter and would lock it when he was done."

Ty groaned again, gaining everyone's attention.

"Is he coming to, Dan?" Kenny questioned.

"I think so. Hey, buddy, can you hear me?" he asked of Ty.

Ty replied with a protracted moan, before trying to grab for his throbbing head. "Oh, geez it hurts! What happened?"

Dan caught his hand in midair and brought it away from the wound. "That's what we'd like to know," he told Ty. "For now, just lie still. Does anything hurt besides your head?"

Ty opened his eyes to mere slits. "Jess? That you?"

"The one and only," she replied, trying to hold back her tears.

"No, babe. Right now there's at least three of you."

"Concussion," Dan concluded.

"Answer the officer, Ty. Do you hurt anywhere else?"

"My cheek, my forehead . . . my right hand." Ty's voice, still weak, took on a panicky note. "I can't feel my fingers!"

Moments later, Tom declared disgustedly, "Jess, you klutz! You're kneeling on the man's hand! His throwing hand, at that!"

Abashed and apologetic, she scooted off his hand, trying not to jar his head in the process.

"So, do you remember what happened? Did you trip? Fall? What?" Dan prodded.

Ty started to shake his head, a move he immediately regretted. Wincing, he rasped, "The last thing I recall is getting Gabe's combination lock undone. I was going to wait for Jess before opening the door, but I thought I'd unlock it, at least."

"And then?"

Ty frowned, trying to remember. "The lights went out, I think. Literally and figuratively. The next thing, I woke up with my head about to split wide open."

"An apt comment, since it actually is split open," Officer Ken noted. "I think we can safely assume someone clobbered you. Did you hear any noises before you got hit?"

"Just Jess when she flushed the john."

"And the lights went off before you were hit? You didn't see anyone, catch even a glimpse or a shadow?"

"I didn't see squat. Why?"

"Obviously someone hit the light switch, and if it wasn't her or you, it stands to reason there was a third party involved. Presumedly, the person who hit you."

"The bag," Ty said suddenly.

"Who? What?"

"The bag," he repeated impatiently. "Gabe's duffel. Is it still in the locker, Jess?"

"What's all the fuss about a duffel bag?" Fred wanted to know.

Jess nodded toward Gabe's locker. "Would one of you officers do the honors, please? It's number twenty-two."

The lock was lying on the floor at the base of the locker, but the door was still shut. However, when Dan pulled the panel open, there was no duffel bag inside. Only Gabe's uniform and protective gear were there.

"What about his shoes?" Jess thought to mention.

"Nope."

Ty let loose a low, careful curse. "Damn! Someone took it."

"The police?" Jess hazarded hopefully.

"Why would we have it?" Dan questioned curiously.

"Your department is investigating Gabe Rome's possible poisoning," she explained. "They searched his house today. We thought perhaps they'd done the same here. You might check with Detective Haggardy, because if his crew doesn't have that duffel, then it's quite possible the person responsible for this whole mess has taken it."

"I'm still not making the connection," Tom stated confusedly. "Is there something in the gym bag that could point to the perpetrator?"

"Bingo." This from Ty. "Give the man a Kewpie doll."

"So the guy Miss Myers heard leaving after the thumps and the lights going off is the one who bonked Ty and took the bag?" Fred proposed.

"That's my guess, too," Jess concluded dismally, "and he's probably guilty of a whole lot worse. Including intentional murder."

"So, why didn't he kill me?" Ty wondered aloud.

Jess shuddered. "For whatever reason, I'll be eternally grateful he didn't."

CHAPTER 22

Amid his protests to the contrary, Ty was transported to the hospital via ambulance. Jess followed in Ty's car, and behind her came the two patrolmen in their police cruiser. Jess was still so unnerved that she stalled the Trans Am twice en route, and was amazed that the officers didn't pull her over and ask to see her driver's license.

As the emergency staff checked the extent of Ty's injuries, the officers questioned Jess again, trying to elicit more details and to verify others. Just when it seemed they were satisfied at last, Detective Haggardy waltzed through the emergency ward doors and the routine began anew.

Finally, Jess had had it. "Look, fellas, I'll carve it in stone if you want, but can we give it a rest? All I care about right now is finding out how badly Ty is hurt."

"One more time," Haggardy urged. "I want to make sure I understand this cockamamie theory you two and the Rome woman cooked up that someone is out to destroy the Knights. Tell me again why you suspect the team doctor, this Johnson."

"Because he's the one who did the drug testing on the team, and had the best opportunity to alter the results," she reiterated wearily. "Also, he might have prescribed Brice Tackett's antihistamine, perhaps in the wrong dosage. We're not certain about that, but we do know that Doc was treating Gabe when he got sick, and diagnosed him with the flu. He'd also given Gabe a special medication for his athlete's foot, in an unlabeled bottle.''

"Which you, being a hot-shot investigative reporter, consider suspicious," Haggardy commented snidely.

"Under the circumstances, yes, and so should you," she insisted heatedly. "Gabe was exposed to arsenic in some manner, whether by absorption or ingestion, and every avenue should be thoroughly explored. Why is it you always suspect the spouse first?" she grumbled. "Corey is as true blue as they come."

"So you keep saying. Okay, say Johnson is our culprit. We still don't have any evidence to support that assumption. The mysterious duffel bag, if there ever was one, is nowhere to be found. Also missing is this supposedly tainted athlete's foot remedy and Rome's football shoes. Am I correct so far?"

Jess gave a brisk nod. "Yes. Look, Detective Haggardy, I realize that all this sounds a bit far-fetched, but believe me, it makes a lot more sense than Corey trying to kill Gabe. Now, if you'll excuse me, I've got to see if I can get an update on Ty and phone Corey."

Ty was admitted overnight for further observation. In addition to a moderate concussion, he had a smaller bump on his forehead and a few slight abrasions to his right cheek, these apparently sustained in his fall onto the concrete floor. When they had him transferred to a private room and settled for the night, Jess stayed until his medication took effect and he fell asleep. Then, sadly in need of a shower and a change of clothes, she drove herself home to her own apartment.

No sooner had she stepped into the hall, than the phone rang. Sure it must be either Corey or the hospital calling, Jess ran to answer it. To her dismay, but not surprise, it was her godfather on the other end of the line, with the requisite lecture she had hoped to postpone.

Without preamble, he commanded, "Jessie, I want you to resign your position as kicker and stay the hell away from the team until all this nonsense stops. It's too dangerous."

"I can't do that, Tommy. I won't," she replied flatly.

"Don't argue with me. If anything were to happen to you, your mom would skin me alive."

"As everyone is so fond of reminding me, I'm a big girl. I can look after myself," she insisted.

"Face it, Jessie, you have a nose for trouble. For your own well-being, it's time you tucked it back into your own business before you get it snipped off."

"No can do, Tommy. As I said, it seems that someone, for whatever reason, is deliberately taking aim at team members, and I'm going to get to the bottom of it if it kills me."

"Which it very well might!" he shouted.

"Don't yell at me. I know you're concerned, but what kind of reporter would I be if I didn't investigate this? Besides, if it wasn't my business before, it most assuredly is now. Whoever is behind these vicious incidents made it in-my-face personal, first by attacking my friends and now by assaulting Ty tonight. I'm not about to ignore it, Tommy, and let him get away with murder."

"Damn it, Jess! If you take this as some kind of challenge, you're bound to regret it. Knock off the hot-shot reporter act and use your common sense for once! Leave it to the police, and stay out of it! Consider that an order, young lady!"

Jess's nerves, stretched to the breaking point along with her temper, snapped. "Stuff it, Tommy. You might mean well, but you're overstepping the godfather role. You have no right to censure me or issue mandates. You're not my father, after all."

"Maybe not, but I should have been!" he shot back sharply. Before she could assimilate that statement, he abruptly hung up.

For several seconds, Jess frowned dumbly at the buzzing receiver in her hand, as if some mechanical malfunction had been at fault. Finally, with a confused shake of her head, she slowly replaced it in the cradle. "Whew! What was that all about?"

As she started to turn away, the blinking red light on her answering machine caught her attention. Deciding whatever was recorded couldn't possibly ruin her day any further, she punched the playback button. There was a short message from her mother, just to touch base. A reminder from her dentist's office that her semiannual checkup and cleaning was due. Corey, asking for the latest update. And a short, succinct threat in a muffled voice, which warned, "You were lucky tonight, and got off easy. Take heed, or you're next, lady."

Jess stumbled backward, away from the machine, as if it had suddenly grown fangs. She stared at it, aghast, as the tape clicked off and a thick, ominous silence surrounded her. Her brain was reeling with the shock, her heart pounding, her knees turning to Jell–O. Having Tommy rant and rave at her, out of the kindness of his heart, was one thing; receiving a threatening message from an unknown source was another matter entirely. Actually, it scared her spitless!

Especially when she realized that she was all alone in the apartment—or hoped she was! She'd flipped on one light in the living room as she'd dashed for the phone, but other than that, the place was dark. Moreover, she wasn't sure she'd taken the time to lock the front door behind her. Just then, the furnace kicked on, and the unfamiliar sound in the otherwise quiet apartment nearly made her jump out of her shoes.

"Get a grip, Jess," she told herself shakily. "You're losing it, girl. You've lived by yourself for years, and it never bothered you before." Still another part of her—the quivering chicken part—reminded her that she'd never received threats via her phone before, either, and was urging her to get out of the apartment. The sooner the better.

Jess gave in with uncommon haste. She yanked the tape from the answering machine, stuffed it into her jacket pocket, and was fishing for her keys on her way out the door. When her fumbling fingers failed to find them in her pocket, or amid the hodgepodge in her purse, she all but panicked. She turned to retrace her steps through the apartment, soon spotting her keys, still dangling from the outside of the lock. Heaving a sigh of relief, she pulled the door shut and the keys free, and made a mad dash for the car. For the first time in years, she checked the backseat before getting in, launched herself inside, and promptly flipped the locks before fitting the key into the ignition switch.

She was halfway down the block before the thought occurred to her that she had no idea where she was going. To Ty's place? She had the keys. Back to the hospital? Or to Corey's to spend the night? To Dayton, and her mother's house perhaps? It would only take an hour or so to get there.

But her mother would take one look at her, her clothes caked with Ty's dried blood, and go into hysterics, so that was out. She had extra clothes at Ty's. She could go there and clean up, but she really didn't want to stay the night by herself, no matter how good security was at the complex. Not tonight. Not without Ty. Corey would put her up, she was sure; but Corey had enough to deal with, and Jess didn't want to add to her friend's burden, or possibly endanger her even more.

Nervously, she checked in the rearview mirror yet again. Was that car following her, or just heading in the same direction by chance? At the next corner, she ran a yellow light, sped forward and changed lanes three times in the next two blocks, then quickly made a left turn, followed by a right at the corner, and another left. Satisfied at last that if anyone had been tailing her she'd lost them, she drove swiftly to Ty's condo.

Safe within the security gates, she parked the Trans Am in the garage and scurried into the house before the garage light went out. Within three minutes, armed with Ty's old baseball bat, she'd turned on every light in the house, checked each door and window to make certain they were locked, pulled all the curtains and blinds, and looked under the bed and in the closets for possible intruders. Had she encountered one, she'd likely have been too busy wetting her pants to swing the bat at him.

Fortunately, the house was empty, and Jess collapsed on the couch, a human heap of jangled nerves. "Okay, calm down, and stop acting like a fidgety female," she instructed herself as she hugged her knees to her chest. "You're perfectly safe."

So, why did her stomach feel as if it had turned into a super-charged popcorn popper?

"Because you're overreacting, you idiot," she deduced aloud. "You haven't had a decent meal all day—a day thoroughly shot to hell from beginning to end—which would make anyone a little raw around the edges. It's just a lousy phone message, for heaven's sake. No more than words, which can't hurt you. Now, pull yourself together and start behaving like an intelligent adult instead of some sniveling scaredy cat."

Her monologue pep talk left something to be desired. She needed to talk to someone, or failing that, simply to be around other people, where she would feel more secure. That decided, she bounded into the bedroom and began rifling through the closet and chest of drawers. Not only did she need a change of clothes, but so would Ty. Even if the doctor didn't release him in the morning as planned, he would still need his electric razor, his toothbrush, bathrobe and undies. A set of pajamas wouldn't have been amiss, but the man didn't have a pair to his name—unless she wanted to stop by the mall and buy some for him, which she didn't, since he'd probably refuse to wear them anyway.

She crammed everything into one small suitcase, his things and hers, shut off most of the lights, and was on her way again, without bothering to shower or change her own attire. She would wash up in the bathroom off Ty's hospital room, and use his phone to call Corey.

This time Jess drove her own car, preferring the familiarity of it. At least she could be fairly certain she wouldn't stall the darn thing if another unforeseen emergency arose.

To her surprise, when she arrived at the hospital, there was a uniformed officer standing guard outside Ty's room. "Oh, no!" she declared, running down the hall toward the man. "What's happened?"

As she tried to push past him, the guard threw out his arm and blocked her entry. "Sorry, ma'am. No visitors allowed."

"But I just left a little while ago. What's going on? Is Ty all right?"

"He's fine."

"I want to see for myself."

"Are you a family member?"

"No, I'm his . . . uh . . . his . . ."

"She's mine, all right," Ty barked from inside the room. "Let her in, or she'll stand out there arguing all night."

The officer pushed the door open a crack and peered in at Ty. "You sure? I've got orders not to let anyone in there."

"I'm sure. I sleep with the woman. If she was going to kill me, she's missed dozens of opportunities already."

Jess squeezed in under the guard's arm. "Kill you? And miss hearing you whistle in the shower? No way. What's with the guard?"

Ty put a hand to his head. "Lower the volume, babe. My head's already exploding." As she came into the circle of light near the bed, Ty's eyes widened. He stared at her blood-soaked clothes in alarm. "Sweet Lord, Jess! You've been hurt! Officer, get a doctor in here right away!"

"No, no! I'm fine!" Jess assured him immediately. "It's your blood, not mine. I had your head on my lap, remember?"

Ty heaved a heartfelt sigh as he relaxed back onto the pillow. "Good grief! You scared the liver out of me!"

"Yeah? Well, you're both doing wonders for my blood pressure," the guard grumbled. "So, is she staying or what?"

"I'm staying."

"She's staying."

"I'm leaving," the man said. "I'll be right outside the door if either of you needs anything."

Jess jerked her thumb toward the departing officer. "What's he doing here?"

"It's a long story," Ty hedged.

"Give me the condensed version."

Ty patted the mattress at his side and waited until Jess had seated herself gingerly on the edge. "Haggardy sicced him on me after someone tried to sneak in here and pump my veins full of air."

Jess's brow wrinkled. "Come again?"

"I was almost asleep when I heard someone tiptoe into the room. I thought it was probably a nurse, coming to check on me. You know how they keep pestering you when you have a concussion, waking you up periodically and checking your pupils and whatnot?''

Jess nodded. "Go on."

"When I felt this hand on my arm, I assumed she was going to take my pulse. Instead, I felt a prick on the inside of my arm, and when I opened my eyes this guy in green scrubs and a surgical mask was standing over me, trying to give me some kind of injection. Don't ask me why, but I knew something wasn't right. I jerked my arm away, but he grabbed it again—roughly, without a word of explanation. So here I am, yelling and trying to fend him off, when a nurse pops in to see what all the fuss is about. She starts firing questions, and the guy runs out of here like his tail is on fire, knocking her to the floor on his way out.

"Next thing, the whole nursing staff is in an uproar, and Haggardy shows up. Turns out I wasn't supposed to have a shot, and the guy trying to give me one probably wasn't hospital personnel. Furthermore, the syringe he dropped was empty."

"Empty?" she echoed. "That doesn't make sense."

"Sure it does." He went on to explain, his expression grim. "An air bubble in your bloodstream can be just as lethal as any drug. Hits your brain or heart, and poof! You're a goner."

"Oh, my God! He tried to murder you!"

"That's about the size of it." Ty drew a weary breath. "Hence, the guard at the door."

"I should never have left," Jess babbled, instantly filled with remorse. She picked up his hand and brought it to her lips, peppering it with kisses. "I should have sat right here and watched over you. Oh, Ty! I'm so sorry!"

"Hey, I didn't expect you to baby-sit me all night." Ty cradled her cheek in his open palm. "Besides, you're here now, and both of us are alive, if not fit. That's all that counts."

"Did they catch him?"

"No. He got away. But at least Haggardy is leaning more toward our theory now."

Another startling thought occurred to her suddenly. "What

about Gabe? Could the killer have gone after him again tonight, too?''

''Not to worry. We've already covered that base, and Gabe is safe. Our would-be assassin had an easier time getting to me than he would have trying to get into that special unit where Gabe is staying.''

''Thank God you're both okay.'' Jess was silent a moment, then asked thoughtfully, ''How do you know it was a man and not a woman? You said he wore scrubs and a mask.''

''His arms,'' Ty told her. ''They, along with the rest of him, were too big, too muscular, and too hairy to belong to a woman. So were his hands, even inside those rubber gloves.''

''In that case, I take it he didn't leave any fingerprints behind.''

''Astute deduction, my dear Watson. And we're right back to square one again.''

''Maybe. Maybe not.'' Jess debated telling Ty about the phone message; but his eyelids were drooping, and she figured it would keep until morning. Hopefully, by then they would both be more rested and alert and ready to deal with all their problems. Meanwhile, with a policeman guarding the door, they were both safe and sound for the night. She could even take a shower without having scenes from *Psycho* flashing through her head.

She leaned over and kissed his forehead. ''Go to sleep, sweetheart. I'm going to take a quick shower in your bathroom. Then I'm going to curl up in that big chair in the corner and spend the whole night with you.''

''You could always climb in with me,'' he countered sleepily. ''There's not much room, but we could make do.''

''Not tonight, darling,'' she told him in a droll voice. ''You have a headache.''

CHAPTER 23

Ty was released from the hospital the next morning, and Jess drove him home to his condo. There, she hovered over him like a mother hen with one lone chick. "Are you hungry? I could fix a sandwich? Or a nice hot bowl of noodle soup?"

"What I really want is a frothy cup of cappuccino."

"Ty, you know the doctor said to slow down on the caffeine for a few days. How about some orange juice, instead."

"Sure. Why not?"

"Shouldn't you be lying down?"

"Shouldn't you be heading off to practice?" Ty countered. "Coach Danvers is liable to have a fit if both of us skip out."

Jess brushed his comment aside. "What will it matter if I kick twenty goals today or thirty tomorrow? If I don't know how to do it by now, I might as well hang up my cleats."

All morning Jess had delayed telling Ty about the message on her answering machine, but with Detective Haggardy due at any moment to question Ty further about the attempt at the hospital, she figured she might as well spill the beans now.

"Uh, Tyler?"

The minute she called him Tyler instead of Ty, he knew something was up. "Yes?"

"Last night, I went home to change my clothes, and I found an odd message on my answering machine. Sort of a threat, actually," she admitted. "At least it sounded like one to me."

He eyed her sternly. "And you're just now getting around to informing me of this? Who was it? What did they say?"

"The voice was so muffled, I couldn't begin to guess who it was. I can't even be sure if the caller was male or female, but I suspect it's a man. He said, and I quote, 'You were lucky tonight, and got off easy. Take heed, or you're next, lady.' I have the tape, if you want to hear it for yourself."

"Under the circumstances, I'd classify that as a threat," Ty concurred. "And I ought to beat your butt for not telling me sooner. Is there anything else you want to confess while you're at it? Anything more you've been keeping under your hat?"

"No, and the only reason I didn't tell you last night is because we already had so much happening, and I figured this could keep until today, when we were both thinking more clearly."

"By 'tonight,' I suppose the caller was referring to last night, at the stadium?" Ty presumed.

"I assume so," Jess agreed, "especially since it was the last message on the tape, recorded after one from Corey wanting an update on your condition—and you were fine before then. Besides, I'd just checked my machine the day before and erased all the previous messages."

"Play it for me. Maybe I'll recognize the voice."

Ty didn't recognize the voice, but he insisted that Jess let Detective Haggardy listen to it when he came. Haggardy surprised both of them by taking the threat seriously, rather than simply dismissing it out of hand.

"I hate to admit it, but I think you two just might be onto something. I'd like to take the tape and have one of our lab men analyze it, if you don't mind. If nothing else, he may be able to tell us for sure if it's a man who made that call, and maybe pick up some other clues like background noises that aren't clear to us now. We're also attempting to locate Dr. Johnson, since last night's attack on Tyler would appear to have been made by someone with some medical knowledge, and thus tie in with your suspicions about him."

"His address should be on file at the Knights' office, if nowhere else," Ty offered helpfully.

"We've already obtained his address and gone to his house, but it's locked up tight with no sign of the man. He didn't show up at his office at the stadium today, either, but we'll keep trying. He's bound to pop up sooner or later, and we definitely want to talk to him. Meanwhile, here's my card with my direct number. If either of you spot him before we do, give me a call."

Jess made it to the team practice the next day. Ty went along, but would be sitting this one out, as well as those scheduled for the rest of the week. Whether he'd be well enough to play in their game Sunday in Miami was yet to be determined.

Since she preferred to wait until the other players cleared out of the locker room, leaving her privacy in which to don her shoes and jersey, Jess was the last one out on the field.

"Okay, you bunch of sissies, hitch up your jock straps, and let's get this show on the road," Danvers commanded gruffly.

"Hey, Jess! You wearin' your jock strap?" one of the guys called out jokingly.

"And your protective cup?" another player added with a snicker. "According to the rules, you've got to be wearing all the required safety equipment, you know."

Jess was used to their ribbing by now, and usually gave as good as she got. Today was no exception. She thrust out her chest and replied with a superior sneer. "I'm wearing two of them, hotshot. Right here in my double-barrel 'jockette' strap."

"Aye, chihuahua!" Chili hooted with glee. "Guess the chica told you!"

"And I'm telling you clowns to get with the program! Now!" Danvers yelled, though he, too, was grinning and shaking his head at her quick comeback.

The practice was long and tiring, and even within the controlled atmosphere of the dome, they trooped off the field afterward dripping with sweat. In reverse procedure, Jess got the locker room first following the practice, since unlike the guys, she simply changed into street clothes and shoes and went home to shower. Normally fast about it, this time she was even quicker, and she reemerged still wearing her uniform. Her face, glowing with color mere seconds before, was now pasty.

"What gives?" Ty inquired hastily.

"There's a note taped to the outside of my locker," she replied, her voice trembling slightly. "Another warning."

Ty dashed inside, his teammates and coach on his heels. He was back in a flash, the note in his hand, followed by Danvers.

"What's going on?" the coach asked. "Ty says this is the second threat you've received in a couple of days."

Jess nodded. "Yeah, and it's already getting tiresome."

Danvers frowned, repeating the words on the note. " 'Keep talking to the police, and you're gonna get yours, bitch' is more than tiresome, Jess. And what's this about the police?"

Ty filled him in on all that had happened Monday, adding, "Didn't the police say anything to you when they were here yesterday looking for Doc Johnson?"

"Not much. I guess they're playing their cards pretty close to the vest. They just asked for Doc's home address and told me they needed to talk to him. I thought maybe it was about Gabe."

"That, too, and a lot more," Ty said. "Look, Coach, I don't know how much Detective Haggardy wants revealed at this point, so I can't say anything else."

"Okay, but if there's any way I can help, just holler. I can't have many more key players keeling over and getting threats like this, or pretty soon I won't have enough to make a decent team. We're already using several of the second-string guys to fill in the gaps." He pointed toward the note, still in Ty's hand. "And I don't care what that thing says, go directly to this Detective Haggardy and hand it over to him. Maybe they can get a good fingerprint off of it, or something, if you haven't already mucked 'em all up."

They stopped by the condo long enough for Jess to get cleaned up, then went straight to the police department. Haggardy, looking as haggard as his name implied, wasn't particularly surprised to see them. "Don't be shocked if we don't get any prints off this thing," he told them as he accepted the note. "If this is Johnson's doing, he probably wore rubber gloves."

It wasn't three hours later, when Haggardy phoned them at Ty's. "Thought I'd let you know the note was clean, just as I suspected. But if Johnson left it, I'll eat my socks. A couple of our officers went by his house again late this afternoon, and found the place still locked up. But his next door neighbor, a sweet, nosy, little old biddy, cornered them before they could leave. She complained about this noise, like a car motor running, coming from Johnson's garage. Said it started shortly after midnight and went on for hours. Kept her awake most of the night. That was enough for the officers to initiate an immediate investigation, and they found the good doctor behind the wheel, dead as a doornail. As things stand right now, it looks to be carbon monoxide poisoning."

"He committed suicide?" Ty exclaimed incredulously.

"I didn't say that," Haggardy clarified. "Could be he did, or could be someone helped him along." He switched swiftly to a related topic. "Here's another thing you might find of interest. That missing duffel bag of Rome's was in the trunk of Johnson's car, along with that bottle of green foot gunk. We've sent it off to the lab, to see if they can find any arsenic in it."

"That was convenient," Ty mused.

"Yeah, I thought so. Too damned tidy, if you ask me. Like maybe somebody else is in on this and setting Johnson up as the fall guy. Could be Johnson had a partner or partners in crime. That would be one way to explain Miss Myers getting that note after the doctor's demise."

"So it's not resolved yet, even with Johnson out of the picture," Ty surmised.

"I'd say not. We'll know more following the pathologist's report. Meanwhile, watch your back, James. I'm pretty sure your little cutie pie isn't involved in this, except perhaps as a future victim, but I've had investigations take stranger twists."

"What's with you, Haggardy? First you blow hot, and then

cold. Pick one and stick with it, will you? Furthermore, Jess
is no more guilty than Corey is. I'd stake my life on that.''

"That's what I'm saying, super jock. It's your neck.''

Jess was appalled, and livid, when Ty related what Haggardy
had said. "Why, that pompous, overblown excuse for a detective!" she ranted. "I suppose he thinks I left myself that
recorded message, and wrote the note myself. And just how
long am I supposed to have been in cahoots with Doc Johnson,
pray tell?''

"Now, Jess, calm down," Ty advised. "I know you're not
involved in any of this, but if Haggardy wants to think so, let
him. Perhaps with him keeping an eye on you, you'll be all
the more safe from the real culprit, and that suits me just fine.''

Jess planted her hands on her hips and glowered at him.
"Well!" she huffed. "Isn't that dandy! So what does that make
me, other than a sitting duck?''

Ty frowned. "I hadn't thought of it in that light, but I'm
sure Haggardy has other suspects he'll be investigating as well.
I simply meant that—''

"I know what you meant, Ty, and I appreciate your vote of
confidence. But I don't like being left hanging out to dry.''

"You won't be, love. I'll be looking out for you, too.''

Jess sighed. "That's good to hear. You guard my back, and
I'll guard yours, and maybe we'll both come away relatively
unscathed.''

After a moment, Ty ventured, "You know, perhaps you
should take your godfather's advice and quit the team, at least
until this guy is caught. You could go visit your mom for a
while.''

"I've thought about it," she surprised him by admitting.
"But I can't let this maniac rule my life, and I can't let him get
away with murder. I'm convinced he—or they, or whoever—is
responsible for Alan's death, and probably Ervin's, too. Not to
mention poisoning Gabe and attacking you. Yes, I'm scared,
but the more I consider it, the more I think our perpetrator
might be equally afraid of me.''

"Afraid of you?" Ty repeated, his brow furrowing. "Care to expound on that?"

"Look at it this way. Did he warn his other victims? Alan? Gabe? You?"

"No."

"But he is warning me away, for some reason. Perhaps he just doesn't like killing women, which would be a definite plus for me. Or, maybe my basic threat to him is not that I've joined up as the team kicker, but that I'm a reporter. He wants me out of his arena, so to speak. Away from the action, before I can discover who he is or catch on to his next devious move."

"That certainly puts a different slant on things, doesn't it?" Ty commented thoughtfully. "I don't know, though. It's plausible, but adding that ingredient to the mix only complicates the whole mess even more. Rather like pouring mud into murky water. The more you add, the less is clear."

Jess shrugged. "It goes that way sometimes. You're cruising along in one direction, turn a corner, and suddenly you're viewing everything from an entirely different perspective. That's what makes investigative reporting so intriguing. Unraveling the mystery, rooting out the rotten apple from the rest of the bushel."

"Yes, but this time you're right in the thick of it," Ty pointed out. "Just one little myopic caterpillar in a whole can of look-alike worms."

Jess got another anonymous warning on Thursday, this time on Ty's answering machine. Again, the theme was the same. "Look out, girlie. Your turn is coming."

"How did he get this number?" Ty wondered angrily. "Damn it all! After the hassle with those reporters, and getting my number changed, now this!"

"I got mine changed then, too," Jess reminded him, "and he still got through somehow. Which leads me to believe it's someone we know, somebody we think we can trust." She arched a brow at him. "Someone on the team?"

"Or who is close to a member of the team, perhaps," Ty

contributed. "Anyone with access to a player's personal phone directory. Hell, Jess! We're still talking about hundreds of prospects."

"What about a former teammate, one who didn't make the cut? In all likelihood, he could still be in contact with a current player, and might have a vendetta against any number of guys who did make the team."

Ty considered this. "That has possibilities. We'll mention it to Haggardy."

"You mention it to him," Jess groused. "He's still on my shit list, just as I'm certainly still on his."

When the team flew to Florida early Saturday, Ty was with them, insisting he was well enough to play in the Sunday afternoon bout against the Dolphins. Regardless, he wasn't about to let Jess go without him, even if Danvers decided not to put him in the game. When they landed in Miami, instead of boarding the shuttle buses with their teammates, Ty led Jess directly to the rental desk, where he picked up the keys to a car already reserved for them. She was all the more confused when Ty drove off in the opposite direction of the hotel where they and the team were registered.

"Where are we going?" she asked, when he failed to volunteer the information.

"It's a surprise."

"Can't you give me a hint?"

With an enigmatic smile, he sang the first few lines of an old song about flying to the moon and playing among the stars.

"That's it? That's my hint?"

He nodded, still humming the tune.

Jess frowned. "We're not heading toward Cape Kennedy, so I guess a rocket launch is out. Stars. Stars," she mused. "Are we going to one of those trendy restaurants owned by a group of actors or something?"

"And have you drooling over a bunch of macho celebrities? No way. Tonight is just for you and me, babe."

"Good, because if you started panting over a pair of silicone boobs with a fake tan, I'd be heartily tempted to give you a swift kick in the butt.''

He slanted her an amused look. ''Is that any way to talk to a man recovering from a concussion? What happened to all that sweetness and sympathy you've been oozing for the past week?''

''I'm oozed out. Give me another hint.''

''A trip to the moon on gossamer wings,'' he crooned cryptically.

''There's that moon thing again. Is there a launch tonight? Is it possible to see one from this far away?''

''I think so, but you're way off base.''

''And you're off-key.''

They were headed toward the bay, but aside from that Jess had no idea what Ty had up his sleeve. She was thoroughly puzzled when he turned onto a private drive and stopped in front of a wrought iron gate. Reaching out, he pressed the call button on an intercom atop a stone pillar, gave his name, and the gates swung open.

''Ty? If we're visiting someone, you could at least have given me fair warning, so I could comb my hair and change out of these jeans into something nicer. I'm travel-worn, to put it mildly.''

''Don't fuss, Jess. You're fine.''

At the end of the mile-long driveway—surrounded by lawn so perfectly manicured Jess wondered if it was artificial turf, and enough statuary to fill a museum—they pulled up in front of a home so magnificent it nearly robbed her of her breath.

''Oh, wow! Is this a house, a hotel, or the state capitol building?'' she exclaimed in awe.

Ty laughed. ''It's a home, albeit a rather large and extravagant one.''

''So, what are we doing here?''

''Staying for the weekend.''

''With whom?''

''I told you before, love. Just you and me.''

Jess was flabbergasted. ''But . . . how? Who? Why?''

''The house is for sale, and I managed to rent it for a couple of days so we could be totally alone.''

''Twenty people could be alone in this place,'' she marveled. ''It's huge! We'll rattle around in it like a pair of marbles in a shoebox.''

Ty grinned. ''No, more like two very pampered minks in a gilded garden.''

Whistling merrily, this time to the tune of ''Muskrat Love,'' he rounded the car, opened her door, and held his arm out for her. ''Madam, welcome to paradise, a la Miami.''

CHAPTER 24

How anyone could call this place a house was beyond Jess. It qualified hands down as a mansion, if not a small palace. The foyer alone, with its gleaming Italian marble floor, was two-thirds the size of her apartment. The living room, or great room, or whatever it was termed, was mammoth by anyone's standards. White stucco walls, a multitude of windows, and an inlaid-mosaic hardwood floor were just the beginning. The ceiling rose three stories high, crowned by a breathtakingly beautiful stained glass dome.

"Oh, my land!" Jess gushed, eyes agog. "I've gone and fallen down the rabbit hole!" She gazed around in wonder. "And the place is furnished, no less!"

Ty shrugged. "I guess when you're a millionaire, you can afford to buy new to go with your new house. Just pack your clothes and split."

"I wouldn't know," Jess murmured, "and I doubt I ever will."

There was a library with built-in, wall-to-wall bookshelves, several large lighted fish tanks, and an oriental rug. An overly spacious dining room with seating for a minimum of forty guests. A music room. An exercise room, still filled with workout equipment. And an immense game room, complete with billiard table, table tennis, dartboard area, two bowling lanes, a miniature golf game, a fully stocked wet bar, and room to spare.

"What? No polo field?" Jess joked.

"That would be out back, probably behind the tennis court," Ty jested.

Jess smacked a palm to her forehead. "Of course, what a dunce I am. No doubt, it's next to the eighteen-hole golf course."

Additionally, also on the ground floor, there was a family room, a sun room/conservatory, a fully equipped kitchen designed to send any cook into ecstacy, a pantry the size of a large country kitchen, three full baths, and a laundry room bigger than some laundromats. That still left the screened-in patio and the glass-enclosed, olympic-sized, in-ground swimming pool, complete with a three-tiered fountain in the center of it.

"Holy Moses!" Jess declared in disbelief. "Who lived here, and why would anyone in his right mind want to sell it?"

"Supposedly, it belongs to some big-name musician," Ty told her, "but the realtor didn't name names."

"You'd think a house this big would have maid's quarters, wouldn't you?" Jess commented.

Ty gestured toward an intercom system on the wall. "There's a caretaker's cottage somewhere on the property. Appropriately placed out of sight and sound of the main house, of course."

"Of course," Jess repeated numbly. "God forbid the servants should be quartered over the garage, or some such nonsense. They probably also have their own little golf carts, the better to rush to the house when they're summoned."

The second floor consisted of a dozen separate and complete bedroom suites, all with their own sitting rooms, baths, dressing rooms, and walk-in closets. Naturally, the largest and most elaborate of these was the master suite, which featured a skylight that encompassed nearly the entire ceiling over the sunken tub and bedroom sections.

Jess gaped. "I'll bet every airplane and helicopter pilot in a forty-mile radius has this place listed on his map, just for the fun of it. I can hear it now. *There's a traffic jam at Forty-fifth and Central, a three-car accident on the southbound freeway, and erotic activity in the bedroom near the bay. They're really going at it, folks. Someone get the hose!''*

Ty doubled over with laughter. ''Geez, Jess! Only you would think of something like that!''

She arched a brow at him. ''You think so? I don't. There are probably a dozen perverts who have taken up parasailing just to get a peek inside this bedroom. I wouldn't be surprised if they pay the birds not to poop on the roof, just so they can have an unobstructed view. Which brings another thought to mind. How in hell do you clean a skylight?''

Ty was still chuckling as he guided her out of the room. ''You let the rain wash it off, I suppose.''

At the far end of the hallway, an open staircase curved upward toward a partial third story. At the top of the stairs was another unique addition to the house—a circular observatory, with a domed glass roof and a large and obviously costly state-of-the-art telescope. Charts and graphs of stellar constellations papered the lower half of the walls, the part below the windows. Even the floor had sketches of star clusters and planetary revolutions etched into it.

''I see it, but I don't believe it,'' Jess breathed. ''Their own private observatory! It's . . . it's absolutely incredible! And just look at the view of the bay from up here!'' Then it dawned on her, and she turned to find Ty watching her expectantly. ''This is what you meant, with all those hints and songs about the moon and stars.''

Ty nodded, grinning. ''Yep. What's more, there's a full moon tonight. I ordered it just for you.''

Jess rolled her eyes. ''I appreciate it, but please don't break into song again. I really don't need to hear a chorus of 'Moon over Miami.' ''

''How do you feel about mooning Miami, instead?'' he teased, his eyes twinkling with merriment.

Jess grinned back, sidling up to him in a fair imitation of a vamp. "I say we go for it, big boy. We'll double-moon them. And if we send a few pelicans into shock, so be it."

Jess soon discovered that Ty had planned this weekend adventure very carefully, down to the finest detail. After they had unpacked, showered, and changed clothes, they took a walking tour of the grounds, and through the numerous decorative gardens. There were rock gardens, shell gardens, rose and flower gardens, even a formal English garden—with a multitude of shady arbors, statues, and fountains sprinkled amid the fragrant blossoms, on either side of the winding stone pathways. Trees and shrubs, mostly palms and flowering varieties, dotted the lawn in between the gardens.

There was no beach along the shoreline at the back end of the lawn. A retaining wall separated the land from the bay. A pier led out to a boathouse. "The realtor seemed relieved when I told him we wouldn't be needing the yacht," Ty mentioned casually, as they detoured the dock area.

Jess gave him a grateful smile. "Thank you, Ty, for being so understanding about my phobia."

"No sweat, sweetheart. You'd do the same for me."

There was no polo field or golf course, though they did pass a tennis court along the way. A peek into the seven-car garage was enough to send any car buff into a fit of envy. Though only four of the stalls were filled, they held, respectively, a Jaguar, a Porche, a Mercedes, and a Lamborghini. Ty was like a kid at a candy store window, all eyes and drool. Laughing, Jess finally managed to drag him away from them.

"Boys and their toys," she said with a wry grin. "You know you can't have one, so why torment yourself?"

"Why can't I have one?"

"Because you're going to be an accountant when you retire from football, and you wouldn't want your clients to think you're on the take, would you?"

He grimaced. "I suppose not, but they sure are sweet to look at, aren't they? Maybe I'll just test drive one, one of these days, just to see how it handles . . . and smells. There's nothing like the smell of leather.''

Jess chuckled. ''So buy an old saddle. It's cheaper. Or a pair of cowboy chaps. Now, I'd really like to see you in a pair of those sometime. Just the chaps. Nothing else but a touch of after-shave.''

Ty wagged his eyebrows playfully. ''Ooh! Getting kind of kinky on me, aren't you? That being the case, I don't mind admitting I'd like to see you decked out in leather sometime, too. But no perfume. I want to savor the scent of the leather when you get it all hot and sweaty.''

Their conversation alone was heating her up nicely. It promised to be a sultry evening, Florida temperatures aside. The sun was setting, painting the sky in a swirl of colors, as they returned to the house, hand in hand. Upon reaching the rear terrace, Jess was surprised to find the patio torches had been lit. A small table was already set for an intimate evening meal for two—complete with tablecloth, china, silver, and crystal. A single fat candle flickered softly in the center of a flower-ringed hurricane shade.

''Who did all this?''

''Would you believe elves?'' he teased, holding her chair and seating her.

''At this point, I'd believe almost anything,'' she rejoined.

Despite her statement, she was caught off guard when a trio of musicians, secreted away in a shadowed corner of the patio, began to play softly, serenading them. Jess's eyes lit up with her smile, and she blushed prettily. ''Ty! How marvelous! You really have gone all out, haven't you?''

''I was hoping you wouldn't find it too schmaltzy,'' he said with some relief.

''Actually, it's the most romantic thing that anyone has ever done for me.'' Her voice wavered slightly as she fought back happy tears. ''I adore it, and you for thinking of it.''

Dinner, all seven courses, was an elegantly catered affair, served by waiters who appeared instantly when needed, but remained out of sight otherwise. Jess was duly impressed, with the food and the service, though by the end of the meal she simply had to decline dessert.

"If I eat any more, I won't be worth anything for the rest of the evening," she warned. "All I'll want to do is sleep off all this delicious food."

"Then we'll save dessert for later," Ty said, pushing his chair from the table. He came around and helped her to her feet. "Come dance with me. That should work off a couple of ounces, anyway."

They danced closely, slowly, swaying to the music. The waiters swiftly and unobtrusively cleared the table, their departure practically unnoticed. The night grew darker, the stars brighter, the moon rising full and fat. The scent of flowers and salt air wafted on a light breeze from the bay.

Jess pillowed her head on Ty's shoulder. He nuzzled her neck with his lips, running his hands over her back and holding her close to him. Finally, with a sigh, he whispered, "I think we'd better send the musicians home, before things get too cozy."

Jess stepped back, reluctant to release him and this magical moment.

He brushed her cheek with his knuckles. "I know. Me, too. But there's more to come, sweetheart. Much more."

Retrieving two goblets and what remained of the bottle of wine, Ty led her off the terrace and into the dimly lit pool enclosure. With a gentle push, he directed her toward a small dressing room to one side. "Your swimsuit should be in there, if you want it. But be forewarned, we're going to wind up skinny-dipping anyway."

"I think I'll start with the suit," she decided, modesty prevailing, "and let you sweet-talk me out of it."

Ty's smile promised he would. "I'll wait here for you."

When she emerged, Ty had already stripped to his skivvies and was standing at the head of a tier of steps leading into the water. Only now, with the pool as a backdrop, did Jess perceive the full extent of the wondrous spectacle Ty had arranged for her. Dazed, she stared in dumbfounded amazement. Dozens of candles had been lit and spaced around the perimeter of the room, their flames magnified as they reflected off the prisms of water shooting up from the fountain in the center of the pool. Multicolored underwater lights further lent to the enchantment, but the crowning touch to this fabulous fantasy were the scores of blossoms floating atop the water. Lilies, magnolias, daisies, roses—all bobbing merrily to the tune of the fountain's spray.

Without a word, Ty held out his hand. Just as silently, as if in a dream, she went to him. Slowly, he led her—step by step—into the midst of shimmering beauty. His arms enclosed her. Hers wound around his neck, hugging him near as her tears joined the droplets of water drifting down on them.

"I hope those are tears of joy," he murmured, kissing a salty bead from her lashes.

"How could they not be?" she replied, her adoring gaze linked with his. "I'm completely overwhelmed! This is unbelievably marvelous! You have to be, without doubt, the most romantic man on the face of this earth, and I'm so happy that you're mine. Here. Now. If I live to be a hundred, I'll never forget this evening or stop loving you for it. With or without armor, you're my shining knight."

He kissed her quivering lips, tenderly and lingeringly. When at last he raised his head, he said, "Let's make it last, Jess. Enjoy it to the fullest. Feed the fire slowly, steadily, until it consumes us."

With his arms still around her, he guided her into a lazy, graceful waltz. The water swirled with them, lapping at her breasts in silken waves. The flowers spun like pinwheels, the petals brushing against their flesh like velvet paws. Jess was entranced, caught up in a dizzy haze, where nothing existed but her and Ty in this blossom-bedecked, watery wonderland. She didn't even think to object when Ty unhooked the bra of her swimsuit and tossed it out of the pool—or when he did likewise with the bottoms and his own briefs. It felt too glorious, having the water rush over her bare skin in an endlessly erotic caress.

At length, they found themselves standing near the center of the pool, caught in the spray of the fountain. Water rained down upon them as they came together in a passionate embrace. Mouth sought mouth; lips met and meshed. Tongues and limbs twined as, like two sleek otters, one wet body slid along the other in glad recognition. Searching fingertips stroked, fondled, aroused.

Grasping her by the waist, Ty lifted her. Against her water-cooled skin, his tongue was a fiery torch as it seared a path across her chest. She cried aloud as he tugged her nipple into his mouth, branding her with its fierce heat.

Wrapping her long, lithe legs around his waist, she anchored herself to him, tugging him nearer. He lowered her slowly, letting her glide down his torso inch by inch until she was fully impaled upon him. She arched backward, relying on his strong arms to hold her as she reveled in the feel of him so deep within her. Water pelted down upon her breasts, exciting her turgid nipples all the more, stoking the sensual flames higher still.

As Jess lay in his arms, her head thrown back, her breasts thrust upward, her face flushed with passion, she reminded Ty of some pagan princess offering herself to the gods. In turn, the sight of her like this struck a primitive chord in him—the urge to claim, to bind, to merge with her so thoroughly that she would remain a part of him forever, and he a part of her. It was all he could do to remind himself to go slowly, tenderly, to possess her with all the love in his heart.

Swaying with the gentle buoyancy of the water, he rocked his pelvis against hers. On a needy moan, she answered by shifting her body, lodging him even more firmly inside her, though that should have been impossible. Then she wriggled, rubbing her swollen nubbin of desire against him like a cat in heat, and Ty lost his fast-waning battle for patience. Clamping his hands to her hips, his fingers clutching her buttocks, he set a driving rhythm that soon had them both panting and grasping amid a froth of churning water. Time and again, he surged into her, as far as he could reach. Time and again, she welcomed him with savage eagerness, until at last the dam burst, hurtling them both down the swirling river of rapture.

When at last they washed up on calmer shores, Ty, weak-

kneed and wobbly, couldn't believe he'd actually kept his footing throughout their wild session of lovemaking. By all right
and reason, they should both have drowned, or at least taken
a good dunking and swallowed a ton of water. To his additional
surprise and satisfaction, rather than being traumatized by all
the splashing and turbulence in the pool, Jess—the lady with
the ingrained fear of drowning—was wearing an expression of
total contentment, reclining against him in boneless bliss.

Pure male pride lent him the necessary energy to carry her
out of the pool and lay her on a padded recliner. He flopped
down beside her on the tile floor, not even bothering to cushion
the hard surface with a towel.

It was several minutes before Jess ventured weakly, "Ty,
we're lying here as naked as Adam and Eve, surrounded by
glass walls. We really should go inside before someone happens
along and catches us in our birthday suits."

"I couldn't move right now if my life depended on it. If
somebody shoved a lit stick of dynamite between my toes, I'd
just lie here and wait for the bang."

She mustered a chuckle. "We already had the bang, and it
was a whopper." Listlessly, she managed to stretch far enough
to snag the towels he'd left on the deck and drag them nearer.
Keeping one for herself, she flopped another atop his belly.
"Here. Cover the important parts, and don't let me sleep past
noon."

"Hah! Think again, sexy lady. You can have a short nap,
just long enough to recharge your battery."

"Then what?"

"Then I'm going to let you seduce me again." He heaved
a theatrical sigh. "Oh, woe is me. Worn to a thread. It's a
tough job, but somebody has to do it." Before she could reply
to that, he said, "Yeah, I know. I'll say it for you. Wagara."

"So you finally figured it out, huh?"

"No, but I thought it must fit the situation somehow."

"Not this time. Not accurately, at any rate."

"I know what it should mean," he offered. "Women Assess
Guys As Really Adorable."

"Ha!"

"Really Amorous?" he submitted.

Jess wagged her hand back and forth, in a maybe/maybe-not gesture. "You would certainly qualify on both counts, but I couldn't say the same about other men, or other women's opinions of them."

"You're prejudiced in my favor," he allowed. "But I'm not complaining." Then, "In honor of the season, does it stand for Witches And Gnomes And Rascals Alert?"

"Cute, but wrong."

He tried again. "Whales' And Gorillas' Aptitude Range Achievement?"

"Not even close, funny man," she drawled past a yawn.

"World Aggregate Guarding Against Running Amok?"

Her sole response was a delicate snore.

Ty's lips crooked in a droll grin. "I really ought to patent this game as an alternative to over-the-counter sleeping aids—best when applied after really great sex."

CHAPTER 25

Forty-five minutes later, Ty woke her with a kiss. Before she could rise from the lounger, he slipped a gorgeous silk caftan over her head. It slid down her naked body in a sensual whisper.

"Ty, this isn't mine. Where did you get it?" she asked, thinking he'd found it in a drawer or closet and mistaken it for hers.

"It's yours," he assured her. "I bought it specifically for you. Do you like it?"

"It's beautiful. Thank you. But you're far too extravagant. Just renting this house must have cost you a small fortune."

"You're worth it," he told her, adding with a wink, "so far."

He carried the glasses and the wine, and she followed him upstairs, thinking they were headed for the bedroom. Rather, he took the extra flight of stairs to the observatory. In contrast to the rest of the house, this room was strictly utilitarian. No fancy furniture or decorative knickknacks cluttered it. Just a worktable, one straight-back chair, and a super-large beanbag chair. Ty lit the fat candle on the table and dragged the bean bag to the center of the room, pulling Jess down onto it with him. He poured both of them some wine and placed the bottle aside, on the floor.

"Here's to us, Jess," he said, offering a toast.

They snuggled together in the semidark, quietly admiring the display of bright stars and the luminous moon overhead. "It's heavenly," Jess sighed in complete contentment. "It just doesn't get any better than this."

"Don't bet on that," he debated. From the pocket of the robe he was wearing, he withdrew a rolled piece of paper, tied up with a silver ribbon, and handed it to her.

"What's this?"

"A star. Your very own star, named after you, and the certificate to prove it. There's also a chart showing where it's located. Later, if you want, we can take a peek through the telescope and try to locate it."

"Oh, Ty!" she exclaimed, throwing her arms around his neck. "How incredibly sweet of you!"

He indicated the paper again. "You want the stars? I'll get them for you." He pointed toward the sky. "You want the moon? There it is."

"You're spoiling me terribly," she warned him, lifting her lips to his for a quick kiss. "Moreover, how can I ever reciprocate, when you're offering such grand gifts?"

"There's only one thing I truly want," he said softly. From the same pocket, he extracted a gleaming long-stemmed rose, fashioned of silver. He held it out to her. "It's hinged. Open it."

She fumbled with the latch on the side seam until it gave and the rose split in half to reveal a velvet-lined interior. Nestled within was the same exquisite ring she had chosen at the Boston jewelers. Her heart skipped a beat. Did this mean what she hoped it did?

She didn't have to wonder for long. Plucking the ring from its nest, Ty reached for Jess's left hand. "Will you marry me, Jess? I love you more than I've ever loved any other woman, or ever will again. You're that other half of me that's been missing all these years, and now that I've found you, I don't ever want to lose you. Please say you'll be my wife."

Jess's free hand flew to her chest, as if to keep her racing heart from leaping free. "I must be dreaming," she murmured wistfully. "That, or that knock to your head did more damage than the doctors thought. Ty, you're the one who claimed you needed more time. Are you sure about this?"

"As sure and serious as death and taxes," he assured her. "I don't need time, Jess. All I need is you, and to know that you feel the same."

"I do," she breathed. "You know I do. I love you with all my heart and every fiber of my being."

"Then, you'll marry me?"

"Oh, yes!" she declared, her eyes glowing with joy. He'd scarcely slipped the ring onto her finger when she launched herself at him, nearly tipping both of them out of their slippery seat. She showered his face with kisses, chattering excitedly between pecks. "Just tell me I'm not going to wake up and find I've dreamed all this, or I'll be totally devastated. Tell me you won't regret this tomorrow. I know there are thousands of women prettier than I am . . . smarter . . . richer . . . with sweeter dispositions."

"But they're not you," he countered sincerely, holding her at bay by securing her face between his palms as he gazed into her eyes. "Not half as sassy, or feisty, or funny, or stubborn, or exasperating . . . or downright provocative. Only you have that unique blend of qualities that lures me like a siren's call. I couldn't stop loving you if I tried."

"Don't try," she pleaded, "because if you ever stop loving me, I'll die of a broken heart. For richer or poorer, for better or worse, you're all I'll ever want, all I've ever longed for— and right now I know I'm the luckiest, happiest woman in the world."

If anyone had previously predicted that they would celebrate their engagement by making love in an observatory in a multi-million-dollar mansion—in a twenty-dollar beanbag chair— they would never have believed it. But, wallowing in spilled wine, with the heavens smiling down on them, that's precisely what happened. Later, as playful as a pair of lovebirds, they found Jess's star, labeling it their symbol of good fortune.

Then they trooped, hand in hand, down to the master suite, where Jess found yet another delight awaiting them. At Ty's bequest, the housekeeper had readied the bedroom. Again, candles provided a soft, flickering light. The bed had been made up with satin sheets, now turned down invitingly to reveal a blanket of rose petals scattered across their creamy surface. Music played faintly, flowing throughout the room from concealed speakers.

The merry gurgle of water from the connecting bath told them that the whirlpool was ready and running, should they care to avail themselves of it. They did, submerging themselves in a flood of bubbles that soon rid them of the last residue of wine their lapping tongues somehow failed to swab clean. They toddled off to bed, much too satiated to make love again.

As they lay nestled together among the fragrant rose petals, Kenny Rogers' ''Lady'' began to play, and Ty sang along with it, making each word, each phrase, his own heartfelt pledge to her. Moved to tears, Jess knew it was true. She had found her knight in shining armor and, amazingly, won his heart for her own. Twined in each other's embrace, they drifted off to sleep beneath a blanket of twinkling stars, and the blessing of a love as full and radiant as the moon above them.

Jess woke the next morning to find her head pillowed on Ty's shoulder, and her left hand splayed across his chest. The first thing to meet her sleepy gaze was the wink of sunshine on the diamond ring gracing her finger.

''It's real!'' She all but sobbed the words.

''It had better be, for the price I paid.'' Ty's voice was just-awake gruff, as his hand clamped over hers, bringing her palm to his lips.

''That's not what I meant. It's just that last night was so marvelous, so absolutely storybook perfect, that I wasn't certain I hadn't fantasized the whole thing—until I saw the ring.''

''Having second thoughts?''

She raised her eyes to his. "No. What about you?"

"I've had third and fourth thoughts already," he admitted, "and I still want to marry you."

She smiled. "My mother may nominate you for canonization for falling in love with her homely daughter. Personally, if I wasn't so utterly giddy over the concept, I'd say you should probably be committed, instead."

"I am," he told her sincerely. "To you."

Jess's face glowed with happiness. "That's what I find so remarkable. You . . . wanting me."

"There's nothing complicated about it, Jess." He turned her hand to kiss her finger and the ring it bore. "I'm finally learning to appreciate quality over quantity, thank heaven. And believe me, lady, you're the genuine article. Nothing false or fake or feigned about you—except a little stuffing in your bra, of course," he taunted with a smirk.

Lying on one arm, with him holding tight to her other hand, she retaliated for that last remark by kicking him lightly on the shin. "Watch it, buster. You're the one who suggested the falsies to start with, and don't you forget it!"

He chuckled. "Hardly. Not with you around to remind me for the next fifty years or so. Maybe you'll mellow with age."

She let loose an indelicate snort. "Don't plan on it. More than likely, I'll be as cantankerous at eighty as I am now, or more."

"That's precisely what I love about you, darlin'," he drawled. "Everything's right up front with you. No trickery. No flattery. No pretense. Just pure, ornery, honest, wonderful Jess."

"That's just part of why I love you," she confessed.

He grinned. "Let me guess. You love my fabulous body."

To his surprise, she agreed with a vigorous nod. "Sure do. You're the most gorgeous, sexy hunk I've ever seen. But I love you for your quick intelligence, too, and your playful, wacky sense of humor, and the fact that you're incredibly romantic— and the way you are with Josh, your loyalty to your friends, your passion and compassion, and a million other reasons."

He laughed heartily. "You make me sound like a big, horny St. Bernard!"

"So trot out a cask full of hot coffee, will you?" she suggested teasingly. "It's too early for brandy. Besides, we've got a practice and a game to play today, and I'm already drunk enough—on love."

They had a terrible practice, followed a few hours later by a superb game. It was just one of those crazy games where everything they did went right, and everything the opposition tried went wrong. For a new team to beat the Dolphins was practically unthinkable, but they came away with a 42-39 victory, nonetheless. Then, like the good sports they were, the Dolphins turned around and invited the Knights to a Halloween costume party they were having that evening.

"They probably want to spike our punch, then tar and feather us," Jess joked as they headed toward the visitors' locker room.

"I noticed they waited to invite us until it was too late for any of us to rent or buy a decent costume," Ty pointed out with some irony. "All the stores are closed."

"No problem," Jess told him. "If you want to go, we'll think of something."

Ty shrugged. "I wouldn't mind putting in an appearance, at least. We wouldn't have to stay long, but it's nice to get together with other players from other teams now and then and catch up on some of the NFL scuttlebutt."

"That's okay by me." She checked her watch. "You're right. Even Kmart is locked up by now." She thought a moment. "If you can find a twenty-four-hour grocery, we can purchase a few things there and make do."

"What sort of things?"

"Makeup, tape, glue, whatever. I'll know when I see it, I guess. Oh, and don't turn your uniform in. Bring it with you."

To say Jess was resourceful was an understatement, Ty soon discovered as he pushed their cart down the grocery aisles. "Aluminum foil? What's that for?"

"For you."

"Pardon?"

"You'll see. Now hush. I'm trying to concentrate, so I don't miss anything we need." She tossed a roll of colored cellophane wrap into the cart and hurried on.

In the automotive section, limited as it was, she found a large metal funnel. Into the cart it went, along with some speckling putty and a small squirt-type oil can. When Ty, trying to be helpful, reached for a quart of motor oil, she smacked his hand. "Don't need that."

"You sure? I'm just guessing here, but don't you have ideas of presenting one of us as an auto mechanic?"

She laughed and shook her head. "Too mundane, James. You've got to be more imaginative than that."

In the stationery aisle, she selected tape, a bottle of glue, a pack of paper clips, and a pouch of colored markers. In the adjacent, if scanty, art section, she rummaged around until she found a single jar of gold sprinkles hidden at the back of the lower shelf and heaved a sigh of relief. "Whew! For a minute there, I thought I'd have to resort to moth crystals, or those thing-a-ma-gigs you hang in the toilet bowl."

"Say what?"

"Never mind." She waved him off and charged onward, a woman on a mission. Locating the guaranteed-to-break-in-five-seconds toy area, she chose a bag of fake coins, a bottle of blowing bubbles and a plastic pinwheel on a stick.

"Lawrence Welk, perhaps?" Ty hazarded, eyeing the bubbles.

"Get real," she scoffed. "Okay, where are the cleaning supplies? I need a new head for a dust mop, a really shaggy one."

"You need a new head, regardless," he muttered, trailing along behind her.

Among what was left of the Halloween novelties, she found three sets of ghoul's teeth. "Ho, ho! Perfect!" With a wicked chuckle, she popped them atop her growing mound of supplies. Next, she tackled the cosmetic rack with a vengeance.

When they left the store thirty-five dollars lighter, and toting a bulging bag of assorted "goodies," Ty was still in the dark as to what was cooking in that screwy brain of hers—and, cute but obstinate cuss that she was, Jess wasn't about to tell him until they reached the privacy of the mansion. And with good reason. He'd likely have caused a six-car collision if she'd confessed while he was driving.

"I'm going as *what?*" he bellowed in disbelief.

"The Tin Man," she repeated sheepishly, waving the aluminum foil box at him. "You know, from the *Wizard of Oz.* You have seen it, I hope."

"Only about a dozen times." He gestured toward the mop head. "Tell me that's not part of my costume. As I recall, the Tin Man didn't have bushy hair."

"No, that's for me," she told him calmly, sounding much like a teacher speaking to a slow student. "This is yours."

He nodded as she produced the funnel. "It figures," he groused. "So, what are you dressing as? Dorothy? Toto? The witch?"

"Nope. I'm going as the Rotten Tooth Fairy."

He shook his head, sure his ears were playing tricks on him. "The Tooth Fairy?"

"No, the *Rotten* Tooth Fairy," she stressed. "There's a difference, you know."

"Actually, I didn't," he admitted in bafflement. "However, I'm sure you'll enlighten me."

"I'm the fairy that collects all the kids' rotten teeth. The ones not worth as much, because they're decayed."

Ty sighed, and pinched the bridge of his nose, where a headache was threatening. "Right. Why didn't I know that?"

"Beats me. Now, we'd better hurry, or we'll never be ready in time." She hurried out of the room, headed for the patio. "Come on. You can help me collect some ashes from the barbecue grill. If there aren't any, I suppose we'll have to burn some paper in it, or something."

He chased after her. "What for? What do we need ashes for?"

"To make the speckling gray. It's part of your costume."

"What part?" he demanded, not sure he wanted to know.

"Your makeup. For your face."

He groaned. "I didn't want to hear that."

"Then why did you ask?"

"Because I'm as nuts as you are, I guess."

An hour and a half later, they were ready to leave the house, and Ty was praying they wouldn't have an accident and end up in the hospital—or worse yet, get mugged. Being robbed would be bad enough, but in this getup he'd be thoroughly humiliated.

"Tin Man, my blooming ass!" he grumbled. "I look more like that character on 'Captain Kangaroo.' What was his name? Tom something."

"That was before my time, I'm afraid," Jess commented blithely, making him feel ever so much more—decrepit.

"Maybe we should just skip this party," he suggested belatedly, catching a last glimpse of himself in the hall mirror. He was wearing his football shoes, minus the cleats, along with his gray uniform pants, socks, knee and elbow pads. From the waist down, he looked pretty normal. It was the upper half that gave him pause.

After some squabbling, Jess had finally agreed to let him wear a T-shirt, over which she'd wound several layers of tin foil—completely covering his chest and his arms with it. She'd left his elbows bare of the stuff, covered only by his elbow pads, so he could at least bend those without crinkling like a cheap TV dinner. Then, she'd plastered his neck, face, and even his hair with gray putty, covered his hands with silver eye shadow, painted two huge circles on his cheeks with bright red lipstick, and pinned the funnel to the top of his head.

"Hey! After all the effort I put into this, we're going to this party," she told him, not about to let him weasel out of it at this late date.

"I look ridiculous!"

"And I don't?" she replied, drawing his attention to her own costume.

Until now, Ty's mental image of a tooth fairy had been of some beautiful winged creature. Nix that idea. Before him stood the most atrocious example he could ever have imagined. After donning her caftan, inside out, Jess had fashioned cellophane wings with the aid of several coat hangers. This, by itself, wouldn't have been too horrible. But then, she'd gone off the deep end by adding the mop head as a wig, creating "warts" made of putty, which she'd tinted dark brown, and applying her makeup in the most hideous manner. Her eyebrows now resembled two squiggly caterpillars over a double arch of neon green eye shadow. Huge purple "bags" beneath her eyes gave the illusion that she hadn't slept in three months. Her lipstick looked as if it had been applied by a preschooler just learning to fingerpaint, and she'd blackened one of her top front teeth.

"You are, indeed, a fright," Ty agreed. "Enough to give any poor kid nightmares for the rest of his life, especially if he found the likes of you hovering over his pillow. He'd probably wet the bed into puberty after an experience like that."

"Yeah, but I'll bet he'd lay off the candy and start brushing regularly," she predicted with a "toothy" cackle. "He wouldn't want me collecting any more of these, would he?" She patted the Zip-Lock baggie hanging from her cellophane belt. It was filled with ghoul's teeth. Another bag contained the play coins, and a third held gold sparkles, aka "fairy dust." She was carrying her bubbles, as well as the pinwheel, her makeshift wand.

"No offense, sweetheart, but you're a real hag this evening."

"You're kind of a rust bucket yourself, fella," she retorted sassily. "Don't forget your oil can. We wouldn't want your old joints to freeze up."

CHAPTER 26

"Lord, I've never seen anyone with such a low tolerance for alcohol," Ty commented with a rueful shake of his head. "You're sloshed."

"I know," Jess agreed, blinking as the white lines on the highway made her even more dizzy, "and I only had a couple of drinks."

"Well, it's a good thing we didn't stay any longer. I was planning on another marathon love session, but it looks as if I'll have to sober you up first—and wash this gunk off both of us. Somehow I can't visualize the Tin Man making love to the Rotten Tooth Fairy."

"I'm . . . I'm starting to feel awfully odd," Jess said, her voice quivering.

"Do you have to throw up? Do you want me to pull the car over?"

"No. Just get us home. Maybe if I lie down, everything will stop spinning."

"We'll be there soon," he promised. In an effort to divert her attention from feeling ill, he began talking about the party. "It was a pretty nice turnout, don't you think? And some of those costumes! Once I got a gander at a few of them, I didn't look half bad. Neither did you, but I thought that crack Bambi made about you actually being a fairy was out of line. Not out of character for her, but definitely in bad taste. So was her outfit, come to think of it, though I have to give her some credit for ingenuity.''

Bambi had pinned palm fronds to her thong/bikini underwear and gone as Eve. She had even carried an apple, and dared to offer Ty a bite of it. He'd declined as politely as possible, but she was still ticked off, though not nearly as mad as when she learned that Ty and Jess were now engaged.

Jess hadn't spoken at all in the past few minutes. He glanced over at her, to find her holding her arms out and staring at them in fascination. ''You still with me, babe?''

''This is amazing!'' she enthused in a dreamy tone. ''I can actually see the blood flowing through my veins. It's kind of bubbly, like Christmas lights, and the colors are really neat! But I wish my heart would stop making those funny little bumps. It feels really weird.''

Her off-the-wall comments stunned him into silence. Then it dawned on him. She was hallucinating! With mounting horror, he concluded that she was likely having heart palpitations as well.

''Oh, holy shit!'' he cursed. He stepped on the accelerator, careening across three lanes of traffic to take the next ramp off the freeway. ''Which way? Which way?'' he muttered to himself, trying to remember which exit along their route was the one for the hospital. They had passed it a couple of times before, on their way to and from the house, but it took him a second to recall exactly where it was. ''Not this one. Two up,'' he decided, hoping that he was correct.

He pulled back onto the highway, horn blaring as they sped along in the right-most emergency lane.

''Oooh!'' Jess clamped her hands over her ears. ''Stop the noise! My ears! My eyes! The blood's pounding so hard in them.''

He didn't doubt it; but he couldn't take the time to soothe her, and he had to warn other drivers to stay out of the way. He saw the sign for the hospital and took the exit on two wheels. By this time, Jess was mumbling incoherently. A chill chased up Ty's spine when he realized she was holding a conversation with her dead father.

"Hang in there, Jess. We're almost there."

He screeched to a stop in front of the emergency entrance and had her out of the car before anyone could come to their aid. Rushing into the hospital with Jess, now unconscious, in his arms, he yelled, "We need help here! Now!"

A pair of nurses answered his panicked call, hurrying up to them. One ushered him past the automated hall doors, into a small room. "There. Lay her on the table."

The second nurse started firing questions. "What do we have here? A wound? Gunshot? Is she bleeding?"

"No," Ty panted out. "We were at a party. I think someone might have slipped something into her drink."

An intern, appearing in time to hear, shouldered Ty aside. "Damn! Another O.D.? I hate this frigging holiday! What did she take? How much?"

"I don't know. Jess doesn't do drugs. She wouldn't touch them with a ten-foot pole. At least not knowingly. Someone must have spiked her punch."

"Yeah, that's what they all say."

"She started hallucinating in the car. That's when I knew she wasn't just drunk," Ty elaborated. "She said her heart was pounding out of rhythm."

Another woman in uniform came in and drew Ty aside while the doctor and first two nurses continued to examine Jess. "Sir, I need your friend's name and address, her social security number and/or insurance information, and a list of anything she might be allergic to. Also, do you know her next of kin and how to contact them?"

"I have no idea if she's allergic to anything," Ty responded tightly, "and I don't know her social security number. Her name is Jessica Myers. We're from Columbus, Ohio—in town for the game. I can't remember the name of our insurance carrier, but it's whichever one covers the Knights."

"The football team?" the intern called out. "She's that Jess Myers? The kicker?"

"Yes."

"And who are you?"

"Ty James. Jess's fiancé."

"The quarterback. Well, Mr. James, if we pull her through this, I'll expect an autograph from both of you."

Ty didn't like the sound of that. *If* we pull her through. "You'd damn well better do something, and fast, or there's going to be hell to pay."

The ward clerk patted his arm, trying to calm him. "They'll do their best, sir, but sometimes these things are touch and go. Why don't you come with me? You can wait in the hall, out of the way. Perhaps you should phone her parents and alert them."

Ty shook his head. "I'm staying. I'll call her mom as soon as I know Jess is going to be okay."

From the exam table, where they were hooking Jess up to a monitor, the doctor grumbled, "What is this tangle of wire she's wearing? Get her out of it."

"Her wings," Ty replied, his voice cracking. "Those are her blasted tooth fairy wings."

"She'll be lucky if she's not wearing another kind before the night's over," the doctor predicted. Then, as if his prophesy had triggered a reaction, he exclaimed, "Damn! We're losing her! There's no pulse! Get the defib over here, stat!"

The ward secretary pulled Ty out of the way as a nurse brushed past him to pull the machine to the table. Ty watched numbly as they readied the paddles. "Please, God. Please, Jess," he sobbed, unable to formulate an actual prayer.

Through his tears, he saw her body lurch off the table as they tried to shock her heart back into action. Once. Twice. On the third attempt, they got a heartbeat, and Ty released the breath he hadn't even known he'd been holding.

"She's back. For now," the intern announced tersely. "But we've got to get this shit out of her system." He jerked his head toward Ty. "You. Go call her mother. Find out if she's allergic to anything, particularly medication. I don't want to save her only to kill her by administering something else she shouldn't have. And get her permission to operate—just in

case. We shouldn't have to open her up, but it's best to be
prepared, on the off chance of hemorrhage or some other com-
plication."

Loath to leave Jess's side, Ty obeyed the directive anyway.
There were no two ways about it. He had to call Claudia.
Though he dreaded telling her, she had a right to know that
her only daughter's life was hanging by a thread—and the
hospital needed information only she could provide.

He tried to compose himself as he dialed the number, but
the moment he said her name, Claudia knew from the sound
of his voice that something was terribly wrong. "Tell me
straight out, Ty. I know it's Jess. Is she . . ."

"She's in the hospital, here in Miami. They need to know
if she's allergic to any medication . . . and they want permission
to operate if necessary."

"What happened? Were you in an accident?"

"No. We went to a party. We think someone slipped her
some drugs. The doctor is working on her now."

There was a stunned silence, then, "Oh, my God! Is she
conscious?"

"Not yet. She was, until just before we got to the hospital.
Claudia . . . her heart quit. They had to . . . to shock her back
to life."

"I'm coming," Claudia vowed through her own tears. "Tell
her I'm on my way. Tell the doctor she's only allergic to
strawberries, and to operate if they have to."

"Wait! The nurse is right here. She needs to hear you give
permission."

He turned the phone over to the nurse and hurried back to
Jess. They were still working over her at a feverish pace. "How
is she?"

"Do us a favor, Mr. Touchdown, and don't ask us that every
two seconds," the doctor said. "We'll tell you when there's
any significant change you should know about. Did you get
hold of her mother?"

"She gave permission for any medical treatment and said
Jess is only allergic to strawberries," Ty related.

"Good. So, this is where we're at. We've pumped her stomach, hooked her up to an IV and the monitor, and now we're going to sit back and see how it goes. You can sit with her, if you want. Talk to her. Let her know she's safe. If she regains consciousness, call the nurse. The monitor will automatically signal the desk if she goes into arrest again, so don't panic and charge out of here with your tail on fire. We'll be on our way before you clear the door.'' He headed out of the room, then turned and added, ''By the way, there's a rest room down the hall if you'd like to wash that gray stuff off your face, assuming that's not your normal complexion.''

''Thanks, but you still haven't answered my question. Is she going to be all right?''

''We won't know that for a few hours yet, but it helps that you got her here as quickly as you did. The longer the wait, the more drugs enter the bloodstream. She's also fortunate that she consumed the drugs orally. Via injection, we're talking a direct hit to the veins. Just for the record, I did check, very thoroughly, for needle marks. The cops always like to know these things.''

''Cops?'' Ty repeated, still in a daze of worry. ''I guess I ought to call them, too, in case anyone else at the party—''

The doctor cut him off. ''We've already contacted them. Primarily, it's a first come, first serve basis, but they'll get around to you eventually. In the meantime, we'll be keeping an eye peeled for any more of your friends who might come stumbling in here in the same condition. So far, Miss Myers is it, at least from your group. Now, if you'll excuse me, we've got a slew of kids, candy, and stomachs to x-ray. God, I hate this stupid holiday.''

Ty moved his car from in front of the emergency entrance, availed himself of the bathroom, and then stationed himself at Jess's bedside, prepared to stay the duration, however long that was. Half an hour later, the police arrived, their demeanor bordering on the blasé as they took his statement, got the location and names of participants of the party, and left. Ty figured they must get this type of call on a regular basis. It was probably no big deal to them anymore, especially compared to rapes, murders, and the like. But they had assured him they would check it out, if only to make certain other people hadn't unwittingly consumed drugs.

"More than likely, Miss Myers got hold of someone else's drink," the older officer presumed. "That, or some idiot thought it would be fun to spike the punch and space everyone out as a Halloween prank."

"An awfully expensive and dangerous prank, if you ask me," Ty said.

"Yeah, you'd be amazed at some of the calls we get, though," the fellow added. He wound his finger aside his head, and quoted, "This is your brain on drugs."

Three hours later, Claudia and John tiptoed into the room, looking frazzled and frantic. "How is she? Did she wake up yet?"

Ty shook his head. "Not yet, but they haven't had to call another code on her, either. She seems to be holding her own."

Claudia approached the bed, leaning over the side rail to brush Jess's hair from her damp forehead. "My poor baby," she crooned. Then, to Ty. "She's soaking wet."

"I know. The nurse told me it's a good sign, that she's sweating the drugs out of her system. We've been wiping her down and changing the pads under her to keep her more comfortable."

Perhaps it was the sound of her mother's voice that finally brought her around. Jess opened her eyes slightly and managed a wobbly smile. "Mom." She winced. "My throat's sore. I don't want to go to school today." Immediately, she dropped off to sleep again.

Claudia, tears filling her eyes, caressed Jess's cheek. "That's all right, sweetie. You just rest and get better. Mom's right here, and I love you."

Ty buzzed for the nurse. Upon learning that her patient had regained consciousness, however briefly, she noted Jess's vital signs again and ran a few quick checks. "Her reflexes appear normal, her pupils are responding much better, and her pulse seems less erratic. All pointing toward recovery. You say she spoke? How did she sound to you?''

"Hoarse," Claudia answered. "She said her throat hurt."

The nurse nodded. "That's typical. We pumped her stomach. But you could understand what she was saying?''

"Her voice was somewhat slurred, but yes," Ty contributed.

"Good. If she's a little disoriented, don't worry. At least she's able to speak and think, which is a definite plus.''

John spoke up. "You thought perhaps there might be brain damage?''

The nurse was noncommittal, saying only, "It's been known to happen.''

Ty drew a shaky breath. "Does this mean she's out of danger?''

"Not necessarily," the woman qualified, "but her chances have improved dramatically. Let me know when she wakes again.''

The three of them kept their faithful bedside vigil, but Jess slept on. Somewhere around one in the morning, the police officers returned to speak with Ty again. "The party was still in progress," they reported. "As far as we can tell, no one else has suffered any ill effects, so it was probably an isolated incident. Likely just a quirk, like we said before.''

"Unless someone deliberately chose to harm Miss Myers," the second officer noted. "Did she, or you, offend anyone there? Was anyone particularly nasty?''

"Only Bambi, one of the Knights' cheerleaders," Ty told them. "But that's nothing out of the ordinary. She's been jealous since Jess and I started dating, and that's been months now, though it didn't set too well when she heard Jess and I became engaged.''

"Since when?" Claudia asked in surprise.

"Since I proposed and gave Jess a ring Saturday night.''

"Maybe we ought to have a talk with this Bambi," the first

officer decided. "Do you know her full name, and where we might find her?"

Jess slept until four o'clock that morning, woke briefly, and went back to sleep for another few hours. Around six-thirty, the same two police officers stopped by for another chat with Ty.

"Tell us more about this altercation between you, Miss Myers, and Bambi Shultz at the party last evening."

"There wasn't any altercation," Ty corrected. "Just a couple of nasty remarks tossed around. Bambi called Jess a fairy, alluding to more than her Halloween costume. Jess returned the compliment by calling Bambi, who came dressed as Eve, a tart. I refused a bite of Bambi's, aka Eve's, apple. Bambi hit the ceiling over our engagement, wishing us both misfortune, and that was that."

"What time did you and Miss Myers leave the party?"

"I can't pinpoint it precisely, but I'd estimate about fifteen or twenty minutes before we arrived here. Frankly, I was driving like a bat out of hell, once I realized that Jess was hallucinating," he admitted.

"Did you speak to anyone just prior to leaving the party?"

"I recall thanking a couple of the Dolphins for inviting us, and Jess stopped on the way out to say goodbye to Pepper, the Knights' head cheerleader. Why? Just where are you heading with all this?"

"We'll ask the questions for now, if you don't mind. Did you, at any time between your arrival at the party and your departure, leave the party and return?"

"No. We stayed for a couple of hours, then left."

"Did you and Miss Myers become separated from each other during this time?"

"Only when Jess went to the ladies' room." Ty frowned. "Would you mind telling me why you're asking?"

"In a minute," the officer said. "While Miss Myers was visiting the bathroom, did you step outside with Miss Shultz for a brief liaison, perhaps?"

Ty glowered. "If that's what Bambi told you, she's lying through her teeth. When is that woman going to give up and stop trying to make trouble between Jess and me? It makes me wonder if she spiked Jess's drink, out of pure spite."

"That's occurred to us, too, along with a few other possibilities. One more question. When was the last you recall seeing Miss Shultz?"

Ty shook his head. "I don't know. Sometime during the party. I couldn't say if she was still there when we left."

"We understand from the nurses that you were quite a mess when you arrived last night. Gray makeup all over your face and hair and hands."

Ty gave a rueful smile. "Yeah. Jess made me up as the Tin Man. I did my best to wash it off, but it's going to take more than a quick splash over the bathroom sink."

"You've still got clumps of it in your hair and behind your ear," the officer commented. "Looks like it smears pretty easy, and tends to stick."

"And your point is?" Ty asked irritably. "Besides the fact that I'm in need of a hot, soapy shower?"

The two officers shared a look and a nod. "Okay, here's the skinny. We had to verify your story against other information we've gathered before we could rule you out as a suspect."

Ty gaped. "A suspect? You think *I* drugged Jess?"

"No, but we did wonder if you might have sneaked out of the party long enough to kill Miss Shultz."

Ty's eyes widened further, his jaw dropping. "What?" He practically shrieked the word. "Where? When? How?"

They ignored his query for the moment, preferring to relate the details in due process. "Despite the argument between Miss Myers and Miss Shultz, we knew your fiancée didn't do it. There was evidence of sexual intercourse, which naturally points to a man as the perpetrator. It appears that Miss Shultz either had a romantic interlude that turned ugly, or someone lured her outside with the intention of murdering her. A couple of guests looking for privacy stumbled over her body on the golf course behind the country club where the party was held. That was a few hours ago, after we last spoke to you."

The second man took up the tale. "Of course, we'd still like to compare your story with Miss Myers', but all things considered, the time frame doesn't really jibe. Moreover, if you were the killer, Miss Shultz should be smeared with that gray paste you were coated with."

"I take it she wasn't," Ty concluded.

The older man shook his head. "Nope, and it would have been fairly obvious, since the only clothing she had on at the time she was found was her bra. It was knotted around her neck. The coroner will be able to supply more details when he finishes the autopsy, and the news media will sniff them out, too, no doubt."

"So, I take it you're not about to read me my rights and haul me off in handcuffs?" Ty deduced, his voice laced with irony. "Or warn me not to leave town?"

"Nah. We know where to find you if we need to. Still, you might watch what you say to the reporters. They're going to have a field day with this one, no *punt* intended."

Ty heaved a weary sigh. "What else is new?"

CHAPTER 27

By late that afternoon, Jess was well enough to be transferred to a private room. After his own recent experience in the hospital, Ty was not about to rely on the hospital staff to see to her safety. He was determined to do that himself, even if it meant literally living in there with her for the next few days.

Jess put up only a weak objection. "Ty, you look like you're about to drop over. You need some rest, darling. In a bed, not a lumpy chair. Besides, Mom and John are here, too."

"John is flying back to Dayton tonight," he told her. "And let's face it. Your mom couldn't whip a bowl of overcooked noodles, let alone a man. I'm staying."

She smiled, and gave his hand a weak squeeze. "Good. I need you near me. I was just trying not to be a thoughtless wimp."

"You?" he teased. "My fearless Amazon reporter? No way."

When Jess fell asleep again, Ty did let Claudia and John take over, while he drove to the mansion and packed up their belongings. At Claudia's insistence, he used her and John's motel room to take a shower, shave, and change clothes. Also at her urging, he called his parents and Josh, told them that he'd asked Jess to marry him, and explained about Jess being in the hospital.

"You don't want them hearing about it second-hand, on the news or in the papers, in the same breath with that cheerleader's murder and Jess's so-called accidental overdose," Claudia admonished him. "The way the media distorts things, your family is liable to think Jess is some sort of junkie, for heaven's sake! Even if they don't believe the worst of her, that is not the ideal way to announce your engagement. As thrilled as I am for both of you, eavesdropping on your conversation with the police was not how I'd envisioned learning of my daughter's plans to marry. It's a wonder I didn't keel over, but I guess I was still too numb with fear that Jess might die for it to make the proper impact."

Jess wasn't released from the hospital until Wednesday, and then with strict orders to rest and avoid any physical or emotional stress for at least a week.

"Ha!" she scoffed. "If that doctor only knew! Stress is our middle name these days. It's become part and parcel of our everyday lives. I'm becoming so used to it that if a week went by without it, I'd be bored simple."

All three of them, Jess, Claudia, and Ty, flew back to Columbus together. Claudia insisted on staying with Jess, at least through the next weekend, to make sure she followed the doctor's orders.

"Mom," Jess protested, "you know how you hate sleeping on that futon . . . and what about John?"

"He can fend for himself for a few more days. Besides, he's already agreed. He'll drive down Sunday to pick me up. Meanwhile, you and I can have a nice little mother/daughter visit and get caught up on things. Like this recent engagement for instance," she added significantly. "Maybe we can get started on some wedding plans."

"Ty and I haven't even had time to decide *when* we want to tie the knot, let alone any of the other particulars. He just popped the question Saturday, and things have been rather hectic since then. We really need some time to discuss it together, at our leisure, first."

"Right," Ty agreed, jumping into the conversation. "Let's not get the cart before the horse."

Claudia was openly disappointed. "Well, it wouldn't hurt to browse through a few bridal magazines, would it? After all, we are talking about my only daughter's wedding, and if I'm footing the bill, I want it to be nice."

"You don't have to pay for anything," Ty assured her, trying to be amicable. "Between us, Jess and I can handle it."

Claudia's face clouded. "Now, listen here you overrated Romeo! I'm not some destitute bag lady. I fully intend to finance this wedding. And if you—"

"Mom, I'm sure Ty didn't mean any offense," Jess inserted hastily. "Did you, Ty?"

"Absolutely not. I simply thought that Jess and I are a little old to be having our parents pay for our wedding, especially when we're capable of doing it ourselves. Lots of couples are taking over that responsibility these days."

"Oh, well, that's different," Claudia said, partially mollified. "But I still want to pay for part of it. It's only proper."

"That's fine with this overrated Romeo," Ty replied with sardonic humor.

"Can we sort all this out later?" Jess submitted wistfully. "I'm supposed to avoid stress, remember? Besides, I'd prefer to handle one crisis at a time, if possible."

Ty went straight from Thursday's practice to Jess's apartment and announced, "I have good news and bad news. Which do you want first?"

"The good," Jess decided. "The bad, maybe never, depending on how awful it is."

"Gabe is out of the hospital. He might even be able to play a series or two in Sunday's game."

Jess beamed. "That's great! We ought to have him and Corey over for dinner, to celebrate. Mom, you'd help me prepare the meal, wouldn't you? Nothing fancy. Maybe spaghetti and meatballs? Of course, I'll have to check first, and make sure Gabe isn't on a restricted diet."

"Whatever we have, I'll do most of the work," Claudia insisted. "You are supposed to be taking it easy, young lady."

"I'm already turning into a lazy sloth," Jess complained. "Tomorrow, like it or not, I'm going back to work."

"Oh, no you're not!" Claudia declared adamantly.

"Try it, and I'll borrow Haggardy's handcuffs and cuff you to your bed!" Ty warned at the same time.

"Gee, you guys! Cut me some slack!" Jess exclaimed. "What's so hard about sitting at my computer and doing a little research? I'll be pounding keys, not railroad spikes, for crying out loud."

"You could have been more specific," Ty said, climbing down off his high horse. "I thought you meant football practice."

"I did, too," Claudia admitted. "I suppose a couple of hours at your computer wouldn't hurt, as long as you don't tire yourself." She turned to Ty with a grin. "Boy! For a minute there I could have sworn I was hearing Jess's dad laying down the law. You sounded just like Mike, Sr., when he had a burr under his saddle about something."

Jess's smile was a little wobbly. "He did sound like that, didn't he? They say, subconsciously or otherwise, a girl looks for a guy like her father. Do you suppose that's one of the reasons I fell for Ty?"

Ty wasn't buying it. "Because I yell at you? What kind of nonsense is that?"

"Nonsense or not, it wouldn't be a top priority with me," Claudia remarked. "Though I do like an assertive man. No mealymouthed wimps for me, thanks."

"Me, either," Jess agreed. "How can a gal have a good argument with a man who won't stand up to her? It would take all the fun out of winning. Which reminds me of something else I wanted to ask you, Mom. Have you talked to Tommy lately?"

Her mother frowned. "No, and what brought him to mind, may I ask?"

"You mentioning Dad, I guess. A while back, Tommy phoned me in his godfather mood and was haranguing me about this and that. I lost my temper, told him he didn't have any right to boss me around, that he wasn't my father. In response, he announced that he should have been, and hung up on me. It sort of rocked me, you know?''

Claudia groaned. ''Don't tell me he's back to grinding that old ax again? I thought once he'd married Anita, that was all water under the bridge.''

''Am I missing something?'' Ty asked in confusion. ''You've lost me.''

''In a nutshell, I met Tom before I did Mike,'' Claudia explained. ''We went out a couple of times, but nothing serious was developing between us, at least not on my side. Then, Tom introduced me to his best friend, and I fell for Mike like a ton of bricks, and vice versa. Though all three of us remained fast friends for over fifteen years, I think Tom has always held a bit of a grudge that he had first dibs and it didn't work out. But what can I say? He just didn't trip my trigger.''

''So he hangs that on Jess?'' Ty said in annoyance. ''Infers that she should have been *his* daughter? That's a crappy thing to do.''

''I thought so, too,'' Jess concurred, ''but I chalked it up to all the stress he's been under since Anita came down with Alzheimer's, and dismissed it. He's been in some awfully rotten moods lately, not his usual jovial self at all.''

''Perhaps I should talk to Anita while I'm here,'' Claudia suggested. ''Get her feel on things.''

Jess sighed sadly. ''She'd love seeing you again, Mom, if she's able to recognize you. From what Tommy says, she rarely has a good day anymore. He's been urging me to go visit, but I've been putting it off. I know I should be ashamed of myself, but I want to remember her the way she was before, so bright and vibrant.''

''You can go with me, if you want,'' Claudia offered. ''If Anita is in a muddled state, I suppose I could break down and talk to Tom personally, though I'd rather not. Still, he is your godfather, and he was there for us after your dad and brother died, even if it was primarily for his own selfish purposes. It can't be easy for him, seeing Anita deteriorate before his eyes.

Maybe I can talk him into joining one of those Alzheimer's support groups. But I swear, if Tom makes the first snide comment about John, I'll pop him one. I've had it with trying to convince him that I made the right choice, twice running, and that I will never want him in any romantic way."

"Good luck," Jess murmured.

"Speaking of luck, or the lack thereof, reminds me. Do you want to hear the bad tidings now?" Ty queried.

"Concerning what?" Jess hedged.

"The Knights. The stadium."

"Might as well," Jess relented. "Lay it on me."

Ty grinned devilishly. "I can't. Not in front of your mother."

"Stop fooling around, and tell us," Claudia directed with a mock scowl.

"While we were lolling around in Miami, some person or persons unknown took it upon themselves to revamp the stadium—and not for the better. They thoroughly vandalized the office area, and most of the vendors' stalls. Stole several rolls of preprinted admittance tickets and assorted merchandise. They upset files, desks, cash registers—everything that wasn't nailed down, and then some. Strew papers and food stuff and souvenirs all over hell's half acre. Then they stopped up the drains and toilets and turned the water on in all the rest rooms, including those in the locker rooms, overturned about half of the lockers, broke out windows, and made off with a variety of team equipment."

"Good grief!" Jess exclaimed. "All that?"

"Oh, that's not the sum of it," Ty proclaimed. "After they finished with the trivial ransacking, they went on to the field. Hacked up the sport turf and tried to set it on fire, broke some of the seats, and shot about a dozen holes in the overhead dome. All in all, the place resembles a war zone."

"So much for hoping to catch Tom in a good mood," Claudia muttered. "Even if the insurance covers most of the cost, I imagine it's going to take a bundle to restore the stadium."

"Not to mention time and labor," Jess added. "How could you even practice, with the field in such shambles?"

"Coach Danvers arranged for us to use the Ohio State field,

for practice only, and only when the Buckeyes aren't using it. Workers are already trying to clean up the mess at the dome. They've been at it since Tuesday morning. Hopefully, they'll get enough accomplished so we can play there on Sunday. If not, we may have to forfeit the game.''

"Where was our handy-dandy night watchman while all this was happening?" Jess inquired curiously.

"As I understand it, he'd taken Sunday off to attend a family reunion. His replacement didn't show up. Apparently, no one realized anything was wrong until a motorist reported hearing gunshots Sunday evening. By the time the police arrived, the vandals were long gone, having saved their noisiest shenanigans 'til last.''

"Wow!" Jess sat back on the couch and tried to imagine the extent of the damage, and the immense task of reparation. "Those were some very busy hooligans! Presumably not our best fans, either. Do the police have any idea who is behind it?''

"Not as yet, but they're hopeful, as always. By the way," Ty added nonchalantly, slanting a quick glance at Claudia before pinning his sharp gaze on Jess, "Haggardy sends his regards. He'll try to get by to see you around the first of the week.''

Jess frowned, but caught on quickly enough to say lamely, "That's nice.''

"Who's Haggardy?" Claudia asked.

"Just a team benefactor of sorts," Ty told her. Swiftly, he changed the subject. "Enough about the Knights and all their woes. I'm starving. Would anyone care to split a king-sized sub sandwich with me? I'll spring for it.''

Beyond all expectations, the work crews had managed to whip the stadium into reasonable shape in time for Sunday's game against the Kansas City Chiefs. The mess on the field had been raked up, and new turf laid. They had roped off the section of damaged seats, lashed tarps over the holes in the dome as a temporary measure, and replaced the broken lighting. Though many of the shops and refreshment stands were still

closed, the locker rooms had been restored enough to use. A
local printer had run off a new batch of tickets for this week's
game and was working on printing up the remainder.

While disappointed that Jess would not be playing, Josh was
tickled to be able to sit with her at the game. He also got to
meet Claudia and John for the first time, and promptly set about
charming the socks off his prospective grandparents.

The Chiefs were in a slump, which should have given the
Knights quite an advantage, if not for the disruptions in their
practice routines. As it was, by the end of the third quarter, the
Chiefs were leading by three points. Even with Gabe back in
action, their defense was effectively keeping Ty and his offense
from gaining much ground.

In the first series of the fourth quarter, the Knights made it
as far as the Chiefs' forty-five-yard line. It was fourth down,
and there was no way Sam Miller, the team punter who was
subbing for Jess, could kick a field goal from that range. It was
a rare kicker who could do it.

With the clock stopped for an injured Chiefs' player, Sam
was gearing up to punt when Jess leapt from her seat. "I can't
stand just sitting here! It's driving me crazy!"

In seconds, she had climbed the railing separating the lower
tier of seats from the team area and, with a hand from one of
the coaches, was down on the ground. Already wearing her
jersey, in support of her team, she marched up to Sam and
demanded, "Give me your helmet."

"What?"

"Just hand it over."

Danvers approached her at a lope. "Jess! What are you
doing?"

"I'm going to kick that sucker through those uprights," she
declared determinedly. "I'm still on the roster, aren't I?"

"Yes, but Ty's going to have a cow."

"Then we'll have beef for the winter, won't we?"

To Ty's astonishment, since he had yet to realize that Jess
was now in the game, the coach signaled for a field goal. "He's
out of his ever-lovin' gourd," Ty grumbled to Gabe. "Set up
for a fake."

That's exactly what the opposing team did as well, certain that's what the Knights' strategy was, now that their star kicker wasn't playing. Everyone was lining up in his slot when Ty looked back to find Jess in Sam's place. If his teeth hadn't been firmly rooted, he would have swallowed all thirty-two of them.

Jess merely grinned. "The ball, Ty. Set it," she reminded him just in time.

Through sheer instinct and all their practice, Ty caught the pitch and placed it properly. As her leg whizzed past his face, he got a glimpse of her bare foot and five pink-enameled toenails. Needing distance versus so much height, the ball skimmed over the fingertips of the Chiefs, who were leaping to block the kick. Like a rocket, it soared into the end zone, clearing the bar by a fraction of an inch.

The home crowd and the Knights went crazy. Jess had just tied the score and accomplished the all-but-impossible—a sixty-two-yard field goal! A mere yard shorter than the standing NFL record! Her teammates, Ty in the lead, converged around her to heft her onto their shoulders and carry her off the field.

"I ought to beat your fanny for pulling a stunt like this!" he bellowed over the cheers echoing throughout the stadium.

"Jess, you're a doll!" Gabe yelled.

"Can we have your foot bronzed?" Chili hollered.

When they finally put her down on the sidelines, Jess rounded on them, her fists on her hips and her features drawn into a scowl. "Okay, you guys, shape up and do the rest on your own! Don't make me come down here again and bail your worthless butts out of trouble. And win, dammit!"

Abashed, but grinning, they saluted her like a troop of well-trained soldiers. "Yes, ma'am!" they clamored as one—all but Ty, who was still glowering at her with smoldering blue eyes that threatened retribution.

CHAPTER 28

Bright and early Monday morning, Haggardy was rapping on Ty's door. Jess let him in, to find him standing there with a box of cinnamon rolls. "What's that? A peace offering?"

"If you want to look at it that way," he said, shouldering past her. "That was some field goal you kicked yesterday. You must be feeling better."

"She was, before she jammed her toe executing that barefoot kick," Ty said as he joined them in the living room. "Which is the only reason I didn't throttle her. I figured she was suffering enough for her stupidity."

Haggardy eyed Jess's bandaged toe and actually chuckled, a feat Jess had thought he couldn't perform without having his face crack into a million pieces. "Well, you won the game, by a single point, so I suppose it was worth it."

He sobered again and announced, "We found out who vandalized the stadium. It was a street gang. Some supposedly unknown party passed a note and a hundred dollars to one of the members. Left it on the counter at a local bakery run by the punk's family. I questioned him again earlier, and he still insists he doesn't know who left the note. Only that it informed him that the stadium would be empty and unguarded that particular night, and if his gang would vandalize it, they would be paid five thousand dollars. They did, and they were. The money was passed along in the same manner.''

"So that's why you appeared bearing donuts," Jess deduced. "Not out of any fondness or remorse."

Haggardy shrugged. "I thought of it as killing two birds with one stone."

"So, are the gang members in jail?" Ty inquired.

"Out on bail," Haggardy replied. "Par for the course." He accepted the cup of coffee Ty held out to him with a nod of thanks. "I've been trying to unravel this mystery, but everytime I think I've got a handle on it, something else pops up. Like that cheerleader being strangled in Miami. It just doesn't fit with the rest of the puzzle, not if we're going on the theory that someone is out to ruin the Knights. The stadium, I can see. Even Jess's overdose could apply, whether this Shultz woman was our culprit or not. But how would killing Bambi do any damage to the team? I mean, she's not a major player, a backer, or even dating one of the players."

"An emotional hit?" Jess suggested. "Another means of reinforcing fear, distrust, and dismal spirits among the Knights?"

"It's a thought," Haggardy conceded, "but my gut tells me there's more to it. I just don't know what."

"You sound as if you're not sure Bambi is responsible for spiking Jess's drink, either," Ty noted. "Any particular reason?"

"Oh, she probably did it, but I have to wonder if the idea was hers or somebody else's, or a combination of the two."

"You think Bambi could have been in on this whole situation from the start?" Jess surmised.

"At this point, I'm not sure who's in and who's out. There seem to be any number of people involved, and my suspects are getting bumped off almost as fast as the victims. First Dr. Johnson is our primary suspect, a person capable of hanging Ervin, tampering with the drug testing, poisoning Rome— perhaps even of shooting Crumrine, and knocking Ty in the head and attacking him at the hospital. But he can't be the one who sent you those last couple of threats, Jess."

He took a breath, and went on. "Now, Miss Shultz could have poisoned Rome. She had access to the locker room, and if she was in league with Johnson, he could have supplied the arsenic. Poison and drugs rank high as preferred methods of murder by females. They tend to shy away from anything involving blood and guts. She may also have killed Johnson, or aided in his demise—and sent you those threats, Jess, as well as dosing your punch. But Ty and the nurse on duty at the hospital both claim *their* assailant was a man. Moreover, Bambi was in the morgue in Miami when the payoff was made for vandalizing the stadium. So, we still have at least one assassin, if not more, on the loose, any way you cut it. It wouldn't surprise me to discover that one of them did Bambi in, for whatever reason. Maybe to keep her from blabbing."

"This is getting awfully complicated," Jess declared, trying to assimilate all of Haggardy's suppositions and mentally file them away.

"Isn't it, just?" Ty agreed. "So, we may have had two previous suspects—Johnson and Bambi—both out of the picture now, and neither responsible for the latest dastardly deed."

Haggardy gave a curt nod. "That's the way it looks."

"Am I still on your most-wanted list?" Jess inquired archly. "Could be I slipped myself a mickey, knowing Ty would save me, just to throw you a curve."

Haggardy smirked. "Then you're not as smart as I'm giving you credit for. As I hear it, you came within a hair of cashing in your chips for good."

"Yes, but Bambi may have done it solely out of jealousy, and had nothing to do with any of the other incidents. Her death may not even be connected to your case—just your run-of-the-mill Miami murder," Jess pointed out. "Which would put me back on the roster of possible criminals, wouldn't it?"

"Holy crap, Jess!" Ty exclaimed, throwing up his hands in exasperation. "Stop egging him on. Do you *want* Haggardy suspecting you?"

Jess released a catty smile. "No, I was just hoping he'd finally admit how asinine that presumption was from the start."

"Okay, so I jumped the gun a bit," the detective conceded. "I was just trying to cover all the bases."

"If that's an apology, I've heard better," Jess groused. "But I accept."

"Where to from here?" Ty asked.

Haggardy enumerated on his fingers. "Back to questioning those gang members, investigating disgruntled players and those cut from the team, analyzing evidence, going through a heap of paperwork with a fine-tooth comb, trying to keep the rest of the Knights alive, looking for more clues and possible motives. Believe me, I've got more than enough to do. Too bad they haven't perfected cloning, particularly for humans. I could use another me right about now."

Haggardy was right. There was at least one more bad egg rolling around loose. On Tuesday, he left a message on Jess's E-mail. "I'll get you yet." It was followed by a note with no postmark, left in her regular mailbox on Wednesday. "Your luck can't last forever." Both messages were addressed to her, not Ty, and both sent to her apartment, though she was spending the majority of her time at Ty's condo.

"I don't like this," Ty told her for the thousandth time. "This jerk has been to your place and personally put that last note in your mailbox. Why else would it have no postmark?"

As a matter of course, they turned the threat mail over to Haggardy, who advised the pair of them to exercise extreme caution, and for neither of them to go anywhere alone.

"We might as well be attached at the hip as it is," Jess informed him wryly. "Ty barely lets me out of his sight to use the bathroom."

Haggardy grunted. "Then he should go in there, too."

Thursday was blessedly uneventful, but the fact that it was only made the day all the more unnerving. Like waiting for the other shoe to drop. Then, on Friday, Ty and Jess arrived back at her place to find that her apartment had been broken into while they had been at practice.

"Don't touch anything!" Ty warned, as they stared at the shambles that stretched from the front door as far as they could see. "I'll call Haggardy."

"H . . . How?" Jess asked, her voice trembling—indeed, her whole body beginning to shake. "I d-doubt we can f-find the ph-phone."

On the off chance that the intruder was still inside, they went back outside. While Ty kept watch on the apartment, Jess used a neighbor's phone to call the police. Haggardy arrived within a quarter hour, with a team of back-up officers. Only after they ascertained that no one was inside, did Haggardy allow Jess and Ty to enter.

"Try not to disturb anything. Just look around, Jess, and tell us if you can spot anything missing."

"In this mess?" she exclaimed in disbelief. The vandal or vandals had gone through the apartment with a vengeance. Much worse than the police had done at the Rome household a few weeks prior. There wasn't a piece of furniture that wasn't overturned, the cushions sliced open and the stuffing torn out. The entire contents of her cupboards and refrigerator lay crushed and smeared on the kitchen floor. Her office had been totally demolished, books and research files ripped to shreds and thrown in the center of the room in a jumbled heap of paper. Her fax machine and computer had been smashed beyond repair—and all of her computer discs were gone!

"That's a start," Haggardy noted. "Now all we have to do is determine why they needed them. What was your current project?"

"I was trying to correlate all the data on the problems plaguing the Knights," she told him. "Doing background checks on everyone involved with the team. That sort of thing."

"Did you come across anything interesting?"

"Not that I could tell. Not yet, anyway."

"Who knew you were doing this?"

"Just Ty. I didn't tell anyone else."

"Then someone, knowing your skills as a reporter, must

have assumed you'd be working on it. That would account for the threats. They were trying to get you to back off. Now they want to know just how deep you've dug, so they've taken the discs. Did you keep back-up discs anyplace else?''

Jess nodded. ''At Ty's. On my laptop, and on a floppy.''

''I'll need copies of those, if you don't mind.''

Her bedroom hadn't escaped damage either. To Jess's mind, this was the worst. Not only had her clothes been yanked from her closet and drawers, they had literally been cut to tatters. Dresses, sweaters, underwear—not a whole piece among them. Her stomach roiled as she viewed it all. Her intimate belongings, handled and destroyed by some madman. She felt violated to the core of her being. If she'd been physically raped, it could not have affected her more deeply.

Then, among the litter of her life, she spotted the photo. It was lying on the floor, the glass shattered, the paper gouged in several places, as if the vandal had ground his foot into it in a fit of rage. With a cry, she fell to her knees, and despite Haggardy's warning not to touch anything, she scooped it up with trembling hands. Ty knelt beside her, holding her shoulders as she broke into anguished sobs.

''Who are they?'' Haggardy asked, not recognizing the people in the picture.

''Her father and brother,'' Ty related. ''They were killed in a boating accident when Jess was young. That photo is her most precious possession. I'd like to get my hands on the guy who did this.''

''Stand in line, James. You realize, of course, that this is no ordinary act of vandalism. This maniac is through messing around. It's personal to him now. In my professional opinion, no one carves up a woman's clothes like this, without visualizing doing the same to her.''

Jess's body stiffened in Ty's grasp as she let out a strangled whimper.

''Jesus, Haggardy!'' Ty exploded. ''What are you trying to do? Send her over the edge? Couldn't you have kept that disgusting bit of information between you and me? Do you get your jollies by scaring women witless, or what?''

"I want her scared," Haggardy went on relentlessly. "I want her to be looking over her shoulder at every turn. I want her to second guess everything she sees and hears from here on out—until we catch this deranged squirrel and lock him safely behind bars. I don't want her to trust anyone, not even her pastor or the little old lady down the block. Her life could very well depend on it."

"I'm aware of that," Ty shot back. "That's why she's moving in with me, where the security is tighter. If I have to, I'll hire a bodyguard for her. I intend to do my part, Haggardy. Now, do yours, and get this lunatic off the streets."

The one bright mark on the day was that among the chaos the police did turn up a couple of vital clues. Until now, all of the threats to Jess had been via phone, fax, E-mail, or notes made up of cut-and-pasted newsprint. Never handwritten or typed. He'd gotten reckless this time, however, and scrawled a message on the sink over her bathroom vanity. "Count the days. I am." More importantly, in the process of slicing up her clothes, the man had cut himself as well. They found several droplets of blood on the shredded fabric.

"I know it doesn't look like it to you, but I think we might have gotten our first big break," Haggardy said. "Even with the gloves and no fingerprints, we now have solid evidence against this bastard. He just screwed up."

Ty wasn't thrilled about having to fly to New York that night for their upcoming game against the Jets, but Jess was terrifically relieved to be getting away from the site of so much hatred and violence. "I really do need the change of scene, Ty," she convinced him. "I need the distraction, so I can regroup and be ready to deal with all of this once we get back home."

Another factor, all but overshadowed in the wake of the vandalism and Haggardy's dire warning, was that this Saturday was Ty's birthday, and Jess had something special planned, with Corey's help. She'd be damned if she'd let this faceless monster ruin it, as he'd laid waste to her apartment.

The flight was a late one, and she and Ty were fairly well washed out by the time they checked into their Meadowlands, New Jersey, hotel, just a stone's throw from the stadium. New York could wait until tomorrow. Tonight, all Jess wanted was to curl up in bed in Ty's arms and forget the trials and tribulations of today.

Saturday brought clouds and drizzle, not a great omen by any means, but Jess was determined to go through with her plans and make Ty's birthday a wonderful and memorable event. She hated seeing him so worried, so burdened, so constantly on edge—and now he'd decided that until this whole disaster was resolved it was too dangerous for Josh to continue his weekend visits to Columbus, which dampened his spirits even further. She was going to change that, to lighten his mood, if only for a couple of days.

After the morning practice, Jess was to meet Corey at Rockefeller Center, presumably for lunch and to watch her shoot a commercial, something which held little interest for Ty. Gabe's assignment was to keep Ty occupied elsewhere while the girls conducted their business on the sly. Corey, who had come to New York in mid-week to do a modeling shoot, had made all the advance arrangements. In fact, when Jess had been trying to decide what to give Ty for his birthday, it was Corey who had come up with the idea.

There were three routes into the city from New Jersey, none of which thrilled Jess—two tunnels and one bridge over the Hudson River. She opted for the bridge, the lesser of the evils in her estimation. Ty tried to convince her otherwise, to no avail.

"Honey, we'll be going out of our way if we take the bridge. The Lincoln tunnel is more of a straight shot. We'll get there a lot sooner, and I'll be there to hold your hand the whole time." He and Gabe were riding into town with her, to see that Jess hooked up with Corey safely. Then the guys planned to take the ferry to Liberty Island, an excursion Jess's fear of boats would not allow her to experience.

"No way," she told him firmly. "I'd be a blithering idiot in that tunnel, imagining all those tons of water surrounding

me. The bridge is going to be bad enough, thank you.'' She
scowled. ''Why did they have to build the blasted city on a
blasted island to start with? You'd think they'd have better
sense.''

Ty and Gabe shared an amused look. ''They've done okay
so far,'' Gabe pointed out.

''What's all that stuff you're lugging with you?'' Ty asked,
changing the subject. Jess was carrying an oversize tote bag,
crammed to the gills.

''Just a few things Corey suggested I bring along. Comfortable walking shoes, my camera, and the like.'' Actually, the
bag held several changes of clothing, though Ty didn't need
to know that. It would spoil the surprise if he did.

Corey was waiting for them when their taxi pulled up. ''You
fellows had better keep the cab while you've got one,'' she
advised. ''Jess and I can walk from here—and don't worry,
Ty. I'll watch her like she was made of gold.''

Ty was going along with this plan very reluctantly. He'd
only agreed because Jess had seemed so excited about spending
some time with Corey and watching her work. He supposed
Jess also needed a little space, away from him for a while, to
do her ''woman'' thing.

Ty consulted his watch. ''Okay, we'll meet back here at five
o'clock, right?''

''Sure thing.'' Jess leaned back into the cab to give him a
quick kiss. ''See you then. Have fun.''

CHAPTER 29

The taxi had scarcely pulled away from the curb when Corey grabbed Jess's arm and began tugging her along at a fast pace. "Come on, or we're going to be late. I told Blane I'd have you there by one, and we don't want to tick him off. After all, he doesn't do this for just anyone."

"Is he one of those temperamental artist types?"

Corey rolled her eyes. "Aren't they all? Even if they're not, they pretend to be."

They dashed into a building and caught the elevator just as the doors were about to close. Squeezed in like sardines with a dozen other people, they got off on the fifteenth floor. Upon entering an office halfway down the hall, the receptionist motioned them on. "Better hustle. He's waiting for you—very impatiently."

They burst through another set of doors, and Jess found herself in a cavernous room with no windows and no light, with the exception of a couple of bright lamps at one end.

"Watch your step," Corey cautioned. "There are wires and cords strung every which way." Indeed, the floor was littered with them. They picked their way through them, toward a man fiddling with one of the lights.

"Here she is, Blane," Corey announced. "Meet Jess Myers, latest darling of the sports world."

Blane strode forward and, without so much as a by-your-leave, caught Jess's chin in his fingers. Saying nothing, he twisted her head this way and that, studying her face. He stepped back, motioned for her to remove her coat, and surveyed her body from head to toe. "Nice and thin," he stated finally. "Good bone structure. We'll have to work on the makeup, though. Enhance her eyes more. And for God's sake, have Emma do something . . ." He fluttered a hand in the air, as if to grab the words from space. ". . . interesting with her hair. I trust you have your outfits and accessories?"

"Uh, yes." Taken aback, Jess couldn't formulate a more complete response, but it didn't matter. Blane was already waving them away.

"Good. We'll go with the uniform first. Corey will show you where to change, and get Emma started on you. Don't dally."

Inside the dressing room, Jess let out a breath. "Is he always so brusque?"

Corey grinned. "According to him, it's part of his charm. Let me introduce you to the real magician of the group. This is Emma, the lady who does our makeup, styles our hair, and helps keep our clothes in order. Emma, this is Jess."

Emma was a tad more congenial. "Glad to meet you, Jess. Now, strip down to your undies, tie this cape around your neck, and we'll get started."

Twenty minutes later, Jess couldn't believe the change, as she contemplated her reflection in the mirror. "I love what you did with my hair, but are you sure we didn't overdo it on the makeup?"

Corey, who was steaming the wrinkles out of Jess's clothes, laughed. "Emma knows best, Jess. Trust her. You have to apply more cosmetics than you would normally, or you'll end up looking like a ghost."

"I don't want to look like a streetwalker, either," Jess protested weakly. "I don't want Ty to be disappointed."

"He won't be, and neither will you when you see the final

results," Corey promised. "Now, shimmy into this top without mussing yourself."

Before Jess could object any further, she found herself back in that big, bare room, standing in front of several blazing hot lights. She wore nothing but her Knights' jersey, which ended at mid-thigh, red satin panties, and a pair of flesh-colored, stick-on supports beneath her bare breasts, designed to push them up and together without benefit of a bra.

Corey was off to one side, in the shadows, and Blane was attempting to arrange Jess's stiff limbs in just the right pose to suit him. "Loosen up," he commanded in exasperation. "That's a camera, not a gun. This is why I rarely work with amateurs. They're so awkward and timid."

By the time he was done contorting her, from her chin to her toes, Jess felt like a department store mannequin with a charley horse—not at all natural or relaxed. "This is ridiculous!" she muttered, trying not to move her mouth, lest Blane come back to readjust it. "I just want some pretty pictures of myself for Ty. This isn't for some magazine, for heaven's sake."

"I don't take pretty pictures," Blane said from behind his camera. "I take great photos, or none at all. Now smile. Show me some teeth. I said a smile, dammit. I'm not a dentist, I'm a photographer. Relax your shoulders. No, not that much. Now, think money. No? All right, how about mink? Diamonds?"

Corey stepped forward. "Let me try, Blane. I know Jess, and what she likes. Fifty dollars says I can get a real smile out of her the first time out."

"I'll pay it, gladly," he muttered.

"Okay, Jess. Think of Josh. You've been teaching him to kick, and he's just landed his first team goal." She pointed toward the camera. "Picture it. There's the ball, sailing into the soccer net, with Josh's footprint all over it, and you're bursting with pride. Show me how much."

Jess, completely pulled in by Corey's soft-touch coaching, reacted automatically. A smile wreathed her face, her eyes going bright and wide as she exclaimed aloud, "Way to go, Josh!" Deserting the pose Blane had chosen, she cocked one knee forward, thrust out her chest, and gave the camera a double thumbs-up.

Blane snapped the shutter. "Now we're onto something," he declared with satisfaction.

After they took a couple more, just for insurance, Jess changed into her caftan, the one she'd been wearing when Ty proposed to her. The nurses had cut it down the front, to bare her chest for defibrillation; but Claudia had carefully stitched it again, and the seam didn't even show. Jess was thankful that the caftan had been at Ty's on the day her apartment had been vandalized, or it would have been irreparable. Likewise, with her smiley-face swimsuit. Her black dress, the one Ty liked so well on her, had been at the dry cleaner's. She'd picked it up just prior to heading home Friday.

Blane could not understand why Jess, via Corey, had requested a big beanbag chair as one of the props, but he honored her wishes anyway. He shot a picture of Jess sitting in it, surrounded by softly glowing candles, her caftan draped in silky folds as she gazed dreamily at the ring on her left hand. For the photo of Jess in the black dress, Blane had her twirl round and round, as if dancing. He caught her on a turn, half-facing the camera, looking carefree and happy, her skirts flaring out around her long legs.

Next came an outfit Corey had picked up for her, so Ty wouldn't accidentally catch a glimpse of it ahead of time. Feeling more than a little silly, Jess wriggled into it and asked, "What do you think, Corey? Would I pass muster as a biker chick?"

Corey grinned. "If Ty's got a penchant for leather and lace, this is just the ticket, girl. He'll flip out. Are you going to model it for him when you get him all to yourself tonight?"

"I'll never tell. But if you hear things going bump in the dark, pay no attention. It'll be us, doing the bunny hop."

The outfit in question was constructed of black leather accented with silver chains. It consisted of a front-zip, sleeveless vest, combined with a pair of extremely short shorts, knee-high boots, and elbow-length gloves. Under it, Jess was wearing a slinky satin teddy, in a shade called champagne blush, decorated with tiny mauve ribbons and touches of lace.

Blane photographed her first with only the leather ensemble showing. He posed her sidesaddle on a big black-and-chrome Harley he'd borrowed for the shoot. Into the swing of it by now, Jess had no trouble portraying a brazen babe, decked out for her hard-riding guy. All she had to do was follow Corey's very innovative and suggestive promptings, and imagine Ty as that man. To her surprise, she was actually starting to enjoy herself.

There followed shots with the teddy half-exposed—then in the teddy alone. For this last set, Blane posed her amid a pile of satin pillows, with Jess half-reclined on them. "Think sex, Jess," Corey told her. "Hot, steamy sex. You're ready and waiting for him. Ty is fresh out of the shower, naked as a jaybird, and walking toward you. Envision him, Jess. Anticipate what is about to happen between you."

Unconsciously, Jess licked her lips. They were still dewy, her face flushed, her eyes gleaming with a come-hither glow, as Blane snapped the photo. Only after he'd caught the shot, did he exclaim huskily, "Damn if I'm not getting hard just listening to you, Corey! Do you have to be so graphic?"

Corey laughed. "Hey! Don't knock it! It's working, isn't it?" Jess slanted an anxious glance toward the photographer, and Corey chuckled anew. "Don't worry, Jess. Blane isn't going to go ape and jump your bones. He's gay, and proud of it."

The final few shots were of Jess alternately sitting and lying on a beach lounger in her smiley-face bikini. Blane changed the background to a sand-and-surf scene, adjusted the lighting to give her skin a slightly tanned appearance, and directed Corey to wet Jess down with water from a sprinkling can to give the effect that she'd just emerged from a pool. "I want languid here," he directed. "Slow and easy, sunbathed and sensual."

"Feel the warm tropical breeze," Corey added softly, "wafting over you like a lover's caress. You're dreaming of him, Jess. Erotic daydreams of the night before."

Back in the privacy of the dressing room at last, Jess heaved a sigh. "Wow! That's some imagination you have, Corey! You should be writing romance novels."

"Thanks for the suggestion. A couple of babies under my belt, and I might not be in shape to model anymore. Besides, I'd want to stay home and be a mommy then."

Jess stripped out of her suit and headed for the bathroom. "Boy, am I glad there's a shower in here. With luck, I can wash all this sweat, makeup, and hairspray off and look halfway normal by the time we meet the guys. If I can remember how I had my hair before Emma rearranged it."

"Not to worry. If Ty notices the difference, we'll tell him she did your hair while you were waiting for me. You know, Jess, these photos are going to turn out terrific. Much better than those glamour shots in all the malls these days."

"I hope so, but I still think it's a bit egotistical to give Ty pictures of myself for his birthday."

"Not at all," Corey assured her. "Besides, Blane is going to enlarge that snapshot of you and Ty and Josh at the zoo. Your first family photo. Ty will love the idea."

"And Blane is positive he can have them processed by this evening?" Jess fretted.

"He promised to have them hand-delivered to us at Windows on the World. I've already reserved a table for four for dinner at eight." After a short pause, she asked, "Are you certain you wouldn't rather dine alone with Ty? Gabe and I can duck out, if you'd prefer."

"No. I'll corner him later, when we get back to the hotel. Oh, and I hope we still have time for a bit of shopping. I want to find a fur-lined jock strap for Ty." She poked her head out of the shower to add, "Do you have any idea how hard it is to find a birthday present for a guy who already has everything? Something you can actually put in a box and have gift wrapped?"

Rain, snow, sleet—they had it all for Sunday's game, enduring four endless quarters of foul November weather, only to go into overtime and lose to the Jets. By the time they dragged their muddy, frozen tails back to the hotel and showered off most of the muck, Ty and Jess were looking forward to a stint in the sauna. Gabe joined them, as did Corey, whose teeth were still chattering from sitting in the stands the whole while. Dressed in men's and ladies' terry cloth wraps provided by the hotel, the foursome trooped into the sauna, fortunate enough to have it all to themselves.

"At least you guys got to run around and work up some heat," Corey complained. "We spectators nearly froze in place, like so many popsicles."

"Oh, stop whining," Gabe told her, giving her a swat on the rear. "You didn't take the battering we did out there on the field, slipping and sliding and getting knocked on our butts."

"No kidding," Jess said, rubbing at her aching posterior through the thick toweling. "I still can't believe I did that. Ran straight for the ball, and wham! Flat on my backside!"

Ty had to laugh. "You did kind of resemble Charlie Brown with that move, and unlike Lucy, I didn't even have to snatch the ball away. You slipped before you even got to it."

"I wouldn't laugh if I were you, hotshot," she retorted. "You spent more than your allotted time sucking up slushy mud pies."

"And I've got the bruises to prove it," he groaned. "Sacked three times! I'm definitely going to have a word with the front line about throwing better blocks and tackles."

"Ah, but doesn't this feel glorious?" Corey nearly purred. "All this blessed heat, soaking into our bones. I thought my toes would never be warm again."

"With me, it was my nose," Jess put in. "I had the biggest urge to hide it in Ty's armpit, until I took a good look at his filthy, sweaty self. I figured frostbite was preferable to asphyxiation."

"You could have borrowed his new jock strap," Corey said with a wide smile, "and worn it as a nose warmer."

"Uh, uh." Ty shook his head. "I was wearing it. By the end of the third quarter, that was the only warm part of my body—especially thinking about these hot photos." Ty and Jess shared an intimate look.

"Speaking of hot, isn't it getting a little too steamy in here?" Gabe asked.

Ty peered around. "Yeah. It's weird, like being caught in a warm fog. Maybe the vents aren't working the way they should."

"Why don't you go investigate?" Jess suggested lazily, too tired to move at the moment. "And while you're at it, turn the heat down a notch. I was cold before, but now I'm starting to roast."

"Would you grab me a bottle of spring water from out there, too?" Corey asked. "I forgot to get one on the way in."

"Sure. Save my spot. I'll be right back."

The problem was, in order to come back, he had to leave first, and when he pushed on the door, it wouldn't budge. He pushed harder, but the door remained in place.

"Hey, Gabe. Come over here and help me, will you? Can heat warp a steel door? It won't open."

Gabe climbed off his perch. "Don't you just love these wimpy quarterbacks?" he quipped. "All brain and no brawn."

But when he applied his muscle to the task, along with Ty's, the door stayed shut. "What the devil is wrong with this thing?" He inspected it more closely. "No inside knob. Just that pull bar on the outside. And no lock, that I can tell."

"There'd better not be," Ty grumbled. "I believe there's a law against having a lock on a sauna, and if there isn't, there should be. It's probably just jammed, like I said."

They rammed their combined weight against it several more times, with no appreciable result. "This is nuts." Ty swiped at the foggy window set in the upper half of the door panel, and peered out. The adjacent room was empty. "Any other time, there'd be people standing in line to use this thing, or stacked three deep in the whirlpool. Where are they now, when we need them?"

"Can you see the outer handle?" Jess asked, starting to get a little nervous over the situation. "Maybe it's caught on something."

Ty rubbed another spot clear on the window. "I can only see the top part, but it looks okay."

"Well, something is keeping that door shut, and it's getting hotter in here by the minute," Corey complained with a worried look. "If I sweat off much weight, all my ensembles for next weekend's fashion show will have to be altered."

Jess got up to tour the perimeter of the small concrete enclosure. "You'd think they'd have an emergency phone in here, or a shut-off valve, or an alarm button. I don't see anything but bare cement walls, wooden benches, and steam vents." By now she was panting. "Is anyone else having trouble breathing?"

"Get down on the floor," Ty told her. "Heat rises. It should be several degrees cooler at ground level."

"Can you break the glass out of the door?" Corey suggested helpfully. "Even if the opening is too small for one of us to crawl through, it would let some cool air inside and make it easier for someone to hear us if we all yelled for help."

"Honey, that's double-thick tempered glass," Gabe informed her. "We can't pound hard enough on it with our bare fists to break it." He tried anyway, succeeding only in bruising his hand.

"The hinges," Jess declared hopefully. "If we can remove them, we can take the whole door off."

"That would work if the hinges were on the inside," Ty pointed out. "This door opens outward, and the hinges are on the other side."

"I'm getting dizzy," Corey said, scooting to the floor to sit beside Jess.

The guys pounded on the door for several more minutes, shouting at the top of their lungs. Then, their energy fast waning, they too had to seek refuge on the floor.

"I wish whoever left that boom box on full blast would come back to get it, or at least turn the damned thing down." This from Gabe, who was breathing heavily. "It's no wonder nobody can hear us, with that thing blaring."

Ty nodded. "Look, I don't want to be an alarmist, but we've got to get out of here, one way or another, before we all succumb to heat prostration, or whatever. We can't afford to wait and hope someone accidentally comes to our rescue.''

Gabe looked around. ''What about the benches? They look pretty sturdy, but if we could pry one of the slats loose, or one of the legs, we could use it as a battering ram.''

The fellows edged closer to examine that possibility. ''Damn! Not only are they bolted together, but they're bolted to the walls and floor, too,'' Ty announced disgustedly. ''I, for one, didn't happen to bring my wrench along with me.''

Corey started to sob. ''Oh, Lord! We're going to die in here, aren't we?''

''No, by God, we're not!'' Gabe exclaimed. ''I didn't recover from arsenic poisoning just to croak in a steam bath! There's got to be some way out of here. Now think, guys. Think!''

That was easier said than done, with the heat steadily robbing them of their power to function, both mentally and physically. Now Jess, despite her effort not to, began to cry, too. ''This is just my luck. I find the man of my dreams, get engaged, and check out before I can even select a wedding gown.''

Ty pulled her close. ''Don't talk that way, Jess.''

She couldn't help it. Tears flowed down her cheeks, to drip on his chest. ''You know what? When Corey first suggested that photo session as a birthday present to you, I thought the idea was ridiculous. Entirely too egotistical. Then I got to thinking that, with everything going on, if something were to happen to me, you and Josh would at least have some nice pictures to remember me by.'' She gulped back a huge sob. ''Oh, Ty! Poor Josh! He loves you so much. Losing you is going to break his heart.''

''No it won't, because I'll be damned if I'm going to go this way, roasted like some Thanksgiving turkey! We're going to get out of here, if I have to claw my way through that metal door!''

He shifted, rising to his knees. Head hanging, he stopped to gather his energy. ''Jess?'' he questioned, his tone tentative. ''What did you do with that key to the locker where we stored our clothes?''

She sniffled. "It's right here in the pocket of my wrap. Why?"

"Give it to me."

She handed it over. The others watched as Ty began scraping at the caulk around the drain cover in the floor beside his left knee.

"Ty, what are you doing? Even I'm not skinny enough to slither through the drain," Jess told him, concluding that the heat was affecting his brain.

"No, but this drain cover is metal. If we can pry it loose, maybe we can use it to break the window. It may not work, but it's sure as hell worth a try."

"At this point anything is," Gabe concurred, shoving his fingertips through the holes in the grate and tugging upward. A couple of minutes later, with a sucking sound, the cover gave so suddenly that Gabe toppled onto his backside at the abrupt absence of resistance.

The girls huddled on the floor as the guys crawled quickly to the door. "Hide your faces," Ty advised. "Safety glass isn't supposed to shatter into slivers like regular glass, but you never know."

It didn't shatter, but it did crack as Gabe hammered the round grate into it. After several whacks, he'd made a large hole in the glass. Abandoning modesty, the men used their terry wraps to carefully pry enough of the shards out of the frame to get a good shot at the second pane. They took turns battering at it until it, too, fractured and finally gave way under the pressure.

Cool air rushed through the hole in the window. They sucked it in gratefully, in huge gulps, like thirsty nomads at an oasis pond. "Watch the glass," Ty warned, as Jess and Corey crept closer. "Don't cut yourselves."

After a brief rest, the men attacked the window once more, enlarging the hole. When it was big enough, and enough of the pane had been removed to make it safe to do so, Ty poked his head out. They heard him curse. "There's a long metal rod stuck through the door handle."

He pulled back inside and stuck his arm out, reaching for the obstruction. On the first attempt, it wouldn't move, but when he pulled the bar in the opposite direction, it slid free. Though it still blocked their exit to some extent, they managed to push the door open wide enough for each of them to wriggle through. Mincing their way past the glass, they collapsed on the nearest bench, a few yards away. Gabe knocked the boom box to the floor, rendering it blessedly silent.

"I've just about had my fill of this," Ty proclaimed, his wrath tempered only by his weakened body. "This was no accident, folks." He pointed toward the door, and the heavy metal rod still holding it part way shut. Not only had the pole been thrust through the door handle, either end of it had been wedged behind the workshop-style shelves flanking the door. Though filled only with towels, the shelving units were bolted to the walls, creating a firm anchor for the pole, which appeared to be the bar from a weight-lifting set. "I'll also bet my last dime that the heat controls have been tampered with. Put on the highest setting."

"This really tears it," Gabe muttered, his dark eyes shooting angry flames. "Messing with me is one thing; but now they've threatened Corey's life, and I'm not gonna let it rest until I've found the bastards. Then, they're dead meat, ground and pattied."

"My sentiments exactly," Ty agreed. "The problem is finding them . . . before they get to one of us again."

CHAPTER 30

Though they hadn't called him from New Jersey, Haggardy was there to meet them when their plane landed at the Columbus airport. "Boy, bad news travels fast!" Ty declared, upon seeing him. "I assume the New Jersey police phoned you? Or did they just put it out on the Internet for everyone's benefit?"

"No one called me," Haggardy said gruffly. "What happened that I don't know about?"

Jess answered. "Ty and I, along with Corey and Gabe Rome, got locked in the hotel sauna, to bake like Idaho potatoes. It was deliberate."

"You can fill me in on the details later," Haggardy said. "At the moment, I have to perform an official duty, and place Ty under arrest."

"What?" Ty stared at the detective in disbelief. "Haggardy, if this is some sort of sick joke, it's not funny."

"No joke," Haggardy stated. "Now, listen up. Officer Agerter is about to read you your rights."

"Wait a minute!" Jess jerked on the detective's sleeve. "What are you arresting him for?"

"Gambling. Placing bets against the Knights with a local bookie, and failing to pay up."

The four friends gaped at him.

"No way," Gabe said. Corey nodded.

"That's absurd," Jess claimed.

"You can't believe that," Ty exclaimed.

Haggardy cuffed him while Agerter read Ty his rights. "Calm down, James," the detective mumbled, leaning close so he wouldn't be overheard. "We've got to make this look good, for whoever might be watching."

Ty relaxed, and drew a shaky breath. Jess, not in on the conversation, was as riled as she could be. "Haggardy, I'll have you charged with false arrest!" She followed close on his heels as Haggardy and two policemen led Ty out of the terminal, Gabe and Corey in her wake. "You can't do this! Do you hear me?"

"You're going to get yourself arrested right alongside him in a minute," the detective warned, "for interfering, if not aiding and abetting."

Jess thrust her hands out, baring her own wrists. "Go ahead. Do it. Even if you don't, I'm coming along to the station with you."

They had reached the police cruiser. One of the officers opened the rear door, placed his hand on Ty's head, and propelled him into the backseat. Haggardy waved her forward. "Get in, Miss Myers. And shut up."

Only now did she hesitate. "I forgot about my car. It's in the long-term lot. I'll follow you."

Haggardy speared her with a hard look. "Agerter, take her keys and the claim ticket, and bring Miss Myers' car to the station." He practically shoved her onto the seat beside Ty.

"We'll be right behind you," Gabe vowed. "Ty, don't say anything until we can get hold of a lawyer."

Ty nodded, as Haggardy slammed the door and climbed into the front passenger seat. The officer behind the wheel put the car in gear, and they were off.

"What? No lights and siren?" Jess sneered. "I'm disappointed in you, Haggardy."

Ty patted her arm. "Ease up, Jess. Let the man explain . . . if he can."

Haggardy turned in his seat to face them. "While you two were gone, we got an anonymous tip claiming Ty was betting against his own team. Now, this in itself is bad enough, but when we contacted the bookie to verify the rumor, he confirmed that several bets had been made by Ty. Furthermore, the bookie wasn't pleased that Ty hadn't paid his debts, having lost a few hefty bets. He's in arrears to the tune of ten thousand dollars to date."

"Oh, for heaven's sake!" Jess exploded.

Haggardy ignored her interruption, and went on, "Of course, all wagers were made by phone, money paid up front via certified check for the first one, with any winnings left to ride on the next bet. Moreover, the bookie couldn't swear the guy who called them in was actually Ty James, though he thought the calls were legit." He paused. "In essence, you're being set up."

"I'm relieved to hear you say that," Ty responded wryly. "So tell me. Why? And by whom?"

"I'm not sure who. As to why, perhaps to get you out of the picture and make Jess a more accessible target. Naturally, if you had both died in that sauna, as you were intended to do, this would be a moot point. As it is, I'm considering putting both of you in protective custody, for your safety's sake. However, if we resort to that, our culprit will probably just lie low until you surface, and the attempts will start over again."

"What about Corey and Gabe?" Jess asked. "All four of us were together this time. Shouldn't they be protected as well?"

"If we decide that's the best route," Haggardy told her.

"What's your—"

Ty's words were cut off in mid-stream as the cruiser, slowing for a traffic sign, was suddenly struck from the rear.

"What the—" Regaining his balance, Haggardy looked out the window to see a car careening past them on the right. A few yards farther, it plowed into a light pole and stopped.

"Hey!" Jess shouted. "That's *my* car!" Automatically, she reached for the rear door handle, only to find there wasn't one.

Haggardy leapt from the cruiser before it had come to a

complete stop. "You two stay here!" he directed them. To the officer, he commanded, "Call this in, and get another cruiser on the way to take us on to headquarters."

He loped toward Jess's wrecked car. Within a minute, he was back. "Agerter hit the steering wheel. The air bag must have been disabled. If he didn't break a couple of ribs, they're at least bruised. Says he couldn't stop. When he pressed on the brakes, there were none. Which would lead me to guess that our murderer is trying to cover all of his bases at once. If the sauna didn't get you, the car would. Failing that, your arrest. This is one busy felon."

"Or more," Ty reminded him. "There have to be at least two, don't there? One here, tinkering with Jess's brakes, and another in New Jersey?"

"Not necessarily. He could have phoned in the tip from New Jersey, and he could have hurried to the parking lot ahead of you and cut the brake line on Jess's car. It only takes a minute."

Jess spoke up, her voice an octave higher than usual. "I'm glad Agerter wasn't hurt more seriously, but that was a brand-new car! I haven't even learned to use all the gadgets, yet!"

Haggardy merely shook his head. "Hope you have good insurance."

Corey and Gabe arrived, and they all sat down with Haggardy to discuss various options and ramifications, the main objective to see that they all survived until their enemy was caught. After taking so much time off work while Gabe was recovering, Corey was reluctant to miss the upcoming fashion show.

"It's not so much that I need the money, or the exposure," she explained, "but my agency is already having fits that I've cancelled so many appearances. They need to know they can rely on me. Besides which, the proceeds from this show are being donated to a children's charity. Also, if I'm in New York, apart from the Knights, I should be safe. Shouldn't I? I really want to do this, if possible."

"Then I suggest you hire a personal bodyguard," Haggardy recommended.

"I'll be her bodyguard," Gabe insisted. "We can leave after Thursday's game, hop a direct flight from Chicago to New York, and Corey will still have plenty of time to get ready for the show Saturday night."

Haggardy frowned. "Thursday is Thanksgiving. The Knights have a game scheduled?"

Ty nodded. "Against the Bears. After which, Jess and I intend to go to Kentucky to spend the remainder of the holiday with my folks."

Haggardy mulled this over. "That might be for the best. Get you out of town, out of the limelight, out of sight completely for a few days. Hopefully, your stalker doesn't know where your family lives—and I am leaning more toward the idea that there's only one assailant left out there now. Meanwhile, until the game, I want you all to lie low and remain vigilant. No unnecessary jaunts to the grocery or the video store. Stay in, lock your doors, make yourselves as invisible as possible.

"On a brighter note," he continued, "we received some interesting data from Miami while you were out of town. They've arrested the man who killed Bambi Shultz. Turns out it was some guy she'd been dating here in Columbus, one of those mafia-wannabe types. This Vince Penny fellow followed her to Miami. Seems he wasn't too thrilled that Bambi still had the hots for Ty, and decided to teach her a lesson."

"Boy, we were way off the mark on that one, weren't we?" Jess remarked.

"In that aspect, yes, but Penny did confirm that Bambi was the one who dosed your drink. She also talked him into making a hit on you a while back. The things a guy won't do for a piece of . . . love, huh?"

Jess frowned. "You lost me, Haggardy."

"That drive-by shooting. Penny and some of his friends were behind that, only they accidentally got Alan instead of you. After that goof up, they backed off. Penny decided it wasn't worth messing with, since Bambi was starting to show signs of having a roving eye."

"What about all the things that happened later?" Ty asked.

"Not to the rest of the team, but aimed at Jess. Her apartment getting wrecked, the threats, her brakes?"

"Nope. They arrested Penny Thursday night. He was still in Miami, taking a little vacation, as it were, when Jess's place was hit. And I doubt his mobster buddies were involved. Why would they only take Jess's computer discs? No, our guy is closer to home, someone affiliated with the team. Someone right under our noses, who has a score to settle."

At this point, a patrolman motioned to Haggardy from across the room. "Stay put a minute," Haggardy told them. "Let me see what he wants; then I'll arrange for a squad car to follow you to your homes, just to make sure you get there with no further mishaps."

Jess glanced wearily at her watch. It read nine-fifty, though it felt more like midnight. "This day seems like it's lasted a week," she sighed. "I'll be glad to see it end."

That was not to be—not just yet. Haggardy's expression was grim as he returned to his desk. "Danvers phoned," he stated. "He was trying to get hold of you, Jess. There's been some trouble at your godfather's house."

"At Tommy's?" she echoed. "What sort of trouble? Is anyone hurt?"

"Your godmother was killed this evening, about half an hour ago."

Jess gaped at him. "Anita? Dead? How?"

Ty immediately asked, "What about Tom? Had he made it home from the airport yet? Has he been notified?"

"He was there," Haggardy said. "Physically, he's fine, but I understand he's pretty much in a state of shock."

"What happened?" Corey queried.

"Danvers didn't know much, just that the officers at the scene couldn't contact Jess, so they called him to see if he could locate her for Nelson. I called down to the desk and got more information. Seems there was a bomb hidden in a florist's box. You know, the long kind they use to deliver roses? It went off when Jess's godmother and her nurse were opening it. Killed both of them."

Jess shook her head in disbelief. "I don't understand. Why would anyone want to kill Anita?"

"To hurt you?" Gabe suggested lamely.

"But she wasn't even my godmother," Jess protested. "I loved her like one, but she only married Tommy about six years ago."

"Could be Tom Nelson was the actual target," Haggardy proposed thoughtfully. "It would fit the pattern, since he's one of the team owners. He told the investigating officers that he found the box on the front porch when he arrived home. He took it inside, handed it over to the women, and headed straight for the bathroom. That's where he was when the explosion took place in the kitchen."

"That doesn't add up," Ty commented. "Florists don't normally deliver on Sundays. Even if they did, why wasn't the box already in the house? Why was it still on the doorstep this late at night? Wasn't Tom the least suspicious?"

Haggardy shrugged. "I guess not. Maybe he was too tired to question it, or to make that connection. Could be he assumed someone stopped by the house to visit and left it there when no one answered the door."

"But, someone is home with Anita all the time," Jess refuted. "Why wouldn't they answer the door?"

"Maybe they didn't hear the bell," Gabe suggested.

Corey agreed. "If the dishwasher was going, or the vacuum, or the nurse was helping Anita in the bathroom, they could easily have missed hearing it."

"We're straying from the main point," Haggardy said, "which is that someone wired the box with explosives and deposited it on the Nelsons' porch to be found."

"And poor Anita and her nurse are dead," Jess finished, fresh tears springing to her eyes. "I can't believe this! I just can't believe it! Anita was the kindest, dearest woman. She wouldn't harm a moth if it was eating the clothes off her back. And she was so talented. She was a concert pianist, you know, before the Alzheimer's hit and she had to give it up."

Haggardy's brow rose. "She had Alzheimer's?"

"What a crying shame," Gabe added. "Who would do such a thing to a helpless, harmless woman?"

"A ruthless, craven killer, with no conscience whatsoever," Ty concluded somberly.

Corey leaned from her seat to Jess's, to give her friend a consoling hug. "If it's any comfort, Jess, think of her in God's hands now, with a new and perfect body. In heaven, there is no sickness or sadness."

Ty stood, holding out his hand to Jess. "C'mon, babe. Let's go home. I'll fix you a hot toddy and tuck you into bed."

"Not yet." She raised sorrowful eyes to his. "First I've got to see Tommy. Even if we have been on the outs lately, he's still family. He needs to know that I care, that he's not alone in his grief."

Jess felt bad about not being able to spend more time with Tommy before Anita's funeral late Wednesday afternoon, but everyone, including her godfather, was adamant that she remain in the background as much as possible. She did so primarily for Tommy, who claimed he would be prostrate with grief if anything were to happen to her, too, especially on the heels of Anita's demise.

Thursday being a holiday, the funeral was held on Wednesday. Despite having to rush the arrangements and burial, there were a sizable number of mourners, some arriving from as far away as Vienna. In addition to family, friends, neighbors, and Tom's business acquaintances, many were fellow musicians who had known or performed with Anita throughout the years. They had come to pay their respects, to applaud her one last time.

Following the grave-site service, Jess and Claudia approached Tom. "We won't be coming to the dinner at the church," Jess told him regretfully, taking his big cold hand in hers. "I'm sorry, Tommy. I wish there was something I could do to make it better, easier. Are you going to be okay?"

Tom nodded, patting her hand. "I'll make it, Jessie girl. Somehow. It's just . . . why did this have to happen now? I

mean . . . with the holidays coming up. It's so damned hard!''
His eyes filled with tears. ''I was going to start my Christmas
shopping this weekend. Look for something really special for
her.''

Claudia stepped forward. ''Tom, you shouldn't be alone right
now. I've been through this. I know. Why don't you drive up
to my house tomorrow, have dinner with John and me? We
can watch the game together on television.''

''It's good of you to ask me, but I doubt I'd be good company.'' Tom sighed. ''I'd rather be by myself, but I suppose
you're right about not spending the day holed up in the house
by myself. I can't bear to go anywhere near the kitchen, where
. . . where . . .'' He took a moment to compose himself. ''If I
don't take my nephew up on his invitation, I'll probably grab
a bite to eat at a restaurant somewhere. Or . . . might wander
down to the soup kitchen and volunteer some time, like I used
to do. Remind myself that others are hurting, too, and in worse
need than I am.''

''That sounds like a fine idea,'' Claudia agreed. ''But if you
change your mind, just call. God knows, there will be enough
food, and hardly anyone to eat it, what with Jess in Chicago.''

''I'll wave to you, Mom,'' Jess promised, ''and to you,
Tommy. I know you won't be attending the game, but you will
be watching it, won't you?''

''Yeah, I suppose,'' he replied dispiritedly. ''It'll help pass
the time, if nothing else.''

The rest of the team had flown out Wednesday morning,
after paying their respects at the funeral home. Tom had voiced
his appreciation, and wished them well at the game. He'd
assured Danvers and the other coaches that he didn't expect
them or the players to attend Anita's funeral. They needed to
get to Chicago and prepare for the big Thanksgiving game.
Only Ty and Jess had remained behind to attend the services.
Jess, out of love and regard for Anita and Tom, would have
had it no other way, and Ty was not about to go to Chicago
without her.

At first, they had planned on catching a late flight on a regular airline, but holiday travel had the seats all booked. They were considering driving to Chicago, a six- to seven-hour trip, when Keith Forsyth had offered to fly them there on his private jet. The business executive had all but insisted. "I won't have any use for it until Monday, at the earliest," he'd assured them. "My wife has a big family weekend planned."

"What about your pilot?" Ty had asked. "Doesn't he have holiday plans, too?"

"I'm sure he does, but his folks live in Evanston. So you see? He'll be going that direction anyway. You might just as well tag along."

To avoid the worst of the air traffic, the pilot wanted to leave at six o'clock Thursday morning, which would get them into Chicago around seven-thirty or so. Kickoff was at twelve-thirty, so even allotting for any unforeseen delay, they would arrive with hours to spare before the game.

Jess was still half-asleep as she and Ty boarded the smart little silver jet. "Ugh! The sun's not even up yet," she complained. "I hate going back to Eastern Standard Time in the winter."

Overhearing her comment from his place in the cockpit, the pilot called back cheerfully. "You'll see a spectacular sunrise as soon as we get off the ground. A bird's-eye view. There's nothing like it on a clear, crisp morning like this. As soon as we're airborne and leveled out, feel free to unbuckle your seat belts and help yourselves to breakfast. There's a fresh pot of coffee in the galley, juice in the fridge, and cinnamon rolls in the microwave. That should tide you over until we hit Chicago."

"Maybe," Jess muttered past a yawn. "If I don't sleep the whole way."

The plane was small, but plush. In place of the usual rows of seats, there was a casual arrangement of swivel chairs and tables. The chairs resembled those in Ty's breakfast nook, except they were bolted down. The galley, rather than being partitioned off, was more of a semicircular, bar-type setting, similar to that in the Miami mansion they had rented. Though compact, it seemed to include all the amenities. Even the rest room, which Jess peeked into before strapping herself into her seat, was more than the standard airline hole-in-the-wall. This one had a closet, an actual vanity, and a shower stall.

"I'm asking for a raise when we land," Jess joked to Ty. "If Forsyth can afford this, he's got money to burn."

The pilot, finished with his precheck, emerged from the cockpit and headed toward the back of the plane. "Okay, we're all set. Buckle up. I've got to signal the ground crew to remove the stairs, secure the rear door, and we're off."

"Aren't you going to give us the usual spiel about flotation devices and oxygen masks?" Jess inquired as he passed.

He grinned. "Nope. I figure as much as you two travel, you could recite it to me, word for word."

CHAPTER 31

The pilot had just reached the door, when a man pushed past him onto the plane, lugging his bulging travel bag with him. "I almost missed you," he panted. "Got room for one more?"

"Sure thing, Mr. Nelson," the pilot greeted. "Welcome aboard."

Jess turned in surprise. "Tommy! What are you doing here?"

"That's a stupid question if ever I've heard one," her godfather replied, plopping into a chair. "I'm going to Chicago."

"But . . ."

"Honey, I just couldn't bear that huge, silent house a minute longer. Everything in it reminds me of Anita. So," he said, with a palms-up gesture, "here I am, bag and baggage. I can eat turkey just as well in Chicago as I can here, and be with people I like. Maybe it'll cheer me up some. At any rate, it can't be as bad as sitting at home alone."

"That's the ticket, Tommy."

"Will you be coming to the game, too?" Ty inquired.

"I thought I might," Tom told them. "If it gets to be too much for me, I'll go back to the hotel and cry in my beer."

There was a short delay while they awaited their turn for takeoff. Then they were up, soaring into the sky. Jess peered out the window. "The pilot was right. Just look at that magnificent sunrise. I hadn't realized we'd see it right away. It's still dark on the ground."

"It's the difference in horizontal angle," Tom explained, as he rose and headed for the galley. "Coffee, anyone?"

He brought the entire carafe back to the table, along with four cups. "Hey, Jimbo!" he called out to the pilot. "You ready for a refill on the java? I'll trade you for a ride in the copilot's seat."

"Bring it on," came the reply from the cockpit.

Tom went forward, leaving Ty and Jess to themselves.

"Does Tom strike you as just a bit too jovial?" Ty asked in a low voice.

Jess nodded on a sad sigh. "He's trying too hard to put up a good front. I wonder if he's really broken down and cried yet? When Dad and Mike died, it took my grandpa several days for the shock to wear off and reality to set in. You have to let the grief out, before you can start to heal. The longer you hold it in, the worse it gets."

Jess and Ty were nodding off when Tom rejoined them. "How you doing back here, kids? Catching your forty winks?"

Ty yawned, not even bothering to open his eyes. "I was wide awake when we took off, but I can barely hold my eyes open now. Must be the change in air pressure."

"Or the movement of the plane," Jess murmured drowsily from her seat next to him. "It's as lulling as sitting in a rocking chair."

Her fingers curled around Ty's forearm, giving it a squeeze. Ty smiled. Then he heard the loud rip. His eyes popped open, but not in time. Tom had already secured his other wrist to the armrest, binding it tightly with duct tape—just as he'd done a moment ago when Ty had thought Jess was touching him.

"Hey! What's the deal here?" Ty exclaimed. He blinked, trying to make sense of it all. His brain was slow to react, his reflexes sluggish. He watched in a daze as Tom swiftly bound first one of Jess's arms, then the other to her own chair. She tried to fight him, to swat his hand away. Tom was stronger, faster. Within seconds he had her secured as well.

Tom stepped back, eyeing his work with satisfaction. "That's better. Now I know you won't be giving me any trouble. No more than old Jimbo will. He's out like a light, thanks to those sleeping tablets I dissolved in the coffee."

"Who . . . who's flying the plane?" Jess asked, her words slurred.

"Ever hear of autopilot, little girl?"

"But . . ." She focused on him fuzzily. Tom had his duffel bag open on one of the tables and was pulling some sort of padded coverall from it. "Whatcha need that for?"

"I'll give you three guesses. The first two don't count. Here's a clue, Jessie. It's called a jumpsuit. And this"—he hoisted a thick backpack—"is a parachute."

"You're gonna jump?" Ty's words, too, were slow in emerging.

"Right."

Jess yanked at the tape binding her arms. "Why, Tommy? What's going on?"

Tom smiled. "I thought you'd have figured that out by now, smart gal that you are. Then again, you weren't smart enough to back off when I warned you to. Now, you're going to have to pay the consequences. You and lover boy, here."

His words finally jarred something in her brain. "You're . . . you're the one," she exclaimed softly, a look of horror coming over her face. "You're the killer."

"Oh, I can't take all the credit," he replied smoothly. He stuffed one leg into the jumpsuit, then the other. "Johnson carried out most of the legwork, at least to start with. But, you already knew that, didn't you?"

"You killed him," she surmised.

"I had to. The cops were after him, and he would have pointed them toward me."

"The spa. You locked us in? Did you cut my brake line, too?"

He nodded, appearing proud of himself. "Surprising what you can learn on the Internet these days. Even how to rig a letter bomb, or in this case, a flower box bomb."

Jess gasped, her face going white.

"Why?" Ty growled. "Why kill Jess? Or any of us?"

"Basically, it all boils down to money," Tom confessed as he zipped up the front of the suit and reached for the parachute pack. "You might say I overextended myself. I need a tax write-off in the worst way. The Knights go under, I get one. Anita dies, I get the insurance, and can pay back the 'loan' I took out at the bank before it's discovered in the next audit. I also altered that policy Jess has with the team. After you, Tyler, I'm her designated beneficiary. Not dear, fickle Claudia."

"Is that what all this is?" Jess surmised incredulously, her voice shrill with fear. "A payback because Mom chose Dad and John over you?"

"That's the frosting on the cake," Tom admitted. He shrugged into the parachute. "Your death is going to be a terrible blow to her, Jessie. Just as your father's and brother's were. It's no less than she deserves."

"You can't do this, Nelson," Ty declared, fighting against his bonds.

Tom's laugh was pure evil. "Who's going to stop me?"

"They'll know this wasn't an accident. When they only find three bodies, they'll know it was you."

"But nobody else saw me come aboard," Tom gloated. "I made sure of that. As far as anyone knows, I'm hiding away, licking my wounds. Just a poor, heartbroken widower." From the duffel, he took a helmet, tugging it on. "Now, let me lay it out for you. As I said, the plane is on autopilot. If it doesn't collide in midair with another aircraft, you'll stay airborne until it runs out of fuel. I dumped most of that, by the way." He chuckled. "Oh, and don't worry about not being able to reach the oxygen masks. We're flying at a lower altitude, as well as a slower speed, to make my jump easier. After all, I haven't done this since my Air Force days."

He reached out to stroke Jess on the cheek, shaking his head at her when she pulled back from him. "Believe it or not, I really am sorry it's come to this, Jessie. If you would just have heeded my warnings. Forsyth talked me into hiring you for that article. I'd hoped you'd make fast work of it and be gone. But you had to stay and stick your nose in where it didn't belong. Sooner or later, you would have caught on to me. I knew it the minute I reviewed your computer discs.''

Tears coursed down her face, blurring her image of him even more. "No, Tommy. Please," she begged. "Don't do this to me. To Ty."

"You won't feel a thing," he told her, his tone soft and loving. "By the time the plane goes down, you'll both be fast asleep. I promise." He started for the back of the plane and the rear door. "Give my regards to Anita when you see her."

They were screaming after him as he unlatched the door and shoved it open. Wind rushed into the plane with a roar, sending debris flying through the interior ahead of it. Tom stumbled backward, before catching hold of the frame. Then he propelled himself through the opening and vanished.

"Oh, God! Oh, God!" Jess was praying between hysterical sobs.

Beside her, Ty was applying all his strength against that of the tape. "Jess! Jess! Listen to me! We've got to get loose, before we pass out."

"H . . . How? There's no way!"

"That glass coffee container," he shouted over the wind. "It's right there in front of you. Can you reach it?"

Not understanding, she wiggled her fingers toward the carafe, which had blown to the edge of the table and was about to tumble off.

"No, Jess! Bend forward. Grab it with your teeth."

She caught the handle in her mouth, just as the glass pot was about to slide into her lap.

"Knock it against the table. Break it," Ty told her.

Jess squeezed her eyes shut. What were a few cuts, compared to the pile of blood and bones she was bound to be after the crash? Lunging forward, she rapped the carafe as hard as she could against the edge of the table. It shattered, sending shards flying back at her. At the same time, the plastic handle slammed painfully against her lips and teeth. Though she tried, she couldn't hold on to it. It fell into her lap.

"I'm sorry! I'm sorry!" she wailed.

"It's okay, Jess. Open your eyes. Help me here, babe."

"I'm tired. So tired."

"Don't conk out on me, Jess. See if you can reach it with your fingers."

She had to bounce her knees to jiggle the handle close enough, but she finally managed to grasp it.

"Good. Swivel your chair toward mine a bit. There. Now, aim that metal ring my way, as close to my arm as you can reach. C'mon, Jess! Stretch! Don't let go of the handle, whatever you do!"

They strained toward each other. The band barely reached the distance between them, just touching the side of Ty's chair. "Now, hold it as steady as you can."

Wobbling to and fro, swiveling his own chair frantically, Ty scraped his forearm back and forth against the sharp edge of the aluminum hoop. Bit by bit, the tape began to fray, until it loosened enough for Ty to pull his hand free. And not a moment too soon. The handle slipped from Jess's limp grasp as she slumped forward, succumbing at last to the drugged coffee.

Working left-handed, it took Ty longer than he wanted to free his right hand. Then, as much as he wanted to do the same for Jess, he dared not take the time. He was getting more and more woozy, and Lord only knew how long they had before the fuel ran out.

Bracing himself, Ty made his way to the cockpit. Jim, the pilot, was slouched in his seat. Ty shook him, slapped him, yelled into his ear. It was no use.

He turned toward the instrument panel, trying to quell his panic as he scanned the complicated array of knobs and dials. The only thing he recognized was a microphone, similar to the one in the police cruiser. Picking it up, he pressed the button and screamed into the mouthpiece. "Mayday! Mayday! Can anybody hear me?"

Nothing. Dead silence. There was a numbered dial near the cord. He turned it and tried again. And again. Finally he hit a channel in use. "Mayday!" he yelled. "Mayday!"

"This is South Bend tower. What's your situation?"

Ty wasted no words. "We're aboard a small jet. Low on fuel. Pilot unconscious. On autopilot, I think."

"Do you know your call letters? Your coordinates? Your altitude?"

"I don't know jack shit, except that we're going to crash!"

"Okay, buddy. Calm down. Now, are you in the pilot's seat?"

"No, the copilot's." Ty launched himself into the seat.

"There should be a headset there. Do you see it?"

"Yes! Yes!"

"Put it on. Can you hear me?"

"Yes."

"Good. I can read you, too. You can let loose of the mike now. Who am I talking to?"

"Ty James."

For once, the man didn't ask if he was Ty James, the quarterback. "Have you ever flown a plane before, Ty?"

"Not in this lifetime," Ty replied shakily.

"We're going to walk you through it, step by step," the voice assured him. He went on to tell Ty where to find the readings he needed in order to determine the location and altitude of the jet. "Gotcha. You're on my screen. Now, you're headed due west. We need to correct that. Here's what you have to do."

Ty located the switch that would take the plane out of auto-pilot and put it in his control—or lack thereof. Feeling as if he was disconnecting his own umbilical cord, he grabbed hold of the "stick" and flipped the switch. The plane tilted sharply to the side, nearly unseating him.

"Whoa!" the radio voice said. "Easy does it." Swiftly, he instructed Ty how to level off again. "Keep the 'wings' on that dial level with the horizon line."

The next quarter of an hour was the longest and most frightening of Ty's life. He was functioning on pure adrenaline, relying on it to counteract the drugs in his system. From what he relayed to them, the tower confirmed that the plane was nearly out of fuel. With luck and a tailwind, they might have enough to make the nearest airfield. If not . . . Ty didn't even want to think about it.

"Hey, fella?"

"Stan."

"Stan, I forgot to tell you something important. I'm about to pass out, too. It was the coffee. Laced with sleeping pills. Tom Nelson did it. He bailed out a ways back. Call Detective Haggardy. Columbus Police Department."

"Later. Let's get you down, first. Then you can call him yourself. Just stay with me, Ty. Not much longer. You're almost there."

Three minutes later, Stan reported, "I don't think you have to worry about that Nelson guy anymore. We just got word about a man smashing through a barn roof about thirty miles east of here. His parachute failed to open."

"He's dead?"

"Affirmative."

"Couldn't have happened to a more deserving bastard," Ty claimed tersely.

At last, Ty spied the landing strip. His stomach clenched itself into knots.

"Just do what I tell you, Ty," Stan said. "That baby can practically land herself, but she needs a little help from you."

"I . . . I'm fading fast," Ty warned. "Can hardly see the . . . dials."

"Pull yourself together, man!" Stan yelled. "Concentrate! You can do this! Just hang on a few more minutes!"

"Trying to," Ty murmured.

Everything seemed to happen in slow motion from then on. Ty saw his hands moving to do as Stan directed, but they seemed to be moving of their own volition, not under any conscious command from his brain. He saw the wings tip, and straighten. He heard the thump of the landing gear as it locked into place. He saw the emergency equipment lined up along the runway, their bright lights flashing. Last, he felt the lurch as the plane touched down, heard the squeal of rubber tires skidding against tarmac.

He tried to hold out—wanted to see how it all ended, if they made it through unscathed—but he just couldn't muster that final ounce of energy. His lids drifted shut; his head nodded onto his chest. He knew no more.

* * *

The ceremony was simple, solemn, sincere. The guest list had been pared to the bare minimum, yet the church was packed beyond its capacity. Claudia clutched at John's hand, mopping her tears with the handkerchief wadded in the other. Across the aisle, Maggie James held her hand to her chest, her emotions running high. Beside her, Wes gazed intently toward the altar.

"I now pronounce you husband and wife," the pastor intoned. "You may kiss your bride."

Ty drew Jess into his arms and kissed her with all the love and longing in his heart. Jess melted against him, her happy heartbeats matching his. When at last they parted, to gaze adoringly into each other's eyes, the minister was announcing proudly, "May I be the first to present to those of you assembled here today . . . Tyler and Jessie James."

Jess's mouth flew open. The congregated guests burst into laughing applause. Ty grinned.

"You horse's rear! You told him to do that, didn't you?" Jess swatted at him with her bouquet.

"You bet your sweet bippy," Ty admitted without a hint of remorse.

"I'll get you for this," she promised, her eyes narrowed in warning.

"Now, Jess, I have witnesses, about five hundred of them, who just heard you pledge to honor and cherish me," he reminded her with a chuckle.

"Wagara."

"Meaning?"

She told him at long last. "Who Actually Gives A Rat's Ass?"

His blue eyes twinkled. "I do. You do. Everyone heard us both say we do. Our vows, remember?"

She gave an exasperated huff. "That's what I get for wanting a traditional wedding. And for being such an impetuous, love-struck fool."

"You know the old saying, 'Marry in haste, repent at leisure.' Well, sweetheart, we've got a lifetime ahead of us for that and

a lot more. By the way, have I told you yet today how beauti
you are?''

"You do throw a smooth pass," she conceded with a w
smile. "Just remember . . . I kick balls.''

"Yeah, but I get to call all the plays, don't forget."

"Your saving grace is that you're great in the sack," she
informed him with a smirk.

"So are you." He offered her his arm. She slipped her hand
into the crook of his elbow. They headed down the aisle, Gabe
and Corey falling into line behind them.

"Jessie James!" she muttered anew. "Honestly, Ty! How
could you?"

"Stick a sock in it, babe."

"Gladly, super jock. Bend over and show me some teeth."

He shut her up the best way he knew how. Without missing
a beat, he swept her into his arms and clamped his mouth over
hers. The crowd cheered.

Josh, mindful of his role as ring bearer and all-around "best
son," scurried to grab Jess's trailing train and hold it off the
floor. He strutted importantly along in their wake, with a wide,
gap-toothed grin.

Claudia followed John out of the pew. She dabbed at her
damp eyes, offering him a misty smile. "Like I told you, John.
Those two were made for each other."